MURDER, MYSTICS, AND MENOPAUSE

EMERALD CITY PARANORMAL COZY MYSTERIES

THERESA CRATER

Murder, Mystics and Menopause

Emerald City Paranormal Women's Fiction

Copyright © 2024

Print ISBN: 978-1-7369571-8-9

Theresa Crater

Cover by Karri Klawiter

Editors: Lori DeBoer & Marilyn King

Crystal Star Publishing

P.O. Box 223

Lafayette, Colorado

USA

www.crystalstarpublishing.com

 Formatted with Vellum

CONTENTS

This one is for Mugs

CHAPTER

ONE

Professor Lauren Olson felt the flush of heat start in her neck and spread up to her cheeks as she lectured to her afternoon literature class. Why did she have hot flashes in front of her twenty-something students? Why couldn't she have night sweats like they talked about in commercials so she could keep her reproductive status private?

No, she had to turn bright red in front of thirty students who tried not to smile and nudge each other or squirm uncomfortably as she turned into a radiating stick of dynamite. And that described her temper these days, too. Easy to set off. She used to pride herself on her professional demeanor.

They were studying women's literature. The important female writers who paved the way forward both in fiction and non-fiction. Some poets, too. The class filled up early every time it was offered. Students appeared, eager to read the books and essays. Some even claimed to be feminists, but did they have any pity for their professor in her current humiliation?

Apparently not.

Lauren, known to her friends as Laurie, cleared her throat and continued with her lecture as if nothing was happening. "Virginia Woolf and her new husband had a challenging first few years when her emotional difficulties resurfaced. The PTSD diagnosis did not exist at that time. Even though Woolf had significant childhood trauma, no one thought this to be the cause of her troubles."

Laurie clicked to the next slide in her PowerPoint and looked down to read the notes. A fat drop of sweat plopped onto her computer. She dabbed her forehead and upper lip with the tissue she always kept in her hand these days and soldiered on.

"Thankfully after this initial rough start, Woolf enjoyed years of stability. The two started a press together." She smiled up at the class, watching a few students pack away their scornful expression at her predicament. Joey Ryan, on the other hand, sat in the front row, eyes fixed on her. Except his focus was not on her face.

Brats, she thought, then chided herself for the thought.

She remembered threading a needle for her mother who could no longer see such small things clearly enough to do it herself. She'd declared she'd never lose her sight when she got old. Her reading glasses slid down her sweat-slicked nose.

Sorry, Mom.

"Self-publishing is not as new as some think." She looked up expectantly. Nobody laughed. She used to at least get a chuckle from that line.

"The Woolfs had successful publishing and writing careers, but Virginia did eventually die by her own hand. She felt the old symptoms returning and walked into the river."

Laurie wished she could walk into a river about now, float in cold water, relax. Early retirement was sounding better and better. With that moderate inheritance from her grandfather, she could almost afford it. She could help save the whales like she'd dreamed of in high school. There was always a cool breeze on Puget Sound.

She forced her attention back to the lecture. "We'll discuss any evidence of this trauma when we talk about *To the Lighthouse* next week."

A young woman raised her hand. "Professor Olson, why do we study Virginia Woolf? I mean, in a class on women's literature, shouldn't we read women who are good role models? Women who were successful?"

Laurie took a deep breath, suppressing the urge to shout. Instead, she smiled and said, "Woolf was a pioneer. She was the first to call for researching and teaching women's history, for example. Her essays connect the rise of fascism in Europe with patriarchal domination of women in the family. She is a founder of modernism. All this and she was not allowed to go to university like you are doing now."

"But she killed herself," another woman piped up.

"I thought Joyce invented modernism," another said from the back of the room.

Joey continued to stare at her breasts, a dreamy look on his face.

Laurie's face flushed bright red, sweat popping out under her arms. She'd had to stop wearing jackets. She wore her summer blouses year round now.

It's nothing to be ashamed of, she reminded herself. It's a natural bodily function. But that didn't help. Her embarrassment added to the flaming red on her cheeks. And her irritation. Why did everything have to be all positive and rosy?

She ignored her anger, her scarlet face, and answered the question. "Yes, she did commit suicide. Eventually. But it's important to understand the challenges and abuses women suffered in the past. Many of these problems still exist." Laurie suspected these questions were a way to hide the fact that they hadn't finished the reading. At the end of term, students tended to slack off.

Laurie realized she'd stopped caring if they finished the novel. She wished she could torture them with a pop quiz. The final would have to do. She remembered early in her career being scandalized by professors who did such things. Good teachers inspired their students to read. They didn't threaten them into compliance.

Oh, how the righteous had fallen.

3

Laurie clicked to her next slide and found it was the end of the presentation. Thank the powers that be. "Looks like that's the end of the hour. Finals are next week. See you then."

Laurie slammed her computer shut, unhooked it, put it into her roller bag, and headed off to her office. Joey followed her down the hall. "Professor Olson, do you have a minute?"

"Sorry, not today. I have a plane to catch."

"But don't you have office hours now?"

Joey had developed a fixation on her. Maybe a crush, but could you say that about somebody who stared at your breasts and never made eye contact? He came to every office hour she scheduled and spent the time talking about anything except the course material.

"I was forced to cancel them, Joey. I can talk to you next week or you can text me any questions you have." She made her escape.

Her department chair stepped out of his office just as she walked by.

He stepped in front of her, his lanky frame somehow taking up the entire hallway.

Stalker.

"Dr. Olson, I was hoping I could get that report from the curriculum committee before the weekend. I have a meeting with the dean early next week and it is on the agenda."

She pushed back her shoulders and tried to match his height with her own five feet, four inches. "I'm still waiting for Jason's section. You might mention how important this is to our new assistant professor."

"I wouldn't want to step on your toes as chair of the committee." His civil tone carried an undertone of threat.

She tried not to huff out a breath. "Of course, Dr. Brown. I'll emphasize the urgency to him. Once again."

Dr. Brown stared down at her, stretching out the silence. "You do that." He treated her to his famous shark smile, then returned to his office. Barbara, his admin assistant, gave her a sympathetic look.

Laurie nodded at Barbara gratefully, then rushed down the hall.

In her office, she grabbed the curriculum committee folder, along with a stack of ungraded essays. She'd have to find some time to work over the weekend. She'd hoped for a real vacation. Stuffing everything into her briefcase, she headed for the elevator at top speed. She had a plane to catch.

LAURIE SAT BACK in her plane seat and let out a sigh. Finally, she could relax. At least until she got to the high school reunion. Why had she let Dana and Skye talk her into going? Thirty years. How could it be that they'd graduated that long ago? The days of *Jurassic Park,* Whitney Houston and Meat Loaf, and the start of *Frasier*. The trio planned to dress up in 1990's clothes for the event.

She hoped to catch up with John Newman and talk about his company. See what opportunities existed to work with the whales or help clean up Puget Sound. Revive her old passion. For the whales, not him. They'd had a fling in high school. Great chemistry, something she hoped was a thing of the past. John would probably be at the reunion with his wife Kimberly, Ms. Prom Queen. Yeah, it had been a shot-gun wedding, but still. It had been 1994, not 1924.

Her seat jerked suddenly.

"Sorry, sorry. Can I get in?"

"Of course." Laurie stood and moved into the aisle to let the late arrival put her roller back up in the overhead bin. Good thing it wasn't full already. She'd been hoping the middle seat wouldn't be taken, but no such luck.

And then the woman picked up a pet carrier and began stuffing it beneath the seat in front of her.

Laurie stood in shock for a moment, then pasted one of those practiced, professional smiles on her face. She loved animals. Much more than people. But people who inflicted air travel on their pets deserved to be consigned to Dante's ninth circle of hell.

Whimpering sounded from the carrier. Then the poor creature started clawing at the metal door.

"Stop it, Mittens," the woman snarled.

Oh, this wouldn't do.

"Why don't you get settled first. Then we can get Mittens comfortable," Laurie said, using what her ex-husband Graham called her teacher voice. Sure to soothe and create obedience. Everybody'd had a teacher in their life and were programed to obey.

The woman glared at her. Bad teacher experience here. Then the late comer harrumph and plopped into her seat, kicking Mittens' cage in the process. Mittens started barking. People in the surrounding seats looked over, some frowning, some shaking their heads in sympathy with the dog.

While the woman fiddled with her seat belt, Laurie broke off a piece of jerky she carried for travel and leaned down, trying to pretend she was reaching for something in her own carry-on. She held it up to Mittens' cage. A squished nose began sniffing. Laurie couldn't really make out what kind of dog it was. A wet tongue licked her fingers, then gentle teeth took the jerky from her.

When Laurie looked up, the woman was glaring at her. "You can't feed my dog."

Laurie just smiled. "I'm Dr. Olson. And you are?" She peered down her nose just a bit. Laurie used her academic title in emergencies such as canceling reservations and, in this case, subduing a clearly stupid human.

"Uh, Pam." Her seat mate had a round face and belligerent stare.

"Pleased to meet you." Laurie glanced down at the cage. "It seems Mittens has calmed down. Have a pleasant flight."

Laurie opened her Kindle and pointedly ignored her. Once the woman settled, Laurie checked on Mittens from time to time. About halfway through the flight, Pam started snoring. Laurie reached into her purse and fed the dog the rest of the jerky.

The plane gave a shudder and the seat belt light came on.

"Please return to your seats. The captain has reported some light turbulence—"

The plane dropped, leaving Laurie's stomach at least two thousand feet higher, exactly where they'd been seconds ago. A few screams came from further back.

Mittens started barking.

The plane shook.

The barking turned into a high pitched wail.

Pam woke with a start. "Shut up, you stupid dog."

The plane rose as suddenly as it had dropped. Then pitched violently to the right. Laurie was thrown against Pam. Mittens clawed at her cage, yowling.

"Shut that dog up," the man in the window seat yelled.

The plane dropped again, then went into a nosedive. Oxygen masks fell from the panel above their heads.

Laurie put on her mask, then looked down at Mittens. Spots of crimson dotted the front of cage. The dog was clawing so desperately she'd drawn blood.

"Stop it," Pam screamed.

Laurie made an executive decision. She leaned down and opened Mittens' cage. She pulled what turned out to be a trembling mop of fawn-colored fur out of her cage.

"You can't do that." Pam scrambled to stop her.

Laurie wrapped her arms around the trembling dog, snuggling her to her chest.

"You can't—"

Laurie fixed her with a stare. "Shut up. I'm rescuing your dog."

The plane shook again. Pam grabbed her armrests, squeezed her eyes shut, and started praying.

Finally, the plane leveled out, trembling from what must be heavy winds.

Laurie tucked her face next to Mittens. "It's okay. I've got you now."

The dog whined, then licked her cheek.

"That's right. We'll be okay."

The plane dipped again. Went into another nosedive, gathering speed.

Mittens huddled deeper into Laurie's arms.

Laurie had not planned to die this way.

A few people had taken out their cellphones and were shouting "I love you" to whoever they'd called. Others implored God for help. One man rocked back and forth, praying loudly in Hebrew.

Did she still believe in God? She'd gone through a goddess phase in college. The chant "Isis, Astarte, Diana" popped into her mind, but she just snuggled tighter with Mittens, tucking her nose under the dog's fur. They panted together.

The plane plunged and Laurie's ears popped. She was having trouble breathing.

Everything went black.

SOMETHING WET SWIPED across Laurie's face. She blinked, trying to remember where she was. She was sitting up. Heard people talking around her. Somebody was crying.

Another wet swipe on her nose and a voice in her head said, "Wake up. We stopped shaking."

Laurie opened her eyes and found two limpid brown eyes staring at her. A flash of pink was followed by another wet swipe. "Mittens?"

The dog squirmed happily and wagged her tail. "We're safe."

"What?" Laurie asked out loud, then looked around. Paper cups, Coke cans, napkins, a few small purses and bags littered the aisles. Half the overhead bins hung open, their contents scattered on the floors. But what Laurie cared about the most was that the plane was level. The plane flew straight. No shivering or shaking.

"Thank God," Pam shouted. "We survived."

Mittens whimpered and tucked her head under Laurie's hair.

The passenger address system made a clicking sound and a deep masculine voice said, "This is the captain. We are out of the storm and flying safely now. The crew is doing a systems' check. Your flight attendants will be around to help you as soon as they can. If you are injured, please press the call button and raise your hand. Do not press anything if you are not injured." He added emphasis to this. "Thank you."

The buzz of the PA system went silent.

Hands reached for Mittens.

"Don't let her take me. Please."

Laurie blinked. Who was talking to her? She looked at the passenger across the aisle.

Pam's hands latched onto the dog.

Mittens whined. "No, please."

"Is that you, Mittens?" Laurie mentally asked the dog.

"Yes."

Pam's fingers dug into the scruff of the dog's neck and she started to pull her away.

Laurie slapped her hand. "No, this dog saved my life. I'm saving hers now."

Pam opened her mouth to object, but Laurie kept talking. "You treat her like crap. You don't deserve her. She's mine now."

"Thank you." Mittens heaved a sigh and relaxed against her chest.

The PA system buzzed again. "We'll be landing in Idaho. Emergency help will be waiting."

Pam stared at Laurie for a minute, then shrugged and sat back. "I got stuck with that dog when my aunt died. I never did like that mutt anyway."

"I am not a mutt."

Laurie nodded at Pam, relieved. She didn't know what she'd do with Mittens either, but she'd figure it out. But first, she needed to work out why she thought the dog was talking to her. Maybe it was the shock.

The PA came on again. "This is the captain. We've got a short runway, so brace yourself."

Laurie checked her seatbelt. The wheels made contact and the pilot braked, almost standing everyone on their head. The jet screeched as it slowed, then taxied to a stop. People stood, grabbing their belongings out of bins and off the floor, then headed for the door, not waiting for directions. Laurie grabbed her carry-on and tried to pick up the carrier. She couldn't manage everything, so she left the dog's cage. Clutching Mittens to her chest, Laurie joined the throng in the aisles.

She reached the exit. Stairs, Laurie thought. Just great. She and Mittens climbed down slowly. A young man behind her kept trying to get around her. She turned and glared at him.

"Sorry," he muttered.

The commercial airliner dwarfed the tiny terminal. Apparently they'd landed in Podunk, Idaho. Inside, emergency workers triaged the passengers. An eager young nurse who walked up to her, scanning for injuries.

Laurie waved her off. "I'm fine. Just a scare."

"You sure?"

"Yes." She headed inside, her legs shaking only a little.

The nurse didn't argue. They had plenty of other people to see to. Around her, passengers were trying to find connecting flights to Seattle or Portland. She was never getting on another plane as long as she lived.

"I need to pee," Mittens said.

"Let's go outside, then."

Wait, she was talking to the dog. The couple standing next to Laurie gave her a confused look, but she ignored them. She led Mittens out the automatic glass doors and found a patch of grass. The dog squatted, a look of relief on her face.

Laurie spotted one car rental office. Other people were headed to it already. She could drive to Seattle from here. It would take most of the day, but she'd get there in time for the reunion. She better hurry before all the cars were gone.

"Let's go then." Mittens trotted ahead of her, tail high.

She was going to need a leash.

CHAPTER

TWO

Laurie pulled up to Dana's Victorian house just in time to run in and get dressed for the reunion. The long drive had calmed her, but frenzy reigned when she walked in the door. Skye and Dana rushed to hug her, but Skye pulled back quickly. "Head to the back bedroom. Your outfit is all laid out."

"Oh, a Havanese. How adorable." Dana leaned down and scratched behind the dog's ear, speaking baby talk to her.

"So, that's what kind of dog she is," Laurie said.

"You don't even know what kind of dog you own?" Dana looked at Skye, who was already halfway down the hallway. "Typical Laurie."

"Would you guys hurry up?" Skye said.

"What's her name?" Dana asked.

"Mittens."

Dana screwed up her face. "For a Havanese? Is she a mix?"

Laurie threw up her hands. "It's a long story."

Dana dug her fingers into her fur. Mittens half closed her eyes, enjoying the scratch. "She needs to be groomed."

"I'm taking the best costume," Skye yelled from the back bedroom.

Laurie told her old friends about the near crash and Mittens' rescue while they sorted through clothes Skye had found at the Goodwill—early 1990s classics.

"Honest to God, I thought we were goners." Laurie stripped off her airplane clothes and pulled on a blue and white plaid mini skirt. A white shell went up top, followed by a red ultra-cropped cable knit vest and matching plaid jacket. Navy blue knee-length socks first, then boat shoes. Laurie looked in the mirror. "Who decided I was the preppy one? Wait, isn't this outfit straight out of—" She snapped her fingers "—what was the name of that movie?"

"*Clueless*," Dana and Skye shouted in unison.

"Why me?"

Skye snorted. "You were late. Besides, aren't you the brainy one?"

Laurie shook her head, then pointed at Skye. "No way. How did you get Madonna?"

Skye twirled in her black jumpsuit topped with a metallic jacket with tiger-striped patterned lapels and cuffs. She'd pulled her fly-away red hair back with a huge black bow. Freckles spread across her fair skin like stars.

"Not fair. You know I'm the true Madonna fan," Laurie said.

"It looks better on me," Skye teased.

Dana and Laurie surveyed their plump, round friend.

"It works on you." Dana said. "Madonna was passé in our high school days."

"Heresy! Madonna is eternal." Skye spun around again, showing off her outfit. Mittens barked and did a lap around the room.

"My new dog approves." Laurie pointed to Skye. "Who was your fav?"

"Nirvana." Dana answered for Skye. "But I was a big fan of Mariah Carey "How do you like my slip dress?" She ran a hand in front of her body like a clothes model.

Skye snickered. "You planning a wardrobe malfunction tonight?"

"That was Janet Jackson," Dana said.

"It happened to Mariah, too. The black satin dress?"

Laurie laughed. "Dana has the body for this dress." Dana's shining black hair framed her petite, V-shaped face.

"Let's get on the road," Skye said. "Where are the kids, by the way?"

"Kevin has them."

Laurie looked at Skye who mouthed, "Tell you later." She went to grab her purse, but it didn't match her outfit at all. She pulled out some bills and her license and stuffed them in the capacious pockets of her jacket like she used to do when she went dancing. Only then it was the back pocket of tight jeans. "Ready."

Then she spotted Mittens. "Will the dog be all right?"

"Of course. What do you think I am? Some feral mut?" Mittens said.

"Do you need to pee?" Laurie asked.

"You're talking to the dog now?" Dana asked, then bent in front of Mittens and asked in a squeaky voice, "Does little Mittens need to go wee wee?"

The Havanese looked up at Laurie. "Adorable, isn't she?"

Laurie was just now realizing how sarcastic this dog could be. Or at least her own mind. She shook her head. Dogs couldn't talk. Why was she still imagining things?

"Sure you are." Mittens turned over on her back and stuck all four paws in the air.

"You are shameless," Laurie told the dog.

"Aw." Dana squatted to scratch her. "I think she's fine. There's water in the kitchen. I cut up some leftover chicken and left it in a bowl in the kitchen."

"She's not too bad after all," Mittens said.

"Let's go." Skye was bouncing up and down.

Dana grabbed a duster to put over her dress. "Ready."

"It's so good to see you guys." Laurie couldn't tell her friends she could hear Mittens. They'd think she'd lost it, and anyway, she didn't know how long it would last. Probably it was a stress response and would go away.

Laurie and Skye piled into Dana's new SUV. Fancy leather seat. A dashboard with more instrument panels than an airplane. Laurie and Skye exchanged a look. Dana must be doing well to afford this car. And the house was nothing to sneeze at, sitting on the northern crest of Capitol Hill with a grand view of Lake Union. She'd get the scoop later.

Laurie sat back to enjoy the luxury after the small rental. This was the first moment she'd taken a deep breath since she arrived. "Where's the reunion being held?"

"The Galactic Conference Center," Skye said, fiddling with the zipper on her nylon jacket.

"Seriously? How did old Jefferson High swing that?"

Dana turned onto 15th. "You remember Walter Pearce?"

"That tall guy who served on Student Council? Didn't he disappear at the end of senior year?"

Dana nodded. "That's the one. Now Walter is a famous author."

"I haven't seen his books," Laurie said, her English professor pride at stake. She didn't admit to reading genre fiction. Not in public. She devoured paranormal women's fiction in private. But these were her friends, she reminded herself, and she wasn't in Boston.

"Uses a pseudonym. Writes mysteries as D.J. Stone," Skye said.

"That's Walter Pearce?"

"Our old geeky classmate." Dana took a few side streets and angled down toward Denny Way.

"His last one was based on a local murder. He takes his plots from the news," Skye explained.

"He's got that series and a movie contract. So the head of Galactic gave him a deal for the reunion." Dana concentrated on making her way through the heavy traffic. She took Lenora to 7th and pulled into the parking garage under the building before Laurie could catch a glimpse of the new globes.

"It will be impossible to find a good spot," Laurie predicted.

Dana pulled into a spot reserved for electric cars with a smirk. "It's like this everywhere," she said. "I always get a space right next to wherever I'm going."

"This car is electric?" Laurie asked.

"Yes, and all-wheel drive. I got one of the first ones available. Had to order it like two years ago." Dana pulled out the key and opened her door.

The three piled out of the SUV and headed to the elevators. They pushed the button for the ballroom floor. Dana tapped her foot while they rode up. The doors opened and "Dream Lover" wafted out. Two tables covered in white cloths spread with name tags sat just in front of the doors to the main event. Three old classmates sat behind them, smiles plastered on their faces. Laurie didn't recognize any of them.

A woman with a blue streak through her hair looked up and turned her smile up a few more watts. "Why Dana Preston, as I live and breathe."

"Matilda. How nice to see you." Dana's tone was prime.

Laurie remembered her now. Always trying to get in with the popular kids, but just a bit too chunky and awkward to be accepted. They'd made fun of her back in the day, but now Laurie felt a little sorry for her.

"You remember Laurie Olson and Skye Yarrow," Dana said, gesturing to them like a model in a game show displaying the prizes.

Matilda nodded enthusiastically. "I see you all dressed for the occasion."

They smiled.

Matilda fished around the table. "Here are your name tags."

Laurie took hers. God, she hated these things, but she and her friends dutifully pinned them on.

She didn't recognize the man at the table who tore tickets off a big roll like they used to have at the movies and handed them each two. "For drinks. First two are on the house, but if you want to drink like it's 1994, the rest are on you." He smiled at his joke.

Laurie wondered how many times he'd said that already. She peered at his tag and saw 'Rudy Gonzales.' The name didn't ring a bell. "Thanks, Rudy."

They pushed through the door. The band switched to "I'll Do Anything for Love." A glitter ball hung over the dance floor, which struck Laurie as a gesture toward an earlier decade. A few couples danced.

Laurie surveyed the crowd. About half had gone with the nineties theme, a lot of the men in dark flannel shirts and ripped jeans. More than a few wore suits, looking like they'd come straight from the office. Others sported leather jacks and tee shirts with their ripped jeans.

More of the women had taken up the challenge. Some wore short black slip dresses over a tight, undersized white T-shirt. Something forbidden at school, she remembered. She spotted grunge flannels and jeans, bright satin shirts, another Madonna, and a few preppy plaid suits.

She grabbed Skye's arm. "I don't recognize anybody."

"I see a few familiar faces, but maybe the name tags were a good idea after all," Skye whispered.

Dana started pointing out people. "There's Sandy Jones. Remember her? Knew everybody. Always getting into trouble for talking and chewing gum?"

"Maybe." Laurie wondered if her memory was slipping away.

"She's a real estate agent now. Apparently doing great."

"Didn't she play basketball?"

Dana squinted her eyes. "Maybe, but she's average height. She might have been a cheerleader." She sounded doubtful.

Laurie and Skye scanned the crowd, standing close to each other for reassurance.

"Oh, and there's Carl Simmons. Always in the library? Quiet but cute. I think he works in a bank now," Dana informed them.

She pointed to a rotund, washed out blond, her cheeks red, carrying a drink with one of those colorful little umbrellas in it. "Remember her? She was on the cheerleading squad. Starred in the class play *Our Town*."

Laurie was surprised. "What happened to her?"

"Big house on Queen Anne. Three kids."

"She must have gained fifty pounds at least." Skye slapped her hand over her mouth. "We're not supposed to notice those things these days, right?"

Laurie shrugged. "I can't keep track anymore. I'm supposed to give trigger warnings about the literature we read. Literature is supposed to disturb people, isn't it?"

Skye's forehead wrinkled in confusion, then she said, "Walter's book is definitely disturbing."

Laurie took a breath to explain what she meant, but then decided it wasn't worth it. She was tired of literary arguments. Tired of academia, in fact.

"Let's go use these drink tickets," Dana said, leading the way through the crowd.

"How can there be so many people here? Our class wasn't this big." Laurie turned sideways to slip between two groups in animated conversation.

"Wives, husbands, domestic partners, plus ones," Dana said. "Walter is a huge attraction and I think Baldwin Cress is putting in an appearance."

"The guy who owns Galactic?" Laurie asked.

"The very one."

They reached the bar and Laurie ordered a Hemingway daiquiri, not that she was a fan, but the guy sure knew how to drink. It had been a day and she needed something to settle her nerves. Skye and Dana both ordered wine from local vineyards. Dana held up her glass of white. "I see Walter isn't skimping. This stuff is expensive."

The three friends strolled around, watching the crowd.

"Look, there's—" Laurie snapped her fingers, trying to recall his name.

"Buddy Smith," Dana supplied. "My first crush. Leather jacket and Yamaha. Now look at him."

"I never understood the attraction. You didn't seem like the rebel type to me," Skye said.

They paused to study the man dressed in navy slacks and a light blue shirt open at the neck. He caught sight of them and held his drink up in recognition, then went back to his conversation.

"Still hot," Dana said.

The band finished their mediocre tour of the top hits of 1994 and the crowd responded with tepid applause. The MC walked up to the mic. "Give it up for Grunge Review," she said, holding her hands out to the group.

"Wasn't she in our algebra class?" Laurie asked. "She could solve any equation."

"Yeah, but I can't remember her name." Skye tapped her finger on her mouth.

"It is my distinct honor to introduce our very own Walter Pearce, known to the world as D.J. Stone."

Enthusiastic applause broke out. "Go, Walt!" somebody behind them shouted. A tweedy man with round glasses and pleasantly tussled hair walked up to the mic. "Thank you, Nancy."

"Right," Laurie said. "Nancy Pansy we called her. I hated algebra."

"He looks better than I remember," Dana said.

The crowd quieted and Walter leaned into the mic. "Thank you all for coming tonight. I wanted to make our thirtieth reunion special. Here's to Jefferson High." He held up a flute of champagne.

Waiters began circulating with trays of the stuff. The three friends grabbed their own flutes from a passing server in penguin black and white.

Once everyone had a glass, Walter raised his high. "I want to thank Mrs. Moss for putting up with me in English class, my dad whose stories of being a police detective inspired me, and Galactic's mystery editors for picking up my first novel." He acknowledged the applause with a modest bend of his head. "But most of all, I want to thank the man who has become my good friend, the owner of this fine establishment, Baldwin Cress."

Wild applause broke out.

Baldwin appeared and acknowledged the applause with a nod of his almost bald head. He was shorter than Walter's six feet plus, his head reaching his famous author's chin, but in all other ways, he outshone Walter. He wore jeans, a white shirt, and simple jacket, but his energy commanded everyone's attention. Laurie found it hard to put her finger on just what made him so charismatic.

With an easy smile, he took the mic. "Welcome, Jefferson High. We're pleased you could join us in our new headquarters. Tonight, we'll give tours of the Galactic Globes."

Cheers went up.

Baldwin held a hand up for the crowd to quiet down. "On the back of your name tag is a number. This is your group. Meet outside the ticket office every twenty minutes starting—" he made a show of checking his watch "—in ten minutes. The link on your app for this event opens a map of the grounds."

The clapping drowned out Nancy's thanks.

"Bunch of suck-ups, if you ask me," Skye sniffed.

Laurie turned over her name tag over. "We're Group Two."

Dana checked her watch. "Let's finish our drinks and get down there."

"I'm going to the bathroom first," Laurie said.

"Good plan," Skye said.

Laurie and Skye made their way through the crowd to the elevator bank and looked around for restroom signs. "Maybe this way," Skye pointed to their right. They'd followed the hall a few feet when a door opened and a figure in dark pants and a black hoodie came out, then headed away from them.

"Strange outfit for this event," Skye said.

"Creepy," Laurie said. "The bathrooms must be down there."

They reached the door the figure had come out of and Skye opened it only to find mops, buckets, brooms and metal shelves filled with cleaning supplies and paper products. "This isn't—"

"I told you I can't do it," a voice sobbed out. A woman walked around the shelf, her face red and tear streaked.

"Uh, sorry," Skye said.

"Oh, my God," she screeched. Her eyes narrowed. A glare replaced the tentative smile. "Lauren Olson."

Laurie went rigid with shock. Here stood Ms. Prom Queen herself. John's wife. Laurie found her voice. "Kimberly. It's good to see—"

"This is all your fault. You have to stop harassing me." Kimberly flew at her, long red nails reaching for her face.

Laurie's ancient martial arts training kicked in from somewhere deep in her brain. She grabbed Kimberly's hands and pulled them away, then turned a shoulder into her and shoved. Kimberly stumbled back. Skye reached out to steady her.

"Get away from me!" Kimberly shouted.

Laurie opened the door and ran into the hall, Kimberly hot on her heels. "What is wrong with you?" Laurie shouted.

But Kimberly didn't attack again. She stumbled down the hall, heading away from the ballroom, away from Laurie, her shoulders heaving with sobs.

Laurie watched her go, anger rushing through her followed by sadness for John who thought he'd done the right thing marrying his pregnant girlfriend. She tried to shake it off. He could have gotten a divorce, she supposed. But still. John was smart and funny. At least he was living his dream with his business, working with whales and the environment.

Laurie turned to Skye. "What was that all about?"

Skye took a tissue out of her pocket and dabbed at Laurie's face. "Here, you've got some blood."

Laurie touched her cheek. Her fingertips came away red.

"Harassing her? I haven't talked to her in thirty years, for heaven's sake."

Skye shook her head. "That was just plain weird. Let's find the bathroom." She tugged on Laurie's arm.

They found the ladies' a few doors down the same hallway. Skye wet a paper towel and cleaned off Laurie's face. Then rubbed hand sanitizer over the scratch.

Laurie winced. "That stings."

"It's supposed to. It will stop any infection."

"Good thing I don't wear much makeup," Laurie said.

They finished up and went back to the ballroom to find Dana. But, just their luck, they ran straight into the man of the hour, Walter Pearce.

"Laurie Olson. You came all the way from the East Coast for my triumph."

"Uh," Laurie blinked. "You mean the reunion?"

Walter waved this away. "Mr. Moss said if anybody was going to write the next great American novel, it would be you. Have you?"

Laurie tried to go around him, but other people had crowded around him vying for his attention. "Have I what?"

"Written the great American novel?"

"No, Walter, that honor goes to you," Laurie said, putting as much sarcasm as she could into her words. She pushed past him.

"Damn right," he spit at her as they made their escape.

"What a jerk," Skye said. "He's held that grudge for a long time."

"Let's find Dana." They pushed through the crowd and discovered her near a grouping of tables toward the back of the room.

"What took you so long? Our group starts the tour in five minutes." Dana put her glass on a table by the door and the three took the elevator to the ground floor. On the way, Skye told her what had happened.

"That woman has always been nuts," Dana said with a decisive shake of her head. "I don't know what John sees in her."

Outside, they walked across the plaza to the ticket office where a few people already waited and settled on a bench between two concrete planters. Small solar lights climbed the trunks of the vine maples growing in them.

"I think he did the honorable thing and married her because she was pregnant," Skye whispered.

Laurie decided to change the subject to something they didn't have to whisper about. She glanced up at the three-story greenhouse, interconnected glass-and-steel geodesic domes filled with plant species from around the world. One interior feature was a green wall that stretched from the bottom of the tallest globe to the top, filled with over 25,000 plants, from what she'd read. Workspaces for Galactic employees were placed strategically inside. "I like the idea behind it. That nature is missing from downtown areas with concrete and skyscrapers. I can't wait to get in there. Have either of you been inside the Globes already?"

Skye opened her mouth to answer, but loud voices drew their attention.

"You're a bastard. A no-good, cheating bastard." The woman stumbled and the man she was with reached out to steady her.

"Take your hands off me." She jerked away, wobbling on her high heels.

Skye glowered. "Not again."

But Laurie couldn't take her eyes off the man. Tall and still fit. His face angular, handsome in a classic sort of way. John Newman. The biggest mistake of her senior year. The quarterback. Voted most popular. Possessor of letter jackets who'd ignored everyone in public except his teammates and girlfriend, the lead cheerleader.

Kimberly Woolridge, said cheerleader, who'd pranced around in his jacket. Blond. Fit. Baby blue eyes.

Complete jerk.

Now his wife, drunk and out of control.

The very same woman who'd attacked her in the supply closet.

Everyone stared, then caught themselves and tried to look anywhere but at the arguing couple. Laurie moved behind the tallest man in the group. She didn't want to feel the emotions welling up. It had been thirty years, for heaven's sake. She tried to force down the memories.

She used to let John copy off her history exams. Once she let him talk her into writing a paper for him.

"I'll take you to dinner," he'd said. "We'll go to Ray's Boathouse. Everybody will see us."

She'd been a stupid teenager.

Laurie peeked between two classmates at the arguing couple. Kimberly whirled around. Laurie had no idea how she stayed upright in those shoes. That cheerleading practice must still be paying off.

Kimberly took in the group, squared her shoulders, and sauntered closer to them.

John seemed at a loss where to take himself, and then he spotted her. "Laurie? Is that you?"

Oh, no.

The tall man she was trying to hide behind moved aside, leaving her exposed.

"Laurie? That slut is here?" Kimberly searched the crowd and found Laurie's now red face.

Why is she pretending not to know I'm here?

John frowned at his wife, then looked back at her. "I'm so sorry, Laurie."

Memories flooded her. They'd actually had a decent time at dinner. He dropped the jock act. They shared a passion for orcas and kayaking. Discovered they loved the same trail in Mt. Rainer National Park. Afterwards, he'd driven her around, just chatting.

Thirty years later, he still looked great in his grey trousers and white Oxford shirt open at the neck. His walnut brown hair now silvered at the temples. His eyes, angered before, were lit with eagerness.

"You should have married her. You two are perfect for each other," Kimberly spit out.

"Hi, John. How are you?" Laurie asked, her voice husky with memory. This was not how she'd wanted things to go.

"It's good to see you." John took another step toward her.

"Now you can get rid of me and finally marry the love of your life," Kimberly shouted. "How are you going to get rid of me, John? Smother me with a pillow while I'm sleeping?"

John's head snapped back as if he'd been struck. His face flushed an angry red and he shouted, "Shut up for once in your life, you stupid cow."

Kimberly's baby blue eyes widened in shock. "You...you." She burst into tears and ran past the guides who had just opened the door to the Globes.

John shook his head. "I'll find you later," he said to Laurie and went after his wife.

The guide huffed out an embarrassed laugh. "Well, I hope our tour can match that excitement."

The group chuckled obligingly and gathered around him.

The Galactic Globes were breathtaking. Walls of green rose high. Water trickled. An elevator woven like a basket took them up one level. All the while the guide explained what they were seeing, but Laurie couldn't focus on him. She was lost in her memories.

On their second date, they'd walked at the park along Elliott Bay and talked about the Orca pod. At the end of the paved sidewalk, they wandered over to the cliff and John leaned down to kiss her. The kiss lit a flame that spread through both of them like a match dropped on dried grass. Don't do this, she kept thinking, but she couldn't stop. Didn't want to stop.

"You okay?" Dana whispered. They'd reached a deck with chairs set in discreet conversation areas.

Laurie just nodded.

Another level up an area offered a flat screen with couches facing it. Walkways draped with vines to look like tropical bridges took them between towering walls filled with plants.

"We'll finish our tour at the top. It's a spectacular sight," the guide assured them.

The three friends stood to the side as people waited for the elevator. "I just can't believe how I react to him," Laurie told them. "Even after all these years."

"When was the last time you saw him?" Skye asked.

Laurie shook her head. "High school."

"Oh, and that wife of his. Drunk as a skunk," Dana said.

"Who do you think she was talking to in that closet?" Skye asked.

Laurie shook her head, pushing it all away. "This place is beautiful. I can't let them ruin it for me."

"That's the spirit," Dana said.

Skye squeezed her arm as they rode to the top tier of the globe. Once outside, the guide explained more about how the place had been built and what kind of plants the greenhouse held. He finished his technical explanation and invited the group to enjoy the view. They all crowded to the railing at the edge and looked around.

"It's quite an engineering achievement," the man in front of them said.

"Just beautiful," the woman accompanying him agreed.

The three friends moved toward the edge of the group for a better view, finally relaxed and enjoying themselves. Then Laurie caught a glance of Kimberly over Dana's shoulder, back to the railing, surveying the group as if she were scanning for someone.

The elevator door opened and another group came out, laughing and talking. The group poured toward the rail, heads craning. Laurie went back to trying to enjoy the tour.

Then shouts went up from the back.

"Stop."

"Hey."

"Wait your turn."

A wall of people surged forward. A woman stumbled and fell. Two men tripped over her, clipping Dana and pushing her up on the railing.

Somebody dressed in black pushed Laurie to the side and rammed into Kimberly. The impact lifted her up and threw her onto the rail. Kimberly collided with Dana, grabbing onto her to stop her fall. She pulled Dana over the railing with her.

"Dana," Skye screamed.

Laurie froze for a split second.

"Help," came a tiny voice.

Skye and Laurie peered over the edge.

Dana hung from a protruding rock about ten feet below.

"Help," Skye shouted. "My friend needs help."

A woman screamed. One hand flew to her mouth. The other pointed down at the bottom of the globe.

Kimberly's body lay sprawled far below, her head twisted at a sickening angle. Her left arm stretched out from her body, a bunch of leaves from the vines clutched in her hand.

CHAPTER

THREE

S kye kicked off her shoes and started climbing the railing. "Hold on. I'm coming."

"No." Laurie grabbed her arm and tried to pull her down.

"We have to help her," Skye shouted.

"You'll fall, too. Do you want to end up like Kimberly?"

Skye's eyes strayed to the ground floor of the globe, then jerked back to Laurie's face. "We have to help Dana," she said, this time in a whisper.

Below them, their friend clung to the vine, fingers white with effort. Her feet swayed over empty space.

"Can you find a toe hold?" Laurie shouted.

Dana looked down and then whipped her head back up, her face blanched with terror. "I don't ... see ... anything."

"Coming through." Several voices came from behind the crowd at the railings shouted. "Make way."

The crowd parted and a young man pushed through carrying a deflated fire hose. More people carried the length behind them. He leaned over the edge. "Ma'am, I'm going to lower this down to you."

Dana nodded and attempted a smile.

The young man slowly fed the fire hose over the railing, the people behind keeping the crowd away. Laurie watched, Skye by her side. The hose reached Dana's level, but she hung from a protrusion that put it just out of her reach.

"Can you grab it?" the young man asked.

Dana stretched out, but the hose was too far away.

"Can you move closer to it?" he asked.

Dana tried to let one hand go, but her body started to swing. One of her shoes fell. She shrieked and grabbed hold again. "No, I'll fall."

"I'm going to swing it close to you. See if you can grab it."

The hose swung past Dana and she tried to snag it with her foot. Her left hand lost its grip and she hung, her body swaying back and forth. When she swung back toward the wall, she reached for the vines, but missed. Dana screwed up her face and threw her hand up to the support. This time she made contact.

"Got it?" he yelled.

Danna nodded, her face now streaked with tears. "Please hurry."

"Okay . I have another idea." He turned to his helpers. "Let's pull the hose back up."

"But—" Skye started to object.

"Don't worry. We're going to save your friend."

Once the hose had been reeled back, the young man tied it around his waist, then looped it around his shoulders. "George, Simon. Can you hold us both?"

Laurie surveyed the broad shoulders and bulging arms of the two men he spoke to. She wondered where they'd come from.

"We can, but is the hose strong enough?" one asked.

"I'll check," shouted a woman next to the wall where the hose had been stored. "It says it holds up to 116 and 290 psi. Whatever that means."

"It's strong enough," one man said. "I'm a volunteer fire fighter."

The young man in the lead climbed over the railing. "Okay , I'm ready."

George and Simon braced themselves and started to lower the rescuer. He inched closer and closer, but Laurie could see Dana's arms were shaking. "Hang on," she shouted.

The young man reached Dana's level and pushed into the vines, looking for the supporting structure. "Okay, I've got a hand hold. I'm going to work my way out to you." Hand over hand, he crept closer.

Laurie could see the sweat dripping from Dana's face even from where she stood. Dana's arms trembled.

"Hurry," Skye whispered.

One of Dana's hands slipped off again and she screamed. Her body dangled over the long drop below her.

Her other hand started to slip.

"Oh my God." Laurie wrapped her arms around herself.

Skye seemed to be praying or maybe chanting under her breath.

The young man reached Dana and grabbed her around the waist.

The crowd let out a collective sigh of relief. Some applauded.

Dana's eyes were wide with terror. Her hand now seemed frozen to the mass of vines.

The young man leaned close and seemed to give her directions, but Laurie couldn't hear what he was saying. Dana's rescuer turned around and backed up against her body. Dana wrapped her legs around his waist, then grabbed his neck with her loose hand.

"The other hand." His voice was loud enough to hear now.

Dana whimpered, then released her hold on the vine and wrapped both hands around his neck. The young man reached up and took hold of her arms.

"Pull us up," he shouted, his voice a bit strangled.

Laurie hoped Dana didn't choke off his airway.

Inch by inch, the two men pulled her friend and rescuer closer. Sweat beaded on their foreheads. Laurie shouted to the people around the limp hose. "Please, grab on and help. Don't pull too fast."

People gripped the hose and pulled. It looked like a lop-sided game of tug of war. In a matter of minutes, Dana's rescuer reached the ledge and grasped the railing. He helped Dana off his back. A few people surged forward to help Dana find her footing. Someone strong stepped forward and lifted her over the rail. She fell into Skye's arms and burst into tears. Dana sobbed in Skye's arms, Laurie petting her shoulder, then straightened and stepped back.

"Are you hurt?" Skye asked.

Dana shook her head no.

Laurie handed her a tissue and she blew her nose. Took another tissue and ran a finger under each eye to catch stray mascara.

Typical tough Dana, Laurie thought.

The elevator opened and two EMTs emerged rolling a gurney between them. Dana spotted them and held her palm out. "No, I'm fine."

"It's protocol, ma'am. We need to have you checked out at the hospital."

"Really, I'm fine." Dana protested. She hardly noticed as the team expertly guided her onto the stretcher and strapped her in.

"It'll be quick. Can we call someone for you?" Dana called as they rolled her away.

"We're with her," Skye said. "We'll go with her."

"You'll need to come with us, ma'am," came an unfamiliar voice.

Skye jumped when she saw the police officer who'd appeared at her side as if by magic. "But our friend needs us."

"She's in good hands. We're asking everyone to wait downstairs to be questioned."

Skye turned to Laurie. "When did we get to be ma'ams?"

Laurie was relieved Skye's sense of humor was returning. "It happened to me a few years ago." Laurie started to follow her friends out, but found a policewoman by her side.

"Could you come with me, ma'am? We need to get witness statements from everyone who saw the events leading up to this death."

A chill ran through Laurie. She'd been so relieved by Dana's rescue, she'd almost forgotten about Kimberly. She glanced down at the floor of the globe. A photographer moved around Kimberly's body. A German Shepherd sniffed her. Dogs had such good noses. Kimberly hadn't been dead long, but still. She wondered if it was bad.

"It is." The thought floated up to her.

Laurie stiffened. Am I hearing this dog, too?

The shepherd glanced up at her, then went back to work.

"There's nothing to worry about." The policewoman said, perhaps sensing her tension.

"It's such a shock," Laurie said, trying to cover her reaction. But then, nobody would imagine she could hear the police dog's thoughts. Laurie wondered when all this would stop. She'd already gone through a close call on the plane. Now this. How much more could she take before she was talking to lamp posts?

The dog gave a snort of derision.

She shook this off as her imagination and followed the group to the elevator bank. The officers herded everyone toward the adjacent Galactic headquarters.

Once Laurie was on the elevator, an anxiety attack hit. Not that she'd ever had one before, but it had sure felt like one. The sight of Kimberly's body and then Dana dangling from the vines kept playing in her mind's eye. Her chest squeezed tight. She couldn't breathe. Then a full-fledged hot flash hit her. She was on fire. Her blouse soaked through, her face as red as the fire engine the young rescuers road around in.

Skye kept shaking her head. "I can't believe it. I mean, I never thought I'd ever see anything like that. She was all—"

Once the group reached the ground floor, most found seats in the lobby. Several had opted to wait in the outdoor plaza adjacent to the doors. Laurie appreciated the cool of the Seattle evening. She'd already taken off her jacket and was close to peeling off these tight stockings.

"Yeah," Laurie said, trying to stop Skye from saying what she was thinking. What she couldn't stop seeing. The image of Kimberly's twisted body, her head at that awful angle, her hand reaching out for something to grab onto to stop her fall.

Skye rummaged through her purse again.

"What are you looking for?" Laurie asked after Skye had done this for the fifth time.

"My cigarettes. Where are my cigarettes?" she answered.

"You smoke?"

"I stopped ten years ago, but this calls for a cigarette." She threw her purse down between her shoes.

"And you still carry a pack around?"

Skye shrugged. "I guess it's like alcoholics keeping a bottle of their favorite around to help them know they're not going to drink it."

This didn't make a lot of sense to Laurie.

"My uncle's was Monkey Shoulder Whiskey."

Laurie reached over and gave Skye's arm a squeeze. "Have you heard anything about Dana?"

"Not yet. Can you believe this?" Skye asked.

"No. Who do you think did it?" Laurie tossed a crumpled tissue she'd used to wipe her face into the recycling can next to her.

"You aren't supposed to recycle those," somebody said.

Laurie fixed this somebody with a look she usually reserved for students who turned in their papers a month late and expected a free ride.

A police detective walked into the plaza and surveyed the people still left from the group who had been on tour when Kimberly had been pushed. "Laurie Olson," he called out in an authoritative voice.

"Oh, shit," Laurie whispered.

Skye gave her an encouraging nod. Laurie stood up and identified herself.

"Ms. Olson, please come with me."

Laurie resisted the urge to tell him she was Dr. Olson. That wouldn't get her anywhere except labeled as someone with an attitude. And she didn't need that. She followed the stocky detective into a small room with a worktable that ran down the middle, a white board on one wall, and flat screens on the other. These Galactic employees had well-equipped meeting spaces.

"Please have a seat, Ms. Olson." The man opened to a fresh page in his notebook and asked her to state her full name, place of residence, and cell phone number.

"So you live in Boston, Massachusetts. What brings you to Seattle?"

"My high school reunion."

"You grew up around here?"

"I did."

"Come back to see your old boyfriend?"

"Excuse me?" Laurie felt a spike of irritation and her face flushed.

"You heard me."

"No, I didn't really have a boyfriend in high school. I came to see friends and go to the reunion."

The officer consulted a piece of paper. "Dana Preston and Skye Yarrow?"

"That's right."

"You three keep in touch?"

Laurie sat back, relaxing a bit. "Yes, we've been friends a long time."

"They in on it, too?"

"What?" Laurie stared at him.

"Did you and John meet before the event? Make plans?"

"John? What the—" The irritation burst into fury. Heat ran up from her stomach. Sweat broke out on her forehead.

"You seem pretty upset. Why the red face?"

"It's just a hot flash."

"Right." The cop drew out the word, his face a sneer.

Laurie suppressed an urge to grab him around the neck and squeeze. She looked him up and down. Muscled arms under his tight shirt. A buzz-cut. Probably mid to late twenties. Way too young to know what he was talking about. Besides, his neck was too thick for her to get her hands around. His mind seemed equally thick.

"Afraid of getting caught?"

Laurie stood up, her eyes blazing. "Listen here, you stupid prick. My whereabouts are accounted for from the time I got on that stupid airplane that almost crashed until we all saw—" she teared up "—poor Kimberly lying broken on that floor."

"Several people said you disappeared right before your group started their tour."

She shook her head. "I was in the bathroom. I had no reason to kill Kimberly."

He leaned in. "And you didn't see Kimberly before the tour of the globes?"

Laurie opened her mouth, then shut it quickly. There were probably cameras in the hallway. "I saw someone come out of what I thought was the bathroom. When we went inside, it turned out to be a utility closet. Kimberly was inside. She seemed...upset."

"Uh, huh," he scoffed.

"She attacked me and scratched my face. Skye Yarrow will collaborate everything I've said. She was there."

They stared at each other for a full minute until the cop broke eye contact. "Where are you staying, Ms. Olson?"

"At my parents' house. I'm sure you have the addresses."

"Don't leave town."

Laurie stared at him, dumbstruck. Why couldn't she leave town? This was what they said to suspects on TV shows. "I have classes on Monday. I have to get back to Boston."

"You are a person of interest in a murder investigation. You cannot leave town."

"But—"

"We'll be in touch, Ms. Olson." He emphasized her name as if to threaten her.

"It's Dr." Laurie said.

The man's eyes flicked up at her. She saw a flash of confusion quickly replaced by bravado.

"Dr. Olson," she repeated.

"Dr.? You're a medical doctor. I thought you were—" he checked his notepad "—a professor."

Laurie let out an exasperated breath. She decided it wasn't worth explaining and stalked back out to the plaza.

CHAPTER

FOUR

"We need to finish our examination before you can question her." The doctor's voice reached Dana where she lay behind a curtain in Bayview's emergency room. Somebody sat in a chair in a corner, but she couldn't quite make out who it was. The face was blurry. Maybe she'd hit her head. She blinked and looked again, but still couldn't see any features clearly.

Before she could ask who was there, a nurse closed the curtain with a snap. "You've had quite a scare," she said. "I'm just going to check your vitals before the doctor comes in."

"They did that in the ambulance. Really, I'm fine."

The nurse gave her a rushed smile and took her arm. She pushed the blood pressure cuff up her arm and pushed a button. The band tightened. Dana tried to relax so she could get a good reading and go home.

"Do you take any medications?"

"No prescriptions. Where are my friends?"

"We called your husband. He's on his way."

Dana was not looking forward that. She hadn't seen Kevin since he'd moved out over a month ago. "What about the friends I was with? Laurie and Skye?"

The nurse slid the cuff off her arm and recorded the numbers.

"What was it?"

"Still a bit high. 140 over 80. But you had a big scare, like I said."

Dana thought it was the mention of Kevin. The nurse ran a thermometer over her forehead and pronounced it normal.

"My friends," Dana reminded her.

"Oh, all the witnesses are being questioned at Global. There are two officers waiting to talk to you."

Dana's gaze shot to the curtain. The haze in the chair next to it seemed more solid. She closed her eyes, but when she opened them again, the smoky cloud was still there.

"What is it?" the nurse asked.

"Nothing. I just want to get back home."

"Follow my finger."

Dana studied the nurse's face. Dark hair pulled back in a tight bun. Her forehead wrinkled with concentration. Bushy eyebrows. She didn't wax. Dana could see every detail. Was her distance vision affected?

"Keep your head still. Follow it with your eyes."

The woman had slender fingers. No nail polish. Dana's close up vision was fine, so what was the shadow in the corner?

"Thank you," the nurse said.

"Can I go now?"

The curtain moved back and a young man in a white coat stood there. Two police officers in blue uniforms crowded behind him. The doctor—Dana assumed that's who he was—stepped forward and closed off her view of the police. She tried not to glance at the chair, but her eyes strayed there anyway. The blob seemed even more solid. She must be hallucinating, but she had no intention of telling them and ending up in the psych ward.

The nurse read off her vitals, the doctor nodding with each

number. He looked up and smiled. His warm, brown eyes helped Dana relax a bit more. "I'm Dr. Joshi. You had quite a scare, I hear."

This must be the standard language for somebody who'd almost fallen to their death, Dana thought.

"How are you feeling? Any pain?" He started to palpate her arms and legs without waiting for an answer.

Dana tried not to pull away. "My shoulders are a little sore from hanging on that vine."

"Sit forward," Dr. Joshi said. He squeezed her shoulders. "Any discomfort?"

"Not much."

He pressed on either side of her spine and the crest of her hipbone, asking the same question.

"Nothing."

"Did you hit your head?"

Dana hesitated a second too long. The doctor reached for her head and felt around her skull. "No lumps. Anything hurt?"

She shook her head. She glanced at the dark shape in the chair and gasped in shock. The outline of a body was forming in the cloud.

"What? What hurts?" Dr. Joshi asked.

"Uh, nothing. I just remembered I ..." She couldn't think of anything to say, but fortunately the doctor was looking at her chart. If she told him she was seeing things, he might want to keep her overnight and she desperately wanted to go home. To be around familiar things. In her own bed. Should she ask for a vision check? Maybe one of her retinas had dislodged or something. But would they think she was hallucinating?

The doctor took out his little hammer and tested her reflexes, then shined a penlight into each eye. "Good. All normal. Feeling up for talking to the police?"

"I suppose so." Maybe that would distract her.

"I'm discharging you. See your personal care physician if you develop any headaches or new symptoms."

"Thank you, doctor." Dana didn't watch him leave. She didn't want to risk another peek at the chair. She'd get an eye exam once she was out of the hospital.

Two police officers walked into the room, young beat cops by the look of them. The taller one seemed somewhat older than the bright eyed, eager one.

"Could you tell us what happened, Mrs. Preston?" the tall one asked. The younger one opened his notepad.

With a sigh, she repeated the story she'd told the EMT workers. "I was just standing by the railing looking at the view from the top floor of the Globes. Then suddenly somebody shoved into me and knocked me onto the railings."

"Did you see who it was?"

"No, my back was turned."

"Then what happened?"

"I'm not sure. I was trying to get my balance, but somebody else went flying into me." Her eyes filled with tears, remembering seeing Kimberly's mangled body sprawled on the stones a few floors below. How she'd clung to the vines, desperate not to end up like her.

Dana heard a little sob from—was it the chair? The other side of the curtain? Please, let it be that.

"It must have been Kimberly since she..." Dana couldn't say the words.

"Did you see the deceased before this happened?"

Dana sat us a little straighter, relieved at the change of questions. "Yes, she was fighting with John."

"John?"

Dana frowned. "Her husband, John Newman."

"Do you know what they were fighting about?"

"Bastard," someone whispered.

Dana shook her head. "Not really. She seemed angry with my friend. Accused Laurie of causing the problems between her and her husband. But Laurie hasn't lived here in a long time. She hasn't been in touch with either one of them for years, so it didn't make any sense to me."

The younger officer opened his mouth to ask another question, but the curtains opened with a snap and Kevin Preston marched in. He stopped in the middle of the space, taking up a lot of room, hands on his hips. "Excuse me, why you are questioning my wife without an attorney present?"

Oh, no, Dana thought.

The two cops exchanged a guarded look. Dana was sure they recognized the state senator. The tall one squared his shoulders and asked, "Why does she need an attorney, if you don't mind me asking?"

Kevin glared at them, but the younger police officer ignored him and turned back to Dana. "What is Laurie's last name, ma'am?"

"I'm sure she's being questioned," Kevin snapped.

"Olson. Dr. Lauren Olson," Dana said, pushing down her fury at Kevin. This was why she'd asked for a trial separation. He dominated every situation. The more his political ambitions grew, the more controlling he'd become. Wanted an accounting of everything she did so he could be sure to counter any gossip. When the children were young, she thought he was being a good father. Keeping track of his family. They'd confer over a glass of wine every night once the children were in bed. His questions about her day seemed like genuine interest.

But lately, he was trying to involve her in intrigues at important business and political gatherings. To be his secret little spy and serve his aspirations to run for the U.S. Congress. Things had gotten worse when her firm had worked on a merger and the investigation seemed to involve state politicians. Kevin started probing her about the case. He'd pushed the matter. That same week, she'd been dismissed from the inquiry. "Possible conflict of interest, Dana. Nothing to worry about, but you should be clear of it," her boss had said.

When they separated, Kevin had insisted they keep it secret. "People don't like divorced politicians, no matter what they say." She'd acquiesced, on this point at least, but she was spreading her wings and trying to remember who she was before the marriage, before the tsunami of two kids and her high-powered job.

"That will be all for now, Mrs. Preston," the tall officer said, bringing her out of her barrage of thoughts. "Here's my card in case you think of anything else."

The younger one closed his notepad and the two left the cubicle.

"Get dressed," Kevin snapped.

Dana stood up and straightened her clothes. "I am dressed."

"That looks like a slip."

"It's a costume. We wore nineties clothes."

"It's indecent. I'm surprised at you, Dana. You—"

Dana cut off the scolding he was about to deliver. "I had a duster. Do you see it?"

Kevin looked around. "Here are your shoes, but nothing to cover you up with."

Dana ignored his tone. She accepted Kevin's suit jacket and slipped on her shoes. Picked up her purse and straightened.

Her eyes strayed to the chair in the corner.

The cloudy blob had sharpened into a clear form.

A blond woman was staring at her, baby blue eyes misty and confused. "What is going on?"

Dana let out a strangled cry.

Kimberly Woolridge sat there, plain as day.

LAURIE HEARD a car pull into the driveway of Dana's house where she and Skye had gone after being dismissed by the police.

Dana's voice drifted up to them. "I'm fine. Just jumpy."

"I can't leave you alone in this state." That was Kevin and he was shouting.

She and Skye exchanged a look. "What should we do?" Laurie asked.

"They separated last month," Skye explained.

"I'm not alone. My friends are here." A car door slammed.

Skye peeked through the curtain and Laurie crowded in beside her. Mittens pushed in next to her.

Kevin walked around the car and tried to take Dana's arm. "How do you know?"

"My car is here. Skye texted me. Said she had my purse, and I told her to take my car and meet me here." Dana turned her back on him and headed for the house.

"Your friends are upset, too. I'm not sure you should be with them. The kids are at my apartment. We could all be together."

"I need to be with the people who saw this. Who helped rescue me."

"You need to calm down."

Dana turned around to face him. "I agree and you're not helping. Just leave, Kevin."

Mittens let out a low growl. Laurie looked down at her, surprised.

Kevin shook his head and mumbled something Laurie couldn't quite make out. Maybe pig-headed was one of the words. He got in his car, revved the engine, and peeled off.

Skye blew out her breath. "Who needs to calm down?"

"Right?"

The door opened and Dana walked into the living room. Mittens greeted her at the door, tail wagging. Dana bent down to pet her. "Such a sweet face." Then she kicked off her shoes and collapsed onto the couch, pulling a plum throw over herself.

Laurie and Skye rushed to her. "Are you all right?" Laurie asked.

Skye leaned over the couch. "What did the doctor say?"

"I'm fine, fine. Stop hovering." Dana waved them off.

Laurie took the armchair across from Dana, and Skye settled on the other end of the couch. "Tell us," Skye demanded.

Dana arched her well-groomed eyebrow. "I need a drink."

Skye frowned. "Did they give you anything at the hospital?"

"Nothing. And they called Kevin. Apparently he's still my emergency contact. So, I need a drink."

Laurie walked over to the cellaret, an antique Chinese cabinet. "What'll you have?"

"Wine, please. My favorite Merlot is on the rack in the kitchen."

"Coming right up." She cocked her head at Skye. "You?"

Skye shook her head.

Laurie walked into the kitchen and found a tortoise-shell cat sitting on the marble island. "What's wrong with her now?" the cat asked.

"We've had a bad night," Laurie answered without thinking.

"We sure have." Dana's voice reached them from the living room.

The cat started grooming herself, unconcerned. Laurie gave herself a shake and poured a glass of Merlot for Dana, admiring the rich red, but opting for Chardonnay for herself. She tucked a couple bottles of spring water under her arm and went back to the living room. She set the drinks on the coffee table.

Dana picked up her glass and sat, swirling the wine around, saying nothing. Skye opened one of the water bottles and took a giant swig. After a full minute, she said, "Okay, what gives?"

Dana gave a little start, then looked up with haunted eyes. "I can't believe I almost turned into a splat on the floor."

Laurie choked on her wine, coughing and laughing. "It's not funny," she choked out. "I don't know why I'm laughing."

"It's the tension. Inappropriate laughter is—" Skye couldn't finish her thought. Laurie's laughter was contagious and soon they were all roaring.

"I mean, I was dangling there in my slip."

"Right, and that guy with the firehose. I mean, he went into action-hero mode."

"I think Buddy was trying to catch a peek," Skye said.

"He should be so lucky." Dana finally took a sip of wine.

"Yeah, but who could imagine this? Kimberly is dead." Laurie shook her head. Dana's eyes flitted over to the empty armchair, then back to Laurie's face.

They sobered immediately.

"It's tragic. I wonder how John is taking it," Skye said.

Mittens barked, her gaze fixed on the empty chair. Dana blanched and took another big gulp of wine.

"Look, I'm sorry the woman is dead. Really." She held her hand up like a girl scout. "None of us liked her in high school."

"That's true, but still," Laurie said.

"By the looks of that fight, John wasn't happy and now he's free —" Skye pointed at Laurie "—and you have to stay in Seattle."

Laurie frowned. "You're awful."

Dana jerked her gaze away from the empty armchair. "What? Why can't you leave Seattle? I mean, you're welcome to stay here. I've got a guest room, but—"

"She's a suspect," Skye said.

"No! Seriously?" Dana fixed Laurie with an incredulous stare.

Laurie called Mittens to come, but the dog ignored her. "The stupid child cop who interviewed me told me not to leave town. It was straight out of *Luther* or *NYPD Blues* or something."

"That guy is so hot," Dana said. The cat chose this moment to jump into her lap and Dana started stroking her.

"She needs comforting," the cat explained.

"Who?"

"The guy who plays Luther. What's his name?"

Laurie was momentarily confused. Who needed comforting? Then she realized Dana was talking about the actor. "Idris something. Are you drunk?" Laurie asked.

"Wasn't he in *The Wire*?" Skye asked.

"That's the guy." Dana lifted her wineglass as if she were giving a toast. "Really hot."

"Even I have to admit that." Skye raised her water bottle. They both looked at Laurie expectantly.

Laurie shook her head in disbelief. "The Seattle cops told me to stay in town. I have an exam to give on Monday. In Boston. I'm a person of interest in Kimberly's murder. And you're asking me if some actor is hot?"

Dana's gaze darted to the empty armchair, then back to Laurie. "I don't think that's legally binding."

"Don't worry. I can see her, too," the tortie said, apparently to Dana.

"Humans never can," Mittens said, looking superior.

Laurie frowned at the animals. What were they talking about? Why was she still hearing them? "Yeah, but our department chair is after me. He'd like nothing more than to get rid of me." She picked up her wine and took a big swallow. Did she want to stay in Seattle? She was tired of teaching. Tired of academic politics. Studies showed universities were some of the most toxic work environments. But could she talk to John about jobs now that Kimberly had fallen...been pushed to her death?

She opened her mouth to say this, but Dana interrupted. "Don't you have tenure?"

"He can make my life hell. He's such an ass."

"So retire," Skye said. "Take up a second career. What did you want to be when you grew up?"

Laurie's stomach knotted in fear. Or was it excitement? "I wanted to save the whales," she answered in a small voice.

Skye raised her water bottle again. "A noble goal."

"I'll drink to that." Dana took another big gulp.

Laurie's eyes misted. "So did John."

"See? See?" Skye kicked her heels on the couch like a kid.

"A woman is dead," Laurie scolded.

Dana's gaze shot over to the empty chair again.

"What are you looking at?" Laurie asked.

"Uh, nothing."

Mittens snorted.

"Skye, we haven't heard about your interrogation. Are you a suspect, too?" Dana teased.

"I got lucky. Sam Peters interviewed me."

"Who's he?" Laurie asked.

"She. Sam is short for Samantha. She's a friend of Jade's, but we didn't reveal that we knew each other to anyone."

"Is that going to get you in trouble?" Laurie asked.

"No," Dana shook her head, the self-assured attorney again.

"Anyway, she just asked me to run through our encounter with Kimberly in the supply closet and then repeat what happened on the upper deck of the Globe. I got her card and asked if she'd keep me updated on the investigation. You know, on the sly."

"Now that will get her in trouble." Dana waved her glass in the air. "More wine?"

Laurie took her glass and her own back to the kitchen for refills. The cat followed, twining between her legs as she stood at the island. "Careful, I don't want to trip on you."

The cat made a sound like a chuckle.

"So, that was the plan?" she asked. Laurie wondered when she was going to stop imagining she could hear the animals. The plane crash had set it all off, and now with Dana's close call and Kimberly lying broken on the stone floor... Had that made it worse somehow? She was on the suspect list for some ridiculous reason and couldn't go back home. But was it really home? Finals were next week. Dr. Brown would find a way to fire her. What if her encounter with Kimberly in the closet made her look guilty? She took a gulp of Chardonnay.

The cat rubbed against her leg as if to calm her.

She went back to her friends, handed Dana her wine, and sat down again. Mittens was still fixated on the empty chair. Laurie guessed the dog had been trained not to get on the furniture. The cat had no such reluctance. She jumped into Laurie's lap and scooted her head under her hand. Laurie stroked the cat's head and down the smooth, dappled side.

A rumbling purr rose.

She thought of Manley Hopkin's poem "Pied Beauty" and her brain began a recitation. 'Glory be to God for dappled things – For skies of couple-colour as a brinded cow.'

46

To stop it, she asked, "What's the cat's name?"

"Liễu Hạnh." Dana waved her goblet, almost spilling her Merlot on the sofa. "She's named after the Mother Goddess of Vietnam. Lele for short."

"Hello, Lele." Laurie continued to stroke her sleek sides.

"Which brings me to another vital point. Mittens? I mean, please." Dana scrunched up her face.

"Like I said, I rescued her. That's what her human called her."

"She wasn't my human," Mittens said.

"She needs a new name," Dana declared.

"I agree," Skye said.

"Something beautiful. I love her fawn coat—" Dana frowned "—once she gets a good grooming." Dana and Skye both stared at the little Havanese mix, then grabbed their phones and started googling.

"The breed comes from Cuba. Named after Havana which means 'heaven'," Skye said. "Angel?"

"I found a list of most popular names for Havanese. Bella. No vampires. Charlie. She's a girl, right?" Dana looked up from her phone.

"Yes," Laurie said, amused by her friends.

"Lucy, Coco, Sophie." Dana continued listing off possibilities.

Mittens turned around and put her front paws on the coffee table. "My name is Rosa Miranda Gomez Diaz."

Laurie choked on her wine.

"What? You don't like Sophie?" Dana asked.

She coughed, then said, "I think her name is Rosa Miranda."

They both stared at her. After a few seconds, Skye nodded her approval. Dana smiled. "Good one. How'd you come up with it?"

Rosa Miranda took her paws off the table and wagged her tail vigorously.

"Well, the dog likes it," Skye said.

"Rosa Miranda it is. But it's a bit long," Dana said.

"Rosa for short?" Laurie addressed herself to the dog.

She barked her approval.

Skye stood up and stretched. "I think it's past time to go home. Want a ride, Laurie?"

"Uh," Laurie didn't want to wake her parents up, explain the dog, which would lead to the near plane crash, then the murder and almost death of one of her besties.

"Stay here. I've got a guest room." Dana tried to stand up, but fell back on the couch. "Besides, I think I might need a hand."

Skye took hold of Dana's arm and hauled her to her feet.

"Okay." Dana patted Skye's arm. She took a wobbly step. "How much wine did I drink?"

Laurie shook her head. "I lost track, but you had good reason."

"We all did," Dana said, "except for Ms. Teetotaler here."

"Hey," Skye objected. "I've got to drive all the way out to Duvall."

"You could stay here, too." Dana said with a silly smile. Her eyes teared up. "You two are my best friends."

"All right, you're going to be embarrassed in the morning," Skye said.

"If she remembers," Laurie added.

The two friends helped Dana up to her room and into bed. Laurie waved goodbye to Skye and watched her drive away.

"I like her," Rosa said.

"Me, too," Laurie answered.

She retrieved her suitcase and got ready for bed. She pulled the covers up, then felt the dog jump up. "You can't sleep on the bed."

Rosa snorted, turned around three times, and settled in a neat circle.

Laurie decided not to argue with her.

CHAPTER

FIVE

Dana woke to pounding on the front door. She jumped up and grabbed her throbbing head. How much had she drunk last night?

"Quite a bit," came a voice.

She froze. Please God, no.

"Oh, yes. Still here." Kimberly waved at her from the chair in front of the vanity.

The pounding downstairs continued. "Seattle police. Open up."

Dana grabbed sweatpants and a shirt hanging on a hook in the closet and threw them on. "You better be gone when I get back." She gave Kimberly a withering look before heading for the stairs.

The door to the guest room opened. Laurie stood there in an old t-shirt and undies. "Who were you talking to? Did Kevin come back?"

"Uh, no." Dana closed her bedroom door and stood against it. Could Laurie see Kimberly? Nobody at the hospital had or last night when she'd lounged in the chair across from her. Only the dog and cat seemed to notice her.

"Mrs. Preston. Please open the door," came a voice from the front porch.

"Who is that?" Laurie asked.

"The police. You'd better get dressed."

Dana ran down to the living room and opened the front door just as a burly officer lifted his fist to pound again. She winced at the pain in her head. "Can I help you officers?"

"Officer Ketts," said the burly one. "This is Officer Fensel." They flashed their badges.

Dana ran her hand through her short bob. Before she could say anything, Officer Ketts asked, "Is Lauren Olson here?"

For a wild second, Dana thought of denying it. But then she came to her senses. "Yes, did you want to ask her more questions?"

"May we speak with her?" the younger one asked.

Dana didn't remember the names they'd just told her. She needed coffee. She ushered them into the living room. "Please have a seat. I'll get her."

She climbed the stairs again and knocked on Laurie's door, then opened it. She could hear water running in the shower. Rosa lounged on the bed. She frowned, almost telling her dogs weren't allowed on the bed. But with this hangover, it was too much trouble. She opened the bathroom door. Steam billowed out. "The police want to talk to you. And don't use all the hot water."

"What do they want?"

Irritation flushed Dana's chest sending a spike of pain through her temples. "How should I know? Just get dressed and come downstairs."

She turned back to find Rosa sitting in the hallway. "You need to go outside?"

The dog started down the stairs. When she saw the police officers, she went over to them, tail wagging.

"Laurie's in the shower. She'll be down soon."

The two men exchanged a look. "Are there any more exits to the house?"

This brought Dana up short. "Just a back door."

Ketts nodded to Fensel, who stood. "Could you show me?"

"Certainly. I was about to let Rosa out." Dana walked to the kitchen, her spine stiffening with suspicion as Fensel followed close on her heels. Why would they want to see the back door?

"Here it is." Rosa shot out as soon as Dana opened it. Fensel closed it for her and seemed to take up station there.

"Uh, I'm going to just make some coffee," Dana said.

Fensel gave her a curt nod. She filled the kettle and poured coffee beans into the grinder. Not a good idea with this headache, but she loved the fresh smell. She set out the French press and mugs and filled the creamer. Fensel watched her every move.

"I'm just going to check on Laurie." She made a break for it.

Upstairs, she found Laurie getting dressed. She made a quick pitstop in the bathroom, then came out. In the hallway, Laurie was way too relaxed. "Hurry up. These guys are spooking me."

"Got any aspirin?"

"Good idea." Laurie went into her room to grab the bottle, but froze at the entrance. She glanced sideways at the vanity table. No Kimberly. That was a relief.

She brushed her teeth, threw some water on her face, then downed three aspirin. Laurie stood in the hallway looking entirely too composed in her jeans and loose shirt. She handed the bottle to her just as the kettle screamed in the kitchen.

Officer Fensel stood with his back to the backdoor, oblivious to the frantic scratching. She picked up the kettle to stop the train whistle. "Could you please let the dog in?"

"Best to let it stay outside." He put his hands on his hips, his leather gun belt creaking as he moved.

Rosa barked. Dana poured water into the French press and set the kettle back on the stove.

Rosa—was that the name they'd settled on?—barked again.

"Come on. It's drizzling outside," which was tantamount to saying this is Seattle.

The man relented and a damp Rosa bounded in. Dana toweled her off before she could head toward Laurie's voice in the living room. Officer Fensel followed. Dana finished preparing the coffee and started to pour when she heard, "Lauren Olson, you are under arrest for the murder of—"

"No," Dana shouted and sprinted into the room where Laurie stood, hands up. "She didn't do it. She was standing right next to me."

Officer Fensel moved in front of her. "Obstructing an arrest is a crime."

Laurie stood, eyes wide, hands still in the air.

Rosa growled.

"Secure your dog, ma'am," Fensel said.

Dana bent down and called Rosa to her. The dog ran to her, whining. "It's all right. Everything's going to be all right."

"Is it though?" Laurie asked in a high, panicked voice.

Officer Ketts finished reading Laurie her rights and took out his handcuffs. "Put your hands behind your back."

"Is that really necessary?" Dana asked.

"It's protocol." Ketts snapped the cuffs on.

Dana grabbed Rosa's collar and stood as straight as she could without losing her grip. "I'm going to need your names for the attorney. Can you please give me your cards?"

"Our names will be on the arrest report. Have your attorney—" Fensel put a sarcastic twist on the word "—pick up a report at the station."

With this, the officers marched Laurie to their waiting patrol car. Dana noticed another police car blocking the street outside. Fury rushed through her. What kind of criminals did they take them for? Sensing her anger, Rosa started barking furiously. Dana picked her up so she wouldn't dash outside to save her new mistress.

Laurie shot a pleading look at her as Ketts helped her into the back of the unit. Dana slammed the front door and rushed back into the living room to find her phone. She had to call Kevin even if it was six in the morning.

"Well, that was satisfying." Kimberly sat perched in the same chair she'd occupied last night, a wide smile on her translucent face.

Dana yelled in frustration, then headed to the kitchen. She'd need to drink the entire pot of coffee if she was going to stop seeing —she shied away from the word that was trying to pop into her mind.

"WE DIDN'T EVEN KNOW you were in town." Laurie's mother stood in the living room of their family home, hands on her hips.

"Do you understand the terms of your bail?" Officer Ketts asked Laurie, ignoring the two silver-haired parents in the room.

Drs. Martin and Larissa Olson were not used to being ignored. "Now see here," Laurie's father stepped forward. Then he seemed to hear what Officer Ketts had said. He blinked. "Bail? What is the meaning of this?"

"They think I killed Kimberly Woolridge," Laurie explained.

"Who in the world is Kimberly—" her mother frowned, her lake blue eyes narrowing. "My daughter did not kill anyone."

Laurie felt a rush a relief when Mittens—no, what was her name? Rosa Miranda rushed into the room, tail wagging.

"What is going on here?" her father demanded in his no-nonsense voice. "And why do you have a dog?"

Dana and Skye arrived behind Rosa, out of breath. "We came as soon as we heard," Skye said.

"WE'LL LEAVE YOU TO IT." Officer Ketts gave Laurie a crisp nod and walked out, Officer Fensel right behind him.

The family dog, a boxer mix, came running into the living room, his whole butt wiggling as he greeted Laurie. She leaned down and tried to hug him, but he was too squirmy. Satisfied he'd greeted her properly, he went to Rosa and sniffed her all over. Rosa stood still under his ministrations.

Larissa surveyed the group, then turned on her heel. "I need a drink."

"Mom, you have to be careful of your heart," Laurie said.

"Which is why I need red wine."

"I keep telling you to try CBDs," Martin scolded.

Larissa huffed. "Everyone follow me."

The group filed into the back of the house, dogs included. The open area included a well-appointed kitchen and spacious family room with a harvest gold sectional and a collection of chairs clustered around it. Windows looked out onto a deck with a glimpse of the sun setting over Puget Sound in the distance.

"Sit," Larissa commanded.

Rosa sat immediately, looking quite pleased with herself. Oliver just plopped down right where everyone needed to walk. Rosa watched Larissa with eager eyes, obviously expecting a treat.

Larissa paid her no mind, so Laurie opened the refrigerator and took out a package of turkey lunch meat. She peeled off a slice and handed it to Rosa and another to Oliver. Rosa gobbled it down in a split second, then woofed for more.

"That's all for now." Laurie scratched the dog's head, then found a seat, steeling herself for the lecture that was sure to come. She shook her head when Skye tried to settle into her mother's favorite chair.

Her mother carried a rather full glass of wine out of the kitchen and settled in the chair Skye had just moved out of. "I'm sorry not to be a good hostess, but I'm sure you'll consider the circumstances. Please help yourselves. There's sparkling water, wine, and soft drinks. The bar is over there." She gestured vaguely with her free hand.

Nobody moved, except Rosa, who came out of the kitchen and sat in front of Larissa, watching her expectantly.

"Where did this dog come from?" her father asked, as if this was the most important question of the evening.

"It's a long story." Laurie settled back into the cushy chair, putting her feet on the ottoman.

Larissa pointed. "What is that around your ankle?"

"It's an electronic monitoring device, Mom. I'm out on bail. They think I killed Kimberly Woolridge."

"But she was pushed by some guy in a black hoodie," Skye blurted.

"I got pushed, too. I was hanging from the vines at the Galactic Globes," Dana explained.

"Black hoodie?" Martin fished this detail out of their responses.

"You were hanging from—" Larissa stared at the three of them as if they'd taken leave of their senses. Her mother took a gulp of wine, not bothering to be dainty. "You'd better start from the beginning."

Laurie told the story from the almost plane crash through the class reunion until the arrest this morning, leaving out the part about hearing Rosa.

"What happened?" Skye asked. "You were in there all day. They wouldn't tell us a thing."

"When did Shanks show up? Was he helpful?" Dana asked. "I mean, you're out of jail, so he must have done something."

"He was in court most of the day, but showed up around three-thirty. Thanks for calling him, Dana."

"Of course."

"We should use our family attorney," Martin said.

"She needs a criminal lawyer, Dr. Olson," Dana explained. "Jonathan Shanks is the best in Seattle. He's a little old fashioned, but is well connected. He knows everybody."

"Imagine that, Martin. Now we need a criminal lawyer." Larissa drained the rest of her wine.

Laurie ignored her mother and turned to Dana. "I took your advice and didn't answer any questions. They kept coming in and asking me all kinds of crazy stuff, like why did I do it? Had I been holding a grudge all these years? Had John and I been in touch? How had we planned it? What happened in the supply closet?" Her eyes teared up and she brushed the escapees away.

"The supply closet?" Her mother's tone was incredulous.

Laurie let out a strangled laugh. "Honestly, I thought I was tougher. It was grueling. And they didn't even feed me lunch."

"We'll use that against them," Dana declared.

"I'll get Jade to keep tabs on the investigation," Skye said.

Martin and Larissa looked at her with confused faces.

"She has connections with law enforcement. Nothing illegal," Skye explained.

Laurie turned to her parents. "I'm supposed to stay in Seattle until this investigation is over."

"Don't you mean trial?" her mother asked. She held her wine-glass to her mouth, but found it empty.

"It probably won't get that far, Mother. I'll have to call my department. Exams are next week."

"You have tenure, though," her father said. "I mean, they can't fire you, right?"

Laurie's eyes teared up again. She looked up at the ceiling to stop them from falling. Why was she upset about this, of all things? She had just been thinking she wanted to retire early. "For a felony? Yes, Dad. I'm afraid that would do it."

Her father just stared at her for a minute. Then his eyes dropped to the little Havanese mix who sat at his feet. "Did anybody feed this dog?"

They all looked over at Rosa, her gaze fixed on Martin, her tongue hanging out.

"Oh, my God." Dana's hands flew to her face. "I forgot. I was so busy getting your attorney lined up that I didn't eat either."

Martin made his way to the kitchen and opened a lower cabinet. He picked up a bag of dog food and shook it. "Larissa, why did you leave an empty bag where we keep the dog food?"

"To remind me to shop first thing tomorrow morning." She eyed Oliver, who lazed in his bed. "This one isn't going to starve.

Martin shook his head at this logic. "Okay, boy. I'll fix you a hamburger."

"It's about time somebody paid attention to me," Rosa huffed.

"Why didn't you say?" Laurie asked Rosa. Out loud.

"Say what, dear?" Larissa asked.

Laurie shook her head at her mother. "The dog is a girl, Dad. Her name is Rosa Miranda Gomez Diaz."

"That's quite some title. Is she pedigreed?" His voice came from the depths of the refrigerator.

Laurie stared at Rosa, but the dog stuck her nose in the air and trotted into the kitchen. "I don't think so."

Martin stood up. "We've got ground beef and fixings for hamburgers. Who wants one?"

Rosa barked.

"Besides you," Martin said.

Well, at least she wasn't the only one talking to the dog.

Everyone raised their hand except Dana. Martin counted, then frowned at her elegant friend perched on the edge of her chair. "What can we make you?"

Dana shrank into herself. "A salad is good enough for me."

"Nonsense. You just said you haven't eaten all day," Martin said in his booming voice.

"Uh, do you have any veggie burgers?" Dana almost whispered the question.

"What?" Martin put his hand up to his ear.

"Veggie burgers?" she repeated slightly louder.

"Uh, Larissa?" he asked.

"I think we have some black bean patties left over from when the Millers came over."

"That would be great," Dana said, but she still chewed her lip.

Laurie decided to rescue her. "How about gluten-free bread?"

Her father frowned. "When did you start that fad?"

Her mother piped up. "I think there's some in the freezer. We keep some on hand. So many people eat that way these days." She shot Martin a look.

"Don't know what's wrong with good ole wheat," Martin grumbled in a voice he probably though was quiet, but everyone could hear.

"Sorry," Laurie mouthed, but Dana brushed it away with a wave of her hand.

"Who's making the fixings?" Martin asked. The three friends scrambled up and made their way to the kitchen.

"Is anybody going to feed me?" Rosa asked.

Laurie patted the little dog on her head. "First patty goes to you."

"She can eat raw meat, you know," Skye said. "My vet recommends it." Rosa wagged her tail so hard it blurred. Skye grabbed a plate and held it out to Martin.

"It's really safe?" he asked.

"Best thing for her."

Martin scooped up enough meat for two patties. Skye put the plate on the rug leading out to the deck, and Rosa scarfed it all in just a few seconds. Oliver lumbered in and sniffed the bowl.

"Is that it?" Rosa asked Laurie.

"For now, yes," Laurie said out loud.

"What are you talking about?" Larissa asked from her chair.

"Rosa wants more, but I told her no."

"How do you know that's what she's thinking?"

"Uh, well," Laurie stumbled, her face heating. "I mean, just look at her. She's staring at Dad."

"I'm glad you haven't gone crazy along with becoming a criminal."

"I'm not a criminal, Mom. I did not kill Kimberly."

"That other one did it," Rosa said.

Laurie almost dropped her glass. Did the dog know who the real killer was?

"Who did it?" Laurie asked Rosa silently.

Skye gave Rosa a second helping and found a plate for Oliver. They ate quickly.

Laurie waited for an answer, but Rosa trotted past her and jumped up into her vacated chair. She turned around three times and laid down, her nose tucked under her fluffy tail. Laurie would interrogate her later.

The group gathered around the island, Skye cutting onions paper thin, Dana taking the tomatoes. Laurie washed lettuce and put it in the spinner. The talk turned to happier topics, like the chocolate cake Larissa had just made.

"But it's wheat flour," her mother told Dana.

"Oh, I'll make an exception." Dana's eyes gleamed.

Laurie couldn't understand how she could eat like a horse and stay so skinny. Dana had always been that way, but one slice of cake would add two pounds to her frame. Laurie cut herself a big slice. Two pounds it would be. She had more important things to worry about.

CHAPTER
SIX

"Is she ever going to wake up?"

"Humans sleep well past hunting time. And they don't let me go out to feed myself."

The thoughts started to penetrate Laurie's awareness. She slowly swam up from sleep. A soft, warm weight sat on her chest. She stretched and tiny pins pricked her skin.

"Ouch. What the—" She opened her eyes and found luminous green eyes with vertical pupils peering at her.

"Natasha?" Her parents' Prussian Blue sat on her chest. She hadn't been around last night.

"Oh boy, she's awake. She's awake." Rosa bounced up and down. "Let me out. Let me out."

"I need to pee," Laurie said.

"Not more than me," Rosa said.

Laurie stumbled into the bathroom. Once done, she started toward her bedroom door. She reached for the doorknob, then realized she only had on a t-shirt. She rummaged through her old closet. Her old flannel robe still hung on a hook behind tailored blouses in different colors.

Rosa pawed at the door.

"All right already." Laurie opened the door and Rosa flew down the stairs. Laurie grabbed the rail, still half asleep. She hurried through the kitchen and opened the back door.

Rosa rushed onto the deck, Oliver right behind her, and into the yard where Rosa let out a mental sigh of relief that sounded entirely too human.

"Dogs," Natasha scoffed. "Too big for a proper box."

Laurie stared down at the cat. "Okay, if I'm really hearing you, then jump onto the couch."

Natasha stared at her as if to suggest she did not take orders. Then she trotted over to the harvest gold sectional and jumped up on the back. She sat and lifted a paw to her face to lick.

"Run around the kitchen island three times," Laurie said to the cat.

Natasha finished cleaning her face and started on her side.

"So I am imagining it." Relieved, Laurie turned her back on the cat and reached for the coffee beans. She put them next to the grinder, then grabbed the kettle. Something brushed against her leg. She looked down to find Natasha dashing around the island. Laurie stood, kettle in hand, her mouth open. When the cat finished her third round, she stalked over to her cat tree, obviously annoyed.

Oh, my God. I'm actually hearing the animals, Laurie thought.

"Of course you are," Natasha said. "Why wouldn't you?"

Laurie stared at Natasha, then heard a scratch on the patio door. On automatic pilot, she let Rosa in.

"Nice yard." Rosa shook all over, dew drops from the bushes flying off her fawn coat. "The sun's out. Let's go for a walk."

"So I've officially lost my mind." She realized she was still holding the kettle. She started to fill it at the sink, then stopped. She shouldn't use tap water.

"It's all right. They got some fancy filter," Natasha informed her.

Laurie froze. The cat was right. Laurie remembered her father going on and on about the new triple-stage filtration system they'd installed. "All the water in the house goes through it." His eyes had gleamed.

So it was real. She could talk to animals.

"Of course you can," Rosa said. "You're not crazy. You're gifted."

Laurie bent down and put her hand under the little dog's chin. Rosa's brown eyes looked up at her, filled with love. "You saved me," she said.

Laurie kissed Rosa on the top of her head. "I'm glad." She put the kettle on to boil, then ground the beans, and got the French press out of the dishwasher. She opened the refrigerator to look for something to cook for breakfast.

Rosa barked.

"You hungry? We'll have to get some dog food."

"Actually, I was just reading—"

Laurie jumped, her hand flying to her mouth. "You scared me."

"Sorry." Her father yawned. "I woke up early, so I googled what kind of dog food is best. Your friend was right. Turns out you should make your own. I made a list of ingredients, so we'll go shopping today."

Laurie stared down at her ankle bracelet, realizing she wasn't supposed to leave the house.

"In the meantime, how about eggs and bacon?" Martin asked the dogs.

"He never gives me eggs and bacon," Natasha complained.

"You can have my bacon," Laurie silently told the cat.

"Dad, you and Mom shouldn't be eating red meat. Not with her heart problems."

"Oh, she eats the turkey kind."

"Blech."

Laurie wasn't sure who had said that. The tea kettle whistled. She grabbed it and finished preparing the coffee. The aroma of Kona beans filled the kitchen. Laurie stood over the pot breathing it in. As soon as it was ready, she grabbed the biggest mug she could find and took it over to her favorite chair.

"How about an omelet?" Martin asked. "I've got onions, spinach and goat cheese."

"Sounds great." Laurie took a big sip of hot coffee and started to feel better about her new realization.

Rosa gave a soft woof.

Martin smiled down at the little Havanese. "I haven't forgotten you. You get scrambled. How's that?"

Rosa wagged her tail and woofed again.

Laurie realized people talked to animals all the time, they just didn't hear their thoughts back. She wasn't so different, not really.

"Just keep telling yourself that."

Natasha really was a bit snide, Laurie decided.

"Don't take I-5. You know the freeway will be packed."

Dana screeched and accidentally yanked the steering wheel to the right, almost hitting the curb. "OMG, are you trying to get us both killed?" She checked for traffic and pulled back into her lane.

"You keep telling me I'm already dead."

Dana glanced in the rearview mirror. Kimberly sat in the back seat studying her manicure. "Looks like I broke a nail."

Dana snorted, then jerked her gaze back to the road. "It's Sunday morning. Traffic should be light." She pulled onto the freeway.

"You're starting to believe in me now."

"No, I'm talking to myself."

"Right," Kimberly drew the word out. "So we're off to see the woman who ruined my marriage?"

"Oh, stop it. You ruined it yourself."

"She's been in love with John forever. That's why she tried to kill me."

"You and I both know that she wasn't the one who pushed you." Dana risked another look at the—okay, she was a ghost. "Do you know who did it?"

Kimberly wrapped her translucent arms around herself and shook her head.

"Doesn't being dead come with benefits? I mean, can't you look through time or something? See who did it?"

Kimberly stared daggers at Dana who was watching her in the rearview mirror.

The car beeped, alerting her that she was drifting out of her lane. She straightened out the SUV. This new technology was coming in handy with her distracting backseat driver.

"The last thing I remember is riding up the elevator."

"You don't remember standing by the rail? Getting pushed into me?"

"Nothing. I was on the elevator laughing with the group, then I woke up in the hospital."

"Why are you still here? Didn't you see a bright light or something? Meet a long dead relative to escort you to the other side?"

After a long silence, Dana glanced over her shoulder. Kimberly had disappeared. She sighed with relief and took the exit to Mercer. Dana made her way through traffic to the Olson's craftsman house with no ghostly company. Maybe Kimberly had gone off to look for somebody to take her on to whatever came next.

Dana grabbed the bag of gluten-free bagels and cream cheese tubs she'd picked up on Broadway and walked up to the front door. Barking announced her before she could ring the bell. Laurie's father opened the door. "Hi Dr. Olson. I brought bagels." She lifted the bag to show him. Dana still couldn't call him by his first name.

"Come in, come in." He stepped back, making room. "We're all in back."

Rosa woofed again and Dana bent down to pet the wiggling mass of fur. "Such a good girl. Let's go see your momma." Rosa ran ahead and announced her with another bark.

"Yes, she's here," Laurie seemed to answer the dog.

"I got your favorite—Eltana's rainbow." Dana set the bag down on the island and grabbed plates and some cutlery. Oliver trotted over to sniff the bag. She scratched behind his ears, then rinsed her hands off in the sink.

Laurie jumped up from her chair and dove into the bag. "Yum. You're my best friend."

"Hey, I thought I was," Skye objected with a laugh. "But I'll forgive you if you bring me a cinnamon raisin one. And some eggs and bacon. Natasha won't let me get up." The Prussian Blue lay on Skye's outstretched legs enjoying the attention.

"You got here early," Dana said to Skye.

"Jade had to work."

Laurie cut the bagels in half and laid them on plates. "What topping do you want?"

"Plain," Skye said, lazily stroking Natasha.

Laurie smeared the olive and herb flavor on her own bagel and added a generous dollop of cream cheese to Skye's plate. She scooped up some eggs and eyed the turkey bacon.

"Either one will do," Skye said.

"You must be psychic," Laurie said.

"Maybe a little, but I saw you hesitating," Skye said.

Laurie handed Skye her plate and settled back into her chair. "No, you can't have cream cheese. It will upset your stomach."

"What? I already have some," Skye said.

The dog woofed again.

"Dad, would you give Rosa some more eggs and bacon, please?"

"Does that dog never get full?" he huffed, but grabbed a dish. Natasha stood up and gave Martin the eye.

"More for the cat, too?" Laurie asked.

Dana watched her from the island where she was grabbing a plate of eggs and smearing the olive and herb flavor on her own bagel. "What are you suddenly, the animal whisperer?"

Laurie stopped for a second, then shrugged.

Dana joined Skye on the sectional and set her plate down on the glass coffee table. She took a sip of coffee, then threw her head back and sighed. "Just what I needed."

"Don't I get any?"

Dana jumped in surprise. Kimberly sat across from them, legs crossed.

Skye eyed Dana. "What's the matter?"

Dana picked up her plate and took a bite of eggs, saving herself from answering.

"You're not vegan?" Laurie asked.

"Mostly, but I eat eggs, dairy, even gluten on special occasions, too" Dana said, "like when my bestie decides to finally pay a visit."

Martin put three plates with eggs and bacon down for the animals. Rosa ran over and scarfed hers down in about two seconds. Oliver seemed to take his in with one lick of his giant tongue. Martin grabbed Rosa's collar when she headed for Natasha's plate, who ate daintily.

Laurie's mother sat at the island and ate a plate of eggs and turkey bacon almost as quickly as Rosa had. She dabbed her mouth with a napkin, rivaling the cat for delicacy, then asked, "What can we do to help today?"

"Nothing, Mom. It's Sunday. You guys should try and relax. My friends and I are going to strategize."

"Only if you're sure. We had a date today to go sailing with the Hendersons. We can cancel—"

"Go, I'm fine," Laurie said.

Her father studied her for a minute. "You sure? We can stay."

Laurie nodded, her mouth full.

"We'll pick up some groceries on the way home," Martin said. "Call if you need anything."

"I will," Laurie said.

The three friends waved goodbye and waited until the Olson's car pulled away. Skye took a set of keys from her pocket. "Jade gave me these."

"Keys?" Dana's forehead furrowed in confusion.

"Keys to the ankle bracelet."

"No," Dana said.

66

"Yes."

"But—" Dana's eyebrows pinched together.

"Jade says the dot just shows the house on the map. Not movement around the rooms. So, as long as the bracelet stays here—" she bent down to Laurie's leg "—they'll think you're home." She inserted the small key, turned it, and the tracking device opened.

Laurie pulled it off and set it on the coffee table. "You're my best friend now."

"Maybe you should move it around when you're here," Dana said. "You know, just to be safe."

Laurie stretched out her leg and did circles with her ankle. "Ah, much better. So what do we know?"

"For one, that you didn't kill Kimberly. You were standing right beside me, for heaven's sake." Skye jabbed her fork in the air, punctuating her words.

"Did anyone get a glimpse of who pushed her?" Laurie asked

Kimberly stopped looking at her broken nail—could ghosts have manicures, Dana wondered—and sat up a little straighter, her interest stirred.

"I only saw someone running away dressed in the same hoodie as the person who ran out of that storage closet," Skye said.

"Somebody wanted Kimberly out of the way," Dana said, "so we need to figure out their motive. Dive into her life and find out what she was hiding."

"Nothing, that's what," Kimberly said.

Dana huffed in surprise and looked over at the chair where Kimberly lounged.

"Jade says to get a list of her known associates," Skye said.

Laurie laughed. "That sounds like some detective show."

Dana settled back, relieved her friends hadn't noticed her reaction to Kimberly. "That's what we need to do. Investigate," she said.

"Oh, boy. This should be fun. The three stooges," Kimberly sneered.

Dana shot Kimberly a look. "We can certainly help Shanks."

"Who?" Laurie asked around a mouthful of eggs.

"Jonathan Shanks. Your criminal defense attorney. Remember him?" Dana made a face.

"She doesn't even know her lawyer's name. How is she going to figure out who kil—pushed me?"

"Oh, right. Shanks. I'm terrible with names and yesterday was not exactly a normal day."

"We know this about you," Dana said.

"I guess we can see if Kimberly was in debt or having an affair." Laurie said.

"Or doing drugs and owed her dealer," Skye added.

This elicited a snort from the indignant ghost. Rosa barked at her. Dana didn't blame the dog. Kimberly was getting on her nerves, too.

"Maybe she knew about a crime and they wanted to shut her up," Skye waggled her eyebrows.

Dana thought her friend was enjoying this a bit too much. "So we get a list of her friends, people she worked with."

"Did she even have a job?" Laurie asked.

"Used to." Kimberly crossed her legs.

"I think she volunteered a lot. You know, gardening clubs, parent/teacher groups—that kind of thing." Dana listed them off on her fingers.

"I wish I knew a good hacker," Skye said.

"I do." Dana's smile was smug.

"Who?" Skye asked.

Dana pointed at Skye. "Do you tell your wife everything?"

"Uh, yeah."

"Then I can't tell you her name." Dana took another bite of eggs.

"Her?" Laurie sounded surprised.

Dana jabbed her fork in the air. "Yes, you thought it would be a man. Fess up."

"Aren't most of those people in Silicon Valley men? I hear they're just awful to women." Skye twisted her mouth in distaste.

"Nah, they're teenage boys down in their mothers' basements with very expensive computer banks," Laurie joked.

"I'll try not to take offense." Dana stifled a laugh. She'd forgotten how much fun her friends could be.

Laurie's eyes went wide. "Wait, it's you?"

Even Kimberly stared at her.

"You can't tell Jade." Dana pointed at Skye.

Skye held up both hands in surrender. "Scout's honor."

"You were a Girl Scout?" Laurie asked.

"Well, no. It's just an expression." Skye rolled her eyes.

Dana went into work mode. "OK, let's divide this up. Skye, can you get Jade to run her record?"

"Like I have one," Kimberly sniffed.

"They've already done that. I can ask her for a copy of the investigation," Skye said.

"I'll check out her social media, work history, get a list of her best friends." Laurie held up her bare ankle. "Then we'll go interview them."

"Shouldn't we go to the funeral?" Skye asked.

"I can't," Laurie said. "I have to pretend I can't leave the house."

"At least one of us. Laurie can hang out in the car and take pictures of who comes. Match them to your list." Natasha jumped up to her favorite spot on the couch, and Skye got up to get more coffee. "Anybody else want some?"

Dana shook her head. "I'll get into her bank and phone records for a start. Our prime suspect, though, is the person in the black hoodie. Could you tell if it was a man or woman?"

Laurie held up her cup. "Couldn't really tell, but aren't men more likely to do something like that?"

"You'd be surprised at the stories Jade tells." Skye carried the pot over and filled Laurie's mug, then carried it back to the kitchen.

"I could try to hack into Global's security footage. See if we can get the tapes." This was the hacker, Dana.

"At first I thought Kimberly was having some romantic tryst, so I'd presume a man."

"Then you'd be wrong."

Dana stared at the apparently empty chair, then blurted, "Wrong about what? That it was a man or that you had some romantic interest?"

"Whoa," Skye said.

"Who are you talking to?" Laurie asked.

Dana looked back at them both, her eyes wide. "Uh, nobody?"

"Come clean Dana nee Leu Thi Dung. What's going on?"

Kimberly tittered. "Poop pants. Poop pants." Kimberly stuck out a translucent tongue.

"Oh my God, you're still in elementary school," Dana shouted at the newly deceased.

"Uh, Dana? Are you all right?" Laurie asked.

Dana dragged her gaze from the childish ghost to her friends. She'd always thought of herself as the rational one. Laurie was an artist at heart. Skye—well, she was like her name. Floating in her own little world. But she had to tell them. "I guess I need to divulge something. I was worried I was going crazy or hallucinating or something, you know, from the stress of hanging from that vine in a slip for heaven's sake in front of all those people and—"

"Honey, you're rambling. Just spit it out." Skye sat, hands on her knees.

Dana took a deep breath. "Ever since the fall, well really since the hospital, I've been seeing—" she glanced at the dearly departed who had her arms crossed and a smug expression on her face "—Kimberly."

"What?" Laurie's eyes went wide.

"You mean she's with us now?" Skye asked in a calm, soothing tone probably meant for people in an asylum.

Dana nodded her head, dreading what her friends would say, but Skye only said, "Ask her who the killer was."

"You think I haven't already?" Dana harrumphed. "She doesn't know. She said the last thing she remembers is riding up in the elevator."

"Then ask her who that was in the storage closet," Laurie said.

Dana felt a rush of relief. Her friends didn't think she was crazy after all. She looked at Kimberly. "You heard what they said. The person who pushed you was wearing the same clothes as the person you had a meeting with. Who was it?"

But the ghost shook her head, then with a whoosh, disappeared.

CHAPTER
SEVEN

Laurie watched Dana talking to the empty chair. How could something so strange be happening to both of them at the same time? Had the clock on their sanity run out? Was it hormones? Just the thought brought a rush of heat. Not another hot flash. At least she wasn't standing in front of a class full of college students.

"Blast," Dana shouted.

"What did she say?" Skye asked.

"She just shook her head and disappeared."

"Maybe she doesn't know." Laurie picked up her coffee and took a sip to steady her nerves.

"More like she doesn't want to tell us."

"We need to get those tapes." Skye looked over at Laurie. "Can we use your laptop?"

"Uh, to hack Global? Bad idea." Dana shook her head. "I'm still wondering why the police didn't confiscate it."

"But it belongs to your university," Skye said.

"I can cover my tracks." Dana explained.

"Can't Jade give you access to the tapes? Copy them on a thumb drive or something?" Laurie asked.

"There would be a record. Besides, she's already risking enough."

"How about the computer in my parents' office?" Laurie pointed upstairs.

"How old is it?" Dana asked.

"I think they just got a new desktop last year."

Dana made a face. "Why would anybody buy a clunky desktop these days? They're old news."

Laurie smiled. "So are my parents."

Rosa jumped up and barked.

"Is someone at the door?"

"Let's explore the neighborhood," Rosa said to Laurie. "Besides, I need to go again."

"You can go in the backyard," Laurie told her.

"A walk, please, pleeease, pleeeease." Rosa's whole body wiggled more and more with each word.

"We don't have time for a walk. We have to find out who killed Kimberly."

"Uh, Laurie, you're talking in long sentences to the dog," Dana said.

Laurie looked up into the worried faces of her two friends. Everyone had just accepted that Dana was seeing ghosts. "I guess I've got a confession to make, too."

"What?" Skye sat back down on the sofa. Dana went to get more coffee.

"Ever since the plane crash—"

"It didn't actually crash," Rosa said.

Laurie let out a sharp exhale and looked down at the dog. "I know it didn't actually crash, but it came close enough, don't you think?"

"You're doing it again," Skye said.

"Yes, that's what I'm trying to tell you. Ever since the plane—"

she looked down at the dog "—dive. Does that suit you? Ever since then, I can hear Rosa's thoughts."

Rosa barked and headed to the back door. "I guess this is going to take a while," the dog said. Laurie let her and Oliver out, then turned back to face her friends.

"You're serious, aren't you?" Dana asked.

Laurie nodded. "I thought it was just the stress or maybe hormones."

"Yeah, menopause is way tougher than I expected." Dana poured a cup of coffee and headed to the couch.

"You're having hot flashes, too?" Laurie felt relieved.

"It's more like brain fog for me. And fatigue," Skye said.

Dana squared her shoulders. "Okay, let's not get distracted. You can talk to your dog."

Natasha jumped up on the back of the couch and let out a protest.

"And the cat, too." Laurie explained the test she'd asked Natasha to perform earlier.

Dana looked at her with narrowed eyes. "How about Lele?"

"Lele, too. I could even hear the German Shepherds at the crime scene." She plopped down. "They know I didn't do it. Too bad they can't testify."

"So you can communicate with animals." Once again, Skye sounded surprisingly calm.

"Does Lele even like me?" Dana asked softly.

"Are you kidding? She loves you," Laurie said.

Dana's shoulders relaxed. "Only cats and dogs?"

"I don't know about squirrels or birds or—" She waved her hand in the air.

"And you've never heard any animals' thoughts before?" Skye asked.

"Never."

"Fascinating," Skye said.

"Oh, my God. You sound like Spock," Laurie said.

"Think about it. You both had a near-death experience. You didn't actually physically die, but you experienced a close call. The shock must have switched on something in your brains. You can talk to animals and Dana can communicate with ghosts."

Dana raised her finger to object. "Only one."

"So far," Laurie said.

Dana crossed her arms in front of her chest. "No, I refuse to talk to more ghosts."

Laurie went to the back door and let the dogs in, then grabbed her laptop, which for some reason the police had let her keep. "I'm relieved you all don't think I'm crazy."

"I think it's normal to communicate with animals," Skye said.

"Okay, back to the investigation. Let's at least check out Kimberly's social media. We can figure out who her besties are—were. Maybe she'll have a picture of someone in a black hoodie."

"Fat chance," Natasha sneered.

Laurie frowned at the cat. "Oh ye of little faith."

"I didn't say anything," Dana said.

"I think she's talking to the cat," Skye said.

Laurie set her computer on the coffee table and squeezed in beside her friends. Dana leaned in and opened Facebook. "Okay, did she use John's last name or her maiden name?

"Such a quaint phrase." Laurie shook her head.

"What?" Skye asked.

"'Maiden name.' It's almost as bad as 'out of wedlock'. My students don't understand George Eliot's first book. Why Hetty Sorrel had to run away when she discovered she was pregnant and not married."

Both her friends stared at her with blank faces. "Who got pregnant?"

"Is that somebody we knew in high school?" Skye asked.

"No, it's a fictional character in a Victorian novel."

"You have lost it," Dana mumbled.

"You're talking about a book? Honestly, can you focus?" Skye looked back at the computer screen.

Laurie burst out laughing. "So I can communicate with animals and that's fine, but you think I'm crazy because I'm talking about a book I teach in Victorian literature."

"Maiden name," Dana mumbled.

"Sorrel. She never married, but died tragically."

"No, dingbat, I'm talking about Kimberly. She used Kimberly Woolridge on Facebook." Dana shook her head.

They all leaned in to read the posts. The most current ones expressed shock and sorrow over her death.

She will be sorely missed.

I can't believe this has happened. We just had lunch last week.

She was so full of life.

Who could have hurt such a kind and gentle soul?

Laurie snorted. "Kind and gentle she was not."

"That's for sure," Dana said.

Rosa trotted into the family room, a leash in her mouth. She dropped it at Laurie's feet and barked.

"Even I understand that," Skye laughed.

"This is going to take some time. Take the dogs for a walk. Enjoy your freedom while you still can." Dana's eyes danced.

"Some friend you are," Laurie said.

"I'll stay and help," Skye said. "Besides, there are bagels left."

"If you need it, the password for the computer upstairs is on the back of the mouse pad."

"Parents." Skye shook her head, but she was smiling. "I've got my phone plus your laptop. That should be enough."

Laurie looked at Oliver, asleep in his bed. "You want to come?" His only answer was a snore. Rosa ran to the door, then back to Laurie and barked.

"You win." Laurie went to the front room and checked for any police cars before walking out to the porch and snapping on Rosa's leash.

The little Havanese mix trotted in front of her, tail up. Laurie started to relax for the first time in two days. She remembered the little park she'd played in as a child and headed toward it. It was nothing more than a copse of trees with a grassy area. Someone had added a swing set. The spinner was new.

Laurie bent down to Rosa. "I'll let you off the leash if you promise to stay in the park."

"I solemnly swear that I am up to no good," the dog said.

Laurie snorted. "So you're a Harry Potter fan. Cute." She unsnapped the leash and Rosa headed off. The dog stuck her nose into the first bush, her tail wagging. "No chasing anything into the street."

Laurie settled on the largest swing and pushed off. She leaned back, watching the sky, remembering her mom bringing her here on summer afternoons. Swinging as high as she could. Sneaking into the trees to explore when her mother fell asleep on a blanket under the shade. How had life gotten so complicated? Growing frustration with her job, then a divorce. Now she was a murder suspect, which was so crazy she almost couldn't take it seriously.

She'd met her ex-husband Graham during her senior year at Beacon Hill University. He'd just started at Fenway Institute of Technology. A nerdy stalk of a guy with a crop of curls and tinted glasses to suggest a nostalgia touch of rebellion. She would have preferred more muscle on his frame, but his wit more than made up for that. He majored in computer engineering. They married and lived happily in a small apartment a few blocks up from Magazine Beach. Laurie commuted to classes and took to jogging along the Charles River.

When he graduated, Apple and Microsoft offered him top jobs, but he opted to stay on and teach at MIT. She laughed at the memory. His parents argued with him nonstop, telling him just how much money he was turning down. But the two of them were idealists and decided to teach. Later came private contracts for Graham and he handed off his classes to TA's. She should have been so lucky.

Had she been jealous? Was that the source of the friction that had grown between them? They'd shared everything when they first met, but more and more, he grew furtive. Work with those corporations and government agencies came with secrets. He had always been the nervous type, but he got downright paranoid after a while, insisting on elaborate security in their house, even putting their phones in a black box at night. In the last year of their marriage, she started calling him Eddie Snow Town, which made him livid. And Laurie suspicious.

And now there was John. Reappearing behind his screaming wife. Handsome, calm even under crazy circumstances. His eyes had lit up when he saw her. And her body had as well. Flushing with the same attraction. This heat was not from menopause.

Rosa trotted out of the trees and sat down in front of the swing set. "Time to go home?"

The dog wagged her tail. Laurie snapped on her leash and they walked back, enjoying the tulips in Mrs. Bennett's garden. Throughout her childhood, she'd relished her neighbor's flowers. When she got back to the house, Skye and Dana presented her with a long list of names. "From what we could figure, these are the people she interacted with the most."

Laurie skimmed the two-page printout. "I see you found the password for the upstairs computer."

Dana snorted. "Like I needed it."

"Who knew you were such a spy."

Skye said, "What you don't know about your best friends."

"This is a long list," Laurie said. "How can we narrow it down? She couldn't have been that close with all these people."

Skye nodded. "We need to find out who her best friend was. Who she told her deepest secrets to."

Skye and Dana both look at Laurie. The silence stretched too long. She had an ominous feeling.

"You need to talk to John," they said at the same time.

CHAPTER

EIGHT

L aurie woke before the sun and somehow Rosa knew before she moved an inch. The dog did a lap around the bed, jumping on Laurie's stomach in the process, then hopped down and gave a low woof. Laurie was still adjusting to west coast time, so she didn't mind getting up early. But she would have appreciated more peace.

"I have to brush my teeth," she informed the little Havanese mix. The dog responded by running down the stairs to the front door and back. She stood wagging her tail as Laurie finished up her morning routine. She threw on some old sweats she found in her drawer, probably left over from high school. The pants were a bit short, but for the most part, they still fit. A minor miracle. Rosa kept running between her room and the front door, brown eyes eager. Laurie crept down the stairs, hoping not to wake her parents if Rosa hadn't already accomplished that. The dog stood still as she snapped on the leash and they headed out into the misty morning.

While she walked, her thoughts circled around the phone call she dreaded. It was Monday and she had to tell her department chair she couldn't come back for finals. She could get her TA to proctor the exams. If she had one. The university had cut back funding and only Dr. Brown's favored faculty had any assistants. Her imagination presented her with one disastrous conversation after another. What excuse could she use? That one of her parents had a medical emergency, but that seemed like wishing bad luck on them. Or that she'd caught some bug and couldn't fly? Same bad luck, but this one sat easier. That she had to go to the funeral of a conniving cheerleader from high school who stole her true love? Maybe not.

They reached the park and Laurie let Rosa off leash. "No running into the street."

"How dumb do you think I am?" Rosa asked before tearing off to the small grove of trees.

Laurie settled on the bench. Rather than continue on this mental mouse wheel, she pulled out her cell and made the first call. Rebecca Joseph, the colleague she was closest to on the English faculty. She would be happy to help. Well, willing was more like it. Becky answered on the second ring.

"Hi, it's Laurie."

"Hey, I'm just heading to my first class. What's up?"

"I'm stuck in Seattle and wondered if you could proctor my exams."

"Stuck? Like in you had too much fun and can't tear yourself away?"

Laurie let out a begrudging laugh. "Actually there's a situation I have to deal with. Friend of a friend died."

"Oh, Laurie, I'm so sorry. Were you close?"

"I was close to her husband in high school, but not her."

"Of course I'll help. Mind if I send a grad student to do one of them?"

"I think I'll post an essay exam online. All you two will need to do is tell them it's there. Of course, I'll post an announcement on the class page and send everyone an email, but half of them won't see it."

"That's easy enough. You calling the prig next?"

"Yes, dreading that."

"Best of luck. See you when I see you."

"Thanks so much, Becky. I appreciate your help."

Laurie ended the call and leaned her head back, taking in the green canopy above. Rosa trotted out of the bushes and sat on her foot, offering moral support. "Okay, girl. Here we go." She dialed the English department number.

"Dr. Olson, hello." Barbara sounded cheerful.

Laurie was almost relieved she'd answered. But it was just one more layer to go through. "Is Dr. Brown available?"

"Sure is." Barbara put the call through, saving Laurie from more chit chat.

"Laurie," Dr. Brown's voice seemed ominous. Or was she imagining it? "I've only got a minute. Off to a chair's meeting."

"I'm just calling to let you know I've had a family emergency in Seattle and can't make it back for exams."

"Oh, that's unfortunate. Who is handling them for you?"

"Becky and her TA."

"You know the Provost complained about faculty skipping out on exam week. She issued a policy that everyone had to be physically present on campus during this week even if they have all online classes. I do hope you have some documentation."

"Tim, seriously?" Dr. Brown's name was Tobias, but he was embarrassed by it and everyone called him Tim. At least to his face. "We don't even ask our students for documentation for absences unless it gets egregious."

"I'm afraid I'll have to have something in case the Provost inquires."

"That seems unlikely." Laurie looked up at the canopy of green to help control her temper.

"You still have some curriculum work to finish. When can we expect you back?"

"The funeral is on Tuesday. Maybe after that."

"Maybe?"

Laurie paused. What should she say?

"He is not a good pack leader," Rosa commented.

Laurie reached down and stroked the dog's side. Rosa leaned into her hand, sending waves of calm.

"Her death was suspicious. My friends and I witnessed the events, and the police have asked me to stay in town."

"What? The police?"

"It's not like I'm a suspect or anything," Laurie lied through her teeth.

"That's a relief to hear because I'm looking at a pretty serious allegation against you here. Harassing a student in your advanced women's lit class?"

"What? Who complained? I never..." Laurie sputtered. "What exactly is the charge?"

"I can discuss this in more detail when you return. In my office," he said, the glee in his voice barely disguised.

A few years ago, several faculty members in the department had urged her to run for chair against Tim, but she had refused. She abhorred administrative work. A few had written in her name on the ballot anyway, just as a protest vote, and he'd held a grudge ever since.

"Of course," she said. There was no other acceptable answer to her boss, but it was not what she wanted to say.

Rosa growled for both of them.

But Tobias wasn't finished yet. "Your post-tenure review is coming up. You should be concerned with covering all your bases."

Rage flashed through Laurie, followed by a full on hot flash. Whoever invented post-tenure reviews should be roasted over a spit. She jumped up from the bench. "Really, Tim, this is unconscionable. A friend has just died right in front of my eyes and you've offered no condolences. Only threats."

"I'm in charge of this department. Money is tight and I can't afford any marks against me. I'll see you next Monday." It was not a question.

Before Laurie could answer, he added, "I cannot be late for the chair's meeting. Goodbye." He hung up.

"Asshole," Laurie shouted into the phone.

Two people walking down the sidewalk stopped and stared at her.

"Sorry." She pointed at the phone. "My boss."

The couple averted their eyes and hurried away. She hoped they weren't close neighbors. Laurie headed back to the house, drenched in sweat. Time for a shower. She'd have to ask her parents to buy her some more clothes if she kept sweating through two or three outfits a day like this. She'd only packed a carry on. Come to think of it though, she hadn't had such an intense hot flash since she left Boston.

They walked up to the house and Laurie unhooked the dog's leash. Rosa bounced through the door and ran up to her father, who stood with the ankle bracelet dangling from one hand, the other on his hip. Just like when she was a teenager and came home after her curfew. "Care to explain this?"

"It was Skye." The words popped out automatically.

Her father scowled. "You always used to blame her. And here I thought you'd grown up."

"Look, Dad. Skye's wife Jade says the GPS on those only shows the house. If it stays here, I'm safe."

"Jade?"

"The police seem convinced I pushed Kimberly. Jade's on the force and she says the detectives on this case aren't seriously considering other options."

"But why? What would be your motive? This just doesn't make sense to me."

"A lot of people think I should have married John Newman. We had a sort of, well—" How could she explain her hopeless attraction to him? The scene from their first time flooded her memory. Their first date after she'd written that stupid paper for him.

They'd walked along Puget Sound. At the end of the sidewalk, with the sound of the water gently lapping the stones on shore, he'd leaned down and kissed her. That first kiss deepened and they moved farther into the shadows toward the rocky cliff. He pushed her against a boulder and his tongue moved into new territory, along with his hands.

'Don't do this' had repeated itself in Laurie's head, a useless alarm. His mouth moved down her neck and he unbuttoned her blouse. Her body flushed with heat, driving thought away. He hadn't stopped, and she hadn't pushed him away. As much as her mind told her to, her body craved his attentions. His hand stroked her leg and moved up her thigh.

She'd moaned against his mouth.

Laurie snapped back from her memory to the present moment. Her hand flew to her mouth automatically to stop herself from making that same sound in front of her father. Her face turned a deep red.

"Why are you flushed?" He moved to put his hand on her forehead.

"Hot flashes. I'm having hot flashes," she blurted out.

"Have you seen a doctor?" He moved back, satisfied she didn't have a fever.

"Not yet. This is normal, isn't it?"

Gynecology was not her father's specialty, but he knew enough to answer that question. "There are ways to minimize the symptoms of menopause. No need to be so uncomfortable." He'd switched to his professional voice. Clinical and detached.

Laurie sagged with relief.

Rosa brushed against her leg. "Your father doesn't approve of your mating choices?"

Mate? Was John her mate? Another blush started. To stave it off, Laurie said something she knew would push the M.D.'s buttons. "I'm going to see that naturopath."

It worked. Her father straightened. "What's wrong with your regular gynecologist?"

"I don't want to take hormones. There are too many potential side effects."

"The dosages are not as strong as they were in the beginning. The research shows..."

Laurie's father started talking about various studies and she let the words wash over her. She'd escaped. Once he finished, she thanked him for all the information. "The thing about the ankle bracelet. We saw someone in a black hoodie running out of a storage closet that Kimberly was in earlier in the evening."

"Storage closet? Are you all still teenagers?"

"Apparently they had some kind of clandestine meeting. Someone dressed the same way elbowed through the crowd when we were at the top of the Galactic Globes. We think he was the murderer."

"But if this person had murderous intentions, why didn't he act on them when he had her in private?"

"Exactly." Actually, she hadn't thought of that. "We need to find out who he is."

"And you say the police aren't taking this seriously? Surely there's security footage."

"We're working on a way to view those tapes."

Her father cocked his head. "I hope you aren't going to do anything untoward."

She huffed a laugh at her father's euphemism. "Not me. Apparently Dana knows how to get in."

He raised an eyebrow.

"She's a lawyer. She has legal access."

He crossed his arms in front of his chest, looking dubious. "If you say so."

"I swear, Dad. Now I've got to get cleaned up. My lawyer is coming at ten. He's probably already gotten access to the tapes and the detectives' work so far." She started toward the stairs, then pointed at the ankle bracelet now sitting on the counter. "I'm sorry to ask, but could you and Mom maybe pick up some clothes for me.

I only packed for the weekend and it looks like I'll be staying longer."

He snorted. "You're free to shop, aren't you?"

"I can't risk being seen."

He frowned at her, then relented. "I suppose that makes sense. Your mother will know what to get."

Laurie gave him a kiss on the cheek. "You're the best dad in the world."

He shook his head. "Such an exaggeration." But she could tell he was pleased.

DANA ARRIVED in a flurry mid-morning and Jonathan Shanks rang the front doorbell only minutes later. While her parents greeted him and Rosa gave him a good sniff, Laurie had just enough time to jerry-rig the ankle bracelet so it looked like it was locked. They took him into the formal dining room, hardly used anymore, where he could spread papers out. Everyone found a seat around the long table while her mother brought in a carafe of coffee, then a bowl of sliced fruit.

Larissa eyed her daughter, silently asking for help, but Laurie was afraid the bracelet would fall off if she walked around too much. She leaned over to Dana and whispered, "Could you help Mom?" then glanced down at her leg.

"Oh, right." Dana jumped up and after a minute carried in cream, sugar, honey, and oat milk, then returned for a plate of mini-cinnamon rolls.

"Thank you so much, Dr. Olson," Shanks said. "This is a nice treat. I had an early start." Shanks' dark hair touched with gray was neatly trimmed, his white shirt starched, and his shoes polished to a shine. His tweed jacket with elbow patches looked more professorial. His round glasses reminded her of John Lennon's. Just like Walter's. What was this John Lennon fascination all about with middle-aged men?

Larissa poured coffee, leaving everyone to add whatever they chose, then passed plates around. Shanks took a roll and started to talk. "First, let me ask if it is acceptable to you, Laurie, for everyone to hear what I have to say."

"Yes, this is my support team. Along with Skye Yarrow. She had to work today."

Shanks nodded, taking a few seconds to chew his roll. He swallowed and said, "I have some good news and bad news. Which do you want to hear first?"

"Good," Laurie said.

He reached into his pocket and pulled out a key. "The police have agreed to release you from house arrest. You can take that bulky thing off your ankle."

"What a relief," Laurie exclaimed. Her father cleared his throat.

"May I do the honors?" Dana reached for the key and hunched under the table. She pretended to unlock the device, then stood up, dangling it from her hand like a long-dead rodent. She laid it in the corner of the room and brushed off her hands.

While she did this, Shanks scarfed a second roll and reached for another one. He downed it and wiped his mouth with a paper napkin. "The bad news. Your arraignment is set for Thursday."

"So soon?" Laurie asked.

"That's not the bad news. It's good to get that over with. The District Attorney's office has appointed Ava Whitehead as the prosecutor."

Dana sucked in her breath.

"I see you're familiar with her," Shanks said.

"She's no-nonsense. Drives a hard bargain in plea deals."

"But Laurie isn't interested in a plea," her mother said. "She's innocent."

Shanks waggled his head in a noncommittal gesture, but didn't comment. Natasha appeared from out of the blue, as cats did, and jumped into Larissa's lap. "She's more worried than you know," the cat told Laurie.

Shanks continued. "The judge is Lincoln Rhodes. An old codger, due to retire soon. That either makes people relax a bit or double down. I'm afraid he seems to be taking the later course. A bit of a misogynist, but not enough to ask for another judge."

Dana chewed her lip, always a bad sign. "What aren't you saying?" Laurie asked her.

"He has a reputation for being tough." Dana turned to Shanks. "I believe Ava Whitehead was one year behind us in high school. Should she recuse herself?"

"Were you close?" Shanks asked.

"I don't remember her." Laurie reached down and scratched Rosa behind her ears.

"How about the deceased?"

"I wouldn't know," Laurie said. She noticed Dana glancing at the empty chair at the other end of the dining table.

"Unlikely," Dana said, although Laurie felt sure she'd gotten a definite no from their ghost. She wondered if Kimberly was taking pleasure in her predicament.

Shanks shook his head. "I'm afraid that's not enough to ask for someone else. We'd have to demonstrate she was close to someone involved in the case and had some partiality."

"How about John? Think he knew her? Everyone wanted to date the quarterback," Laurie explained.

Shanks made a note. "We'll look into it, but we'd have to have a strong reason to ask for another D.A. Plus, they don't take kindly to such things. This judge will press for a speedy trial."

"How fast?"

"Within a month." Shanks picked up his coffee and took a sip, watching her over the rim. "He has tickets for the south of France."

"What?"

"That's ridiculous," Dana said.

"We need more time."

"So my fate will be decided by his vacation plans?"

"Retirement celebration."

Laurie heaved a sigh of exasperation and sat back. "What can we do?"

"They wouldn't schedule the trial so quickly if they didn't think they had a strong case," Shanks said. "We'll get discovery by the end of the day. Probably right at five, so I'll get my team on it tonight. In the meantime, tell me everything." He clicked his phone to record and took out a yellow legal pad. He looked up expectantly, his round glasses completing his studious look.

Laurie leaned her head against the high-backed chair and let out a sigh. She looked at her parents. "Do you mind?"

"Of course." Larissa gathered Natasha up. The cat glared at Laurie. Her parents went upstairs.

Shanks wanted to know about her relationship with Kimberly and John. "Have you been in touch with either of them recently?"

"No, not since high school. I found out John is doing environmental work. It's something I've always been interested in and did a web search of Seattle job possibilities in the field. Saw his firm. I wanted to talk to him about opportunities, but then this all happened."

"What about high school? Tell me about your connection to them then."

Laurie told the whole humiliating story about her crush on John. How she'd helped him with homework, even written a paper for him. The one dinner date he'd taken her on. "We found out we had a lot in common. We loved whales. Kayaking. Wanted to save the planet. Well, at least Puget Sound." The rest of the memory she'd pushed away earlier when talking to her father flashed by in a rush. She refused to have a hot flash in front of her new attorney.

John had touched her in places only she had explored before. And he'd done more than she'd dared to imagine. They walked in silence back to his car, their hands intertwined, the Sound rising and falling under the gibbous moon. He'd taken her home and given her a polite kiss on the cheek after she whispered her parents would be watching. At school, Kimberly still strutted on his arm, but he went to

Laurie again and again. They had chemistry. As soon as they touched, their bodies lit up. They couldn't resist each other.

Until Kimberly caught them one time hiding behind one of the school's out buildings. Kimberly spread stories, calling Laurie a slut. Worse. Saying she wasn't good enough for John. Kids snickered at her when she walked by. But the worse thing was John never came to Laurie's defense.

"We were great, babe," he told her privately, "but I've got to stay with Kimberly." His eyes seemed sad, but he drew himself up and walked away.

Rosa whined, pulling Laurie out of the memory. She gave herself a shake and looked up at her lawyer, giving him the sanitized version. "We became lovers, but kept it secret. John suddenly dropped me and I found out later Kimberly was pregnant. Their parents forced them to get married. I got a scholarship at Beacon Hill University where I stayed for graduate school. Like I said, I hadn't been in touch with either of them until I ran into them at the reunion."

Dana refreshed their coffee, giving Laurie another minute.

"I know I seem shaken, but really, I'd forgotten about it all until Kimberly yelled at me when we stumbled across her in that janitor's closet."

"Closet?"

Dana repeated the story for Shanks. Then Laurie explained how Kimberly had told her everything was her fault and even yelled at her in front of the tour group. "In the janitor's closet, she flew at me and scratched my face. Drew blood."

"I didn't know that," Dana said.

"Skye cleaned it up."

"So, she assaulted you and Skye witnessed this?"

Laurie nodded.

"Good. It seems like Kimberly was the one holding the grudge," Shanks said, making a note. "Go on."

"After the fight she had with John in front of our tour group, I

MURDER, MYSTICS, AND MENOPAUSE

didn't see her again until we were standing at the top of the globe. The same person in the black hoodie elbowed through the crowd and rammed into Kimberly, pushing her over the rail."

"You're sure it was the same person?" Shanks asked.

"I think so. Same clothes."

He studied her a moment, then closed his notebook and picked up his phone. Pushed a couple of icons. Laurie assumed he was stopping the recording. "My goal is to avoid this trial altogether. To find enough evidence to discover the real killer and for the charges against you to be dropped."

Hope surged through Laurie. She sat up straight. "You think that's possible?"

Shanks gave her a clipped nod. "I do. Now, I've got another appointment. I'll get Skye and Dana's story later, but we need to move quickly. I'll get my team on it. My secretary will be in touch." He stood to go.

"I'll make time," Dana said. "I know Skye will." She ushered him out the front door, then came back and gave Laurie a hug. "I've got to get back to the office. Clear my schedule a bit so we can focus on finding the real killer, as the man said."

"You don't have to—"

"Yes, I do." Dana glared at the empty dining room chair. "I'll be damned if I let some ignorant cheerleader send one of my best friends to prison." She slung her messenger bag over her shoulder, then paused and addressed the chair again. "And don't bother following me. Try to be useful and remember what happened."

"Bye," Laurie called after her. Then she looked down at Rosa. "Is the ghost still here?"

"No. Let's go outside."

Laurie realized she was free now. She ran upstairs and found her parents in their adjourning offices. "Looks like I can shop for myself, Dad." She held up her ankle, now free of the cumbersome device.

He snorted. "So glad you don't have to worry about being seen."

91

Her mother leaned in the doorway, a hand on each side, stretching out her back. "Being seen? What's that about?"

"Tell you later," her father said.

"I guess you wonder what the story is," Laurie said.

Her mother straightened and held up her hand. "We heard."

Laurie took a breath to object.

"Sorry, but you are my daughter. I need to know what you're facing." Her face softened. "I'm sorry to hear about your relationship with John. He must have broken your heart."

Laurie was surprised by the sudden hot tears. Why was everything hot these days? She wiped her face. "Yes, but I got over it."

Her mother looked doubtful.

"It's menopause. I seem to overreact to everything."

Her mother nodded sagely. "Be glad you're still thinking clearly. My mind was total fog for a while."

"We'll have to talk," Laurie said. She pecked her mother's check and gathered her purse and the keys to her rental. "Meanwhile, I think I need some retail therapy." She didn't tell them she had a lunch date.

Larissa laughed. "Don't be too late. I'm making paella."

"Yum!" Laurie looked at her father. "What did we do to deserve such a good cook?"

"Just lucky, I guess." Then his face grew serious. "Let us know how we can help. This is just some big misunderstanding."

"Thanks, Dad." Laurie gave him a swift hug, then headed down the stairs before she started crying again. Rosa beat her to the door and sat, tail wagging. "I'm sorry, but you have to stay."

Rosa yipped in protest.

"You don't want to have to sit in the car."

Rosa circled her, then stood in front of her, her brown eyes pleading.

"Oh, all right." Laurie picked up her leash and opened the door. The dog made a beeline for the Honda and waited for Laurie.

CHAPTER
NINE

Laurie arrived early to the little bistro she and John had picked in the University District for their meeting. She'd have to remember to buy some new clothes since she told her parents she was going shopping. The cloudy and cool Seattle spring made it safe to leave Rosa in the locked Honda. The only economy car left where they'd landed in Podunk, Idaho had darkened windows. She was glad of that now. The little dog curled up, tucked her nose between her paws, and gone into dreamland.

Once seated in the restaurant, Laurie ordered a rose lemonade and sipped it. She kept an eye on the door and noticed a dog sleeping under a table. Laurie grabbed the attention of a passing waiter. "Excuse me, my dog is in the car. Can I bring her in?"

"Is she a service animal?"

"Well, no, but I recently rescued her from a near plane crash and she's a bit nervous."

The young man glanced toward the front, chewing his lip. "I'll explain it to my manager. I think it will be all right."

Laurie retrieved Rosa from the car. "You have to be quiet,

though." The little Havanese scooted under the table, put her head on Laurie's foot and closed her eyes.

College students chatted or stared at laptops, then typed in furious bouts of inspiration. Or maybe they were desperate, trying to meet a deadline. Two men behind her talked in nasal tones about mimesis in literature. She slammed her lemonade down on the table. Pretentious snobs. Couldn't she escape academia at least for this weekend? Why had she agreed to meet here?

"Nobody I know goes up there anymore," John had said. He didn't want to be seen with her. She felt a prickle of irritation, but shook it off. Of course, they should keep this private given the court case. She wondered if it was too soon to talk about possible jobs in Seattle. The man's wife had just died. Skye and Dana said she needed to figure out who Kimberly's close friends were and to see if he could have been involved at all. And she had to admit she wanted to see him. Hear about his life. Listen to his voice. See if there was still a spark between them.

The bell on the bistro door rang and there he stood. He wore a t-shirt with his company logo and cargo pants. His broad shoulders filled it out and he looked like he'd stayed in shape. A flush of heat rushed up her torso. Please, don't let me have a hot flash here, she begged. Exactly who she addressed her request to, she couldn't tell. Was there a goddess of menopause? It would have to be one of the crones.

But it wasn't that. The rush left her tingling in places she hadn't thought about for a while. He stood straight, his presence commanding, but not in a domineering way like her department chair tried for and failed.

He searched the crowd and found her. A smile lit his face and he threaded through the tables to hers. "I'm glad you called. I was afraid with—" he waved his hand in the air "—with everything that you'd leave before I got to see you."

"No chance of that. Did you hear?"

He frowned. "Hear what?"

"I'm a suspect."

His mouth dropped open. "A what?"

"Suspect. In the—" she stumbled. What was she thinking bringing this up right off the bat? "—you know, in the accident."

"But..." he shook his head. "They think you had something to do with Kimberly's...fall?"

"The police think I pushed her. They told me I can't leave town. "

He stood dumbstruck, eyes wide.

"Sit."

John pulled out a chair, the legs scrapping against the floor. "When they questioned me, they seemed to think it was an accident. Why on earth would they suspect you?"

Then he hunched just a bit. "Oh. Because of that." He dropped heavily into his seat. Rosa lifted her head. He held his hand out for her to sniff. "You have a dog?'

"It's a long story."

He scratched Rosa's head, then looked back at Laurie.

"He didn't do it," Rosa said.

Laurie glanced down at the dog, momentarily confused by her comment. Then with a little shake of her head, she looked back at John. "The police seem to think I've held a torch for you all this time and finally decided to—"

He smiled, his face wistful just for just a second before they stumbled over each other to cover the awkwardness.

"How have you been?" he blurted as Laurie asked, "How are you holding up?"

They chuckled.

She took him in. His walnut hair was trimmed neat, but not too short, and he sported a dash of gray at the temples. Laugh lines had sprouted at the corners of his mouth and his brown eyes shot with amber. Laurie pushed a strand of her own hair behind her ear. She had to admit her blond was starting to silver. Well, had almost finished, if she told the truth.

"It's so good to see you," he said and reached across the table.

All her self-consciousness fell away. She squeezed his hand. "John, I'm so sorry about Kimberly. It must be such a shock."

He shrugged. "Yeah, I sure wasn't expecting that."

"Where were you when it happened?"

"Downstairs in the bar." He gave her a sheepish look. "We had a fight. She said she had divorce papers drawn up."

He let go of her hand and took a sip of water. The waitress showed up to take their order. Laurie ordered littleneck clams and John went with a veggie burger. He pointed to her lemonade. "And another one of those."

After the waitress walked away, she asked, "You're vegetarian now?"

"Mostly," he said. "I eat fish from time to time. It's Seattle, after all."

She nodded.

"Everybody thinks I should be devastated. I lost my wife, but we drifted apart over the years and had been living separate lives for quite some time now. When she told me she was in love with somebody else and wanted a divorce, I was actually happy for her. The saddest part of all this is she didn't get to be with the man she loved. The man she was compatible with."

Laurie's eyes filled. Here was a good man.

"But murder? Who would want to kill her?" John's forehead wrinkled.

"The police are pretty sure I pushed Kimberly over the railing because she was standing right next to us," Laurie said.

"They must have something more substantial. That sounds completely random."

Laurie finished her lemonade and held up her glass for the waitress to see, stalling. She wasn't sure why. She looked back at him. "I ran into her earlier. At the reunion. I left the ballroom looking for the restroom. Somebody was coming out of a door, so I thought it was one of those unisex bathrooms. Turns out it was a janitor's closet and Kimberly was in there crying her eyes out."

"What? That's crazy."

"Right? When I came in, Kimberly thought the person had returned. When she saw it wasn't him, she started yelling at me. Then she attacked me. Drew blood."

"Blood?"

"She's got—had those long nails."

"You okay?"

"It was just a scratch."

"Be sure to tell the police."

"My lawyer knows. Anyway, after Kimberly fell, I saw a man running away dressed in the same dark hoodie as the one we saw earlier."

"Have the police found out who he is?"

"I don't think so. I'm afraid they aren't taking it seriously." Laurie shook her head.

"You didn't want this?" the waitress asked, holding two lemonades.

"Yes, I did. Thank you," Laurie said. The waitress set them down on the table.

Laurie looked around to see if anyone was listening to them, but everyone was either focused on the people with them or staring at their electronic devices. "The cameras in that hallway seemed to have been turned off. We're going to double check."

"That's suspicious. You had no way to mess with Galactic's security system."

"Exactly, but they arrested me. The cameras did pick up two people in hoodies in the crowd around the railings. Claimed neither one got close enough to push her."

"You saw him, though."

"Skye and I both saw the guy running away. But not his face."

"And Dana?"

"She got pushed over the railing, too, but she grabbed a thick vine. Some young men managed to save her."

John sat forward in alarm. "Is she all right?"

97

"Yes, shook up, but she wasn't hurt."

"That's a relief."

"The police seem convinced I had motive and—what do they say? Opportunity or something."

"That's just ridiculous. I mean after all these years."

Their eyes locked and Laurie felt the old tug stronger than ever. He put both hands flat on the table and leaned forward. "How can I help?"

Laurie's shoulders dropped in relief. Her eyes filled. She hadn't realized how scared she was. "Honestly John, you've got a funeral to deal with. And kids, relatives. Probably lots of legal stuff."

He waved this away. "I'll do anything."

"We need to talk to her friends. The people she was closest to."

"Who is 'we'?"

"Same old gang. Dana and Skye are helping me. Dana got me hooked up with a good criminal attorney."

"Think they'll forgive me?"

"Who? Forgive you for what?"

"The posse. That's what I used to call you three. Forgive me for dumping you and marrying Kimberly."

"You didn't exactly dump me. We were never official."

His brown eyes softened. "We should have been, Laurie. You were the one."

So he loved her after all. Was love too strong a word? Laurie rushed to cover the mix of hope and sadness welling up in her. "We knew she was pregnant. You did the honorable thing."

He looked down and Laurie realized he was close to tears. "I wasn't in love with her. Not really. We were stupid teenagers. She was the head cheerleader and I was the quarterback. It was in all the scripts. We were supposed to get married and live happily ever after."

Laurie reached for his hand. "We were just kids. We didn't really know what we were doing."

"It was the biggest mistake of my life." He shrugged. "But then I wouldn't have my two fabulous kids."

"That's true." She picked up her lemonade. "I'm sorry to harp on this, but I need to stay out of jail and we don't have a lot of time. The judge has scheduled the trial in a month."

"So soon?"

"My attorney wants to see how much evidence we can gather to get the charges dropped when we find the real killer."

John opened his mouth to say more, but Laurie jumped in. "Kimberly didn't talk to anybody particular on social media. She chatted with everybody. Just casual. We already looked. Her Instagram is full of garden pictures. And the two kids. They look great, by the way."

John shook his head slowly. "They're just getting their feet under them. Sylvia works for a medical research firm and Josh is trying to get a script produced in Hollywood." He rolled his eyes.

Laurie smiled. "Maybe he'll grow out of it."

"Or become a movie mogul. Who can say? But what a time to lose your mother."

"I hope your kids will be all right."

The waitress brought their food and asked if they wanted anything else.

"We're fine. Thanks," John said.

They settled down to eat. After a few minutes, Laurie looked up to find John watching her. "Will you be all right, though?" he asked.

She shrugged. "I have an excellent lawyer. So Dana says anyway. But we've got to find out who did this. Do you know who Kimberly confided in?"

"I'll have to think about it. We were basically roommates, so I don't know who her friends were really." He put his burger down and wiped his hands with his crumpled paper napkin. A pile of them was growing next to his plate.

"I'm sorry, John."

He gave her a wistful smile. "I should have reached out. I thought about you often."

"You must have been lonely," she whispered.

He shrugged. "I had the kids. And the whales, of course."

This made her chuckle. "We'll have time to talk about that. Looks like I'll be here a little while." Another tingle of energy washed through her. She took refuge in her food. She opened another clam and almost moaned in delight at the taste.

"If I could get into her phone, I could see who she called the most. Who her contacts were. Thing is, she never told me the password and—"

"She's gone," Laurie whispered. "Dana probably can."

"Dana?"

"Turns out she employs an expert hacker. Who knew?" Laurie didn't say that it was actually Dana who did the hacking, but she thought Dana must have backup.

John snorted. "She looks so innocent."

"Right?"

"The funeral is tomorrow."

"So fast?"

"Her family have a tradition of burying someone within three days after their death."

"That seems old fashioned."

"They are a bit, but it's fine. Pretty much everyone lives locally. After that, I can give her phone to Dana." He crumbled up his napkin and put it on his now empty plate.

The waitress appeared almost instantly, carefully laying the check in the middle of the table. John pulled out his credit card and put it under the metal clip. She thought about protesting, but decided not to.

"You coming?" he asked.

"To the service? Dana and Skye think we should hang back. Watch from a distance." She smiled. "I was under house arrest, but Skye got a key to the ankle bracelet from her wife. She's a cop."

He guffawed. Two customers jerked their heads up and frowned. A black lab sporting an orange vest designating him as a support animal looked up at Laurie. "Tell your friend to keep it down."

"He's fine now," she sent to him. The dog put his gleaming head back on his paws and closed his eyes. Laurie wasn't going to spring this new ability on John quite yet. Maybe never.

John ignored the frowns of the impertinent college students at the table beside them. "So you've been free to run around on the sly?"

"Pretty much. Just can't be seen. But my attorney arranged to set me free this morning."

"I swear. You three. I've missed you."

"I'm missed you, too," she said softly.

His eyes lit up. "You know, there is one person Kimberly was close to. Peggy—" he snapped his fingers, trying to remember "—Peggy Anderson. She was on the cheerleading squad. I'll find her number for you."

"Thanks. Maybe she'll know more."

They stared at each for other another minute. Laurie bit back the words she wanted to say. She pushed back her chair instead. "I guess we both have a lot to do."

John nodded. "Keep in touch. I want to help as much as I can."

Laurie reached for her purse instead of him. "I will. Thank you again."

LAURIE SPENT the afternoon shopping at some discount stores for jeans, t-shirts, and a couple of sweatshirts. She texted Graham to ask if he'd pack her clothes, including some business suits, and ship them. He agreed. He still had a key for emergencies. Then she took Rosa for a long walk in the arboretum. Once they got away from the parking lot, she let her off the leash. Laurie figured it was safe since she could talk to her dog. "You have to stay close," she admonished.

Rosa immediately stuck her head into the bushes lining the trail, stopping to sniff deeply, her tail wagging.

"Back at my parents' house, you said something like the other one did it and then you said John didn't do it. What did you mean?"

Rosa backed out of the bushes and trotted by her side. "I could smell them."

"Who?"

"On your clothes. It smelled like somebody else."

"But I was around a lot of people that night. How could pick out one person?"

"Humans." Rosa's tone was derisive.

"Yes, lots of humans."

"Dogs can smell way better than humans. Somebody pushed against you. They were frightened and angry. They smeared their scent all over you."

"Could you identify them if you smelled them again?"

"Of course," Rosa said. Her whole body suddenly tightened, then she took off into the bushes.

"We agreed you'd stay with me," Laurie shouted, running after her, trying not to step on any flowers.

'Rabbit' came a faint thought.

"Oh, for heaven's sake," Laurie mumbled. She sat down in the middle of a grassy spot and waited.

After a few minutes, Rosa appeared, her tongue hanging out. "That was fun."

"I hope you didn't kill it."

Rosa didn't answer. She started back toward the car, head held high.

"You're going to get us a ticket running off like that."

On the drive home, Rosa stuck her head out the window, ignoring Laurie and enjoying the wind on her face. Laurie smiled at her obvious pleasure, forgiving her antics.

When they walked in the front door, the smell of her mother's paella hit her. "We're eating at the dining room table." Larissa served up full bowls and then held up a finger. "No talking about this situation at the table," she declared.

Happy to forget about her impending trial for a while, Laurie agreed. She stuffed herself to the gills, thinking she just might grow some herself with all the fish she'd been eating. She sank back in her dining room chair, replete.

"Dessert?" her mother asked.

Laurie rubbed her stomach. "Maybe later."

TEN

"The squad stuck together." Peggy flipped her still blond hair behind her back.

Dana wondered what shade she used to color it. Probably got it done at an expensive salon if she could judge by this neighborhood overlooking Lake Washington.

"The cheerleading squad? From high school?" Skye asked.

"Most of us stayed friends." Peggy held her head high, almost daring them to make fun of her.

"I know you must really miss her." Dana struggled to make her tone sympathetic. Kimberly sat beside her best friend attempting to pat her on the back, although her hand kept sinking into her friend's shoulder. Dana tried her best to ignore the ghost.

Kimberly had been hanging around her living room this morning but had remembered nothing else about that evening at the Galactic Globes. Dana had disliked her in high school and, even though she was dead and all, wished Kimberly would tell her who she had been meeting so they could be done with the investigation. Get Laurie freed. Then the ghost could move on and she could get her life back to normal.

Skye voice brought Dana's attention back to the room. "What a shock it's been to all of us." Her tone was sepulchral.

Peggy didn't take well to this offer of sympathy. She eyed Skye's mid-section before sucking in her own rounding stomach. "We kept in shape. Kimberly and I belonged to the same gym. Several of the girls ran together a couple days a week. Her absence will be felt."

"What a bitch. Her best friend's dead and all she can think about is how fit she is?" Laurie's voice whispered into their earbuds.

Skye had her phone switched on but hidden it in the pocket of her duster. They both wore regular earbuds that connected them. It seemed normal. People ran around with earbuds in their ears all day long. Laurie had stayed in the car. They decided her presence might make Peggy clam up.

Dana risked a glance at Skye, who was biting her lip to stop herself from laughing. Relieved Skye's feelings weren't hurt, Dana turned back to see Kimberly giving her chubby friend a smug look. You'd think death would give a person a wider view.

"We all worked to stay healthy. She should have lived a long life." Peggy wiped a tear off her cheek. "We were best friends."

Kimberly tried to put her arm around Peggy to comfort her, but it passed through her shoulders again. The ghost jerked back, frowning at her arm.

Dana put down her mug of coffee. "That's why we wanted to talk to you. Anything you could tell us might help."

"Why are you asking? Wasn't it an accident?"

"The police don't think so. They're investigating it as murder."

Peggy's eyes rounded with shock. "Murder? Who would want to hurt poor Kimberly?"

"That's what we want to find out. Kimberly deserves justice," Dana said. She paused to let this statement sink in. After another sip of Peggy's mediocre coffee, she asked, "Do you know if she had any enemies? Knew anyone who had a score to settle?"

Peggy leaned back on the couch, oblivious to the ghost beside her. "After the kids were out of the house, Kimberly went from group to group volunteering. Nothing really stuck."

"So no bad feelings in any of those places?" Skye asked.

"I don't think she was there long enough." Peggy paused, then spoke in a gossipy tone. "Just between us, Kimberly could be a little flighty."

The ghost huffed and disappeared.

Serves you right, Dana thought.

"She didn't work?" Skye asked.

"Had some reception jobs once the kids were in elementary school, then took a program to become a legal assistant. She got a good position, but the firm let her go. She couldn't find work in the same field after that."

Kimberly blinked back in, choosing a chair across from her supposed friend. She crossed her arms over her chest, her face scrunched up.

Great, Dana thought, now she's pouting. Dana realized she could see Kimberly much more clearly. She wondered what that meant, but didn't have time to think about it while dealing with Peggy.

"What do you suppose happened?" Skye asked.

"I don't think the work really held her interest. Plus, there was a problem with a case."

Skye and Dana leaned forward at the same moment. Dana picked up her coffee to cover their eagerness.

"Finally," Laurie whispered in their ears.

Skye sat back, letting Dana take the lead. "Do you know what happened?"

"A bad divorce. The wife thought Kimberly had lost something—a piece of evidence maybe." Peggy lifted an elegant shoulder as if to suggest such minor details were beneath her notice.

Dana shot a questioning look at Kimberly, but the ghost ignored her.

"She seemed to think someone was stalking her, but the firm didn't take her seriously."

"Did John?"

Peggy shook her head. "Not really. He told her she was imagining it. Trying to feel important."

"What did you think?"

"Well, she had a flare for the dramatic, but I believed her."

"Do you remember the name of this stalker?"

Peggy's eyes lit up. "I might have it in my diary. I can look." But she didn't move.

"That would be great if you could let us know what you find. Or the name of the company."

"That I remember. It was Carter & Williams."

"They're a reputable firm," Dana said.

Peggy looked down her aquiline nose. "Of course. Kimberly only worked for top people."

Kimberly suddenly appeared beside her friend again, mollified by this comment.

Skye sat forward. "Sounds like John wasn't very sympathetic to her. How was their relationship?'

Peggy studied the two of them. "She wanted a divorce. She was going to take him for everything. Maybe the police should check John out."

Dana nodded sympathetically. "I agree, but the lawyer told us he has an alibi."

"He was downstairs when this happened," Skye explained.

Peggy lifted a perfectly waxed eyebrow. "Maybe he hired somebody?"

"Oh, please!" Laurie shouted in their ears.

Dana winced against the squeal from her earbuds. She hoped Peggy couldn't hear anything. She tried for a normal tone. "I suppose that's a possibility."

Skye went for a deeper question. "Was she seeing anyone?"

Peggy picked up her coffee mug and found it empty. "I need a refill. How about you two?"

"Uh, sure," Skye said.

"How do you not throttle her?" Laurie asked in their ear. "Can you guys hurry it up? Hiding in an SUV sounds easier than it turns out to be."

After a minute, Peggy came back with three brimming mugs, handling them like a pro. Dana wondered if she'd ever been a waitress. She decided to drop some more information. "I heard Laurie is a suspect."

Skye followed up. "Actually, I think she was arrested."

Peggy's smile was spiteful. "About time, I say."

Dana dug her nails into her palm to keep herself from reacting. "Why do you say that? She's been gone for so long. Surely she's not an issue anymore."

"And as soon as she comes back, she pushes Kimberly to her death."

"I was standing right next to Kimberly. I got shoved over the railing, too," Dana said.

"How did you—"

"Survive? I grabbed onto a vine and held on for dear life."

"Sounds awful." Peggy gave a little shake.

"Earlier we saw Kimberly meeting with somebody," Skye said.

Peggy shrugged. "There were lots of people there."

"This was in secret. In a janitor's closet down from the main event," Skye said.

"What? Kimberly didn't hang out in dirty closets." Peggy reached for her coffee.

"We saw a man in dark clothes run away before we arrived. We thought it was the restroom, so we went in and found Kimberly in tears."

Peggy stopped, mug halfway to her mouth. "What did she say?"

"At first she thought the man had come back, but when she saw Laurie, she started screaming at her," Skye said.

"Does this make any sense to you?" Dana asked.

"No, I'm sorry." Peggy set her mug down decisively and got to her feet. "I can't share the name of the man she was in love with. He would never have hurt her." She walked toward the front door. "Now if you'll excuse me, I have things to do before the funeral this afternoon."

Dana and Skye got up and mumbled their thanks for her help. Peggy didn't meet their eyes as she held the door open for them.

On the way to the car, Skye said, "She's hiding something."

"Yeah? How do you know?"

Skye hesitated, then said, "Just a feeling."

"I tend to agree."

LAURIE PULLED the raincoat tight around her and opened an umbrella. The drizzle wasn't enough for any Seattle native to take notice of, but she didn't want to be recognized, so she pulled down the umbrella so it almost covered her face. Rosa sat huddled next to her, leaning on her leg to stay dry. "I don't like this rain."

"You get used to it." Laurie was getting accustomed to speaking mind to mind with the little Havanese mix. Plus her parents' cat and Oliver, who'd opted to stay home with her father.

Kimberly's funeral had been well attended at the church. Dana snuck into the back and blended with the crowd once the service started. Skye said it would be weird for her to show up since they hadn't kept in touch and their relationship in high school had been anything but friendly. Laurie couldn't go for obvious reasons. She and Skye had kept watch from Dana's SUV, studying faces as people arrived, observing how people interacted. They'd seen nothing suspicious so far.

Fewer people had followed the hearse to the graveside ceremony. They gathered around the open rectangle of ground, listening to the minister. Laurie lurked behind a tall vertical stele that marked the last grave in a row up the slope from the service. Dana and Skye stood beneath a tall yew tree, blending in well enough not to be seen. They were all too far away to hear anything.

The deceased's family clustered together. John put his arm

around their daughter and pulled her tight to his side. The son stood, stoic, staring at the ground. A few of Kimberly's friends huddled on the other side of the grave. Laurie had spent the evening with Dana and Skye studying faces from Kimberly's social media pictures. She recognized three members of the old cheerleading squad, someone from the gardening club she belonged to, a few neighbors.

Laurie caught movement in her peripheral vision and looked over to see a man peeking around the corner of a small mausoleum. "Psst." Her two friends glanced over at her and she jerked her head in the man's direction. Skye held small field glasses up to her face and whispered something Laurie couldn't hear. Dana pointed the camera she'd brought with a telescopic lens at him and took a series of pictures. Laurie thought they were starting to look like real detectives. Maybe they needed a name.

Skye walked out from the trees. "I'm going to see if I can talk to him."

Laurie frowned. "Do you think that's a good idea?"

"Who knows? It's worth a try." She handed her field glasses to Laurie.

"Use that app Mania installed. Then we can listen in," Laurie said.

"Let me off leash," Rosa said. "I can sniff him out. See if he's the one who brushed against you."

"That's a great idea, but you can't be off leash. They'll call Animal Control and you'd end up at the shelter."

"Shelter sounds good."

"No, that's where they put homeless dogs and cats in cages."

"You mean prison. Like where you were."

"Wait," she called to Skye. "Take Rosa with you. She wants to sniff him and she might pick something up from his thoughts."

Skye gave her a thumbs up and started her stroll down the aisle of graves, head down, shoulders slumped, the perfect picture of mourning. Except for the little dog who stuck by her side.

Laurie put in her ear bud and the link chimed. Dana joined her behind the granite stele. Skye wandered over to the mausoleum and stood near it, her gaze still on the ground. Taking out a tissue from her pocket, she dabbed her eyes. Still focused on the gravestones, she edged around, making her way to the marble wall the man leaned against. She had to pull Rosa back so she didn't spoil her stealth approach.

Laurie put the field glasses up to her face. He wore a dark suit and white shirt, but kept pulling at his buttoned up collar, obviously not comfortable in dress shirts and ties. When Skye neared the end of the wall, she looked up and gazed around. She gave a little jump when she saw the man. "I'm so sorry to intrude on your grief. Please excuse me." She turned as if to go.

"Did you know her?" he asked.

"Know who?"

"He's sad," Rosa said to Laurie and sat in front of the man. He leaned down to pet her, then gestured toward the group of people down the slope.

"No, I visit my husband every week. Is that who you are here for?"

He nodded.

Rosa turned and sat on his foot. Laurie recognized this as her way of consoling humans.

"Rosa, leave the man alone. Come." Skye patted her leg.

"She's fine. I like dogs."

Skye nodded. "My deepest condolences. A recent death is so difficult. And you couldn't bear to be with the others." Skye said this as if it weren't a question.

Laurie widened her focus so she could watch them both.

"I can't be seen." The man wiped his eyes with a white handkerchief. "We were going to be married, but—" A sob escaped. He turned away as if embarrassed.

Skye put a tentative hand on his shoulder. "Please, there's nothing to be ashamed of. You loved her. Deeply."

"Yes," he choked out.

"May I ask her name?"

"Kimberly. We met only a few months ago. She was filing papers for a divorce."

"Had she been unhappy in her marriage a long time?"

"Yes, but our relationship reignited her passion. We had plans." He studied Skye. "I was her personal trainer. She was healthy. Her dying was the last thing I could imagine happening."

He broke down again and Skye patted his shoulder, making comforting sounds. Rosa stood and put her front paws on his leg. After a minute, he blew his nose. Squared his shoulders. "I don't know why I'm telling you this."

"We all need to share our grief with someone. I understand."

"Thank you. It was just so sudden."

"If it's not an intrusion, may I ask how she...passed."

"She fell. At the Galactic Globes."

"Oh, I think I read about that in the paper."

"I thought it was an accident. She was so full of life. She might have been careless. But the police suspect foul play." He said these last words in an ominous whisper.

"Good Lord, this guy is a bit of a cliché." Dana stood at Laurie's shoulder, squinting at the two.

"Maybe not the brightest bulb, but perfect for good ole Kimberly," Laurie said.

Skye continued her questions. "But you weren't at the Globes that night?"

"She went with her husband. Said she it was her last official act as his wife."

"Such a sad story."

"If I knew who killed her—" he squeezed his hands in front of him "—I'd like to wring his neck."

"Oh, dear. I understand." Skye tsked. "Do you have any idea who did it?"

"I thought it was her husband, but the police say he has a rock solid alibi."

Dana scooted closer to Laurie and whispered, "He must watch a lot of detective shows."

Skye waited a beat. "Makes you wonder who else would have done such a terrible thing."

The man's head jerked up. "You seem awfully interested. What did you say your name was?"

"Oh, I'm so sorry. My name is Jane. I lost my husband early, but it was to cancer. I'm just imagining how shocked and angry you must feel."

He stared at her for a moment. Laurie felt a tinge of fear, but the man's shoulders sagged. "Yeah, it's a lot. I'm Tommy. Tommy Johnson."

Skye shook his hand. "It's nice to meet you, Tommy. May I pray for you?"

Laurie snorted. Skye was not religious.

"Good cover," Dana said.

Tommy paused. "Uh, yeah. I'd appreciate that."

The mourners at the grave started to make their way to their cars, John and his family staying longer. Skye said her goodbyes to Kimberly's secret lover and meandered around to the yew trees, Rosa scampering as Skye let out her leash. Tommy didn't watch her go. His eyes were fixed on the grave.

The three friends ducked back through the trees and through the gate in the wrought iron fence. They climbed into Dana's SUV. "We didn't learn much from Tommy," Laurie said.

"At least we can check him off the suspect list," Skye said.

"You sure?" Laurie asked.

"He didn't hurt Kimberly," Rosa assured her. "Didn't smell right."

"Rosa agrees with you, Skye," Laurie told them.

Rosa sat in the back with Skye, who scratched behind her ear. "Such a good girl."

"Still, maybe we should do some background on him. See if he jilted anyone for Kimberly. Or if he has a criminal history. We can do it at my office." Dana started the engine.

"Let's drive through the cemetery. See if anyone else is lingering." Dana turned into an entrance and followed the winding single lane through the graves. She stopped at the top of the hill near where they'd hid out. One lone mourner knelt at the open grave, his shoulders heaving in his black suit. The grave diggers stood at a discreet distance, waiting to finish their work.

"Poor guy," Skye said.

"Yeah. Too bad Kimberly didn't get to have a happy relationship," Laurie added.

Dana turned out of the cemetery gates, negotiating around an old chevy parked too close to the exit, and headed for Capitol Hill.

"I agree. Not to be too insensitive, but I was hoping we'd see somebody in a black hoodie lurking around," Skye said.

Dana snorted. "Surely he's changed his clothes by now. But this guy said he was a personal trainer. They dress that way."

"Nah, he's too big. This figure didn't have those shoulders." Laurie held her hands apart to demonstrate. "Plus he passed the smell test."

"He doesn't seem to be devious. I got a strong feeling he was telling the truth," Skye said.

They drove in silence for a few minutes, then Dana said, "Nobody look, but—"

Both Laurie and Skye looked out the rear window.

Dana let out an exasperated huff. "Didn't I just say not to look?"

Skye laughed, "Sorry. What are we not supposed to be looking at?"

Dana shook her head. She drove another couple of blocks, then checked the rearview mirror again. The chevy was no longer following them. "Well, either I was imagining it or you both scared them off."

Laurie leaned forward. "What did you see?"

"There was an old Chevrolet parked near the exit. So close I had to be careful pulling out. I figured it was some distraught mourner. But then I saw it behind us a couple of times."

"But it's gone now?" Skye asked.

"Yeah."

"Could you see who was driving it?" Laurie took a small mirror out of her purse and was trying to angle it so she could see if anyone was following them.

"Medium height. Wearing sunglasses," Dana said.

"On this cloudy day?" Skye asked.

"I couldn't see the hair. Maybe wearing a—" Dana's eyes flew wide "—oh no, a black hoodie."

They all sat up straight, even Rosa. "Should we turn around? See if we can find them?" Before anyone could answer, Dana took a sharp left and backtracked through a residential street.

"What color was the car?" Skye asked.

"Blue. An older model," Dana said.

"With fins?" Skye asked.

Dana laughed. "Not that old."

Skye and Laurie craned their necks, looking down every street they passed. "Nothing," Laurie said.

Dana drove a few more blocks, then turned left to the street they'd been on before. She drove another block, then turned into the neighborhood on the opposite side of the one they'd just searched. She slowed and they all kept scanning.

After they'd gone a few more blocks, Laurie said, "Looks like Mr. Hoodie is gone now."

"Maybe." Dana cut over another block, then another, but their search turned up no blue Chevrolet. After about fifteen minutes, Dana drove back to her house.

CHAPTER

ELEVEN

Dana pulled into her driveway, and the three friends clambered out of the SUV and into the house. Rap music blared from a bedroom upstairs. A soccer uniform and equipment lay strewn across the living room floor. Dana huffed and marched up the stairs, shouting rapid-fire Vietnamese. The only words Laurie made out were Hoa and Minh, the names of her teenagers. Rosa went in search of Lele. Or some food.

The music volume cut in half and Dana walked downstairs. "Time to eat. Should we order out?"

A tall boy with a shock of black hair appeared in the living room and grabbed his clothes. "Pizza," he shouted.

Dana switched to English. "You're going to turn into a pizza. That uniform needs to be washed. Don't just stuff it into your gym bag."

"Mom." The complaint reached them from halfway up the stairs.

Rosa barked and ran after him. "We got a dog?"

"Dog?" a female voice asked. "We have a dog."

"She belongs to Laurie."

"Who's Laurie?" This from the boy.

"Stop shouting and come here to greet my guests."

Two teenagers appeared along with Rosa, the girl a spitting image of her mother. "Hoa, Minh." The boy dipped his head when his name was called. "Meet Dr. Olson. She's visiting from Boston."

Hoa stepped forward and bowed her head slightly. "Pleased to meet you."

"Is she the person who got arrested here?" Minh asked, his eyes shining with intrigue.

Dana heaved a sigh and said something in Vietnamese that made the boy stand up straighter. "I apologize for my rudeness," he said in a monotone. "I'm pleased to meet you."

"No pizza for you."

"Mom," he objected.

Dana shooed them both away. "We have serious business to talk about."

"Pizza actually sounds good," Skye said.

"Sweet." Minh's voice sounded from the stairwell.

"There's a place nearby with gluten-free crust and—"

Minh made a retching sound.

Dana ignored him. "—a good veggie one."

Rosa woofed. "Sausage," she said to Laurie.

"What does she want?" Dana asked.

Laurie repeated Rosa's request. "But really, some scrambled eggs or whatever you have."

"Sausage sounds great," Minh said, his voice suspiciously close.

Dana shook her head. She headed to the kitchen and handed Skye an old-fashioned takeout menu from the drawer. "I give up. You order."

Skye took out her phone and walked back into the living room. Dana studied the small wine rack and pulled out a bottle. "Merlot?"

"Got any beer?" Laurie asked.

"I think there's some in the fridge." She pulled out a corkscrew to open the wine.

Skye came back into the kitchen. "I ordered three. Two veggies and one meat lovers for the kid and Rosa."

Rosa barked her appreciation.

"Wine? Beer?" Dana asked.

"What else you got?" Skye asked.

Laurie handed Skye an organic peach soda and took a beer from a local brewery. They settled around the island.

"Did anybody get the license plate of the chevy?" Dana asked.

"I didn't even see it," Laurie said.

"Me either. Mind if I text Jade to come here after her shift?" Skye asked.

"Will it compromise her position if she gets involved in the investigation?" Laurie asked.

"She's not assigned to it, so that's not a problem."

"Sure. I haven't seen her in ages," Laurie said.

Skye shot off a text. Dana stared into the deep red of her wine but didn't take a sip. After a minute, she looked up at Skye. "I've got a question for you. And you have to tell the truth. I mean, we've told you about seeing ghosts and hearing animals' thoughts."

"Okay." Skye drew the word out.

"You said you thought Peggy was hiding something."

"That was kind of—"

Dana held up a finger, looking very much like a parent. "Wait, there's more. You were certain that Tommy wasn't the murderer."

Skye took a breath, but Dana shook her head. "You didn't seem surprised that I was seeing Kimberly's ghost or that Laurie could talk to Rosa."

The cat jumped up on the island. Laurie laughed. "And Lele."

Dana nodded, then continued. "In high school, you knew Peggy Anderson was the one who left me that nasty note."

"Peggy turned out to be a mean girl." Laurie made air quotes as she said these last words, probably referring to the movie.

Dana pressed on. "I'm starting to think there's something you're not telling us about yourself."

Skye studied them both for a long moment, then a mischievous smile formed. "You're right. I should come clean."

"I knew it." Dana thumped her wine down and it sloshed close to the rim.

"What is it?" Laurie asked. "Can you hear people's thoughts?"

"Not exactly."

"Ooh." Dana rubbed her hands together.

"I can feel other people's emotions."

"What do you mean, like when they're angry or sad?"

Skye finished her soda and set the glass down carefully. "I'm not sure exactly how it works, but when I walk into a room, I can feel the emotional atmosphere. When I teach classes, I can tell how my students are reacting."

Laurie piped up, "I need that."

"In the shop, I tend to know what customers are looking for. Not the item so much as the feeling they want to satisfy with a purchase. As soon as they see it, I feel the shift in them."

"Amazing," Dana said. "That would be great in a courtroom."

"The best part is I can tell when people say something that doesn't match their inner state."

"You mean you can tell when they're not telling the truth?" Laurie asked.

Skye nodded.

"So, you're basically a human lie detector," Dana said.

Skye shifted, a bit self-conscious. "Pretty much."

Dana rubbed her hands, a devious look on her face. "Now that does come in handy."

Laurie and Skye laughed. The doorbell rang and before Dana could move, she heard Minh pound down the steps and throw the door open. She walked into the living room just as Minh took the stack of pizza boxes from the delivery boy. Dana tipped him. "Thank you." He gave a little salute and bounced back down the porch steps.

When she returned, Laurie was taking out plates and Skye fishing out paper napkins from a drawer. Minh grabbed three slices as soon as he opened the boxes. Hoa appeared and chose a slice from each type, then disappeared up the stairs. "Leave something for Rosa," Dana admonished.

"I'll give her a couple slices. Can I scramble some eggs, too?" Laurie asked.

"Sure, but eat first," Dana waved a hand.

Rosa pawed at Laurie's leg, so she put some pizza on a plate and placed it on the mat at the back door. They each grabbed a slice and ate in silence for a minute. Laurie reached for another one. "I didn't realize how hungry I was."

Dana wiped her hands and mouth fastidiously with her napkin and picked up her wineglass. She motioned to Skye with the other hand. "How long have you had this ability?"

Skye put down the new wedge of pizza she was about to take a bite out of. "Pretty much all my life. My mother is like this and my great aunt. It kind of runs in the family."

"So you come from a psychic family?" Laurie asked.

"I'm an empath, not a psychic."

"What's the difference?" Dana asked.

"For one, I can't tell the future. At least not without Tarot cards and that's really a glance at the energies surrounding a person or situation, not a solid prediction. Can't scry in crystal balls like my grandmother and cousin."

"Scry?" Laurie asked around a mouthful.

"Wait, crystal balls are a real thing?" Dana asked.

Skye nodded. "If you know how to use them. Scrying is a way of seeing the answer to questions in crystal. You form an intention, go into a light trance, and look into a crystal. Images will appear. Clear ones are best, but it's never been my forte."

An uncomfortable silence followed.

"I can feel you're skeptical, especially you." Skye dipped her head at Dana.

"Next you're going to tell us those little magic eight balls are for real," Laurie joked, lightening the mood again.

Skye shook her head and finally took a bite of her pizza.

"So you know Peggy was hiding something and that Tommy had nothing to do with Kimberly's death," Dana summed up. "Did you pick up anything from the people at the reunion?"

"I know that John had nothing to do with it. His shock radiated off him," Skye said.

"You saw him?" Laurie asked.

"I passed him in the hallway after I was interrogated," Skye explained. "I can't read well in such a crowd. I recommend we interview the people at the front tables to see if they saw anything suspicious. People who volunteer for things like that tend to keep in touch with classmates. They could be a wealth of gossip."

Dana nodded, a glint of hope returning. "You can come?"

"The store is a family business, so I can get somebody to cover my shifts."

"I always thought that store was just for fun. You know, filled with pretty stones and curiosities," Laurie said.

"That's what we want the normies to know," Skye said.

Laurie's eyebrows shot up. "Normies? You mean like ordinary people?"

"Muggles," Minh exclaimed.

Dana jumped. "What have I told you about eavesdropping, young man?"

"I just came down for more pizza." His face was the picture of innocence.

Skye put her hand over her mouth and smothered a laugh.

"Get your food and go," Dana said.

Rosa woofed.

Only two pieces of the meat pizza were left. "Take the box and give the dog another slice." Dana shooed him off. He ran up the stairs, Rosa hot on his heels.

Dana reached for a veggie slice. Carbs usually settled her nerves. She'd run an extra mile in the morning. At least Kimberly had kept away tonight. She glanced around, worried just thinking of the ghost might bring her, but she was nowhere in sight.

Skye sat back. "My family brought the old ways with them when they came from Ireland during the potato famine."

"When was that?" Dana asked.

"Mid 1800s," Laurie said, then turned to Skye. "You mean your family are all into Wicca?"

Skye waggled her head. "You could say that. There are a lot of branches of paganism, but my family's traditions have been passed down for a long time. People think our shop is New Age, but I call it Old School."

"Amazing," Laurie said.

Skye turned the conversation back to their investigation. "So, let's interview the people who volunteered at the reunion—at least the ones at the front table. I can guarantee John is innocent, but Peggy is hiding something."

"Right. We'll interview those three volunteers and see what we learn." Laurie grabbed a notepad out of her purse and wrote down their names. "Also the woman who wanted to sue Kimberly's law firm. Anybody else?"

"Not yet," Dana said, recovering from Skye's revelation. "We need to look at the security footage from Galactic."

"And we should try to find out who owns that old Chevy," Skye said.

"That sounds like a needle in a haystack," Laurie said.

Skye shook her head. "Not really. That car is old. We can search the DMV for registrations. Jade can get in for us."

The doorbell rang again. "Just in time." Skye ran to open it. She ushered in a woman dressed in jeans and a sweatshirt. Solid and well-muscled, the woman stood a head taller than her wife. Skye introduced them. "You know Dana. This is our friend who tried to escape to the east coast, Laurie."

"Please to meet you." Jade's accent held faint hints of the south.

She handed a white box to Skye, then pushed an errant curl off her face. "I brought dessert."

Dana moaned. "You are my favorite person."

Jade settled next to her wife and surveyed the table. "Any pizza left?"

"Two veggie slices. Want me to heat them?"

"Nah." Jade scooped them up.

Dana opened the pastry box. "Cupcakes," she announced.

"I want a chocolate one," Skye called.

"They're all chocolate," Dana said.

"Smart woman," Laurie said. "Skye's been telling us about her special ability."

"Ah, so you came out of the psychic closet," Jade teased.

"I'm an empath, not a psychic," Skye said, sounding a bit pedantic. "Besides, this one talks to animals and Dana has a ghost following her around."

"Do tell." Jade took a big bite of pizza and studied them, her dark brown eyes sparkling.

"You mean she hasn't divulged our secret already?" Laurie asked.

"I can keep things to myself when I need to," Skye objected.

Rosa came rushing in and sniffed Jade's pant legs. "She didn't do it."

Laurie burst out laughing. "Rosa just cleared you."

"She what?" Jade asked.

"Rosa knows what the murderer smells like."

"We're taking her along on all our interviews," Dana said.

Skye brushed her nose and pointed at Dana.

"What?"

"Frosting," Skye whispered.

Dana wiped her nose with her napkin and looked at the smudge of frosting wistfully. "What a waste."

"You are a total sugar junkie," Skye said.

Dana laughed. "You've known me how long and you're just now figuring this out?"

Laurie just shook her head at Dana, but a smile played on her lips. "Just get another one."

Dana grabbed a cupcake with lots of frosting.

Laurie turned her attention back to Jade and told her an abbreviated version of the near crash and hearing Rosa's voice.

"What a good girl you are, Ms. Rosa," Jade said.

The dog wagged her tail, looking up with adoring brown eyes.

"Her name was Mittens when we first met her—" Skye continued the story "—but she told Laurie her full name was…what was it?"

"Rosa Miranda Gomez Diaz," Laurie said.

"Quite fitting," Jade said.

Lele jumped up on the table and meowed in protest.

"I think we all understand that," Jade said. The cat rubbed under Jade's chin and presented her butt to be sniffed. "I don't think so," she said, nudging the cat to turn around. She stroked her side.

"She's such a diva," Rosa said. The cat fixed the dog with a look. Laurie called Rosa to her side and scratched behind her ears.

"So, Dana, you're seeing ghosts?" Jade asked.

"Just one. Kimberly."

"The murder victim? That's helpful," Jade said.

"Not so much. She doesn't remember anything. Just riding up in the elevator and then sitting in the chair across from my bed in the hospital."

"That is typical."

They all stared at her. Except Skye, who looked like somebody sitting on a secret.

"Okay, you two. Spill it," Laurie said.

"Skye's not the only one from a magical family," Jade finally admitted. "I'm from New Orleans, after all."

"You did seem comfortable with our revelations." Dana gazed wistfully at the cupcakes.

"I figured somewhere in the South," Laurie said.

Jade laughed. "This accent lingers. My ancestors brought over the old ways and some still practice some."

"You mean like Voodoo?" Dana asked, a bit alarmed.

Jade shrugged. "It's really a mix of Vodou and Santería these days. We don't go in for blood sacrifice, so don't worry. Let's just say dealing with spirits, talking to animals, and having visions is something I grew up around."

"Are you psychic, too?" Dana asked.

"Empathic," Skye objected.

Jade fidgeted with the pizza crust on her plate.

Skye came to her rescue. "She doesn't like to talk about it too much. I mean, she'd get a lot of crap at work if it got out. Maybe even get fired."

"Really? These days?" Laurie asked.

"Yeah, there's still a lot of prejudice there, and if they found out my grandmother was a manbo, I'd never hear the end of it."

"Did you say mambo? Like the Mambo Kings?" Dana asked.

Jade laughed. "It's sometimes pronounced that way, but a manbo is a female spiritual leader. So I don't doubt your experiences. About your ghost. I learned a few things watching my grandmother that might help your ghost."

Dana sat forward. "You think she'd go away after that?"

"Wow, you're really eager to get rid of her," Skye said.

"She probably has unfinished business. Her death came as a surprise," Jade explained. "She needs help coming to terms with what has happened to her. Then we can help her find her ancestors and move on."

"Good, because I want out of the ghost business." Dana sat straight, brushing her hands together to get rid of the cupcake crumbs and maybe Kimberly, too.

"And I need help getting cleared of a murder charge," Laurie reminded them. "Could your grandmother Zoom with the ghost?"

Jade and Skye broke into peals of laughter. Inspired, Rosa ran a lap around the kitchen and living room.

"What's so funny?" Laurie asked. "I didn't kill her."

"We know, sweetie." Skye wiped a tear from the corner of her eye. "But powerful psychics tend to blow out electronics."

"Plus, my grandmother passed away about ten years ago."

"That's disappointing." Dana's shoulders drooped. "I mean, I'm sorry for your loss."

Jade waved this away. "Is Kimberly's ghost here now?"

"I haven't seen her all day. She must have dead people business."

"Once we solve this, let's make a date to help her move on." Jade's voice seemed somehow amplified as she surveyed the room.

Dana looked skeptical. "You think that will work? I mean, she just shows up with no rhyme or reason."

"That you can tell. We might need her input until we know who did it. But don't worry. She won't stick around forever." Jade sat back and fished for her keys in her pants pocket. "Ready, babe?"

"Wait, there's one more thing," Laurie said.

"An old chevy followed us from the funeral," Dana explained. "Skye suggested you might be willing to help us find it. Check how many are registered in King County."

"Whoa," Jade said. "That's a bit risky, but for Skye's friends, I'll try. How big was this chevy? Small, large?"

"It was boxy, like the car in *The Blues Brothers.*"

"Yeah, but that was a 1974 Dodge Monaco." Minh's voice sounded from the stairwell.

"Young man, how many times do I have to tell you—" Dana started toward where he was lurking.

Jade cracked up. "He's right, though."

Dana stopped and shook her head. "You might as well come in."

Minh crept around the corner, eyes wide. "You can really see ghosts, Mom?"

She raised her hands in the air. "I give up. Just one, okay?"

"Sweet."

"Now about this car," Jade said. "How do you know it was a chevy?"

"It had the logo. I mean, everybody recognizes that."

Jade looked skeptical, but didn't question Laurie. "What color?

"Blue."

Jade took out her phone and pulled up different years and models. They all huddled around her, shaking their heads, arguing.

Laurie squinted at the screen. "Can you enlarge these?"

"Let's use my iPad. The screen is bigger," Dana said. "Minh, go get it."

"I've got it." Hoa walked to the table, holding out her mom's device.

Dana stared at her, then put her hands on her hips.

Hoa looked at her brother. "Uh oh."

"You can't tell your father anything about any of this. If he finds out—" she shook her head, not finishing her sentence. Somehow the threat seemed worse not being voiced.

"We promise," Hoa said. Her brother nodded.

Dana took the iPad and noticed Minh had already pulled up images of Impalas. "I don't know what I'm going to do with these teenagers," she mumbled.

Skye smiled. "They can't be as bad as we were."

Dana shot her a look. She put the device on the table and saw that Hoa had tabs for each year of the 1980s.

"Smart kids," Jade said and opened the first tab. They all gathered around. Jade made her way through the first couple pages.

"They all look the same."

Minh read from his phone. "The seventh generation was produced from 1977 to 1985. Both ends of the car got shorter."

Jade sat back. "Here's what I'll do. Compare registrations of that model of Impala with the class lists from—is it Jefferson High?"

"Yes, but that sounds like a huge list."

"I'll limit the students to the years you all were there, so that helps." Jade put her hands behind her head and stretched her back. "The real problem is these are considered low-riders, so that might up the numbers."

"Rudy Gonzales," Dana and Skye said at the same time.

"Let's pay him a visit tomorrow," Laurie said.

Rosa barked and took another run around the room.

CHAPTER

TWELVE

Skye pulled her old Subaru up to a rambling blue farmhouse bordering the Duwamish River in South Park. A white extension had been built on one side and several cars were parked along the street in front. "Is Rudy a mechanic?" Laurie asked, pointing to a long building in the back. It looked like a garage or work shed.

Skye shook her head. "No idea."

Two brown dogs of indeterminant breed stood stiff-legged in the front yard, ready to protect their home turf. Rosa squirmed in Laurie's lap. "Let me go, let me go."

"They don't look all that friendly," Laurie said.

"Who?"

"I'm talking about the dogs."

"What does Rosa say?"

"She wants out, but I'm putting her on the leash just to be safe."

"Humans," Rosa huffed.

Skye opened the door and ambled to the front gate so the dogs could get used to her. The canines approached, heads extended to smell this newcomer. Rosa scampered to the fence, rear wiggling.

The two sniffed her face through the fence. One turned and peed on a nearby bush. Rosa gave a woof.

"We're cleared," Rosa said.

Laurie gestured to the dog just putting his leg back down. "Rosa says we've been approved for entry."

Skye rolled her eyes and opened the gate. Laurie followed, still hesitant. The two dogs ran toward the house, then back again, tongues lolling. The female crouched down and wagged her tail, inviting Rosa to play.

"Seems Lucy likes that fancy dog of yours," someone called from the side of the house. "You can let her off leash."

Laurie looked up and found the same round face she'd seen at the reunion smiling in welcome. "Hi, actually she's a mix. Not that fancy."

"Mine, too. Heinz 57. Some cur, some shepherd—you know." He walked toward them. The dogs ran a circle around him and took off again.

"Rudy, great to see you." Skye said. "You remember Laurie from biology class. Always getting A's."

Rudy wiped his hands on a rag and nodded. "I do. Nice of you to drop by." His voice held a question.

"Got time for a chat?" Skye asked.

"I guess." Rudy kicked at the dirt, studying them.

"We wanted to ask you about the reunion. About Kimberly's murder."

He shook his head. "Awful. Just awful."

The front porch door opened and an older woman stepped out. "¿Rudy, que pasa? ¿Quiénes son?"

"Amigas de la escuela secundaria." Rudy looked back at them. "That's my mother."

The woman gave them a tentative smile.

Laurie gave a little wave. "Hola, señora."

Rudy's mother gestured for them to come into the house.

"Is that okay with you?" Skye asked.

"She'll insist," Rudy explained.

"Does she know what happened?"

Rudy nodded. "Whole family's heard about it."

Laurie called Rosa to her side, but Rudy said, "Let her stay. They'll be fine out here." He held the door open and they entered a smallish living room crammed with two sofas and a couple of recliners all clustered around a big screen TV. Rudy gestured for them to take a seat.

Skye and Laurie settled on a mauve sofa. His mother came in from the kitchen carrying two ice teas and handed them to her guests.

"Gracias," Laurie said. Skye smiled and dutifully took hers.

The woman nodded and retreated into the kitchen. Rudy settled on one of the recliners. "What did you want to know?"

"I guess I'll get right to the point," Laurie said. "You might have heard that I'm a suspect in the murder."

Rudy's brown eyes softened. "I did hear that. Don't make no sense to me."

Laurie's shoulders dropped. "Thank you."

"I mean, you liked that John fella, but you left, right?"

Laurie nodded. "I went to college on the East Coast and stayed. Married somebody from there."

Rudy shook his head in sympathy.

"I was near her when it happened, but I didn't do it. Somebody in a black hoodie pushed her over. Dana got knocked over the rail, too."

"She's okay, though," Skye said. "She grabbed onto a vine and some young guys rescued her."

"Gracias a Dios," Rudy murmured.

"Si." Laurie twisted her fingers together. "The thing is—I hate to ask such a thing, Rudy—but somebody followed us from the cemetery yesterday. They were dressed in a black hoodie and drove an old model Impala. Do you know anybody who owns—"

"You think it was me?" Rudy stood up, pointing to his chest. "You think because I have a low-rider it might be me?"

131

"No, no—" Laurie began, but Rudy kept going.

"I have a big family here." He spread his arms wide. "We've lived in this same spot for four generations. I have my own garage out back. A good business. You think I would risk all that for some skinny white girl?"

Rudy's mother came rushing in from the kitchen. "¿Qué pasa? Cálmate."

Rudy answered her so fast Laurie couldn't follow what he said. His mother turned sad eyes on the two women, shaking her head.

Laurie felt like an idiot. "I'm so sorry, Rudy. I realize how this looks. It's just that I'm desperate." Tears leaked out.

Skye stood up. "We deeply apologize for the offense. We just wanted to know if you knew anybody from our class who drives a blue 1980s Impala. We never suspected you."

Laurie tried not to respond to Skye's little lie.

Rudy relented somewhat. "My low rider is a Cadillac Coupe DeVille."

"Sounds nice," Laurie murmured.

"It is. Lots of people have old chevies they've upgraded. Nobody from Jefferson that I know of."

"We appreciate your time, Rudy," Skye said, standing up and edging toward the door.

"I went to Jefferson because Seattle was trying to integrate the schools," he said, chin high.

Laurie's face flushed as red as a ripe tomato. Oh, God. Another hot flash on top of this humiliation. "I can't tell you how sorry—"

Rudy cut her off with a chop of his hand. He took a deep breath, steeling himself. Then he looked up at the two. "If I hear anything, I'll get in touch with Dana. I know her best."

Laurie saw his mother hovering in the kitchen door. "Lo siento," she said, her hand to her heart. The woman gave her a tentative nod.

Skye opened the door and the two spilled out onto the porch. "God, I feel like such a jerk," Laurie whispered.

The two family dogs stood close to the steps, one growling low in his throat. "Looks like I need to escort you to the gate," Rudy said.

Rosa rushed up. "What did you say to make him so mad?"

"I'll tell you later."

Rosa sniffed Rudy's pant legs. He reached down and gently pushed her aside. She stuck her head in his palm and sniffed again. "He didn't do it," she announced.

"Yeah, we kind of figured that out, but thanks," Laurie mentally replied.

Skye jumped in the car and pulled away as quickly as she could without spinning gravel. "That was awkward."

"No kidding."

"But we needed to clear him."

"Rosa said he didn't smell like the murderer."

"He wasn't hiding anything. He didn't have anything to do with it. Who's next?"

"Peggy never coughed up the name of the woman who got Kimberly fired, but Dana dug through some court records and found her. Michelle Warren. Lives in Greenwood." Laurie put the address into her phone and asked for directions. "Says it will take forty-five minutes."

Skye snorted and floored it. Laurie grabbed the rollbar. She'd always thought of her friend as laid back, but apparently not when it came to driving. "I'll keep an eye out for traffic cops."

"I've got a speed alarm. Keep watching for old Chevrolets."

Half an hour later, they pulled up in front of a modern gray duplex and parked across the street. "Did we call her?" Skye asked.

"Dana thought just showing up might work better. Said she works a swing shift at the hospital, so she's probably home."

They pushed open a gate in a new wooden fence not yet darkened by the rain. Laurie checked the address and pointed to the door on the right. A figure appeared behind the frosted glass-paned door. It opened to reveal a woman in blue scrubs. "I don't want to buy anything," she said.

"We're not selling anything, Mrs. Warren," Skye said. "We'd like to speak with you if we can."

"It's Kaplan now. I went back to my maiden name." She started to close the door.

"We have a question about Kimberly Woolridge," Laurie said just before the door shut in her face.

The door opened wide enough to show the woman's surprised face. "What? That case closed years ago."

"Yes, it did. Have you heard about Kimberly, ma'am?" Skye eyed Laurie for calling the woman ma'am, but Laurie ignored her.

Rosa sat up on her hind legs and whined.

"Aw," Michelle said. "What a cutie. She's part Havanese, isn't she?" She bent down and started petting the conniving canine who was busy sniffing Michelle.

"Yes," Laurie said, biting her lip to keep from smiling. "Her name is Rosa."

"Good name for that breed. What's the other part?"

"You know, I'm not sure. I recently got her. The owner inherited her from her aunt, but was mistreating her."

Michelle looked up at Laurie, her face friendly now. "I guess you can come in for a minute, but I've got to leave for work soon."

"Thank you," Laurie said.

Michelle pointed a finger at Rosa. "But you can't chase my cat," Rosa wagged her tail.

"You'll behave, won't you girl?" Laurie gave Rosa the eye.

They walked into a small living room, modern and sterile as an operating room. Laurie took a seat and noticed a scruffy Maine Coon on the window ledge.

"Oh, goody. Company," the cat said and jumped down to the back of the sofa. The two animals sniffed noses and Rosa wagged her tail. The cat jumped to the floor and rubbed against Laurie's legs. She reached down to stroke his side.

"She was sad until I came," the cat said.

"He likes you," Michelle said. "I'd offer you something to drink, but like I said, I'm headed to work."

"No worries." Laurie had picked up the phrase from her students a few years back.

Michelle nodded. "So, what's this about Kimberly?"

Laurie opened her mouth to explain, but Rosa interrupted her train of thought.

"She didn't do it," the dog sent.

Skye noticed her hesitate and jumped in. "Jefferson High just had a reunion and Kimberly was pushed over the railing at the Galactic Globes."

Michelle's hand flew to her heart. "And you think I was involved?"

Laurie caught Skye's eye and gave a small shake of her head. "You told us you hadn't seen her since the case closed, so no. Did you find out anything about her during the case? Someone who might want to hurt her? Any enemies?" Skye asked.

Michelle shook her head. "She just made a stupid mistake, but it cost me a few million. My ex was loaded." She looked around her small condo.

"I'm sorry to hear that," Skye said.

"I tried to sue so I could get more in the settlement, but it just didn't work. He had a bevy of lawyers." Michelle made a face.

"Sounds awful." Laurie thought about how Kimberly wanted to take advantage of John in their divorce.

"I've moved on. Frankly, I don't think Kimberly was smart enough to make any real enemies."

Laurie felt a stab of sadness for John.

Michelle reached for her key ring. "I've really got to go."

Laurie stood up. "Thanks for seeing us."

Michelle walked toward the door, then stopped. "Can I ask why you're investigating? You don't look like detectives to me."

Laurie answered her honestly. "The police think I did it because she married my high school crush."

"That seems ridiculous," Michelle said. "They don't have any other evidence?"

"Not that I know of," Laurie said.

Michelle opened the back door and they followed her out. Laurie watched as she locked up, then took a key fob between her fingers. She drove a recent model car, then. Old chevies didn't have automatic locks like this and certainly no alarms.

Michelle clicked the button and the headlights of a Honda Accord flashed. Skye walked out into the parking area behind the duplex complex and was scanning the cars.

She paused before starting her car and rolled down the window. "Well, you don't seem like the murdering type to me. My cat has impeccable taste in humans."

Laurie laughed. "Thank you. I wish he could testify."

"Best of luck," Michelle said. She gave a little wave and backed out of her parking spot. Laurie and Skye walked to the front of the complex and crossed the street. "Seems like a waste of time, but at least we've crossed two people off the list," Skye said.

"No new leads, though."

"True. Jade says a lot of detective work is boring like this." Skye drove Laurie to her parents' house and dropped her off.

CHAPTER

THIRTEEN

L aurie opened the door to her childhood home and the smell of roasted sesame oil and cayenne pepper greeted her.

"I made Szechuan stir fry with tofu and those little mushrooms your father loves," her mother called out. "Ready in ten minutes."

Laurie walked back to the kitchen. "You shouldn't have waited for me."

Her mother glanced at the wall clock. "Nonsense. It's just after eight."

"I've never known you to cook so much."

Larissa looked over her shoulder, her face flushed from the steam rising off the wok. "I like having you here. Besides, I need to do whatever I can to help."

Laurie gave her mom a spontaneous hug. "You believe me. That's enough."

"Okay, okay." Her mother broke free. "Don't want anything to burn." She wiped her eyes with the corner of her apron. "It's the cayenne."

"Right," Laurie mumbled. She reached for the lid on a pot and her mother brushed her hand away.

"That's rice. Not ready yet."

Rosa scratched at the back door and Laurie let her and Oliver out. Natasha darted for the opening, but she grabbed her up. "You know you're not allowed outside."

"It's not fair. She gets to go."

"She's too big for a hawk to grab. You're not." Laurie was getting used to these silent conversations. She deposited the disgruntled feline on the couch. Natasha jumped onto the back and started grooming herself, something Laurie realized was her way of salvaging her pride. She left the feline to her recovery process and ran upstairs to splash water on her face. She noticed a new bag on the bed and dumped it out to discover more clothes—twill pants and a matching shirt. Her mother really was worried. Laurie went back down and set the table in the adjacent dining room.

"You want to eat in there?" Larissa asked.

"Sure. The island's a little crowded for the three of us." She went back for silverware. "You want chopsticks?"

"I do, but your father will want a fork."

Laurie grabbed the utensils and kissed her mom on the cheek on her way to the table.

"What's that for?" Larissa asked.

"You got me new clothes. You're going to spoil me."

"You need some things to wear. Did you bring any business suits?"

She laid the fork next to her father's plate. "No, I just packed a carry-on. Didn't expect to be arrested for murder."

A loud clatter came from the kitchen. Laurie ran back to find her mother surrounded by what smelled like soy sauce, her shoulders heaving, hands on her knees.

"Oh, Mom. It's going to be all right."

Her mother sobbed, then shook her head, trying to stop the tears. "I'm sorry. It slipped."

Frantic scratching came from the back door. "It's okay. I'll clean it up." Laurie turned off the heat under the wok. "Wait, Rosa. There's glass."

Her mother started to move. "No, you've only got socks on. Let me get it up first."

"I'm sorry. I'm trying—" Her mom pressed her fingers to her mouth. Laurie crouched down and started picking up the big pieces of the broken bottle. "Careful. You'll cut yourself."

"I'm fine." Laurie threw the glass in the trash and spread paper towels on the dark liquid.

"I'm buying bamboo towels now," her mother said in a quiet voice. "Better for the earth."

"Good job," Laurie said, realizing she was repeating words her mother used to say to her when she was a child. She gathered the sopping mess up and threw it in the trash, then cleaned up the remaining liquid. She swept up the tiny shards. "All better now."

"I'm sorry. I hate wasting a whole bottle." Her mother was subdued.

"Don't cry over spilled tamari." Laurie turned around to see her father standing in the archway, a sad smile on his face. "Smells delicious. What's for dinner?"

Larissa peeled off her wet socks and looked at her damp pant legs. "Guess I better change. Your daughter will serve up the surprise."

"Go, sit." Laurie shooed her father out of the kitchen doorway. She let the dogs in. Rosa ran up the stairs, probably to comfort her mother. Oliver sniffed his food dish, then went to his bed. Laurie dumped the stir-fry into a huge teal and purple ceramic bowl her mother had no doubt bought from a local potter. The rice went in a smaller, equally beautiful bowl, and she put them on the table.

"What do you want to drink?" she asked her father who sat, hands folded, watching her.

"Water's fine."

"Japanese beer for me," her mother called.

Laurie gave the dogs scoops of the freeze-dried food her father had bought and checked Natasha's bowl. She got another beer for herself and carried the beverages to the table. Her mother sat at her regular spot, putting on a brave face. Laurie served up the food, enjoying the aroma. They sat and ate quietly for a while.

"This is so good, Mom." Laurie took another helping.

"She's been taking some cooking classes since she cut back at the clinic. I had to add a mile to my run just to keep from getting fat." Her father patted his belly.

Her mother snorted. "This man's metabolism would rival a bonfire."

"Good, she feels better." Natasha said, then jumped up on the table and sniffed the stir-fry. "How do you humans eat that stuff?"

Laurie laughed.

"What?" her mom asked.

"Natasha doesn't like spicy food," Laurie said.

"No cayenne for cats," her father said.

Laurie's phone rang and she checked the name.

"Remember when people didn't call at dinner time? Who is that?" her mother asked.

"It is a bit past when most people eat. It's my lawyer."

"Can't it wait?"

She declined the call.

Five seconds later, her phone announced a text. *Pick up. We have a situation.*

The phone rang again. Laurie moved out to the deck to talk. "What's happening?"

"Dr. Olson, I can't represent you effectively if you don't tell me the truth."

"I did."

"We found a series of emails between you and Kimberly Woolridge."

"No, I never—"

"Seems you opened a secret account? Threatened her life?"

"What are you talking about?" Laurie shouted. "I never did any such thing."

"I'm looking at the emails right now."

Laurie paced the length of the deck. "I'm telling you it wasn't me. I didn't know her phone number or email address."

"This explains why the DA thinks this is an open and shut case."

Her father opened the door and stood watching her. Rosa slipped around him and paced with Laurie. "What's happening?" he asked.

She waved him off.

"You need to come down and look at these. Do you have your university laptop with you?"

"Yes, why?"

"Bring it. I'll explain when you get here."

"You mean you want me to come—"

"Now," he interrupted her. "We're on a tight schedule. How soon can you get here?"

"I'm on my way." She turned to find both parents standing in the doorway, her father with his arm around her mother. "I have to go to my lawyer's office."

"It's late," Larissa objected.

Laurie explained what was happening.

"But—" her mother started to say, but her father had already gotten the keys. He held them up. "Let's go."

Laurie and the dogs jumped into the back of her parents' older Subaru Outback and her father peeled out of the driveway before she could buckle her seatbelt. She took out her cell and called Dana. Her parents listened as she explained the situation.

"But you have the kids with you," Laurie said.

"They're old enough to look after themselves," Dana explained. "I'll be right there."

Laurie called Skye. "Can you come?" she asked. "I'm scared."

"I'd love to, but by the time I drive in from Duvall, you'll already be done." Skye's voice soothed her.

"How are we going to prove these emails are fake?" Laurie asked.

"We'll figure it out. Don't worry. We've got your back."

"Really?" Laurie hated the whine in her voice.

"Yes. I'm going to talk to Jade now."

"I don't want to get her in trouble."

Skye chuckled. "You don't have to worry about my girl. She's tough as an alligator's hide."

The analogy seemed apt given Jade's hometown. Maybe she could get her mother to cast a spell or something. Then realized she would have scoffed at such a thought only a week ago.

"Good idea." Rosa climbed on her lap and licked her face.

Somewhat reassured, Laurie hugged the dog to her. "Okay, we can figure this out, girl. Too bad you can't smell email trails."

They arrived at Shanks' downtown office in the Smith Tower and took the ancient elevator up. She'd forgotten the leashes, but the dogs stuck to her side. Nobody thought to object to their presence.

Shanks ushered them to his conference room. Several copies of the email exchange were spread in front of chairs. "Thank you for coming at such short notice, Laurie. This new evidence upends your case. Did you bring your laptop?"

She handed over her MacBook.

"I'm giving this to my tech. He's going to check for spyware. Any tampering."

"Good," Martin said. "Because my daughter is not lying."

"I appreciate your concern, sir." Shanks turned back to Laurie. "We may have to keep it for a few days. Even until the trial."

"And you should address my daughter as Dr. Olson," her father added.

Shanks turned his palms up. "Yes, but there are three of you."

Laurie ignored her father and handed over the computer. "I suppose I can use my parents' computer, right?"

"Of course," the second Dr. Olson said. Her mother was in high umbrage now.

"We're doing our best to clear Laurie," Shanks reassured her.

"It's okay, Mom."

"It will be okay when you are cleared of these ridiculous charges."

"Now, please have a seat and read through these emails." Shanks indicated Laurie should sit in front of some printed pages.

"I'm telling you, it wasn't me," Laurie said.

Shanks held up a finger. "Just read, then we'll talk. My assistant is here if you need anything." He gestured toward a youngish woman standing in the corner of the room, hands folded in front of her.

Laurie settled in a chair and pick up the print-out. Her parents sat across from her and did the same. Shanks had printed out a few copies. Rosa busied herself sniffing everyone in the office. She came back and assured Laurie that they were all innocent, then leaned against Laurie's leg. She appreciated the dog's warm weight.

LO: *It's been a long time, but I've never forgotten how you humiliated me.*

KW: *What are you talking about? Who is this?*

LO: *You spread lies about me, then stole my one true love.*

"One true love?" Laurie blurted out. "I'd never use that phrase."

"Keep reading," Shanks said.

Dana arrived and Shanks ushered her to a seat, then explained the printouts in a hushed voice. Laurie gave her friend a wave and continued reading.

KW: *I don't know what you're talking about.*

LO: *You told everyone I was a slut. That I was sleeping with the entire football team.*

KW: *Lauren Olson? Is this you?*

LO: *You were the slut. You got yourself pregnant. That was the only way you could keep John.*

"It takes two people to get pregnant. I think a man wrote this," Laurie said. She looked around, but everyone else was focused on the text in front of them. She continued reading.

KW: *You're crazy. I'm blocking you.*

LO: *I'm coming for you. I'm going to take back what's mine. I'm getting rid of you.*

KW: *What do you mean?*

LO: *Better stay circumspect. You'll never see me coming.*

Laurie looked up. "This is so childish. I never wrote this."

Dana finished reading and tapped the table. "But 'circumspect'? That word seems out of place."

"Yeah—" Laurie started to say more, but Shanks interrupted her.

"The police found this on Kimberly's phone. The IP address is in Boston. From the university you work for, in fact."

"No, that can't be. I never sent them, I'm telling you. Plus, there's no explicit threat of murder here."

"Could be enough to convince a jury," Shanks said. "We'll get our cybersecurity guy right on this."

"I'll help," Dana whispered to Laurie.

"Is there anyone at your university who might have motive?" Shanks asked.

"My department chair despises me. Thinks I tried to take his job, but he doesn't know anything about my high school crush on John."

"Does anyone at your work know about it?"

Laurie thought about it. "No, the only person in Boston who knows about John is my ex, Graham Barker. But we had an amicable divorce. He's in cyber security—oh." Her eyes went wide. "I guess that could be seen as a problem."

Shanks studied her for a minute, his round glasses belying his serious expression. "Or he might be able to help. We're going to have to interview them."

"Just what I need. Dr. Brown will use this to try to get me fired."

"I can help with that," Shanks said. "We'll have to talk to the computer security team at the university as well. Is there anyone else we should speak with?"

Laurie shook her head. "Not that I can think of at the moment. I'll let you know if I remember something."

"Thanks for coming in."

"Can we take these copies of the emails?" Dana asked.

Shanks hesitated. Rosa let out a little bark and he reached down to scratch her head. "Since you're also an attorney, I can allow it. Just don't let them get into the wrong hands."

"We'll be careful," Dana reassured him.

Laurie's father held the door to the conference room open. "Thanks, Dad." Laurie patted the side of her leg "Let's go home, girl." Rosa walked out with her. Oliver stuck with her father. The others followed, subdued by this news.

Outside, Dana put a hand on Laurie's shoulder. "We're going to figure this out. Get some sleep."

Laurie just nodded, fighting back tears. Things just kept getting worse.

The family was silent on the drive home. Laurie let her head rest on the seat, wondering how on earth she was going to prove she had not wanted to kill Kimberly. Rosa put her head on her lap, watching her with worried brown eyes. Her father turned off the interstate and drove up the winding streets of Queen Anne Hill. Laurie caught the flash of headlights in the rearview mirror. She turned around and spotted a car following them.

"Dad, can you take a little detour?"

"Why? Do you want to see something in the neighborhood?"

"I think someone may be following us."

Her mother sat up in alarm. "What?"

"Don't look."

Her mother turned around with a huff. Laurie explained about the chevy that had trailed them from the cemetery. "I want to see if it's the same car. We need to get a license plate."

Martin took a sharp right.

Larissa grabbed the roll bar. "I'm living in a detective novel."

"I never knew you were so dramatic, Mom."

"My daughter is accused of murder, her attorney finds strange emails sent to the victim, and I'm not allowed to be dramatic?"

Laurie didn't bother to answer. She crouched down and peeked over the seat, keeping her head mostly behind the headrest. The car took the same turn. She only glimpsed a low, boxy shape before the headlights flashed in her eyes.

She lowered her head.

Her father adjusted the rearview mirror. "They're behind us."

"See that streetlight at the end of the street? Can you pull over and stop?"

"That doesn't feel safe," her mother said.

"It will be all right, Larissa." Her father's voice was soothing. At the last minute, he pulled to the curb. An old blue chevy flashed by.

Laurie caught a glimpse of a figure with what looked like a hoodie. She tried to read the license plate, but it was in shadow. "C. That's all I can see."

"I couldn't catch anything," her father said.

Her mother shook her head, fighting tears. "I'm sorry. I thought I was tough."

Rosa whined and climbed over the center console into Larissa's lap. She licked her face until Larissa hugged the dog to her chest. "Such a good girl. You'll protect us, won't you?"

Oliver growled. Rosa whined again, her whole body wiggling with the need to comfort Larissa. "I'll bite their legs off," she said.

Laurie laughed and told them what Rosa had said without thinking.

Her mother got out a tissue and wiped her face, fending off the dog with her arm. "How do you know that's what she's thinking? Maybe we need a Rottweiler. Oliver would just lick them to death."

"Don't insult them," Laurie said. "Rosa could do some damage. People are afraid of boxers and Natasha has very sharp claws. I can attest to that."

"We'll be fine, sweetheart." Martin reached over and patted his wife's shoulder. "Everything is going to work out."

Laurie hoped to whichever deity was overseeing her that this was true.

CHAPTER
FOURTEEN

Laurie woke to a ding from her phone. The old clock radio read nine-thirty. She hadn't slept this late in ages. She'd had trouble getting to sleep last night, plus she missed Rosa's warm weight. The little dog had opted to sleep with her mother, saying Larissa needed to be reassured. Laurie picked up her phone and found a text from John.

JN: I find myself thinking about you.

Warmth filled her that had nothing to do with 'the change', as her grandmother had so tactfully phrased it. Rosa came running in and jumped on the bed. "Is that your mate?"

"Why do you call him that?" Laurie scoffed.

"Why don't you want to admit it?" Rosa asked.

She ignored the little Havanese and pondered what to say. Should she tell him about the texts? About the car?

LO: Same here.

The phone dinged immediately.

JN: I'm free today. Can I see you?

LO: Yes. Where should we meet?

JN: Our favorite park?
LO: Is it still there?
JN: LOL! Not really. How about The Market?
LO: Give me an hour.
JN: It's a date.

Laurie jumped out of bed and ran into the shower, her heart lighter than it had been in ages. Rosa yipped and did a full lap around the house. Laurie toweled off and picked out her clothes, glad her mother had gone shopping. Spring in the Pacific Northwest. Layers, she needed layers. The new pants and shirt. The fleece vest. She threw a rain jacket in her bag and ran downstairs. Her keys were on the table next to the door. She grabbed them up along with Rosa's leash.

Her father appeared with a mug of coffee. "Where are you off to? We let you sleep in."

"I'm meeting John at Pike Place Market."

Her father frowned.

"I know, I know. I've got emails to investigate, people to interview, but—" she grabbed the mug and took two gulps "—I need a break, Dad."

His eyes softened. "Your friend Dana called us to say she has her best hacker tracing the emails and Skye's wife is checking out car registrations."

Laurie lifted her mug. "See? Everything's being taken care of."

"Skye says you three are interviewing some woman named Matilda—" he frowned, trying to remember the last name "—something. Anyway, she said meet at Dana's at five."

"Perfect." Laurie drank the rest of the coffee, then handed her father the mug. "How come you know this and I don't?"

"Your mother called them this morning before she left for the clinic."

"She's still working?"

"They like to consult with her on difficult cases. And she needed the distraction."

Laurie's phone rang. She almost answered before she caught the name. English Department. The area code was from her school's part of town. She let it go to voice mail. No way was she talking to Tobias Brown today. "Thanks for the coffee. Oliver, you coming?"

"Leave him home with me."

"Okay. See you later."

"You sure it's a good idea to see the husband of the woman you supposedly murdered?"

Laurie blew out her breath. "I'm going. It's a big city. Nobody will see us together."

"No breakfast?"

Laurie gave her father a look. "Goodbye, Dad."

"All righty then." He raised his hand and gave her a little wave.

On the way, Rosa hung out the open car window, her tongue lolling. "Faster," she kept saying.

"I can't afford a speeding ticket on top of everything else, little one."

Laurie pulled into the parking garage. To heck with the cost. She was splurging today. They hadn't said where to meet, so she walked to the famous fish stall to watch the hawkers throw salmon and listen to the tourists ooh and ahh at their skill. Rosa watched, eager for them to drop one. After a few minutes, she felt like someone was behind her. She turned to see John observing her, his eyes lit with pleasure. "How long have you been standing there?"

"Long enough," he said.

She took his hand. "Long enough for what?"

He shook his head, a soft smile on his face.

"How are you?" she asked, not pressing.

Rosa ran to him and stretched her front legs up, resting them on his thigh. He reached down and cupped the dog's chin in his hands. "Are you taking care of our Laurie?"

"Of course," she said.

"Such a good girl," John said, not realizing Rosa had answered him.

"He didn't do it," Rosa told her once again.

"I know. Do you like him?" Laurie asked her dog.

Rosa sniffed, refusing to answer such a silly question. "He's sad. He needs a walk."

Laurie held out her hand. "Shall we?"

John took it and headed down the middle of the cobblestone street, dodging people. The place was too packed for easy conversation, even on a Thursday morning. John put his arm around her and pulled her close so they could move through the crowd more easily. Laurie snuggled into his warmth, matching his pace. He smelled of musk and cardamon with an undertone of something that reminded her of the sea. She almost closed her eyes, but had to watch her step on the uneven stones. Rosa trotted just in front, tail up like a flag leading them on.

John turned left toward the end of the street and opened a door that led into a stairwell. They descended two flights to another door and emerged onto a long walkway lined with restaurants. A sea breeze smelling of salt water, rotting seaweed, and cooking fish greeted them. Laurie blinked in surprise. The Market had spread like kudzu since her last visit. They strolled, enjoying the views of the Sound and Olympics Mountains rising blue and misty, capped in white. Seagulls sat on the railing, watching the tables being readied with their beady black eyes, waiting for lunch.

The birds reeled off when John and Laurie got too close to them. Rosa gave chase, her eyes bright, her red tongue lolling. Neither of them seemed inclined to break the silence. John steered them toward a bench and they sat, staring out at the water as it swelled close to shore and broke in small, smooth waves.

"How are the whales?" Laurie asked.

John laughed in surprise. "L-pod had two calves this year. A male and a female."

"Great. What's the population?"

"Last count in July, the Center for Whale Study counted seventy-five orcas."

"In which pod?"

"All of them."

Laurie caught her breath. "Seriously?"

"Yes, so a new female is great news, although she'll have to be a teenager before she can give birth. Still, it's progress." His eyes shone.

"But you seem happy."

"We bought a ranch on the Elwha River where the Chinook spawn," he said, as if this would explain everything.

"Who is 'we?'"

"The Center for Whale Study. I'm on the board."

"Good for you." She squeezed his arm.

"You heard they got rid of two dams about ten years ago? Good for the Chinook run."

"I haven't been keeping up." She looked down, a little regretful.

He shrugged. "But you asked about them."

"Do you still kayak out to see them?"

He laughed. "I have a boat now. I'll take you out—" his face fell "—but you'll be going back to Boston."

As if on cue, her phone rang. She looked at the display. Another call from her department. There was a dot next to the voice mail button. She refused the call and stuffed the phone back into her pocket. "Who knows. There were some emails that got routed through my college server."

"Emails?"

Laurie told him about the fake messages. "I can't imagine who would have planted them. I didn't even know I was coming to the reunion until about a month ago."

"That's sounds bad."

"It is. They're going to have to investigate, which means talking to my department chair who already has it out for me."

"Are you saying you could lose your job?" He smiled, then seemed to realize he shouldn't be happy about this news and adjusted his face. "Don't you have tenure? They can't fire you."

Laurie shrugged. "He can try. He already told me there's some complaint against me."

Her phone rang again. She pulled it out of her pocket and silenced it.

"That might be important."

"It's actually my college. Probably Dr. Brown." She imitated the self-important way he spoke. "I'm sure he just wants to lord it over me."

John reached down, put his finger under her chin, and pulled her face up to meet his. "You're going to get through this. You're innocent."

"To tell you the truth, I'm tired of teaching."

His gaze strayed to her mouth and for a moment, Laurie thought he was going to kiss her. Then he pulled back. "That reminds me." He reached into his jacket pocket and took out a mobile phone. "This was Kimberly's. I promised to let Dana snoop through it."

"Thank you. This is great. Maybe she can see if the emails originated from Kimberly's account." Laurie slipped the phone into her purse.

He handed her an envelope. "This is a list of her usernames and passwords. I found them in her computer cleverly disguised under the title 'Passwords.'"

Laurie smiled at this. She folded the envelope and stuffed it into her purse. Then her phone vibrated with an incoming call and this time she answered it. "This is Dr. Olson."

"Good," John whispered.

The shouting from the phone hurt her ear, so she held it out. Even John could hear it. "...and not only has one of your students complained that you sexually harassed him, now the Seattle Police Department is calling to investigate your emails."

"Sexually harassed?" John repeated in a quiet voice.

Laurie shook her head. She switched her phone to speaker.

"Apparently you threatened a former high school classmate's life? And now she's been murdered?"

Laurie took a breath to answer, but Tobias marched on. "I've spoken to the Provost and President. He's called an emergency meeting of the Board of Trustees. You are on unpaid leave starting immediately. I fully expect you to be terminated."

Laurie flashed on the word 'terminated' and thought of thriller movies. But they called it something else when they killed people. She sank back on the bench and closed her eyes. Rosa jumped up and growled at the phone. Laurie set it down next to her, wondering what the little dog would do.

"Do you have anything to say for yourself?" His angry voice sounded tinny coming up from the bench. The distance made him sound just like the petty dictator he was.

She picked the phone back up and straightened her spine. "My attorneys will be in touch." She ended the call, her palm itching to slam down the receiver like she could with old-fashioned phones.

"That was—" John's eyebrows climbed high "—something. Are you going to be all right? I mean financially?"

Laurie snorted, stopping the hot tears that were threatening. "I will. My grandfather passed away last year and left me a little nest egg. Actually, I've been thinking about environmental jobs. Here in Seattle."

"Good. So maybe you can go out on my boat after all." John smiled at his feeble joke.

He leaned in, his breath warm on her face. His musky scent filled her and he kissed her lightly, just enough to wake her body's memory. Her stomach gurgled and they both broke away laughing. "Time for lunch?" John asked.

Her eyes roamed over his face and she pushed a lock of hair off his forehead. "I skipped breakfast."

He pulled her to her feet, tucking her under his arm. "I know the perfect place." He took Rosa's leash in his hand. "Come on, girl."

"It's about time." Rosa's bark was exuberant.

John found a table on the patio at his favorite restaurant at the Market. Rosa laid on Laurie's feet, her weight reassuring. Laurie let

John order for them both, needing time to let her whirling thoughts settle.

"And something for the pup?" John pointed at Rosa.

"Certainly, sir." The server gave a crisp nod.

Laurie fought against their instant familiarity, telling herself she didn't really know him. It had been thirty years. Three decades. They'd both changed. Had a lifetime of experiences.

"They'll bring a meal for Rosa?" she asked, trying to anchor herself in the present moment. To find her sardonic professor self, but it was getting harder to find her.

"Yes, they know who's important, don't they girl?" He reached down and scratched behind Rosa's ear. Her tail thumped.

"Traitor," Laurie sent to her.

"Chicken," Rosa answered.

Laurie decided to relax. After all, there was a table between them. What could happen in public? They spent a leisurely two hours, first eating escargot and fried brie salads talking about his kids and his troubles settling the estate. He was sad about Kimberly's death and guilty at his relief at suddenly being free. Then they ate scallops and seared salmon in honor of the orca pods and drank a bottle of wine while she talked about her life in Boston, her career, her divorce. His eyes lit up at this word.

Rosa enjoyed her own fish.

Even though the spring breeze off the Sound was still slightly chilly, Laurie warmed under John's attention. For dessert, they indulged in crème brûlée and talked about his degrees in Environmental Engineering, founding his firm Living Earth Design. How he'd been able to pursue his passion. At least that one. He smiled mischievously at her when he said this.

Then they just sat, enjoying coffee, watching the sun sparkle off the water, a rare sight in Seattle. She dreamed of freedom, staying in her hometown with old friends. Perhaps an old flame. Watching the whales. Maybe writing articles and reports to advance her favorite causes. Perhaps he dreamed of the future just as she did, not daring to say too much about the hopes that seemed to be rekindling in their hearts. At least, that's what Laurie felt and Rosa assured her John was feeling the same.

CHAPTER

FIFTEEN

Later that afternoon, the three detectives piled into Skye's older Subaru. She turned on the car and then slapped her forehead. "I forgot. I need to stop for gas."

"Gas? That's so twentieth century," Dana joked. "Let's take my car. There's more room, plus it's electric. Not old fashioned like these hybrids." She winked at Skye.

"I beg your pardon," Skye said, but she smiled.

They all piled into Dana's new SUV. Rosa jumped into the back with Laurie and Kimberly harrumphed at the intrusion. The dog pawed at the window.

Dana eyed the ghost and the canine. "No offense, Ms. Rosa Miranda, but I don't want scratches on my new car."

"Rosa is part of the detective team. She knows what the murderer smells like," Laurie explained. "We could get back in Skye's car."

Dana relented and Rosa pressed her nose against the window. Laurie reached over to pull Rosa back and felt a patch of cold air. She wrapped her jacket closer. "Why is it so chilly back here? It's pretty warm out."

Dana decided not to announce Kimberly's presence. She was operating under the current theory that attention just encouraged the ghost. "I'll open the window. Besides, Rosa is smearing her nose all over the glass."

She pushed the button to open the back window a bit, then told the computer Matilda Hutchison's address. Off they went. "Time to catch up. Skye, you go first," Dana said.

"Bossy much?" Skye whispered.

"Hanging from that vine made her more assertive, don't you think?" Laurie joked.

Dana snorted.

Skye started off as directed. "Jade ran a search. 'C' is an old number for a license plate, which makes sense for an old Impala. We thought that would be good, but she found a surprising number of registrations that matched the data."

"How many?" Dana asked.

Skye hesitated. "Like, twenty pages."

"For real?" Dana asked.

"Yep," Skye said. "Maybe they'll follow us again and we'll get lucky."

"Right." Dana drew the word out.

Dana studied Laurie in the rearview mirror. For a murder suspect, she seemed remarkably calm. Dreamy even.

Laurie met her eyes in the mirror. "What?"

"You seem to be lost in your own little world. What's new?"

She hid her smile behind her hand. "I'm now on unpaid leave for sexual harassment and—"

"Wait, what?" Skye shouted.

"Sexual harassment? What kind of—" Dana sputtered, searching for a word.

"I can't imagine who filed that. Except maybe Joey. He sits in the front row and stares at my breasts all through class," Laurie said. "Plus takes up all my office hours."

"Sounds like he's sexually harassing you," Dana said.

Laurie shrugged. "I guess."

"You seem pretty chill about it." Skye turned around and studied her.

"Dr. Brown heard about the emails. He's convening a committee to get me fired."

They both studied her.

"And?" Dana asked. The car beeped a warning that she was drifting out of her lane. She steered back and risked another glance at Kimberly, who was being uncharacteristically quiet.

Laurie shrugged. "I realized I'm tired of teaching anyway. I got a bit of money when my grandfather died."

An uncomfortable silence followed.

"Something happened," Skye said to Dana.

"For sure," she answered.

"She had lunch with John today. He kissed her," Kimberly announced.

Dana gasped.

"What?" Skye looked around, bracing her hand on the dashboard.

"You saw John today," Dana said.

Laurie's head snapped up. "How did you know?"

"Let's just say a little bird told me."

"Kimberly! You mean she was watching us?" Laurie asked.

Dana shrugged. "I guess."

"Creepy much?" Laurie looked around the SUV. "Where is she?"

Dana shook her head. "Don't encourage her."

"Has she remembered anything more?" Skye asked.

Laurie looked around, addressing the air. "If you're going to hang around, at least you could be useful."

Dana tried not to laugh.

"As a matter of fact, I have. But I'm not telling since nobody appreciates me." With that, the ghost disappeared.

"Ugh," Dana said. Now she'd have to figure out a way to get this new information out of her unwelcomed guest.

"What did she say?" Skye asked.

"That she's remembered more, but won't tell me. She disappeared. Apparently, we insulted her."

"That's easy enough," Laurie said.

Dana squared her shoulders. "If we want her help, we have to try to be nicer."

"God help us," Laurie murmured.

The computer in Dana's SUV announced they had arrived. She parked on the street and as soon as Laurie opened the door, Rosa ran up the steps ahead of them. Matilda Hutchison answered before they could knock, her eyes ablaze with excitement. "Welcome, welcome. I'm so happy you've come to interrogate me."

"Well, I wouldn't put it that way, Matty," Skye said, shrugging off her coat once they were inside. Dana remembered Skye had been closer to Matilda than the rest of them and called her by that nickname in school.

"Dr. Lauren Olson. I've never had a murder suspect as a guest before."

"Uh—" Laurie looked like she was going to run for the door.

"See any old Impalas on the way over?"

They all stood stock still, staring at her.

Matilda burst out laughing. "You suspected Rudy of all people? He called me up as soon as you left."

"We thought he might—" Laurie started.

"We had to—" Dana stumbled over her.

"He knows people who own low riders, Matty," Skye said. "It was a long shot."

She guffawed. "Had you going there. We have so much to catch up on." She held out her arms, and Dana was afraid the buxom woman was about to pull them into a group hug. "It turned chilly on us today. Let me take your coats."

Rosa returned from wherever she'd been investigating and sat in front of Matilda, brown eyes eager. The blue streak in Matilda's hair had been replaced with a purple that almost matched her blouse. But not quite, Dana thought, feeling a little dizzy from the effect.

"Would you look at this face?" Matilda leaned down to pet Rosa, who sniffed her all over, then licked her face for good measure.

Matilda pulled a tissue out of a pocket. "A little enthusiastic."

"Rosa." Laurie patted her leg, calling the little Havanese mix to her.

Rosa came to her and sat, looking perfectly innocent. Laurie seemed to be having a silent conversation with the dog. Dana would ask later.

"Honestly, Laurie, nobody believes you killed Kimberly. I mean, why would you?" Matilda said.

Laurie looked up. "Thank you."

Their host leaned forward, a mischievous look on her face. "Word is she was going to divorce John. Try to take him for all he was worth."

Laurie's face flushed bright red.

"Hot flashes?" Matilda tutted sympathetically. "I've been taking some herbs. They help a lot. I'll give you the name."

"T-Thanks," Laurie stuttered.

"Fell in love with her personal trainer. Kimberly did love athletic men." She winked at Laurie.

Dana felt dizzy with the rapid shifts in topic. As if that wasn't bad enough, Kimberly suddenly appeared.

"But I'm being a bad hostess. Sit, relax."

Kimberly took her at her word and settled in a wingback chair by the window. "I've got coffee, tea—that fancy stuff with rose petals. I do love these Bridgetown blends. And wine. Red or white, Dana?" Matilda waggled her eyebrows.

Dana sat next to Skye, whose sides shook like a bag of cats as she contained her laughter. "White, please."

"Just water for me," Skye said.

"Nonsense, I have sodas, too. Aren't you an organic girl?"

"Uh, I am."

Matilda pointed at Laurie, who said. "I'll try the tea. Thank you."

Their hostess disappeared down a hall they assumed led to the kitchen. "How does she know so much?" Laurie whispered.

"She was always a busybody. Big gossip in school," Kimberly said. Dana whispered to her friends what the ghost had said.

"So she's back?" Skye looked around the living room. Laurie opened her mouth to say something, but must have remembered they were supposed to be nice and shut it again.

Matilda returned from the kitchen, still talking. "It was such a shock. I mean, did you see her sprawled there?"

"Did she just say that?" Kimberly asked Dana, who nodded her head.

"Just terrible," Skye agreed, giving Dana a look.

Matilda carried a big goblet of wine and a tall glass of something bubbly that she set before Skye. Dana tried not to be judgmental about being served white wine in a glass designed for red. She took a big sip. "Wow, really delicious. I'll have to get the name before we leave."

"Hypocrite." Kimberly said, looking at her nails. Dana wondered if a ghost could get her manicure fixed. Matilda rushed back into the kitchen and, in her absence, Dana shot Kimberly a dirty look.

Laurie looked at the empty wingback chair, then back at Dana. "Seems like she's still a busybody. Lucky for us."

Dana frowned. "Who?"

Laurie pointed back at the kitchen just as Matilda returned with a tea tray. She set it down on the coffee table and sat down, heaving a sigh. "We'll just let that steep a little."

"You didn't have to go to all this trouble, Matty. So nice of you," Skye said.

"Oh, cookies." She grabbed the arm of her chair to get up.

"No, no. You've done quite enough," Dana said. "Unless you want some."

Rosa gave a little disappointed whine, but Matilda sat back, a look of relief flashing across her face. She rearranged it into a scandalized expression and started to chatter again. "We all suspected John, of course. I mean Kimberly treated him terribly."

"What does she know about it?" Kimberly objected.

Matilda continued. "But several people confirmed he wasn't even up there on top of the Globe when it happened."

Laurie nodded. "The police say he was down in the bar."

"Right. So who do you think did it? What's your theory?" Matilda surveyed them.

The three friends exchanged a look. Dana nodded at Skye, who told the story of the mysterious hooded figure. Matilda poured tea for Laurie and herself as she listened. Her expression grew more delighted as the tale unfolded. "Do you have any idea who it was?"

"No, that's what we wanted to ask you. You saw everyone when they came in. Was anyone dressed like that?"

Matilda shook her head. "I didn't see anyone with a black hoodie on. I would have noticed. I mean people were dressed up for the event, but a hoodie? That would have stuck out."

"Did you notice anyone follow Kimberly when she went down the hall?" Laurie asked.

Matilda looked disappointed. "We were probably packing up by then. Or getting ready for the raffle."

"Well, thank you." Skye gathered her purse.

Matilda caught the gesture and started talking again. "It's so strange this happened when Walter was celebrating his movie contract. You know, he got Galactic to give us their ballroom for free. I'm sure he didn't like a scandal overshadowing his event."

Skye settled back on the sofa, eyeing the other two. Matilda bent down to pet Rosa and Dana gave a little shrug while she was distracted.

Matilda sat up like she'd just remembered something. "Ooh, I wonder if Walter will write about this murder. He seems to take his plots from the headlines."

"What do you mean?" Skye asked.

"Have you read his book? That best seller?"

Dana and Skye nodded. "Not me," Laurie said, then bit her lip. Dana stifled a laugh. Such a literary snob.

"Stole the plot from that suspicious death a couple of years ago," Matilda said.

Laurie shook her head. "I haven't been around. What suspicious death?"

Matilda looked over at Skye. "You remember, don't you? Our old English teacher from Jefferson?"

"Mr. Moss? What happened to him?" Laurie asked.

Skye filled her in. "They ruled it a suicide, but you remember him, right?"

"I did. He loved books. Inspired me to study literature," Laurie said.

"He would never have killed himself," Matilda said, setting down her teacup.

"Unless he had some awful terminal disease," Dana suggested.

"No, nothing like that. He was older, but healthy. I used to visit him from time to time. He loved my banana cake." She squared her shoulders, apparently proud of her baking.

"I seem to remember Mr. Moss telling Walter once in class that he was a terrible writer," Dana said.

"He could be tough at times, but I liked that about him," Laurie said.

Matilda lowered her voice. "I shouldn't say, but Mr. Moss was an author. He wrote romance."

"No way," Skye exclaimed.

"Romance?" Dana repeated. "Proper Mr. Moss?"

Laurie looked around, her face a big question mark. "Do men even write romance?"

Matilda squirmed in delight. "Under a pseudo—what's it called? Pen name."

They all stared at her. Skye finally said, "Spill it, Matty."

"Raven Wynter." She rocked back, laughing.

Skye's eyes flew open. "Get out of town."

"Wait, you know these books?" Dana asked.

Skye nodded. "Raven Wynter writes paranormal romance. We carry them in the store. The pagans love—him, I guess."

Laurie grabbed her phone and looked up the name. "Wow. Two series. Fifteen books in the first one. I'm stunned." She held up her phone so everyone could view the picture. They scooted to the edge of their seats to see better. A mysterious woman with long black hair, dark mascara, blood red lips, and a star tattoo on her cheek gave the camera an enigmatic look.

Dana squinted at the phone. "I wonder who that is."

"Probably some model his publisher hired," Laurie said.

"No wonder we could never get her—uh, Raven—to do a reading at the store."

"Yes, but you're supposed to be finding out who pushed me," Kimberly complained to Dana.

She looked over at the pouty ghost, not quite ready to steer the conversation back to this question.

"I don't remember the plot of Walter's book. How did it match the demise of Mr. Moss?" Skye asked.

Matilda poured herself more tea and offered to fill Laurie's cup. She put her palm over her cup, but smiled. "The murder victim was an English teacher at a private school. Mean. Punished her students. Not like Mr. Moss at all. The body was found in the back of a used bookstore on Capitol Hill in a compromising position. Mr. Moss was found in a grove of trees about two blocks behind that same bookstore. Nothing sexually suggestive at all."

"Did they do a sexual assault forensic exam on the corpse?" Skye asked.

Dana made a face at her.

Matilda sat up, startled. "How should I know? But I heard there was poison involved."

"What kind of poison?" Skye asked.

Matilda's teacup clattered when she put it back in the saucer. "My stars, you ask such questions."

Dana felt compelled to explain. "Her wife's a police detective."

"I see. Maybe your wife can get the report. I have no earthly idea. Anyway, we'll see what Walter's next book is like."

Kimberly huffed. "He better not write about me."

Dana tried to steer the conversation back to the reason for their visit. "So you didn't see anyone wearing a black hoodie or following Kimberly?"

"No, like I told you. Whoever it was must have come out after we closed up the table. But you know, Walter," she said, not willing to let the subject go, "he's so successful now. And confident. Remember him in high school? He was such a geek. Too skinny for football. He tried out for basketball. He was tall enough, but tripped over his own feet." She sat back, a smug look on her face.

Dana was beginning to dislike this woman, but kept the sentiment from showing. She had lots of practice at that dealing with distasteful corporate types.

"Kimberly made fun of him. If you ask me, the cheerleaders and football players pulled that prank on him," Matilda continued.

Laurie frowned. "Prank?"

"Ooh, you don't remember?" Matilda dove into the tale with relish. "It was in the papers and everything. He disappeared from a school dance and was found the next morning stripped naked tied up on Matthews Beach."

Dana glanced at the wingback chair to catch Kimberly's reaction, but the ghost had disappeared.

"You mean it was the cheerleaders who pulled the prank on Walter?" Laurie asked.

"You sure it was them?" Dana shook her head. "I heard it was some jocks."

"What happened exactly?" Laurie asked.

Dana shrugged. "I'm not sure, but his father hushed it up. Pulled him out of school right after it happened. It was a month before graduation, too. I heard his father threatened to sue, so Walter got his diploma."

"Geez, must have some clout," Skye said.

"Well, that's something to think about." Laurie stood and called Rosa to her. "We've got to get going, but you've helped us a great deal. I can't tell you how much I appreciate it."

"Oh, don't go," Matilda lumbered to her feet. "I haven't heard anything about what you three have been up to."

"We'll pay you another visit," Dana lied. But then again, the woman might be helpful. Her life seemed to revolve around keeping track of everyone she went to high school with. She glanced around and saw family photos on the credenza. Wedding and baby pictures. More on the mantel of older children holding up ribbons and what looked like certificates. Matilda seemed like a proud mom with a happy family. She'd never have pegged her for digging up dirt on Jefferson High alums. Could she have done it, Dana wondered.

Matilda followed them to the door. "I could help with the investigation. Just let me know."

"We sure will," Laurie said. "Thank you for sharing so much information."

Matilda pulled her into a hug. "You poor dear. Of course I'll help."

Dana's heart softened. The woman sure loved to gossip, but her concern for Laurie seemed genuine. They settled in the car and Dana sat, pondering the visit. "She knows too much," she said at last.

Skye looked over at her. "She's always been like that."

Dana gave a decisive nod. "I think we should put her high up on the suspect list,"

Laurie sat forward. "Rosa says she doesn't smell like the murderer. She told me Matilda is innocent."

"Are you sure, Rosa?" Dana asked.

The dog snorted and curled up in a ball, her back to Dana.

Laurie laughed. "You've insulted her."

"Well, you insulted my ghost." Dana pulled away, privately unwilling to believe Matilda wasn't somehow involved in the crime.

CHAPTER

SIXTEEN

Laurie stepped into the antique elevator at the Smith Tower and took a big swig of her Starbucks coffee, hoping it would wake her up enough to face her department chair and the Provost. Eight o'clock was too early for a meeting. At least too early for her. Full professors usually left eight o'clock classes to the new hires. Of course, it was late morning back in Boston. Her interrogators would be comfortably awake. This thought made her even grumpier. She looked down at Rosa, who watched everything with eager brown eyes, her red tongue visible as she panted softly.

Dana had called late last night to tell her that she and Skye were off to talk to Gloria Ingram, the former cheerleader and high school actress, who had somehow become a well-regarded therapist. Gloria was booked solid for the whole week, then she was going out of town. Her only opening had been at eight this morning. This left Laurie on her own.

"Except for me," Rosa reminded her.

Shanks was waiting for her in his reception area. "Come in. We'll set up here." Instead of the conference room they'd met in before, he ushered her into a room filled with law books. A computer sat on the long table with two chairs in front of it. Shanks' assistant sat at the far end with a notebook. She gave Laurie a wave.

Rosa wandered down to the assistant to get petted. And give her a good sniff. Laurie rolled her eyes.

"Just being thorough," the dog said.

Laurie settled in one of the chairs. "Is this background of books meant to intimidate them?"

Shanks gave a little nod. "Of course. Now, this shouldn't take long. The most important thing is that you stay silent."

Laurie started to object, but he held up an imperious finger. "Not one word. I'll do the talking."

"Okay, but this whole claim that I sexually harassed a student is beyond ridiculous."

"Yes, it is, but it is the least of your worries."

"What do you mean?"

Shanks chuckled. "Well, you're on trial for murder and the trial is coming up in just three weeks."

"Have you traced these emails yet?"

Before he could answer, the computer signaled a call coming through. Shanks turned his eyes forward and straightened up. She had to admit he looked impressive. Laurie tried to look just as professional, but she wasn't sure she pulled it off as well as her attorney did.

Shanks connected the video call and the smug face of Dr. Tobias Brown swam into focus. Laurie gripped the arms of her chair, fighting to keep her face neutral. "Laurie, I'm glad to see you could make this meeting," suggesting she'd failed to come to others. Fictitious ones, in her opinion.

"Dr. Brown I presume?" Shanks said. "I am Dr. Olson's attorney, Jonathan Shanks. I see there are other people with you. Would you be so kind as to introduce them?"

Tim looked like he'd swallowed something sour. He hesitated, looking unsure how he'd lost control of the meeting so quickly. Tim's boss stepped in. "I'm Provost Barlow. This is our legal counsel, Benjamin Hartel."

"Mr. Hartel, my client denies making any sexual advances to any student. This is a baseless, spurious claim. Placing her on unpaid leave violates your university policies as well as employment law in your state. We will be seeking compensatory damages."

"We have video, Mr. Shanks," Provost Barlow said.

"How was this video obtained? We'll need to see the evidence."

"Certainly. We'll forward it to you along with all supporting documents," Hartel said.

"Thank you. We'll be sending our counter suit naming Dr. Brown for making threats against my client. Being accused of a crime does not constitute guilt. He cited the police investigation into the fraudulent emails that threatened Mrs. Woolridge's life as a reason to have her terminated. We hope he meant her job."

"That is patently ridiculous—" Tim shouted before the university's attorney put a restraining hand on his shoulder.

"My client is no murderer," Mr. Hartel said.

"Furthermore, if the police discover that someone at your university was involved in fabricating these emails—" Shanks turned his palms up and sat back "—who can say how many more felony charges will be filed."

"The university is fully cooperating with the Seattle Police investigation."

"I'm glad to hear it. We expect Dr. Olson's salary to be reinstated forthwith." Shanks stared at Tim, who shrank back in his chair.

The Provost glanced quickly at Tim, then back at the screen. "I'll see to it personally."

"Excellent. Mr. Hartel will send the student complaint and all supporting documentation to my office by—" Shank's voice lifted in a question.

"You will have it by close of business today." Hartel seemed unruffled, which bothered Laurie. What did they have on her? She couldn't remember making comments that could be interpreted as sexual. And video?

"Then I believe this meeting is over?" Shanks asked.

The university attorney nodded. "It is."

Shanks pushed the leave meeting button before anyone else could. He smiled at her. "Happy?"

Relief rushed through Laurie. "Yes. Thank you." Rosa stood up and licked her hand. She scratched the dog under her chin.

"My staff is pouring over the security footage from the Galactic Globes," Shanks said. "The police are doing the same. We should find some clues there."

"Good." Laurie nodded. Dana had enlisted a talented hacker named Mania to get the security tapes from Galactic after Shanks had refused to share them. "It's too big a risk," he'd said. "Could blow up our case." Mania probably had the footage already. Dana had dropped the name with a chuckle. Laurie didn't mention any of this to Shanks. Instead she asked, "Do you really think we should sue Dr. Brown?"

"Why not? He looks like a pompous little prick."

Laurie chuckled. "You got that right."

"Not just him, but also the provost and president. Maybe even the student who made up this sham complaint."

"Sounds like a lot of trouble."

"It will never go to court. They'll settle and you'll make a few million."

Laurie's eyes widened. "Seriously?"

"If we can get you cleared of murder."

"There is that." Laurie slumped back in her chair.

Rosa whined.

Shanks patted the little Havanese on her head. "Don't worry, Rosa. We're working hard to keep your mistress out of jail."

"So are we," Rosa said.

Shanks gave Laurie an encouraging smile. "Keep your chin up."

· · ·

AT SIX-THIRTY THAT SAME MORNING, Dana stepped out of the shower and wiped the condensation off the mirror. Kimberly stood behind her. "Really? You visit me in the bathroom?" This ghost had no sense of propriety.

"I want to tell you what I remembered. I might forget again. I'm having trouble keeping track of things." Kimberly looked frantic.

"Can I at least get out of the bathroom?" Dana felt ridiculous wrapping herself in a towel, but it helped her regain some sense of control. She couldn't stop Kimberly from popping in any time she got it into her head. If she still had a head. Her ghost form had thinned out a bit lately. Dana walked out of the bathroom and sat on the edge of the bed. "All right. What have you recalled?"

Kimberly stood in front of Dana and looked her up and down. "You've kept in good shape."

"Honestly, Kimberly, you're a bit too obsessed with body image for someone who doesn't have one anymore." Dana pulled the towel tighter.

"You don't have to be mean," Kimberly pouted.

Dana tried to soften her tone. "Let's stay focused. What have you remembered?"

"I remembered why I was in that supply closet. I was meeting somebody. I was supposed to give them—" Kimberly frowned "—something important. Something to keep them from talking."

"Talking about what?"

The ghost gave her a haughty look. "That's not important. I got upset because the person who came wasn't who I was expecting."

"Who were you expecting?"

Kimberly shook her head. "I can't remember exactly."

Dana wasn't sure she believed her. "Laurie didn't push you over that railing. You know that. We need as much information as we can get to clear her."

"I know, I know," the ghost whined.

"What else can you remember, then?" Dana tried not to let her impatience creep into her voice.

"That's all. That it wasn't the right person."

"What were you supposed to give them?"

Kimberly's eyes widened in alarm and she disappeared.

Dana threw a slipper at the space where the ghost had been standing. "Argh. Insufferable woman." At least her memory was returning in little bits at a time. She hoped more would trickle into her flighty head. Dana dressed for work since she'd go to her office after the interview with Gloria.

She let the kids sleep. Some new research claimed teenagers needed a ridiculous amount of sleep. Almost as much as Lele. The fluff ball looked up from her where she was curled up on Kevin's empty pillow, blinked, and went back to sleep. She wondered if the cat had heard her thoughts. And what she might say back. Kevin was either in Olympia or campaigning for his U.S. House run, so she'd gotten used to being on her own with the kids and her cat. In fact, she was beginning to prefer it.

Kimberly didn't appear again on her drive to Queen Anne. Skye leaned against her green Subaru, waiting. Dana told her about the new information from Kimberly.

"So there might be two people involved," Skye said.

"Maybe," Dana said. "We'll watch the security tapes carefully when we get them."

The two walked across the street to a well maintained Victorian house, the exterior painted in salmon and blue with butterscotch trim. "Ooh, I hope her office is in the turret," Kimberly gushed.

"Oh, for fu—" Dana stopped herself from cursing.

"What?" Skye looked down at the porch steps, maybe thinking Dana had stumbled on a crack.

"She's back."

"Who?" Skye's confused look turned to realization. "Kimberly? Well, Gloria won't know."

Dana opened the front door, a heavy oak affair with mullioned windows. Dana's low heels clacked on the polished oak floor. Skye checked a sign that indicated Gloria's office was indeed in the turret to the right. Dana put her hand on Skye's arm before she could leave the entryway. She kept her voice low. "What I was going to say is that Gloria might not be able to tell us anything about her clients. Anonymity lasts after death."

"That's a relief," Kimberly said.

Dana glanced over her shoulder at the ghost. "What are you trying to hide?"

"She's nervous?" Skye asked.

"Seems that way."

"Good. Maybe we'll learn something useful."

"If Gloria can talk."

They walked down a short hall and knocked on the door with a neat metal plaque that just read 'Office.' Gloria Ingram opened the door immediately. She looked more professional than she had the night of the reunion, tucked into her navy suit and pearl earrings, her fading blond hair pulled back in a neat bun. "Dana, Skye, please come in."

A low couch took up the wall next to the door replete with pillows in mauve, gray, and silver. Dana didn't have time to peruse the scattered titles on the bookcase, but a figurine of a woman looking down into a round bowl that seemed to be an extension of her body caught her eye. A sense of peace washed over her. Gloria indicated the couch with a wave of her hand and settled in the rocking chair across from it. The chair and little statuette lent a maternal air to the room, somewhat muting the effect of Gloria's office attire.

"How can I help you ladies?" Gloria asked in a rich contralto voice.

Perfect voice for a therapist, Dana thought. Kimberly huffed at not having a seat, so she went to the far corner where a desk sat just beside a private alcove. The ghost flounced into the office chair, looking anything but professional.

"Thank you for seeing us so early," Skye said, covering Dana's distraction, "and congratulations on your successful practice."

Gloria received this with a gracious nod.

Dana gave herself a shake. "I mentioned when I called that we wanted to discuss the events at the Jefferson High reunion. As you probably know, our friend Laurie Olson has been arrested for Kimberly's murder."

"So they've decided it was a homicide," Gloria said, her voice somehow soothing even when discussing such matters.

"Yes," Dana confirmed. "I was pushed over the ledge as well, but it seems I was collateral damage. Thankfully, I grabbed a vine and was rescued. We wondered if you were in the group on top of the Globe. Or maybe you were with another group on a lower tier? If you saw anything? Noticed someone in a black hoodie running away?"

Dana tried to stop the flood of words. She prided herself on being succinct, but something about Gloria's silent, careful attention was making her talk too much. Must be some therapy trick. She forced herself to wait for a response. The silence grew weighty, and Dana opened her mouth to break it just as Gloria said, "I did hear about the arrest. Unfortunately, I was not anywhere near the event. I'm grateful you survived."

Skye stepped in. Thank heaven for her tag team partner, Dana thought. Skye told Gloria about the encounter with Kimberly in the janitor's closet before her death. "There's been some speculation that this attack might have something to do with a prank pulled by the cheerleading squad and some football players in high school. That someone might be seeking revenge."

Gloria's face remained neutral. Interested, somehow encouraging more words. When Skye didn't elaborate, Gloria said simply, "There were several pranks."

"We thought you might know more about this since you were a cheerleader. You remember Walter disappearing at the school dance and turning up tied up naked on Matthew's Beach the next morning? We've discovered Kimberly planned the whole thing and got her clique to carry it out." Skye leaned forward.

Gloria shifted her weight and started the chair rocking. She knitted her hands together in front of her.

If Dana were a therapist, she'd certainly take note of this reaction.

Then Gloria decided to speak. "Why would you think this awful —" she struggled to find a word, then settled for what Skye had used "—prank has something to do with Kimberly's death?"

Damn therapists, Dana thought. She took over. "I'm an attorney. Of course, I'm not representing Laurie since I'm her friend and I do corporate law, but her defense counsel has asked for help with the case. It's being fast tracked for reasons I can't disclose. One line of evidence leads to that group of friends being involved in some scheme to extort money from Kimberly."

"She had money?" Gloria asked, then sat back, perhaps realizing she'd breached confidentiality."

Dana just raised a shoulder in answer.

Gloria took up her gentle rocking again, her gaze fixed inward. Skye took a breath to say something, but Dana held up her hand to stop her. After two minutes of silence, Gloria looked up and fished into her purse that sat next to her chair. She pulled out a one dollar bill and held it out to Dana.

With a smile, Dana reached out and took the money.

"What's that for?" Skye asked, but the two ignored her.

Dana spoke to Gloria instead. "Anything you say to me will be held in the strictest confidence of attorney/client privilege."

"Oh," Skye whispered.

"I must ask, however, that you allow me to share what you tell me with Jonathan Shanks, who heads Laurie's legal team."

Kimberly was suddenly in front of Gloria. "I knew I could never trust you. You were always the weak link."

Dana tried not to react to Kimberly's sudden outburst, but Skye must have noticed a change in the room. She tried to catch Dana's eye, but Dana kept her eyes trained on Gloria—through Kimberly's semi-transparent form.

"I can't testify," Gloria said. "It might ruin my reputation. People need to trust me as a therapist."

This woman must have some damning information, Dana thought. "I'll do my best," she said, "but it is a murder charge."

Gloria pushed herself out of her rocker and walked over to her desk, oblivious to the ghost following close on her heels. She picked up a wicker basket and went back to the couch where Dana and Skye sat. "Please take out your cell phones, turn them off, and put them in the basket."

Skye straightened up in surprise. "You've got to be kidding." But Dana pulled her cell phone out of her coat pocket and switched it off. Skye watched as she placed it in the basket, but still hesitated.

"Just do it," Dana said. "If she divulges anything about a client, it's her license." With a nod, Skye switched off her phone and laid it beside Dana's.

"I don't have any recording devices on me," Dana said. "Everything you say will be held in the strictest confidence. Only shared with Laurie and Jonathan Shanks." She elbowed Skye.

"For heaven's sake," Skye mumbled, then said in a clear voice, "I'm not recording anything either. Same as she said about Shanks."

Gloria put the basket with their phones back on her desk, then settled back in the chair. She rocked back and forth as if to soothe herself for a while before she braced her feet to stop the motion and looked up at them. "I don't know why Kimberly had it out for Walter, but she picked on him all through high school. It escalated in our senior year to what I'd call torment. Leaving foul things in his locker. I don't know how she got the combination. Spreading lies about him masturbating in the library and ejaculating into a book. Accusing him of sneaking into the girls' bathroom and cornering her in a stall. Feeling her up until she fought him off. Then turning around and saying he was gay and was having sex with Mr. Moss."

Skye's head snapped up when she heard this name.

Gloria looked confused. "Mr. Moss was married, of course. He was kindhearted. I don't think he ever cheated on his wife."

"His death was tragic," Dana commented, observing the therapist closely. But she simply nodded. Either she had no suspicion about his death, like most people, or her profession had made her adept at hiding her reactions.

But Gloria's eyes looked weak and watery. She started the chair gently rocking again. "Kimberly just wouldn't let it go. I finally asked her why she was so focused on Walter, what he'd ever done to her, but she never answered. Now with my training, when I think back, it seems likely she'd been hurt by someone else. Probably molested."

"Liar. You had such a dirty mind," Kimberly screamed.

Oblivious to the ghost's reaction, Gloria continued. "Maybe a family member. Some older man who Walter had the misfortune of resembling."

Kimberly stuck her face in Dana's. "She's making this all up."

Dana blinked and sat back. Fortunately, Gloria was too emersed in her own memories to notice. But Skye certainly had. She shot Dana a questioning look. Dana just shook her head.

"Maybe Kimberly was attracted to Walter at some point and he rejected her. I don't know. He wasn't her type. She planned that last prank—attack really—for weeks." Gloria steeled herself. "Kimberly lured him outside and two linemen from the football team bundled him into the trunk of the car she'd borrowed from her father for the night. They took him out on a sailboat." She squinted her eyes trying to remember. "I think it belonged to Peggy Anderson's family."

Dana could feel the tumblers clicking into place. Peggy had been hiding something.

"Kimberly got some of the cheerleaders to strip him down. She talked two boys into assaulting him with promises of—well, you know. Then Kimberly joined in." She shook her head, unable to finish. The tears that had been swimming in her eyes spilled down her cheeks. "That was the end for me. If you could have seen the look on her face. Flushed red and scrunched up in rage. I'd never experienced anything like it before. I wanted to jump into Lake Washington and swim for it, but we were so far out and I still had on my prom dress. It would have soaked up enough water to drown me." She looked up at them and gave a husky laugh. "I suppose it prepared me for the horror stories I sometimes hear in this very room from clients."

"I'm so sorry," Skye said.

"Liar!" Kimberly shouted over Skye. The ghost closed on Dana. "She's making it all up. You can't believe her."

"It sounds awful." Skye frowned at Dana, maybe wondering why she wasn't saying anything. It was all Dana could do to cope with the ghost screaming at her. She shook her head, trying to get Kimberly out of her face.

Gloria continued, "Afterwards, they left him tied up and naked on Matthews Beach. Rumor was this where lots of gay men hung out. I guess she thought this would humiliate him even more or explain his bleeding..." She squeezed her eyes closed, unable to continue. "That the police would think he'd been attacked by a man at the beach."

"Kimberly was homophobic in high school. Was always saying snide things to me," Skye said.

Kimberly screamed so loud a light bulb in the ceiling fixture shattered.

They all jumped and stared at each other.

"Goodness," Gloria said, the shock pulling her out of the fugue of memory. "I'll have to clean that up before my nine o'clock."

Dana closed her eyes, trying to recover from the ghost's onslaught. She heard Skye move and opened her eyes to find the other two women standing. Dana glanced around. The ghost was gone. She pushed herself to her feet and forced herself to speak calmly. "I can't tell you how helpful you've been, Gloria. And I'm sorry that you had to witness that awful—" she screwed up her face "—rape I guess is the only word."

"I agree," Gloria said. "The worst thing is Kimberly threatened us all. Said she'd blame it on anyone who breathed a word of it."

"Have you ever talked about this before?" Skye's tone was compassionate.

"Oh, yes. I spoke to my own therapist about it years ago. He was excellent. He was the one who inspired me to go into this field. But of course that was all confidential—" she gave each of them a pointed look "—as this meeting must be."

"Of course. I will talk to Jonathan Shanks about it, but this is hearsay. It wouldn't stand up in a court of law. We'll have to investigate, find direct evidence."

Gloria gave a satisfied nod. She returned to her desk, retrieved their phones and handed them back. "Now, if you'll excuse me." She looked over her shoulder at the glass that lay in shards beneath the ceiling light.

"We'll see ourselves out," Skye said. Dana let Skye take her by the arm and ushered her into the hall, closing the door quietly behind her. Dana took a breath to tell Skye what had happened, but her friend just shook her head and whispered, "Wait until we're in the car."

Dana let Skye lead her outside to the SUV and even fasten her seatbelt before she went tucked herself into the passenger seat. "Can you drive? There's a little park just a couple of blocks up. We can stop there."

Dana took a couple of deep breaths and started the engine. She drove up the street, following Skye's directions and watching the parked cars on the side of the street, careful not to get too close. She didn't quite feel herself yet.

"Pull in here." Skye pointed to a right turn.

Dana parked in front of an expanse of emerald green dotted with trees. Someone was throwing a frisbee to a golden retriever. She watched the dog retrieve it and deposit it at the human's feet, eagerly waiting for the next throw. "Well, that was interesting," she finally said.

Skye's hearty laugh helped bring her fully back. Dana explained how Kimberly had reacted to Gloria's story. "I never imagined she was so vicious. Poor John. I wonder how she treated him."

"I wonder if he was the father," Skye said.

Dana's jaw dropped. "You think she made good on her promise to those two guys?"

"Too bad we didn't get their names," Skye said. "I guess this late in the game it wouldn't be worth it to get a DNA test from the oldest kid."

Dana shook her head. "No, that would open up a can of worms. Laurie would be furious."

"God, can you imagine?"

"What does this tell us?" Dana asked.

"Maybe somebody was threatening to expose what happened that night," Skye suggested. "Maybe they were blackmailing her."

"Kimberly remembered she was supposed to give something to the person who met her in the janitor's closet. Only the person who showed up wasn't who she was expecting."

"It feels like we're finally getting somewhere," Skye said. "We have to find a way to identify the man in the black hoodie."

"I have some good news," Dana said. "Mania broke into Galactic's files. He's sending the security tapes over in the morning. You and Laurie are invited. Maybe we'll be able to discover who it was. My office. Eight o'clock."

CHAPTER

SEVENTEEN

L aurie arrived too early at Dana's law office in the Columbia
Center downtown. Another eight o'clock meeting. Did attorneys like to torture their clients? Did they think it made
them look industrious? But her friends were helping her and she was
beyond grateful. If they didn't, she'd have plenty of time to sleep in
prison. Or did they get the inmates up early, too? She nodded at Skye,
who was waiting by the revolving glass doors, looking annoyingly
fresh. Laurie hadn't slept well, not after Skye and Dana had shared
what they'd learned from Gloria yesterday.

What bothered her the most was John's part in it all. How
involved had he been? And even if he'd just watched it all, how could
he have then married Kimberly, no matter if she was pregnant with
his child? If it was his child. She'd promised favors to two of the team
for assaulting Walter, and Laurie thought the cheerleader had slept
around. How could the authorities have labeled it a high school
prank? The only explanation was that Walter hadn't revealed the
extent of what had happened to him. He'd probably been drenched
in shame.

Dana had left badges for them at the front reception at in the lobby. The young woman handed them over, but frowned at Rosa. "I'm sorry. Is she a service dog?"

Momentarily startled, Laurie hesitated, but Rosa stepped on her foot. "Oh, yes. An emotional support dog." She winced internally, but kept a smile on her face. Wait, did people who used emotional support dogs smile like this? She wiped the smile away.

The receptionist looked doubtful. "Service dogs are supposed to have vests to identify them."

Think fast, she told herself. An idea popped into her head. "I know, but she rolled in something on the way over—" Rosa sneezed to add to the story "—and we had to take it off her."

The young woman actually leaned over the desk. Laurie had a moment of panic thinking she was going to sniff Rosa, but the little Havanese wagged her tail and gave the woman an adoring look.

"You are such a ham," Laurie sent to her.

"Ooh, she is so cute. I guess it's all right this time. Take the elevator to the twentieth floor. Ms. Preston is in 2023."

"Thank you so much. I've been under such stress since—"

Skye grabbed Laurie's arm and pulled her away. "Don't overdo it. We got in," she said in an undertone. They rode up in silence, surrounded by people in suits who didn't make eye contact or even acknowledge Rosa as she sniffed everyone's ankles.

"What are you doing? Nobody here is a murder suspect," Laurie mentally told the little Havanese.

"You never know," Rosa answered.

They arrived with no one voicing an objection to the nosey little mutt, although Laurie got a couple of looks. Just as Laurie raised her hand to knock at Dana's office door, it opened immediately.

"Come in, come in." Dana ushered them into a conference room. "Meet Gary. We're just loading the security tapes." Three junior assistants sat around the table with him, but Dana didn't introduce anyone else. Something Laurie was grateful for since she had such trouble remembering names.

Gary turned to greet them, his steel-blue eyes serious, the effect softened by a well-trimmed beard and somewhat messy curls reaching to his shirt collar. He rolled up his sleeves. "Greetings, ladies. I'll project the video recordings on the screen on the wall in front of us. This is uncut footage, so it may get a bit tedious, but we can fast forward it. Back it up when we spot something we want to take a closer look at."

"Coffee first," Dana said. She pointed to a small kitchen alcove tucked away in the back. Skye made a beeline for the coffee and frowned at the pods. "You do know these are bad for the environment."

Dana spread her hands. "I'm not in charge of that. But—" She pulled out a bag of dog biscuits and handed Rosa two. The dog scarfed them and waited for more, her butt wiggling.

"I like her," Rosa told Laurie. The little Havanese mix wandered over and gave Gary a sniff. "He didn't do it."

Laurie dunked her tea bag up and down in the almost hot water, shaking her head at the dog's antics. She walked back to the table, only now noticing the expansive view of the Seattle Wheel. She stared out. Puget Sound sparkled in the morning light, the still white tips of the Olympics rosy in the early sun.

"Sorry, but we have to draw the blinds to see the video." Gary pushed a button on a remote and shades crept down from the ceiling. The room darkened and Gary switched on his computer. Twelve squares popped up on the screen. "These squares are from different security cams. I'm going to run all these angles at once and I'm going to speed them up. That's the best way to identify someone dressed like the perp."

Skye glanced at Laurie and mouthed 'perp'. Laurie bit her lip to stop herself from snickering. Rosa and Skye were cheering her up.

"As everyone knows, we're looking for a person dressed in a black hoodie. Once we find someone matching this description, we'll slow down and watch him on the full screen. Ms. Yarrow is assigned the first vertical row, Ms. Preston will take the middle four, and Dr. Olson the last."

Laurie gave Gary points for calling her by her academic title.

"We've also got three more people as backup, so don't worry about missing something. We can watch it as many times as we need."

The others at the table gave little waves. Laurie ducked back to the snack area to add cream to her tea, then hurried to her seat.

"The best way to view a fast video feed is to blur your eyes. Kind of like scanning a printed page. Ready?"

Laurie nodded, along with the others. Rosa gave a little woof, which caused a few giggles. Gary started the video. Laurie instructed her brain to scan for a black hoodie. She sat back and made herself relax, watching without focusing too closely. Her camera angles covered the elevator and welcome table. She watched people pour out of the elevator and mill around the table, picking up their name tags, greeting old friends. Sometimes only a few people arrived. Other times a whole crowd. After about ten minutes, she noticed a dark figure toward the back of a packed elevator sneak off down the hall rather than come to the welcome table. "Got something," she shouted.

Gary stopped the video and rewound it slowly. Everyone focused on the feed Laurie pointed out. Once they saw the figure dart away, Gary paused the recording. "Anyone see this person from the lobby cameras?" he asked.

"Nothing," said one of the assistants.

Gary ran the feed backward quickly. Laurie closed her eyes against the jumble. "Okay, we've gone back half an hour. I'll run it at twice the normal speed. Watch for big bags or backpacks as well as a black hoodie."

They all leaned in, watching intently, but nobody who came into the building matched their description. Gary returned to the footage near the reunion and checked all the camera angles available to them. Nothing.

"Did somebody disable the security cameras on the other

hallway where this alleged confrontation took place?" one of the staff asked.

Laurie bristled at the word 'alleged,' but Dana patted her arm and whispered, "It's just lawyer talk."

"There's a report in the Galactic files that those cameras were malfunctioning a few days before the reunion. For some reason, they weren't fixed before the event took place."

"Who reported the camera problem?"

"A Mr. Fuentes. Been with the company for four years. Good record."

Dana turned to Gary. "Could they have been disabled remotely?"

Gary thought for a minute. "Maybe, but they've got a gnarly firewall."

"Think we're dealing with someone in-house?" she asked.

"Could be, but there are some good hackers out there who might be able to get past their security. I mean, we have this footage."

"Let's go back to the full spread of camera angles and see if we pick up anything else," Dana said.

They settled back and watched. After ten minutes, Laurie felt herself drifting. She sat up and focused on the feed. Just then she saw a figure creep down the hallway on the opposite side of the building from the supply closet wearing jeans, a jacket and a baseball cap pulled low over his face. "Got something," she shouted again.

Gary stopped the videos and checked what Laurie pointed out. "See? And he's carrying a duffle bag."

"Could be an employee," somebody muttered.

"Maybe," Gary said. He blew up the image and they watched the person creep out of an unmarked door. Once he got closer to the event tables, he straightened and strolled along.

One woman sat forward. "Wait. That's not a man."

Everyone leaned in. The person's jacket opened a bit and Laurie noticed the hint of breasts filling out the t-shirt. She sat back in her chair with a thud. "Oh, my God."

"Well, now," Dana said. "This changes things."

"Let's follow her," Gary said. He tracked the figure through the cameras as she got on the elevator and rode down to the lobby, where she walked out of the building. She never lifted her head, so the baseball cap kept her face in shadow, but she had dark brown hair, was around five and a half feet tall with a compact build. They watched her walk down the street and out of camera range.

"She left," Skye exclaimed. "So, is she the one who pushed Kimberly?"

"She might be headed for another entrance to the Globe," Gary suggested.

"But she's walking in the opposite direction," one of the assistants said.

"I'm switching over to the top of the Globe." Gary's eyes darted back to Dana. "You ready for that?"

"Of course," Dana said, but Laurie watched as she crossed her arms in front of her stomach and grabbed onto her forearms.

Gary started the feeds. This time they were looking at the whole top floor of the Globe. Laurie's feed seemed to be the back hallways. She watched diligently, but saw nothing. She heard Skye gasp and risked a glance. The woman, back in her black hoodie, rushed out of the elevator. She slid around the crowd, graceful as a leopard, and rushed toward her intended victim. The woman made contact with her shoulder, her whole weight behind the hit, but when Kimberly only landed on the railing, she grabbed her flailing legs and pushed her over. The momentum pushed Kimberly into Dana who fell over, too.

Laurie tried not to look at Dana, but kept her eyes locked on tracking the dark figure. She ducked into the crowd and Laurie lost her. She searched the video, hoping she'd reemerge. An exit door opened and closed, but the crowd obscured everything except the top of the door. She couldn't see who had gone through it.

Skye's phone chimed and she checked her texts. "Dana." But their friend didn't hear Skye at first. She was riveted to her rescue.

Gary turned toward Skye, frowning. "Can you pause the feed?" she asked. "I've got some new information."

This caught Dana's attention.

"Jade's found something," Skye said. "You can see your rescue later."

"In my office." Dana pointed to a door at the end of the conference room and turned to her assistants. "Can you three watch this video? Scour it until you're sure you've seen every place where our murderer appears. I don't care how long it takes."

"Yes, ma'am," they said almost in unison.

Dana settled behind her desk and Laurie took one of the chairs in front of it. Skye seemed too excited to sit. "Jade found the car."

"What?" Dana sat forward.

"The chevy ran a light. The traffic cam caught the front license plate and the driver. It's Carl Simmons."

"Carl Simmons?" Dana repeated, her face crinkled in disbelief.

"That mousey guy who was always in the library?" Laurie asked.

"The very one," Skye confirmed.

Dana looked between them. "How could he be involved? He was so shy he hardly spoke above a whisper."

"Something must have happened, because we've got him on film."

"We need to go talk to him. Do we know where he works?" Dana fished in her purse.

"I think he's a banker, but we can't charge into his office," Laurie said.

"It's Saturday. Banks are closed on Saturdays, remember?" Skye said.

Dana rolled her eyes. "People who didn't have to work weekends aren't real professionals. At least in my opinion."

Laurie just shook her head. Dana had turned into a workaholic, just like Graham.

"Let's call and set an appointment for tonight," Dana suggested.

Skye shook her head. "He's definitely involved. I think it should be a surprise visit to his home."

The three studied each other for a minute, then nodded. "Seven?" Dana suggested.

Gary ran into the room.

"Good. Gary, please find the address for Carl Simmons. Get all the information available on him," Dana said.

"Sure, but—"

"And—"

"Boss." Gary interrupted, his voice firm.

"How many times have I asked that you not call me that?" Dana asked, a slight smile on her face.

Gary wiped her objection away with a sweep of his hand. "There are two of them."

"Two of what?" Dana asked.

"Two suspects. The second person in the black hoodie, the one who pushed you and Kimberly, is at least half a foot taller than the first one."

BY THE END of the day, Dana's staff had scoured the tapes and found every place that the two suspects appeared. She called Laurie to give her the news. "It's definite. Two people in black hoodies. One who talks to Kimberly and another who appears at the top of the Globe."

"Did you ever see their faces?"

"No. They knew how to avoid the cameras for the most part."

"Does Jonathan Shanks know yet?"

"That's a little touchy. We got the tapes through..." Dana hesitated. She couldn't say she used an illegal, not to mention underage hacker on her office phone. "Let's just say Shanks needs to look at the tapes in a way that will hold up in court. I think the Seattle police have gotten a warrant for them as well. It's best if you speak with him. Just tell him to look carefully at the height of the people in the hoodies."

"OK, I'll give him a call. Did you get the information on—"

"Yes. Best not to say more on this line. I'll talk to you both tonight. My house at five, then we'll pay our friend a visit."

"It's Saturday. Think he'll be home?"

"If he's the same as he was in high school, probably." Dana ended the call. She needed to go home and get the kids settled before this evening's investigation. She grabbed her jacket and purse, then stuck her head in Gary's office. "It's four o'clock. Has everyone else left?"

"About half an hour ago."

"Thanks for coming in on the weekend," Dana said.

Gary just shrugged. Apparently, he was as used to it as she was. Dana felt a guilty pang. She would have to pay more attention to how often she asked people to work on Saturday and Sunday. But then again, Laurie's case was coming up soon.

"I'll call if I need you, but have a late Monday morning. Can you tell the others?"

Gary's face lit up. "Thanks, bo--, huh, Ms. Preston."

"You're welcome. Thanks for your good work today." She tapped the door frame, thinking she should put in for a promotion for Gary, then left for home.

EIGHTEEN

Laurie polished off the last of the sandwich she'd made for dinner and rinsed her plate off in the sink. She ignored the pang of guilt telling her she should wash it. Rosa sat by her now empty dish, licking her lips. Oliver lumbered over to his bed. From her perch on the back of the couch, Natasha looked up from cleaning her front leg. "Nothing for me?"

"Your dish is half full." Laurie pointed to the gray ceramic bowl with red poppies. Her mother had bought a matched set just for the cat.

"Half full?" Somehow Natasha put emphasis on the first word. Laurie swore her eyebrow was raised in disdain. With an exasperated sigh, she scooped up more of the freeze-dried mix her mother swore by and filled the bowl. These animals ate better than she did.

Natasha went back to cleaning her other leg.

"You're welcome?" Laurie said.

The cat ignored her.

"Cats," Laurie grumbled. She turned to Rosa, who sat with her ears perked. "Ready?"

The dog gave a little yip and ran the front door, her plume tail held high. The older boxer mix trotted down the hall to join them. Laurie shrugged into her rain jacket. Grabbed her purse and the leashes, not bothering to attach either one. She opened the door and they both ran for the car. Rosa pawed at the window and Laurie opened it.

Two suspects. It was too much to think about. And her old job. She already thought of it in the past tense. Was she going back to Boston to live? She'd always wanted a place in Seattle with a good view of the sound and maybe the city. With the inheritance, maybe she could afford a small cottage in Magnolia.

"You'll be able to afford a big house. Hasn't your lawyer got your old pack leader cornered? Isn't he asking for more money from where you used to hunt?" Rosa said. The dog's complex sentences amazed Laurie.

"Hunt?"

"You know, spend your time for food?"

"Oh, my job." Laurie chuckled. "That makes sense. Yeah, Shanks threatened to sue them, but I doubt anything will come of that."

"We'll see." The dog sounded like a wise prophet.

Laurie turned off Broadway and headed toward Dana's. She had a great view of Lake Washington. Maybe something on north Capitol Hill. Then she spotted the blue Impala a block away parked under a maple with bright spring leaves. Laurie pulled over, fished her phone out, and called Dana.

"I see him." Her friend's voice was hushed.

"How did you— He's not even— Where are you?" Laurie stammered.

"I was driving home from the office and spotted him when I turned onto my street."

"So you're to the north of him?" Laurie asked.

"I don't do directions. I usually turn on Prospect."

"We need to call Skye," Laurie said. "How do you do a three-way—"

Dana's laugh was a touch bawdy. "You mean a conference call?"

"You know I didn't mean—"

"Hang up. I'll do it. Answer when I call next."

Laurie ended the call and looked over at Rosa, who sat, ears perked, her mouth open, red tongue lolling. Even her white teeth looked eager to sink into somebody's leg. "The prey is in sight," she said. "What are we waiting for?"

"We're going to coordinate," Laurie said.

"I could pen him down for you."

"He's in a car, Rosa. He might run over you." Her ring tone sounded, a whale song. She needed to change it. She could never hear it in a crowd. Laurie answered. "Dana?"

"Yes."

"I'm here, too." Skye's voice sounded hazy.

"Where are you?" Laurie asked.

"Just turning onto Bellevue."

Dana cut in. "Here's the plan."

"Bossy much?" Skye said.

Laurie smiled. "She is."

Laurie could hear Dana's huff clearly. "So who wants to plan this?"

"Me, since I live with a cop," Skye said. "Let's box him in. Dana, he'll pull out and head towards you, so block him. I'll stop beside him. Laurie, you stop behind him so he can't back out. We have to do it together. Perfect timing."

"Sounds good." Dana still sounded slightly miffed.

"What if he has a gun?" Laurie asked.

"A gun?" Dana asked. "Honestly, you've been watching too many spy movies."

"I'll take a bullet for you," Oliver said.

Not to be outdone, Rosa looked up at her from her place on the passenger floorboard. "I'll jump on him and bite his hand."

Laurie's eyes teared up.

"Let me know when you see Laurie's rental," Dana told Skye.

"Is that you in the brown Honda?" Skye asked.

A green Subaru pulled up beside her. Skye rolled down the window and gave her a wicked smile. "Ready?"

Laurie put the phone in the cup holder and shouted, "Ready."

"One, two, three. Go." Skye's car hurdled forward and Laurie followed. Rosa yipped in excitement.

"I'm coming," Dana's voice sounded faint.

Laurie raced down the street, staying close behind the green Subaru. When they were almost on top of the chevy, Skye swerved into the middle of the street and slammed on her brakes. Laurie threw her arm out to brace Oliver as she followed suit. Rosa hunkered down on the floorboards.

The Chevy's engine fired and the car pulled forward, trying to squeeze past the Subaru. Laurie tensed, waiting for the collision. "You better not hit my new car." Dana screamed, distorting the speaker on Laurie's phone.

Only the Chevy driver couldn't hear her. The car came to a sudden stop, pitching forward. The passenger door opened and out sprang Carl Simmons. He looked around wildly, then ran to the back of his car and took off down the sidewalk.

The dogs erupted, barking and growling. Laurie reached over to open the passenger door, but fumbled with the handle. She jumped out of the Honda, intending to run around and let the dogs out, but they darted out her side of the car and took off after Carl. Laurie ran after them. Skye appeared at her side, keeping pace.

"You're in good shape," Laurie said.

Skye shot her a dirty look, then pulled ahead.

Rosa reached Carl and sank her teeth into his pant leg. She shrank back on her haunches, trying to stop him, but the fabric tore and the man pulled free. Oliver jumped on him, the boxer's weight pushing Carl off balance. He tripped, arms flailing, regained his balance and took another step before Skye slammed into him, pushing him to the ground. She and Oliver sat on him, a rather unceremonious pile. Rosa ran to Carl's head and crouched, snarling.

"Don't bite him," Laurie shouted as she arrived, panting from the sudden exertion.

Skye shot her a cocky grin. "Who's in good shape?"

"Let me up, please. You're going to break my ribs," Carl pleaded.

"Will you come with us peacefully—" Skye asked "—or do I need to snap on the cuffs?"

"Cuffs?" Laurie and Carl asked at the same time.

Skye's laugh edged toward manic. "I've always wanted to say that. Jade gets all the fun."

Dana arrived, giving Skye a withering look. "Carl, will you please come into my house so we can talk like civilized human beings?"

He nodded vigorously. Skye and Oliver both got off Carl's back. Laurie gave him a hand up, then latched on to his arm. Skye took the other side and they frog marched him up Dana's stairs and into the living room.

Lele sat on the back of the sofa watching, clearly unimpressed. "I could have stopped him faster."

"Oh yeah, I'd like to see that," Rosa shot.

Oliver ignored them both, making his way to the kitchen where they soon heard him lapping water.

"Eew, dog slobber. I'll have to have fresh."

Laurie frowned at the cat. "Oh, for heaven's sake." Everyone was too focused on Carl to notice her talking to Lele. By the time Laurie looked back, Dana had already arranged Carl in an armchair across from the couch, the one farthest from the door. Skye sat in the one next to him, her hands on the arms of the chair, ready to stop him from making a break for it Laurie imagined. She settled next to Dana on the couch. Lele stayed where she was. Rosa closed off the circle, sitting dead center between the couch and chairs. Oliver moseyed back in and stretched out beside her, his head resting on his paws so he could keep an eye on the culprit.

"What is the meaning of this?" Carl started up. "I was minding my own business—"

"Were you now? Were you minding your own business when you followed us from Kimberly's funeral?" Skye shot out.

"I never—"

"You tailed us when I left my attorney's office Wednesday night," Laurie added.

"And now you're parked near my house. Were you waiting for us to come home or did you break in?" Dana asked.

Carl's eyes went wide. "I'm no burglar. I was sitting in my car. I had to pull over to answer a call."

"You know we can have your phone records subpoenaed, don't you?" Skye said, seeming to enjoy her role.

"You can't do that. You aren't cops."

"Actually, Carl—" Skye leaned close to him "—the police have identified you and plan on bringing you in for questioning to find out why you are following a murder suspect around."

Maybe Skye should have been the cop instead of Jade, Laurie thought.

"I'm not— I just—" He pulled himself up straight, his thin frame trembling. "You can't possibly know that. You're lying. I could have you prosecuted for kidnapping, you know."

"Why are you following us?" Dana asked in her calm, courtroom voice.

"You can't hold me against my will," Carl declared and stood up.

Oliver let out a low, rumbling growl.

"I like this dog," Lele said to Laurie.

Carl took two steps toward the door. Rosa got to her feet and added an alto growl.

"Call off your mutts."

Oliver stood up, his growl turning to a snarl. The three women just watched him.

"You can't let them hurt me. They'll put them down if they attack me."

Both Oliver and Rosa took a step closer to him.

"I don't know, Carl. Boxers were bred to hunt bears. A human is more fragile."

Carl blanched and fell back into the chair, squeezing his legs together.

"You better not pee on my chair, Carl Simmons," Dana said.

A titter came from the stairs.

"Help," Carl shouted out to the sound.

Dana looked over her shoulder and frowned, then turned back to stare at Carl so fast Laurie worried she'd give herself whiplash. "Why are you following us, Carl? Did you push Kimberly Woolridge over that ledge? Did you almost kill me?" Dana hissed.

"Are you the murderer, Carl?" Laurie asked.

"Okay, okay. Call off your dogs." Carl held his hands out in front of him, fending off an imagined attack.

"You can relax, guys. He's not going anywhere," Laurie said.

Both dogs laid back down.

Carl stared at her like she was some sort of magician. Once he was sure the dogs weren't going to lunge at him, he took a deep breath. "I was just supposed to follow you—" He stopped himself, realizing what he'd said.

Dana leaned forward. "Who asked you to do that?"

"I had nothing to do with Kimberly getting pushed over the railings at the Globe. I swear." His eyes were tearing up. "I had no idea that was going to happen."

"What did you think was going to happen?"

"Oh, all right. I was just supposed to follow you and report back who you were talking with. She knew you were investigating. What exactly, I didn't know for sure."

"How much was she paying you?" Dana asked.

"Nothing," Carl said, looking offended. "She told me she'd made a mistake in high school. That she'd been attracted to me, but her cheerleader friends made fun of me. That nobody would like her anymore if she went out with me."

Laurie realized she was staring at him, her mouth gaping. She gave herself a shake and asked, "Who are you talking about?"

"Sandy. Sandy Jones." He looked at them like they were dullards.

"You had a crush on Sandy Jones?" Skye asked, a smile spreading over her face. Laurie could feel a laugh of sheer surprise surfacing and fought to stifle it. She didn't want Carl to clam up.

"I've loved her ever since elementary school," Carl declared. "She said if I could help her out of a jam that we could finally start dating." He stared earnestly at Dana, then shifted his gaze to Laurie. Something about him reminded her of Don Quixote. Maybe because he was tall, thin, and hopelessly optimistic.

"So you've been following us and reporting back to Sandy," Dana said.

He nodded, his lower lip quivering. "But now my chances are gone."

"Maybe not." Skye jumped in. "Maybe we could all help her out of her jam."

A light went back on in Carl's eyes. "You think?"

Honestly, this guy was still a teenager, Laurie thought. Emotionally stuck in high school. "If we knew more about it, maybe we could. I'm in a jam, too. Maybe these two problems are related."

Carl shook his head. "She wouldn't tell me anything. Said she didn't want to see me get hurt."

Dana gave their captive a shrewd look. "When are you supposed to talk to her again?"

"Tomorrow in one of the empty houses she has on the market. There's an open house, so she thought it wouldn't look suspicious."

Laurie remembered Sandy was a real estate agent now.

"What's the address?" Skye asked.

"Why?" his eyes flew open. "You want to follow me?"

"We need to talk to her. We'll say we've been talking to a lot of people who were at the reunion."

"But she might figure it out," Carl objected.

Skye reached out and patted his hand. "Our friend has been framed for murder, Carl."

"I know you're a good guy and you want to help," Laurie added.

Carl's eyes filled and he blinked the tears away, embarrassed. "I don't want to lose her."

This poor guy, Laurie thought. He imagines he has a chance.

"You have to stop following us." Dana's tone brooked no objection.

NINETEEN

The next morning, the three friends rendezvoused in West Seattle where Sandy's open house was scheduled to end soon. They found parking two blocks away and huddled on the sidewalk planning their attack. The house rose three stories, painted the stormy blue of rain clouds with large windows on all levels. It dwarfed the older bungalows and craftsmen surrounding it.

"Skye and I should take the front," Dana said. "You and the canines cover the back to make sure she doesn't make a quick getaway once she sees us."

"Roger that." Laurie started down the street, Rosa and Oliver on either side. She checked the front windows, but didn't see anyone inside. A couple walked down the drive and gave her a nod, probably wondering if she was going to beat them to making an offer. A low wooden fence surrounded the front yard which sported a long table and manicured narrow beds for bushes. Paving stones edged with gravel covered the ground. She skirted around the garage and found more pavers in the small back yard. Hardly any grass around. The house wouldn't be good for dogs. Then she realized a tiny part of her mind was house shopping. Had she decided for sure she was leaving Anthony University?

"I don't like it, either," Rosa told her, referring to the house. Oliver trotted happily beside her, images of biting people's ankles flashing through his mind.

Laurie risked a glance through the kitchen window. This floor was open concept, so she had a view to the front door. Sandy bent over the dining room table sorting through paperwork, getting ready to leave. When the front door opened, she frowned, but then caught herself and raised her head, her dark brown hair catching the light. She put on her high-beam realtor smile. Until she saw who had come through the door. "Dana, Skye, so nice to see you. I hadn't realized you were in the market for a new house." Sandy looked between them, waiting to see who her customer was.

"Actually, we wanted to talk to you," Dana said.

Skye saw Laurie peeking through the kitchen window and gestured for her to come in. Laurie opened the back door and the dogs ran in. Oliver inspected the ground floor. "Nobody else here," he announced to Laurie.

Rosa ran straight up to Sandy and sniffed her all over. "Aren't you a friendly one," she said, her posture stiff with distaste. She looked up at Laurie. Her gray eyes matched the Seattle skies, but she tried for a smile. "Actually, animals aren't allowed in. The house has been thoroughly cleaned and staged."

Laurie started to say something, but Dana ignored this and pulled out one of the maroon brocade chairs around the dining table. "Why don't we have a seat?"

Sandy stood, hands on her hips. "It's great to see you and all, but couldn't you have called my office to find a more convenient time? I have an appointment with another client."

"Carl's not coming," Skye said, subtly maneuvering so she blocked Sandy's way to the front door.

"What? Carl? Carl who?"

"Come off it, Sandy. We caught him following us around. I'm a lawyer and Skye's wife is a police detective. We know how to scare somebody into a confession."

Sandy's mouth worked as she tried to come up with a rejoinder. "He's lying. I never—"

"How cruel. You used his feelings for you to force him to spy on us." Skye tsked.

"After all these years, he's still in love with you. You were never going to have that date with him that you promised." Laurie moved so that she blocked the exit to the back.

Sandy looked back and forth between them, searching for an escape, but they had her hemmed in.

Dana leaned forward, locking eyes with their culprit. "Why are you watching us?"

"I never asked him—"

Dana banged her hand on the table and Sandy blanched. "Yes, you did."

"I've been accused of murder," Laurie said, her voice shaking. "You know I had nothing to do with Kimberly's death. I need help, Sandy. If you have a compassionate bone in your body, please tell us what's going on."

"Look, I wasn't involved in Kimberly's death. I thought it was an accident until I heard you'd been arrested."

Rosa brushed up against Laurie. "She's lying. Her scent is on your clothes. It's fainter than the other one, but she was there and bumped into you."

Laurie looked up from Rosa's brown eyes and found Skye watching her. Was her friend psychic enough to know what had passed between her and her little Havanese? Wait, she'd said she wasn't psychic, but—what was it? Empathic. Laurie gave Skye a small nod.

Dana had not noticed this exchange. "So what were you involved in?"

Sandy tapped her foot as she thought. After a full minute, she pulled out another chair and sank into it, her shoulders falling.

"Okay, I'll tell you, but this story can't get back to anybody."

"We aren't going to reveal what we know or do not know just yet. We've talked to a lot of people already," Dana assured her. She settled her arms on the table and fixed Sandy with an appraising look.

The realtor straightened up. "About six months ago, I sold a luxury house in Shoreline. Ten bedrooms. As many baths. Two swimming pools. Tennis court. Overlooking Puget Sound and the Olympics. The whole package."

"Wow," Laurie whispered.

"Yeah. Big wow." Sandy glanced at her, then focused back on Dana. Maybe she considered Dana to be the big roller in this group.

"It was a cash deal. Sold to a trust fund, but the identity of the buyer was never disclosed. At the closing, they came in two-K short. Said it was a cash flow issue." She snorted in disbelief. "Highly unlikely in a scenario like that."

"I'll say," Dana agreed.

"Anyway, my percentage was significantly more than that, I can tell you. There was no way I was going to lose this sale, so I fronted the money with a promissory note to be refunded."

Laurie felt a tad queasy. These people were way out of her league. Sandy and Dana talked about millions of dollars like it was an everyday thing.

Skye caught her eye. A wave of something reassuring passed from her. Energy? Laurie didn't think in these terms. Rosa whined, leaning against her leg, and Oliver gave a low woof.

Dana kept Sandy's attention on her. "I take it you were never paid back."

"No, the man who'd brokered the deal approached me and said the money hinged on me doing a simple little job for them. Said there was a clause in our agreement to cover this contingency."

Dana's eyebrows shot up. "Was there?"

Sandy waved her question away. "By this time, it didn't matter. I needed the two million and do you think taking a multi-millionaire to court would work for a small firm like mine?"

Sandy took a deep breath. "He wanted me to collect money from a blackmail scheme involving Kimberly Woolridge."

"Kimberly? How were these people connected to her?"

"That's the thing. I never quite figured out who was at the bottom of the well. We investigated a series of shell companies behind the deal. One night my private investigator was walking to his car. A man stepped out from behind a pillar in the parking garage. Such a cliché." Sandy made a face. "Anyway, he told him to stop the search. That if he didn't, his life would be in danger. He made it clear he was packing."

Dana turned back to Sandy. "Could your PI ID this man?"

Laurie followed these acronyms. Reassuring, and she didn't hang in these kinds of circles. At least, she didn't use to.

Sandy shook her head. "He's not willing to get any more deeply involved."

"Okay, back to Kimberly. What do you think they were threatening her with?" Dana asked.

"That part was easy to figure out. Exposure. She had a new lover. They were planning to marry after Kimberly left John. Apparently this guy is a real straight shooter and Kimberly was afraid that if he found out about her past, he might leave her."

"What exactly about her past?"

"You know Kimberly was a total bitch in high school and didn't really change. She had to leave her job as a legal assistant because of some crap she pulled with a client. Lost the woman a lot of money. And there was that scandal after the senior prom."

"Were either of the victims associated with the shell companies you uncovered?"

"Not exactly, but we didn't get many names. Whoever was behind this demanded quite a sum from her. Close to a million." Sandy's eyes sharpened with anger. "Like whoever this is needs money. That's just spare change to them."

"What was their plan?" Dana asked.

"The broker of the real estate deal wanted me to collect the blackmail money from Kimberly at the reunion." She crossed her arms over her stomach, shaking her head. "I couldn't just walk away from what they owed me, so I agreed. I was instructed to wear a black hoodie they provided to cover my face from security cameras. I added a mask." She looked around at them in appeal. "Some people are still wearing them."

Skye nodded in understanding.

"I came in dressed for the event, but went into the ladies room to change. I met her in the janitor's closet. You saw me leaving." She pointed to Laurie and Skye.

"What happened when you met Kimberly?" Dana asked.

"She was desperate. Said she couldn't come up with all the money. That it was impossible for her. She promised she'd have it after the divorce. I was supposed to threaten her with—" Sandy shook her head, not able to finish "—but I couldn't bring myself to do it. I told her I thought these people were serious. That they would tell her new boyfriend and ruin all her plans. Maybe even do worse." A tear escaped and she wiped it away, then said in a whisper. "Even after I heard about the accident, I never imagined it could have been murder."

She looked up at Laurie. "Then I heard you were arrested. I just didn't want my part in this to come to light. It would ruin my reputation. People don't trust real estate agents as it is. Just imagine if people knew I'd cooperated with blackmailing a woman who ended up being murdered. So I asked Carl to keep an eye on you once I realized you were investigating on your own."

"Have they paid you the two million from the house sale?" Dana asked.

"No," Sandy spit out. "They said I was not successful. Like it's my fault the woman didn't have that much money."

Dana sat back, deep in thought. Laurie and Skye sank into the chairs at either end of the teak table. After a minute, Dana cleared her throat. "Laurie's future is at stake. If she's found guilty, she'll likely spend the rest of her life in prison."

Hearing Dana state this so starkly shocked Laurie. She wrapped her arms around herself. Rosa whined, wiggling to be picked up. She scooped up the dog, burying her face in her fawn fluff.

Dana pressed on, pointing a finger at Sandy. "You're owed quite a sum of money. Did you dig up any information at all that might help us figure out who was behind this?"

Sandy's gray eyes lit with a predatory gleam. "When we were investigating the shell companies, we found the name of a Seattle environmental firm. Living Earth Designs, I think."

Laurie froze. Her breath came in quick gasps. Rosa licked her face. It couldn't be. Living Earth was John Newman's firm.

MONDAY MORNING CAME, leaving Laurie with nothing to do. Dana had another case to prepare. Skye needed to put in a few shifts at Star, Stone & Flower, her family's store. Laurie walked the dogs down to the little park, sitting on the spinner while they sniffed the bushes. But once she got home, Laurie was left with her thoughts. What did the future hold? She realized she could never go back to Anthony University, not after they'd conspired to fire her. And the students. How could anyone construe such a ridiculous complaint? That she had sexually harassed a student. She taught feminist theory, for heaven's sake. It was more believable that she could have murdered a student for such stupidity than Kimberly. Academia was as vibrant these days as three-day-old soda.

Her mind shied away from orange jumpsuits. Not her color, but maybe Tobias would look good in one. She'd have real murderers as cellmates and terrible food for the rest of her days. She couldn't face that. Better to steal a boat and make for Canada. Except they'd just send her back. If she got caught. Could she live in the Yukon Territories, build an igloo, eat fish forever? Rosa and Oliver could be her sled dogs.

"She's losing it," Rosa said to the boxer mix.

"Just ignore her. Humans imagine all sorts of things that aren't real," he replied.

No, she should head south. Grabbing her laptop, she goggled countries with no extradition treaties with the U.S. within sailing distance from Seattle. The list was short and didn't include any countries in Central or South America. Except Cuba. Maybe she could get there in a sailboat, but she'd have to go through the Panama Canal and they'd probably catch her there. She briefly considered the Vatican. Monks might make good neighbors. The current pope seemed to be a good guy. But how would she get there? She wished she could reanimate Kimberly and push her over that ledge herself. Next time the ghost visited Dana, Laurie would give her a piece of her mind.

John's face swam up in her memory. Those laugh lines around his mouth. Walnut brown hair, the silver at his temples making him more handsome. How she fit right under his arm, like they were made for each other.

She pushed the memories away. Romance had been invented by a society bent on controlling women, brainwashing them into looking for the perfect man instead of leading their own lives. She was swearing off men. But he knew how to kiss, how to—she stood up and marched to the kitchen. Wheeled around. She wasn't hungry. What was she doing?

Laurie had agreed to meet John that afternoon to go sailing on the Sound. Another romantic fantasy, but she had to get a grip on reality. It would be cold out there. She remembered visiting Wisconsin in the middle of July. Ninety degrees at least. She and Graham had attended a Shakespeare play one night. A buzzing swarm of mosquitoes drowned out the actor's lines. Then they'd come to Seattle and put on puff jackets, wool hats and gloves, and wound wool scarves around their necks to go whale watching. And they'd needed it all to stay warm.

She made herself a sandwich and watched Rosa's feet twitched as she dreamed about chasing rabbits no doubt. How could John be involved in blackmailing Kimberly? He was married to her, for heaven's sake. It didn't make a hill of beans of sense. But had he been involved in planning her demise? Rosa had sniffed him out and given him a clean bill. "He didn't do it," she'd said. Had he hired somebody to do the deed? Was he involved with other people? Or was somebody trying to set him up? The whole thing was ridiculous, but Sandy had been sure. One of the companies hidden among the shell corporations in the real estate transaction had been Living Earth Designs.

Plus, there were the now less frightening questions. Had John been involved in the assault on Walter? If so, what had he done exactly? And if he wasn't on Peggy's boat that night, how much had he known about the events? And—she shrank away from this thought even as she thought about it—was he sure he was Sylvia's father? Could she even ask him such a thing?

Her cell phone played a whale song. His name showed on the screen. She rolled her eyes at her naïveté. He was calling to firm up their plans, but she couldn't imagine being alone on a boat in the middle of Elliott Bay with him. Not after what she'd learned.

"I thought we could sail south. I've heard J-pod is making their way up from Olympia." John's voice still sent warm ripples through her.

"That sounds wonderful—"

"Great, I'll pick you up in about half an hour."

"Actually, I've learned some things in our investigation that are disturbing."

"Then being on the water should help soothe your nerves. I can only imagine how being a suspect is affecting you." His voice was sympathetic, pleased to be helping her relax, if only for the afternoon.

How she would love to be distracted. The peace of the Sound, the chance of seeing the orcas, watching him unfurl the sails, resting in his strong arms. His strong, murderous arms. She gave herself a shake and stuck to her plan. "I'd rather meet you at that little coffee shop near my parents' house. You know the Cup and Saucer?"

John didn't answer immediately. "What's this about, Laurie?"

"I'd rather we talk face to face. Can you meet me there in half an hour?"

"If that's what you want." John's ardor had cooled, replaced with worry, if she was reading him right.

"I appreciate this. See you soon." Laurie ended the call and looked around for the dogs. Rosa sat watching the squirrels in the backyard and Oliver snored on his bed by the unlit fireplace. Natasha was a gray circle, nose tucked under her paws. "Who wants to go for a walk?" she asked.

Rosa ran to her and sat, tail wagging. Oliver lifted his head, then lowered it again. "I'm sleeping."

"Just us, then." Laurie scratched the little Havanese behind her ears.

Rosa closed her eyes and leaned into her hand. After a minute, she sat back up. "So are we going or not?"

The neighborhood coffeehouse sat on the corner a few blocks south of her parents' home. The owners had converted an old storefront into a cozy spot complete with coffee, tea, treats, a few shelves of books, and spaces for local artists to display their work. The morning was brisk as only early Seattle springs could be, with a damp that sank to the bone. Laurie found herself drinking more coffee in this city than in Boston, but the chai at the Cup and Saucer was too good to pass up. She opened the door and was enveloped in warmth and the smell of baking bread.

Amanda, one of the owners, looked up when the bell over the door rang. "Laurie, welcome. You're just in time. The scones are coming out of the oven in a minute."

"They smell incredible."

Rosa let out a little woof.

"I haven't forgotten you, little one." Amanda dug into the dog treat jar on the counter and gave Rosa two dog biscuits, a specialty of this shop. Laurie knew her mother bought them regularly for Oliver. Natasha had sampled them, but turned her nose up.

"Where's your big brother?" Amanda asked.

"Too lazy to get up," Laurie answered for Rosa since Amanda would be surprised to learn the dog talked. She studied the woman for a moment. Maybe she would take talking pets in stride.

Laurie made her way to the back of the shop and settled in a corner that offered two overstuffed, scruffy chairs with reading lamps and a small table between them. A cheerful fire crackled nearby. She was glad they'd kept the stone fireplace. Amanda arrived with a mug of chai and Laurie settled back, taking in the aroma of cardamon, cinnamon, and honey with a hint of black pepper. She took a sip and closed her eyes. Warmth spread through her. Perfect for this weather. Laurie shed her coat, knowing the tea and fire might bring on more than warmth. This confrontation would be stressful enough without adding a hot flash on top of it.

The bell above the door to the shop rang, announcing an arrival. A low voice ordered a decaf cappuccino, then something she couldn't make out. Laurie took another sip of chai, closing her eyes to enjoy the complex flavor before her peace was disturbed.

"There you are."

She looked up at John, his hair messy and face flushed from perhaps rushing here. His kissable lips turned up in a grin as he gestured toward the other chair. She waved her arm toward it, giving permission for him to sit. He was asking permission? She wondered why.

He settled and Rosa jumped into his lap. "Careful, girl. Don't spill this on me." He hastily put down his mug and stroked the little dog's sides. She leaned against him, eyes closed.

"Turncoat," Laurie sent to her.

"Nincompoop," Rosa sent back. The dog's vocabulary continued to surprise her.

Amanda arrived with a tray of fresh scones, Devonshire cream, and strawberry jam. She set it down on the table between them with a flourish.

"I took the liberty of ordering cream tea," John said. He studied her face, seeming to search out if he'd made a miscalculation. "For the British lit professor."

"You do take liberties," Laurie said.

John's smile faltered. "You don't want any?"

"How could I pass this up?" She leaned forward, helping herself to the feast. She cut a fresh scone in half and piled on the cream, thinking she might as well get fat. Become a grouchy retiree and surround herself with cats.

Rosa jumped off John's lap and yapped at her.

Okay, dogs and cats.

John watched her take a huge bite. "Has something happened with the investigation? Have you lost your job? You sounded serious on the phone."

All Laurie could do was nod while she finished chewing the enormous bite she'd taken, now realizing she'd done it because she didn't want to have this conversation. She'd rather stuff herself with Amanda's scones. Fluffy with hints of rosemary and lavender. She swallowed and took a swig of chai. "I still have my job." It was easier to answer the second question first.

"That's a relief."

"In fact, Shanks is suing the university for—" she waved her free hand "—I forget the specific charges, but it's something to do with cutting off my pay and threatening my tenure."

John's face lit up. "So if you win, you could make a lot of money and move here. Work with the whales. We could—"

Laurie cut him off. "Like I said on the phone, I've discovered some things that are disturbing." Her stomach knotted. Maybe the scone hadn't been a such a good idea.

His face fell. He sat back, picked up his mug and held it in front of his stomach like a shield.

She found herself circling the topic like Oliver circled his doggy bed before settling. "We've been interviewing people who worked at the front table at the reunion and might have seen the person who Kimberly met. Whom."

John smiled. "Always the professor."

"And people who were friends with her. Anybody who might have held a grudge against her."

"The posse at work."

"Thing is, somebody was following us."

"Are you safe?"

She waved a hand. "We tracked the car and discovered him waiting for us outside Dana's house. We snuck up on—"

John sat forward. "You did what? That's dangerous. You had no idea who he was. If he had a gun."

Laurie raised her voice to stop his bluster. "He didn't. It was Carl."

John gaped at her. "Carl Simmons? That mousy banker?"

"The very one."

"What was he doing following you guys around?"

"You remember Sandy Jones?"

He looked up at the ceiling, apparently searching his memory. Laurie wondered if he was putting on a show. "No." He shook his head. "I can't remember her."

"You sure?"

Her tone must have alerted him because he frowned. "I'm pretty sure, why?"

"She was always talking, chewing gum. Knew everybody."

"It's been a while since high school. What's she got to do with all this?"

"She asked Carl to follow us."

"Why would she do that?" John picked up a scone and smeared some jam on top of it.

"Seems Carl has harbored a crush on her all these years. Obsession, really. She promised him a date if he would keep an eye on us. Tell her who we were talking to."

John chewed fast and swallowed. "That's suspicious," he said, a few crumbs falling onto his shirt as he spoke. He brushed them into his hands and put them on the plate.

"We thought so too, so we confronted her at her open house yesterday."

"Confronted? You three are going to bite off more than you can chew one day."

Laurie smiled, considering he'd just done exactly that.

"Seriously, this is a murder investigation. If you find the murderer, you might get yourselves hurt. Even—" he stopped and frowned, his eyebrows pinching together.

"Killed?" she asked.

He reached for her across the table. "Laurie, please. I don't want to lose you again."

"Sandy turned out to be the one who confronted Kimberly in the janitor's closet."

"She did it?"

"No, somebody was extorting money from Kimberly. They forced Sandy to collect from her at the reunion." Sandy had asked them not to disclose this, but Laurie had to know. She had to know if John had something to do with his wife's murder.

"How did they accomplish that?"

"They withheld two million dollars on the purchase of some mansion up north. Promised to pay Sandy the balance if she helped them collect the blackmail money from Kimberly."

"Blackmail money? That makes no sense," John sputtered. Some coffee splashed into his lap and he winced. Set his mug down and wiped at his pants.

"That's what we thought at first. Did you know Kimberly was being blackmailed?"

"By somebody who was buying a multimillion dollar house?" he asked, eyes wide.

"Exactly," Laurie said, somehow glad to see him so riled up. She piled more fuel on the fire. "Do you remember senior prom?"

"What? What in the world does that have to do with—"

"Do you remember what happened after the prom?"

John threw his hands up in the air. "What are you talking about? Why do you keep asking about the prom? You're not making any sense." His face turned bright red as he spoke.

Was he having a hot flash, Laurie wondered. Could men even have hot flashes? She was glad she wasn't having one. She sat forward. "Do you remember the morning after the prom?"

John's face wrinkled in confusion.

"Walter Pearce was found tied up on Matthews Beach. No clothes. And he'd been—" She watched John closely, looking for any signs of guilt. Any awareness of what she was about to say. Seeing nothing, she dropped the last word, "—abused."

He shook his head. "Abused how? You mean more than being found naked on a beach in public?"

"You don't remember?"

John's eyes flew wide. "Remember? You think I had something to do with this?"

"Did you?"

John rounded on her. "How could you accuse me of this?"

Rosa let out a low growl of warning, not liking John's tone.

"We've discovered that Kimberly was behind this whole thing. She talked some cheerleaders and football players into inviting Walter onto a boat and partying with them."

John collapsed back into his chair, the color draining from his face.

"Some of the football players—" she put emphasis on these two words "—stripped him. An eyewitness says they molested him and that Kimberly joined in."

"No."

"So you weren't involved?"

"I remember Kimberly said she was going to get back at Walter for something he'd said about her. Spread some nasty rumors or something. After Walter left school, I asked her if she'd done anything to him. She denied it. That's the day she told me she was pregnant. That's the day my life changed." John stood up and paced to the fireplace. He put his hand on the mantel and lowered his head.

Rosa ran over to him and put her front paws on his leg, whining. Laurie looked around the shop, relieved to see they were the only customers. Amanda seemed to have made herself scarce. After a minute, John turned raised his head, his eyes sad. "So Walter Pearce was behind this? I never realized he had enough money to buy a house like that."

"We don't have any evidence tying him to any of this. But…" Laurie took a deep breath, subdued by his demeanor. She was relieved he hadn't been involved in the attack on Walter, but then why was his firm listed in the sale of that house?

John shook his head, watching her with sad eyes. "I can't tell you what is more upsetting. That Kimberly followed through on this plan of hers or that you thought I was involved."

"John, there's more."

He frowned at her. "What?"

"Sandy traced the corporation that bought the house. Her investigator found a series of shell companies. All of them were fake except one."

John blanched. "No."

"Living Earth Designs."

His mouth worked. His face drained of color. "How could you— I never— My company? You think I—" He pointed to his chest. Then he stared at her, rage clear on his face. His words were precise, quiet, menacing. "Has it even occurred to you that Sandy Jones is lying? Somebody's trying to set me up. Right along with you."

Before she could answer him, John picked up his coat and walked out of the coffeehouse.

CHAPTER

TWENTY

Dana came home from the office to a pile of dirty dishes in the sink. Loud music boomed from upstairs. She could shout at her teenagers, cajole them to clean up after themselves, or just do it herself. The last option would take less time and energy. She thought about sticking them in the dishwasher—the dishes, not her children—but there weren't that many since the three of them had eaten takeout. Again.

She was flunking in the mom department, although Hoa and Minh weren't complaining. They enjoyed the parade of pizza, General Tso's chicken, saag paneer, and tacos. And that was just this week. She'd go to the grocery store and stock up. Cook something tomorrow. Maybe roasted chicken and potatoes, green beans, and salad. Basic American food for a change. She filled the sink with soapy water and started in. The warm water soothed her, slowing her down. Her shoulders dropped and she fell into a mindless rhythm.

"I see you're feeding your kids out of boxes." Kimberly's voice dripped with judgment.

Dana whirled, slopping water onto the kitchen floor. "It's about time you showed up. I've got some questions for you."

"Whoa. Easy there, tiger. I've been waiting for you to be alone." Kimberly perched on the kitchen island, examining her ghostly manicure. "It's harder to connect with you when you're surrounded by people. So many chaotic emotions." She waved her hand.

Dana opened her mouth to say that of course everyone was upset, but what came out was, "What is it with you and your nails?"

"I had pretty hands when I was alive," Kimberly said, her tone nostalgic.

This took some of the wind out of Dana's sails. Kimberly seemed to have accepted that she had passed on, although really, here she was so... "I'm sorry your life was cut short."

The ghost studied her through pale opal eyes, the swirling colors in her irises sending a shiver through Dana. This woman, ghost—she hesitated to use the word spirit, but she had to admit it—Kimberly was becoming more otherworldly.

Kimberly considered Dana a moment more. "I'm getting used to it."

Could this ghost read minds now? That could be a problem considering how many disparaging thoughts she had about her current guest.

But Kimberly just said, "I could explain what it's like, being dead and all, but I think you have other concerns."

Dana stared at her. She was tempted. How many other opportunities would she have to learn about the afterlife? Did everyone see a white light? Were people waiting for you at the end of that tunnel they always talked about? But Kimberly hadn't gone anywhere. Not yet. Dana wiped her hands on a dish towel. "I do have other concerns, but do you know what's keeping you here?"

Kimberly nodded, then flinched and glanced behind her. Lele had snuck up on the kitchen island that Kimberly perched on and started swatting at her. Her paws went through the ghost, which fascinated the cat.

"Lele, don't be rude," Dana said.

"That hurt," Kimberly said, surprise lighting her face. "I could feel it, but I can't touch anything. My hands go right through." She demonstrated by trying to pick up a small decanter of olive oil Dana kept on the counter.

"Interesting," Dana said. "Can you feel the cat?"

Kimberly turned to Lele and held out her hand to be sniffed, but the cat just sat watching her. She reached out and rubbed the top of her head. Lele closed her eyes and pressed her head into Kimberly's hand.

"Ooh, that's so wonderful." Kimberly ran her hand down the cat's sleek body.

Dana watched the two for a minute, mesmerized. "I wonder why you can touch cats."

In typical feline fashion, Lele decided she'd had enough. She moved a few steps away, laid down, and proceeded to groom herself.

"Wow, what a treat. People just don't appreciate the world, you know," Kimberly said, looking back at Dana.

"I'm sure you're right. You said that something is keeping you here. Do you know what?"

"I'm supposed to help John. I owe him."

This surprised Dana. "That's good to hear. We've discovered some new information. Someone is trying to implicate John in your death."

Kimberly shot off the island. Lele leapt away. "He's innocent. He wasn't involved."

"We didn't think he was. Do you know who was behind the blackmail attempt?"

Kimberly shook her head. "No, some man got in touch with me first, then a woman said she'd collect the money."

"You are remembering more. Did you know that woman was Sandy Jones."

Kimberly's form thinned. She held her hands out to stop Dana.

"She didn't do it either. Listen, I came here to tell you something important. Don't distract me."

"Okay," Dana said in a calming voice.

"The person who pushed me whispered in my ear 'You tried to ruin my life. Now I'm taking yours.' Then he shoved me over the railing."

"'He.' You're sure it was a male voice?"

"Certain."

"Whose life did you ruin, do you think?"

Kimberly's shoulders drooped. "I'd say John's, to tell you the truth. Now that I've had time to think about it. But he would never have hurt me like that. I don't know who I pissed off enough to actually murder me, though."

"Thanks for telling me this, Kimberly. This is helpful. Maybe that's what you were supposed to do—pass this memory on—and now you can leave."

As if to contradict her, the ghost's form grew more visible and she smiled. "We don't really leave, you know. It's easy to contact people who are still alive. If they have your talent."

Dana didn't think of her ability to talk to Kimberly as a talent. It was more of a burden. "Once we're finished with—" Dana waved the kitchen towel again "—this obligation, whatever, then I can go back to normal."

A sardonic smile formed on the ghost's face. "Whatever you say."

"Just out of curiosity..."

Kimberly's opal eyes kindled with that eerie light again.

Uneasy, Dana looked away. "You said you were supposed to help John. How do you know that?"

Kimberly tapped her finger on the marble island. It made no sound, but didn't sink in. After a pause, she said, "I suppose I can tell you this. After the funeral, I saw more people. Family who've already passed over. Friends. And this tall person connected with me—he's a really bright light. Anyway, he—" she screwed up her face "—let's say he came to talk to me about my life here. He's like some kind of after-life therapist I suppose. We talk about the choices I made. What worked out. What I could have done better."

She jumped back up on the island and gave Dana an earnest look. "I was a good mom and my children are going to have such great lives. Josh is going to—" she slapped her hand over her mouth "— I'm not supposed to tell the future."

Dana smiled at the return of the childish Kimberly, but then realized what the ghost had said. "You know the future?"

"Some of it. I do like my spirit helper. The best thing is, he's not judgmental or condemning like I used to be, especially when I was younger. I like that." The ghost's body brightened.

"I'm, uh, happy for you. Is that the right word?" Dana asked.

"Yes, it is. I can always visit. See my kids. I can't wait to explore this new spirit plane, I guess you'd call it."

"You've already been helpful, Kimberly. This new information is great. If you remember anything else, don't hesitate to call ... uh, show up."

"Thanks, I will. I know there's one more thing I have to do before I'm free."

"What?"

Kimberly shrugged her shoulders. "Don't know yet."

Dana sighed. "That's frustrating."

"Tell me about it," the ghost said. And with that, she disappeared.

LAURIE SAT in her chair in the family room, fury battling shame over John walking out on her. She was supposed to have walked out after confronting him with his part in the prank on Walter. But he hadn't been involved after all. Or so he claimed, and somehow she believed him. Maybe Kimberly had known he wouldn't participate or let it go as far as it had. And when he discovered she'd been behind it, she pulled out her big news—that she was pregnant.

Laurie hadn't asked if John was sure the baby was his. It was too much. She'd wanted to reach out to him. Wrap her arms around him. Tell him she was sorry it had all worked out this way. But the news about his firm appearing in the list of shell companies had sent him over the top and he'd stormed off. He hadn't called or texted her since. She wondered if it was over between them before it had really started again.

She rocked back and forth, staring unseeing at some program her parents were watching. Something about discoveries of possible life on Mars. How Earth was going to lose all its water just like the red planet had if humanity didn't stop pumping greenhouse gases into the atmosphere. She should be out marching in front of some oil company instead of worrying about her love life. Protesting while she was still out of prison for murdering the bitch who had ruined her life and John's.

Okay, that was a bit extreme. She'd had a pretty decent life so far. Had loved Graham, even though they'd never had the chemistry she had with John. She'd put that down to raging teenage hormones. But now she knew better. John lit her up like fireworks on New Year's Eve. And now she'd driven him off. Except had he been involved with the blackmail scheme or even Kimberly's death? Or was he being framed just like she was? He'd accused her of swallowing Sandy's story whole, but she'd seemed genuine at the time. So upset about it. Maybe she was a good actress.

They needed to check out Sandy's story. Dana had the staff for it. Laurie reached for her cell to call her, but the phone rang before she could punch the button for Dana. Skye's name appeared on the screen. "We're meeting at the shop. I have some new information."

Laurie hauled herself out of the chair and her father cut her a look. "Where you off to?"

She resisted the automatic teenage response that popped into her head—that she didn't answer to him—and just told him Skye had called with some possible help with her case. Rosa danced up to her, but Oliver said he wasn't interested in going.

"But it's Skye's shop. You'll like it," she told the boxer.

"What?" her mother asked, eyeing her as if she had doubts about her grip on reality.

Laurie shook her head. "Sorry. I'll be at Skye's store."

They both nodded, speculative looks on their faces. Laurie knew they'd be convinced she'd gone off the deep end if she told them she was answering Oliver's question, so she just smiled.

"Humans," Natasha sniffed from her place on the sofa.

"But they feed you," Oliver said and closed his eyes again.

Laurie headed over to the University District once again and found a parking place only a block from Skye's store, a sure sign of divine intervention. She hoped more would come. Laurie pushed open the glass door and was greeted by the sound of gongs and chanting coming from speakers spread around the room. Incense smoke, maybe sandalwood, wafted across her face. Rosa sneezed.

The store was packed with books. Her eyes ran down the bookshelves on the right-hand side of the store and saw labels for Wicca, Druidry, Voodoo, esoteric Christianity—it went on and on. Another bookshelf offered instruction in channeling, psychic development, meditation, rituals. Jars filled with dried herbs, flowers, and roots lined more shelves, inviting customers to create their own magical potions, spells, and incense. Candles in various shapes, sizes, and colors sat next to a bewildering array of crystals and gemstones. Little cards announced the type of stone and its properties. Laurie noticed a black stone that was supposed to repel negative energy. Maybe she should get one and carry it around. This situation was turning her into some kind of woo-woo nut job.

She leaned her elbow on a glass display case containing a collection of crystal jewelry, including pendulums, necklaces, and bracelets. Laurie looked away, not wanting to be tempted. Crystal pendants might get turned into shanks in prison. Was that the right word for it? She'd have to bone up on prison jargon. A nearby table overflowed with tarot and oracle decks, runes, and scrying tools. Maybe Skye had done a reading and wanted to tell her about it.

Just as she thought this, her friend appeared from behind a blue curtain swirled with constellations and beckoned for Laurie to join her in the back. Rosa gave a joyful yip and tugged at her leash. Laurie reached down and unsnapped her lead. The little Havanese ran straight to Skye, her whole body wiggling. Some of her gloom lifted as she watched Rosa stretch herself up Skye's leg to get her ears scratched. Dogs knew how to live.

The bell rang as the door opened and Dana rushed in, her two teens in tow. "All right, only fifty dollars each and don't make yourself a nuisance," she instructed.

"Is that fifty from you only? Can I use some of my allowance money?" Minh asked.

"Only if you already have it. No advances on future payments." She turned to the young woman behind the counter, most likely one of the college-aged nieces, and whispered, "Keep an eye on them. They're teenagers and everybody goes through a klepto stage at that age."

The girl's eyes widened slightly, but she answered, "Yes, ma'am."

Dana saw Laurie and asked, "Now, what's the big discovery?"

Skye waved them through the swirly curtain to the inner sanctum of the store. A series of tables lined one wall, each covered with fabric decorated with stars or astrological signs or Celtic designs. Some had more swirls. One table held a large crystal ball, another several tarot decks. "We do readings and private sessions back here," Skye explained. "Use this open area for larger classes."

She kept walking toward the back and opened a door marked 'Employees Only.' Boxes of unopened merchandise filled the wall on the right. On the left, Skye opened a door to a drab room filled by a conference table. Skye waved her hands, indicating they should sit.

"Thanks for coming." Skye frowned at Laurie. "You look...upset."

Laurie looked down at herself and realized she still wore her old, torn sweatpants and hadn't brushed her hair. She shrugged.

"Don't let this case get you down. I think I have good news."

"John left me," Laurie blurted out.

"What?" Dana asked. "I didn't realize you were together already."

Laurie shot her a look. "We weren't. Exactly."

"What happened?" Skye asked.

Laurie explained her encounter with John in the coffeeshop. "He thinks Sandy is lying. He stormed out."

"Did he deny his involvement in the prank?" Dana asked.

Laurie rested her forehead on her hand. "He said he wasn't there when the other football players ganged up on Walter. That Kimberly thought he wouldn't let it go that far. Seemed like he didn't know the details."

"Speaking of Walter. I decided to reread his first novel," Skye announced.

Rosa came trotting into the conference room, her face decorated with cobwebs. *What have you been up to?* Laurie asked.

Lots of interesting smells in here. No mice, though, the little dog said.

"Rosa says you don't have mice." Laurie took out a tissue and wiped the cobwebs and dust off the dog's face.

"That's good to know," Skye said. She squinted her eyes and studied the ball of fluff. "I hope you didn't open any packages."

Rosa turned her face away, making no comment, and stretched out beside Laurie.

"I guess we'll see," Skye said, eyeing the little Havanese mix. She turned her gaze back to the humans in the room and settled in her chair. "You remember Matilda talking about Mr. Moss' alleged suicide and how it was similar to the murder in the book?"

They both nodded.

"I read the details of the scene where they find the woman's body and then when they figure out who killed her. I told Jade about it, and she suddenly rushed into the living room and grabbed the book. She was so excited I had to take it away from her before she tore a few pages."

Dana frowned. "What was that all about?"

"Get this. There is a detail somewhere in those two descriptions that the police didn't share with the media or public."

Laurie shot up. "Wait, you mean Walter knew something the police were keeping secret?"

"Looks like it." Skye crossed her arms, a dangerous glint in her eye.

"What exactly?" Laurie asked. She sat back on the edge of her chair.

"Jade wouldn't tell me. Top secret." She drew a finger over her lips.

Laurie and Dana stared at Skye for a minute. "Holy cow," Laurie summed up.

"Let's not get ahead of ourselves. He's a novelist. He might have a police informant," Dana cautioned.

Skye shook her head. "An informant on the force would never reveal something the detectives kept from the press."

The case had been declared a suicide, but with this evidence.... "Do you think Walter had something to do with murder of Mr. Moss?" Laurie named it correctly.

"Maybe." Skye drew the word out. "Jade is taking this to her captain. She thinks they'll reopen the investigation."

CHAPTER

TWENTY-ONE

"You girls have got to be more careful," Jonathan Shanks said. He sat behind his massive oak desk, frowning. "I mean, I'm grateful for the help from your office, Dana. But you are a friend of the accused. And you, Skye. Well, your wife is a police detective. Granted, she's not assigned to this investigation, but still."

A general silence followed this admonishment. Then Dana lifted a well-groomed eyebrow. "Girls, Jonathan? Did you just call us girls?

Shanks sputtered, his face a mix of chagrin and annoyance. "Yeah, bad habit. Sorry, but you know what I mean."

Dana gave him an easy smile. "Just jerking your chain."

Shanks nodded, a look of relief on his face. "Thanks. I appreciate all that you've discovered." They'd just finished filling Shanks in on their conversation with Sandy Jones and Skye's discovery in Walter's book. Dana left out what she'd learned from the ghost. "But you shouldn't be involved at all, Laurie. Except you three seem to be joined at the hip."

Skye cleared her throat.

Shanks eyed her. "I do need the help since the judge refuses to budge on the date for the trial. We've got just over two weeks by the way, and I only have so many people I can call on. I appreciate your efforts. Just try not to get noticed by anyone who will report your activities to the prosecuting attorneys."

"Of course. We want Laurie to be exonerated as much as you do. More, in fact, since as you've pointed out, we're joined at the hip." Dana repeated his words with a bit of humor.

Shanks put the pen he'd been toying with down on the desk. "Good. I just needed to say it."

"Message received," Laurie said. "You don't think John had anything to do with this, do you?"

"I doubt it. I'm sure he's being framed, but we'll investigate his firm's finances thoroughly."

"Thank you." Laurie widened her eyes to stop the tears that were threatening.

"So, I have news," Shanks said.

They waited a beat for him to continue. Laurie tried not to roll her eyes and asked, "What's the news, Jonathan?"

"Men," Rosa sniffed.

"Tell me about it," Laurie said under the cover of Shanks' rustling papers on his desk. Oliver had stayed home with her father this morning.

"I miss my dog," her father had explained. "I want to take him for a hike." Laurie had offered Rosa the opportunity to go with them, but the little Havanese had opted to stick with her, explaining she was her emotional support dog.

Shanks spoke up at last. "We've traced the emails between Laurie and Kimberly and have proof they're fakes."

They all perked up and so did Rosa's ears.

"That's great news. Did you find out where they originated from?" Dana asked.

"I was just about to tell you that," Shanks said.

He seemed touchy this morning, Laurie thought. Maybe his wife had him in the doghouse.

"And what would be the problem with that?" Rosa sniffed.

"Whoever did this sent us on a merry chase through Boston to London, then Singapore, Auckland, Johannesburg, Lima, New York, and finally—" he paused for effect "—Galactic."

They all sat up in surprise. "You've got to be kidding," Dana said.

"Galactic? That is just—" Skye searched for a word.

"Do we know which part of Galactic? I mean, they are—" Laurie waved her hands, searching for the right word. She gave up. "—galactic. You know, really big."

Her friends frowned at her ineloquence. Shanks tried to stifle a laugh but failed.

"Hey, cut me some slack. Being a murder suspect is stressful."

Dana looked back at Shanks and rephrased the question. "Could you trace the source from inside Galactic?"

"Yes," he exclaimed, eyes bright behind his round glasses.

They waited.

"Think you could maybe tell us, Jonathan?" Dana's sarcasm threated to strip the varnish off the desk.

"It's just so delicious." His smile reminded Laurie of the Cheshire Cat. She ran her gaze over Shanks, checking for any evidence he might be high. His pupils seemed to be the normal size. No odd stains on his hands. It couldn't be drugs. He'd been sharp so far.

"The office of Baldwin Cress."

"Holy shit." Laurie felt like she'd gotten an electric shock.

"Geez Louise," Skye whispered.

"Now we're getting somewhere," Dana wiped her hands like she about to dive into something delicious.

Shanks held up a cautionary finger. "Except we don't know if his assistant uses his computer. Or for that matter, how many other people in his office use it. It could even be someone in IT who made it appear the emails came from there."

"But what possible motivation could Cress have to want to come after me?" Laurie asked.

"I want to do background checks on everyone who works in his office. We already checked out the IT department. Only two people warranted extra investigation."

"That must have been a huge job," Laurie said.

"Yes, but we have some—" he steepled his fingers and looked over them like the same Cheshire Cat pleased with a mouse at its mercy "—outside help, shall we say."

"Mania," Dana explained.

Shanks blew out a breath, annoyed Dana had stolen his thunder. "Yes, but we also employ a white-hat hacking firm from time to time."

"You can get those people to work together in an office?" Skye asked.

They all chuckled. "I don't inquire too closely as long as they get the job done," Shanks said. He fidgeted with some papers on his desk. "Now, if you ladies—"

Skye shot him a look.

"Uh, women would just exercise more caution in your investigations, it would be helpful. I'll let you know as soon as we know more. And thank you, Ms. Yarrow, for signing your DND form—" he looked over his round glasses, which seemed an impossible feat to Laurie "—at last."

Skye snorted. "You're welcome."

On their way out of Shanks' office, Dana's phone buzzed. She rolled her eyes. "This must be my office. They seem to think I have to approve every little thing." But when she pulled the phone out of her pocket, she stopped in the middle of the sidewalk in surprise. "It's Sandy Jones."

"Answer it," Laurie said over her shoulder. Rosa pulled her toward the shrubbery next to the building entrance.

The little dog walked behind a bush and squatted. After half a minute, she trotted back to Laurie. "All buildings should have dog bathrooms,"

"Umm, good idea." She joined her friends who'd walked into an alcove.

Dana kept repeating "Uh, huh" while she listened. She ended the call and looked up, her eyes sparkling. "Sandy has more information. We're meeting her at an open house. More privacy that way."

DANA FELT like the pied piper driving over the bridge to Bellevue. She hadn't given the toll a second thought before heading that way, but wondered if Skye would mind. Her friend lived out in Duvall though, so they must have some kind of monthly pass if they were available. Watching the water and seagulls diving relaxed her a little.

Minh and Hoa seemed to be doing well in school. She remembered being their age, how much she'd kept secret from her parents. Minh had just gotten his driver's license and who knew what he was up to. She didn't worry about him as much as his sister. Maybe that was sexist, but girls could suffer more serious consequences from indiscretions. They had to be careful about so many things—walking at night, going to parties, watching their drinks for roofies.

Adrenaline shot through her. She better not be drinking. Hoa had just turned fourteen, and girls that age were still impressionable, wanting to go with the crowd. The female singers the kids listened to set a good example as strong women, although they could certainly put on a few more clothes. Dana chuckled at herself, realizing she sounded like her own parents fussing about the rock stars of her day. She'd survived being a teenager and so would her kids. They were smart.

Then there was Kevin. When he'd been elected to the state legislature, he started spending more time in Olympia than home, even when the legislature wasn't in session. She had to admit she didn't miss him as much as she thought she would. When he did come home, he was distracted. They weren't close anymore. The trial separation proved more comfortable than she'd anticipated. If she decided to move on from the marriage, they could co-parent and she'd be freed up. But did she want to date? Maybe, but this was a moot point. He had big political plans, running for the House of

Representatives first, then on to the U.S. Senate. Just last month, he'd asked that they withdraw their separation agreement, stay married but live separately. It would be an impediment to his election if they were divorced. She dreaded the public scrutiny when this happened. They'd have to figure it out.

She checked her rearview mirror to see if her ducklings were still following behind. Skye's Subaru rode her bumper, too close for comfort, and she spotted Laurie two cars back. She glanced out over the water again. Mt. Rainier's majestic white cone peeked through the clouds, almost a ghost.

"You rang?" Kimberly asked in the back.

Dana jerked in surprise, but kept her hands on the wheel steady. "You need a doorbell or something. I was thinking about the mountain."

"Rainier is out today. Well, sort of. Like a ghost." Kimberly tried to mimic Dana's voice.

"You're listening to me nonstop? Could I have some privacy please?"

"Relax. I don't spy on you all the time. I felt a tug. What's happening?"

"We're off to see Sandy Jones. She has some news."

"Ugh, the one who tried to blackmail me."

"She was only the courier. Besides, she wants this settled as much as we do. There's more. We just discovered the fake emails you received from Laurie—"

"They weren't fake. I got them. I read them." Kimberly's tone was indignant.

"Yes, but she didn't send them. We found out they originated from Galactic. From the CEO's office."

"Galactic? That doesn't make any sense."

"It is strange. We're putting the picture together, though. I think Sandy will have another puzzle piece."

"That's why I'm tagging along. I still can't see who was behind all this."

"You're welcome to come, but please don't interrupt. This is important and I don't want to be distracted. We can talk afterward."

The ghost pushed out her translucent lips in a pretend pout. "Okay, I can do that for you."

Dana thought that death was doing Kimberly some good.

"I heard that," the ghost said and disappeared.

"And here I thought you were interested in who killed you," Dana mumbled. She followed the directions from her GPS to the open house, which turned out to be another three-story contemporary made up mostly of floor to ceiling windows. Eager to check out the views, Dana parked in the side driveway and tapped her foot as her friends tried various parking places and took their time getting out of their cars.

Laurie let Rosa off her leash and seemed to be having a conversation with her. The little dog woofed, ran behind some newly planted bushes, and squatted. She came back and received what Dana considered exorbitant praise for performing a basic bodily function. Cats were so much easier. Finally, they joined her on the driveway.

"Wow, this place is something." Skye tilted her head back, trying to take in the soaring walls in front of them. Not many windows on the street side.

Dana nodded. "Sandy's selling some high end real estate. She seems to be doing well."

"I hope she's with a client so we can pretend to be shopping and see the whole house," Laurie said.

Dana wasn't entirely sure she was pretending. They opened the double door in front and walked through a short hallway to an open kitchen, dining room, and family area. But they didn't linger. The view drew them to the vast array of windows. Lake Washington lay spread out in all its splendor. The clouds had cleared and Mount Rainier rose in the distance, pure white against a blue sky.

"Oh, my goddess," Skye breathed. "Would you look at this view."

"It's amazing, isn't it?" They turned to find Sandy with a well turned out couple beside her. She flashed her high-beam realtor smile at them. "Why don't you ladies look around while I finish chatting with these folks."

"We'd love to," Dana said. Since Kevin wanted to live separately, she might just sell the house and move. Start fresh. She peered down at the lake and spotted a private landing. Oh, yeah.

"Dogs are not supposed to be in the house." Sandy pointed to Rosa, who trotted over to her and sat at attention, her eyes bright.

"We'll be extra careful, won't we Rosa?" Laurie said.

"As long as you keep an eye on her." She gave Laurie a dark look her customers couldn't see.

The wife bent down and offered her hand for the little Havanese to sniff. "May I?"

"Of course," Laurie said just as Rosa licked her fingers politely.

"I just adore Bichon Frise dogs."

Laurie blinked in surprise, but only said, "They're the best."

Good for the professor for not correcting her, Dana thought. The alleged Bichon Frise gave both of these new people a good sniff. Rather too thorough, in her opinion. Then she remembered the dog had smelled the killer on Laurie's clothes because he'd run into her while pushing Kimberly to her death. She watched Rosa return to Laurie. Something seemed to pass between them. Dana caught a faint smile from Laurie.

Dana waited until the wife stood, then ushered them into the family area where she had brochures laid out on a coffee table. They sat and started negotiations. Dana felt a surge of possessiveness. Was this her new house? Was she kidding herself?

The four of them explored the double oven, eight burners on the stove, and two-section refrigerator with glass doors. Just as Dana ran her hand down the granite countertop, admiring the swirls of color, she heard, "Of course, we want to replace that granite with white crystal."

"Naturally," Sandy replied.

Skye's eyes boggled. "Holy shit. Let's get out of here," she whispered in Dana's ear.

They walked back through the hallway, Dana poking Skye to hurry so she wouldn't make faces at the richer echelon. Palatial stairs led to a hallway with a series of doors along it, all open for convenient viewing. A sprawling master bedroom was the last, offering an even more spectacular view of the lake and Seattle's skyscrapers to the right.

Oh yeah, Dana thought.

"Check out this sink," Laurie called from the bathroom.

Dana joined her. "Nice. An erosion sink. It's the latest thing. Concentric, slightly irregular circles mimicking what water running over stone does over years."

Laurie ran her hand over the ridges. "It's beautiful, but do people really need this kind of luxury with the world like it is?"

I wouldn't mind it, Dana thought.

Skye rushed to the doorway. "This closet has a bar in it."

"Like an exercise bar?" Laurie asked.

"No, like a give-me-a-whiskey-sour kind of bar."

Laurie shook her head. "I can't even."

"They're called California closets. I heard some advertisement where some woman was swooning over how her new closet was like an oasis." Dana mimicked her gushing voice.

"Up until the Restoration or even later, most people had two sets of clothes they hung from hooks on the wall," Laurie declared.

"Restoration?" Skye asked. "Is that some kind of remodeling thing?"

"Eighteenth century Britain when King Charles—"

"I heard he's sick and he's just been crowned," Skye interrupted. "It's sad, waiting all this time—"

"Not that King Charles," Laurie objected.

Dana put her hands on her hips. "Thank you, Professor. Shall we go see if Sandy is free to talk?"

Laurie looked down at Rosa. The two must have exchanged a comment, but Dana ignored them and marched out of the room. They ran into Sandy coming up the stairs. "Let me tell you what I've discovered before anybody else comes. I thought this would be a quiet day since it's Tuesday, but it's a hot property."

"Pretty spectacular," Dana said. She loved the view, but had to be realistic. She'd be rattling around in this huge house when the kids moved out. They trooped down the stairs and settled in the family area where Sandy had set up for business talks. Dana glanced at the brochure and caught the sales price. Nine million plus. That took the wind out of her sails.

Sandy got right to the point. "My staff did some digging into the shell corporations. Guess what we found?"

A flash of movement caught Dana's eye. Kimberly appeared in an empty chair next to Sandy, leaning in. So she was interested in who killed her after all. Dana sat forward. "Do tell."

"They lead back to Galactic."

"Oh, my," Laurie said.

"Geez Louise," Skye exclaimed.

Sandy pulled back in surprise. "Who?"

"It's just an expression," Skye explained with a wave of her hand.

Sandy looked dubious, but continued. "Galactic seemed awfully cooperative about holding our reunion at their facility. The committee asked me to find a deluxe location at a good price. When they told me Galactic had contacted them and volunteered, I thought it was a bit odd. They're doing community events, but high school reunions? Not the usual charity venture. But who would turn that offer down, know what I mean?"

Dana nodded. "We've just discovered some other incriminating evidence that leads back to Galactic." She explained a bit about the fake emails without giving away too much information.

Sandy listened, her face eager. "That seals the deal for me at least. I think Baldwin Cress might have helped with the blackmailing scheme."

"What? How could anybody there possibly have any interest in Kimberly?" Laurie asked.

Sandy jabbed her finger at Laurie. "Exactamundo. But who is their new prize racehorse?"

"He's investing in racehorses?" Laurie asked, looking confused.

Sandy gave her a condescending look. "No, who is his latest and greatest new author? Selling millions? Multi-million dollar movie contract?"

"Walter Pearce!" all three of them said at once.

The three friends glanced at each other, no doubt thinking of Skye's latest discovery about the clue in Walter's first book.

Sandy didn't notice their conspiratorial look. "That's the only thing I can figure. You remember the prank the in-crowd pulled on him after the prom?"

"Yes, we've heard several versions of it," Dana said. Actually, they'd only heard two. Really only one and a half since Peggy hadn't told them the whole truth.

"Now that Walter is enjoying so much success, my theory is he's taken it into his head to pay back the people who humiliated him in high school. Apparently Kimberly was the prime organizer of that little stunt and maybe he was the one blackmailing her. But he covered his identity by going through Galactic."

"That stunt wasn't so little," Skye murmured, but Sandy was focused on Dana now.

"Why would Galactic put itself at risk like this?" Dana asked.

Sandy's gray eyes turned icy. "Baldwin Cress gives Walter a lot of perks. One is using his personal yacht for parties. Not the ginormous one. One of the guys who captains his ship whispered to me one night—"

"How did you—" Dana started to ask.

"Never mind that," Sandy said firmly. "Walter hires women, lots of them. He's into some kinky sex. I'd say bondage, but he takes it too far. A couple women have been badly hurt."

"This is some twisted stuff," Skye said.

"Isn't Baldwin worried this will cause trouble for him? That there will be a criminal case or something?" Laurie asked.

Sandy snorted. "Yeah, try suing that guy. These women live on the fringes. They can't press any charges. They can barely afford medical treatment."

"Do you suspect the two of them are in this together?" Dana asked.

Sandy lifted a shoulder. "There's no evidence of that, but who can say?"

The three looked at each other. Shanks might have the evidence.

"Do you think Walter has something on Baldwin?" Skye asked.

Sandy frowned. "I think he's just pampering Walter. Letting him use one of his boats. Announcing his movie contract at the reunion. Walter seems to have a lot of access at Galactic. I hope this will help clear you somehow, Laurie."

"Thank you," Laurie said.

"This is helpful," Dana said.

Rosa jumped to her feet and barked.

Dana laughed. "Even I understand that."

She looked over at Kimberly, who had been silent, listening intently during Sandy's revelation. But the ghost was studying Laurie, a mixture of sadness and was it envy on her face? Kimberly must have felt Dana's attention. She looked over at her and gave her a nod. Now they were getting somewhere.

CHAPTER

TWENTY-TWO

The three friends convened at a local coffeeshop to digest the day's news. Laurie clipped the leash onto Rosa's collar and locked the car. Inside, she ordered a latte at the counter.

"I'm sorry, ma'am. Dogs are not allowed in here," the seventeen-going-on-forty year old behind the counter told her.

She eyed his head, shaved on two sides with a bird's nest of curls on top. She'd heard the boys were getting permanent waves these days, as her grandmother had called them in the 1950s. "Who does your perm?" she asked.

He flushed. By this time, Skye and Dana had joined her and they were all studying his hairdo. "You ladies can sit outside with the dog."

"Did he call me a lady?" Skye mumbled, just loud enough for him to hear.

Dana pointed to the patio seating. "It's raining."

The boy looked confused. He opened his mouth to say something, maybe to explain it was Seattle and of course it was raining, but seemed to think better of it.

"She's an emotional support dog," Laurie added.

He heaved a sigh. "What else can I get you—" he gave Skye a wary glance "—two."

They settled at a table in a corner and when their drinks arrived, so did a treat for Rosa. The ball of fluff gave his hand a sniff and scarfed the dog biscuit. "He didn't do it."

Laurie rolled her eyes. "You do realize everyone is not a suspect. That kid was nowhere near the reunion."

Rosa eyed her. "I'm just lifting your leg."

"You mean pulling my leg?"

"Whatever." Rosa jumped up into the empty seat and curled up. Her human glanced around to see if anyone noticed.

"The floor is dirty," Rosa explained.

"It's okay. Nobody's objecting," Laurie said. She looked up to find her two friends watching them, amusement clear on their faces. "She says the floor's too dirty," Laurie explained.

They both looked down. "Can't say as I blame her," Dana said, her lips pursed in distaste.

Instead of launching into a recap as usual, everyone just sat back, sipping coffee or chai as the case might be. Skye perused the local weekly, one leg crossed over the other, swinging back and forth. Laurie leaned back and let all the latest revelations wash over her. Neither Shanks or Sandy had discovered an explanation for why John's corporation had been found in the shell companies buying the mansion up in Shoreline. Maybe she should apologize to him. Explain the new discoveries about Galactic and Walter's close connection with their owner. That she didn't suspect John now.

But this rankled. He should have understood the pressure she was under. Should have shown sympathy for her. Explained that his company wasn't buying any mansions. Not just stomped out of the Cup and Saucer. If he thought he was shocked at Sandy's accusation of his possible involvement, he should imagine how shocked she'd been when she was accused of murder. And then arrested.

Laurie took a sip of her latte. The warmth soothed her. She was surprised how much she wanted John back. Had lived quite happily without him all these years, thank you very much. She was still pissed at him. Damn it, where had her independence gone? She was doing just fine on her own. Rosa opened one eye to study her, then closed it again, apparently satisfied she was not going to do something crazy.

Laurie wondered how Baldwin Cress was tied up in all this. Maybe he wasn't. Maybe Walter had wormed his way in with a few people at Galactic and used them to plant Living Earth Designs in that list. Gotten to somebody in IT who sent the fake emails.

"We should check Galactic's IT to see if anyone there was in high school with us," she said, "or insulted Walter in some way. I know Shanks says they've already cleared them, but I think we should take another look."

Dana nodded. "We'll get Mania to check, but hundreds of people could have insulted Walter over the years."

"Or he could have imagined they did," Laurie added.

"All right," Skye said, rattling the newspaper she was holding.

Rosa opened both eyes.

"What?" Laurie asked.

"Says here that D.J. Stone—" she said the name with sarcasm "—aka Walter Pearce is doing a reading from his new novel tomorrow night at the latest Galactic Bookstore in Pioneer Square."

"I'll bet Elliot Bay Books doesn't appreciate them being in the neighborhood," Laurie said, fond memories of sitting in their downstairs café and writing in her journal floating by.

"They closed down ages ago," Dana informed her.

"That's sad. I loved that place." Laurie took another sip of her latte.

"He's got readings the rest of the week and a big gala on Saturday night at—" Skye's smile was smug "—our favorite place, Galactic."

"We should go," Laurie said. "We're on a tight schedule."

"I'll bring the kids. They need some culture," Dana said.

Laurie studied her friend to see if she was being sarcastic. I mean, they were talking about D.J. Stone here, not Thomas Wolfe. "Maybe they can peruse the shelves while he reads to find some culture."

Dana shot her a look. "So tomorrow night?"

"Tots, as my niece says. Bring Rosa. She can give him a good sniff, can't you girl?" Skye reached over and scratched the little Havanese under her chin.

Rosa gave a woof and several customers at the other tables looked up, one frowning, but two more smiling. Two approached, wanting to pet her.

"Sounds like a plan," Laurie said.

"We'll get Mania to check that IT list. See if there's anyone else to —" Dana's eye cut to the young man making cooing noises at Rosa "—interview for the position."

"Good." Laurie stood, getting ready to leave, but she had to wait for an older woman to pet the dog.

"You're slowing me down." She sent the thought to Rosa.

"Can I help how adorable I am?"

Laurie snorted, earning her a look from the older woman. "She's a bit of a diva, but I love her to pieces."

This seemed to mollify the dog lover.

GALACTIC HAD INDEED TAKEN over the space of the old Elliott Bay Books. A young woman suffering from terminal excitement pointed them up some stairs that opened into a big room taking up the entire second floor. Apparently, the company had bought the whole building. Gotta spend that money somehow, Laurie thought. Wooden floors gleamed under tastefully placed ceiling lights. Half the chairs were already filled and the low buzz of conversation filled the space. Posters of the book cover and movie ads dotted the walls. They must have taken the usual art display down for this event.

"I thought we were early enough to get places toward the front," Skye said as they settled in aisle seats halfway back from the raised platform serving as a stage.

"We'll have to figure out a way to get Rosa close enough to smell him," Laurie said.

"I have quite a good nose." The little dog sniffed as if to demonstrate.

"Yeah, but there are a lot of people here. How can you pick out one smell from all the rest?" she asked.

A woman dressed in a tweed jacket turned her head and frowned at Laurie. Laurie realized she'd said that out loud. Get a grip, she told herself.

"You get a grip," Rosa answered.

Laurie just shook her head. Two men scooted into their row of seats from the other side, coming toward them quickly. Laurie poked Skye. "Hurry up. Save three more seats." Skye put her backpack on the seat next to her, then spread her coat over the next two.

One of them stopped and raised an eyebrow. "Are people allowed to save seats at these events?" he asked his partner.

The more burly of the two just shrugged. "Let's sit here. I've got a good view."

Laurie and Skye waited in silence, hesitant to talk about the case in public. Laurie searched for a neutral topic. "How's Jade?"

"Good. She got assigned to help with the case she brought to the captain's attention."

So they were going to talk about the case, after all. "That's good, I guess," Laurie said.

"It is. She wants to move up the ladder. They've made some progress." Skye waggled her eyebrows.

Laurie felt a stab of irritation. She couldn't ask for details in this crowd. Maybe a text. She took out her phone, but realized that wasn't a good idea. They would subpoena all her electronics. She'd have to wait. Rosa settled her head on Laurie's foot to comfort her.

Dana arrived, Hoa and Minh tagging along behind, and scooted down the row to the saved seats. The two men who'd objected earlier looked somewhat mollified.

"I can't believe she made us come to this lame reading," Minh complained to his sister.

"It's your fault. You snuck out of the house last time she was out at night. Then tried to sneak back in at two in the morning." The teen let out a dramatic sigh.

"It's not my fault. You're the one who—"

"Hush," their mother said and pointed to the front where the excited woman who had greeted everyone approached the mic. She tapped it and a loud squeal came from the speakers. Rosa barked. A couple of people in the row in front of her nodded in agreement.

"Oh, sorry." The woman grimaced. She grabbed the mic and it squealed again. Backing off, she took a deep breath and approached the mic as if it might jump at her. She leaned forward. "Welcome to the first public reading of D.J. Stone's novel *Long Awaited Fall*." Satisfied the mic would not bite, her eagerness returned. "It's just awesome to see so many people here. But before we get started, I want to tell you about some other events Galactic is sponsoring."

"That title is a dead giveaway," Skye whispered.

"Pure hubris," Dana mumbled.

Laurie just nodded. She tuned out the woman at the front and looked around to see if she recognized anyone. All the seats had filled and people lined the walls. Surely they were over capacity, but given what she was learning, the fire department would probably let it go since Baldwin Cress was such a big deal to the city's economy. She wondered if he would put in an appearance.

Dana gave a few little waves to people she knew, but Laurie didn't recognize anybody. She'd been gone most of her life. She had to admit that John had been the one luring her back to Seattle. Taking up their teenage vision of saving the whales along with the planet now that they were old enough to know what to do. It seemed John had been pursuing his goal all along, probably salvaging one dream after having to give up so much by marrying Kimberly.

After their last meeting, though, maybe she should just stay in Boston. Then she glanced over at the two women sitting by her side.

Her friends who'd stuck by her from the beginning of this disaster. They'd kept up with each other all their lives. Been there to celebrate marriages, jobs, children. To help each other through deaths in their families. Who were there for midnight calls when something terrible happened. She couldn't think of anybody in Boston who was this loyal, who knew her so well, who was so much fun. Reaching over, she gave Skye's hand a squeeze.

Skye looked up, surprised. Then a look of understanding came over her face. "We've got you, kid," she said and squeezed back.

Laurie blinked back a sudden rush of tears. Good Lord, this whole thing was turning her into a hot mess. She tensed as the word 'hot' went through her mind, but her body did not heat up this time. One thing was for sure, though. She was done arranging her life around men.

Then she saw him. Leaning against the wall, watching her. His dark eyebrows arched over stormy brown eyes. Stubble graced a sharp jaw softened by those familiar lips. Had he gotten so upset he'd stopped shaving? Under a brown leather jacket, a white T-shirt stretched across his chest. His thumbs rested in the pockets of distressed jeans, more old than stylish.

Whoa. How had she not realized how smoking hot he still was? Heat kindled in her core. But was it him or an impending hot flash? She tore her gaze away and leaned down to check on Rosa.

"Your mate is here," the little dog informed her.

"Yes, I saw." Then with a shake of her head, she asked. "Why do you keep saying that?"

"Why do you keep resisting?" Rosa sniffed and put her head back on Laurie's foot. Even though the little Havanese thought she was foolish, Laurie found her closeness comforting.

The excitable young woman on stage had finished her rundown of all the awesome events they should all go to in the next month. "If she says 'awesome' one more time, I'm going to throttle her," Skye said.

Two people in the row ahead of them nodded in agreement.

Minh leaned over and whispered, "Awesome."

Skye shot him a look and Dana took a sharp breath to say something, but the woman on stage cut her off. "And now please welcome our awesome author—"

Skye growled and Laurie couldn't hold back a snigger.

"—D.J. Stone." She held both arms out to her right and the famous author walked on stage.

As a picked-on teenager, Walter had stooped, hiding his six feet and some inches frame. But now he stood tall, shoulders back, head held high. His pleasantly tussled hair had been styled, replacing the tweedy professor look with a man in full command of the room. He still had the round glasses, though, which he pushed up his nose after leaning down to the mic.

Why did all middle-aged men wear round glasses, Laurie wondered.

An assistant ran out and adjusted the mic to accommodate his height. Walter looked around. "Wow, what a crowd. I can hardly believe it. Thank you all for coming."

More applause broke out and he basked in it for a moment before pushing his hands down to quiet everyone. "Thank you, thank you. As you know, my first novel is a major motion picture—"

Minh and Hoa snickered at this old fashioned phrase. At least that's what Laurie assumed.

"—to be released in the fall. Tonight, I'll be reading from my next novel, *Long Awaited Fall*. My friends at Galactic rushed it to print and we're happy to report I'll be signing copies later." Walter looked at a teleprompter and cleared his throat.

"He looks just like a politician," Dana whispered.

Laurie couldn't concentrate on the reading. Worries about the trial kept running through her head replacing Walter's words. Then fury followed next at the idea that this nerd had set her up for a murder he might have committed. And here he was, trying to extort a million dollars from poor Kimberly when he was finally making good money himself. Had she just thought 'poor Kimberly'? She'd started this craziness with that scene on the boat. This led to images of Walter entwined with young Eastern European women caught up in the sex trade. She screwed up her face in disgust.

All the while, John stood there, sexy as all hell. She glanced up and found him staring at her. Laurie's body stirred. She jerked her head forward. How could she respond to him while this pervert was up front reading to them? Laurie shifted in her seat. Rosa sat up and started scratching her neck. Her tags jingled. Laurie would have to get her new tags, but she needed to decide if she was moving here first. If she was in prison, her parents would take care of it. She had to find out who really killed Kimberly. She glared at Walter.

Rosa scratched again, her tags loud in a sudden pause in the reading. A few people stirred in their chair. One looked around and saw the little Havanese. He frowned at the noise. Walter started reading again.

The third time Rosa set her dog tags jangling, at least ten people turned and gave her the evil eye. How could this little dog be making so much noise? Laurie gave up. Reaching down, she unbuckled Rosa's collar and left it beside the little Havanese. "Lie down and be quiet, please," Laurie sent to her.

Heads turned back to the reading. Blessed silence reigned.

Or at least silence from Rosa. Walter's self-absorbed voice boomed out as he approached the climax of the scene.

Eww, Laurie thought as that word flashed in her mind. An unbidden image of him shouting his release as he banged some unwilling young woman on Baldwin's yacht. Honestly, they had to find solid evidence against him.

Rosa trotted up the steps to the stage, tail held high. Laurie felt her mouth fall opened in shock. She couldn't believe her eyes.

Oh, no. She rose halfway out of her chair.

"Holy shit, is that Rosa?" Skye asked, forgetting to whisper.

The little dog ran across the stage, stopped next to Walter while he was at the height of his finish, and started sniffing his right leg.

Laurie froze. Like an idiot, she looked down at her feet where the collar and leash lay on the ground by her shoes. Then back up at the stage.

Rosa had moved to Walter's left leg. A confused look crept over the author's face. Getting carried away, the little dog put her front legs on his thigh and stretched up to sniff more of his body.

"Aww," a few murmurs swept through the audience.

Well, she was cute, Laurie thought. "Rosa," she called, her voice strangled.

Walter looked down. His face turned bright red. "What the hell? Get away from me, you mongrel." He shook his leg, flipping Rosa into the air. She yelped, but landed on her feet and tore around the infuriated Walter.

"Oh, no," someone shouted from the front.

"Poor puppy." A few boos and hisses came from the crowd. Seattle liked its dogs.

Walter looked up at his audience, his face switching fast. "I'm sorry. The dog surprised me."

The moderator jumped to her feet. "Whose dog is this?"

But Rosa ignored the interruption she'd created, trotting down the aisle, her fawn tail held high, heading straight for Laurie. She arrived and sat at attention like a soldier who had accomplished a dangerous mission, her pink tongue hanging out.

"Is she hurt?" someone asked.

Laurie ran her hand down Rosa's side, then looked up. "She seems fine."

Chaos reigned at the front. Walter sputtered his apologies in the mic. The assistant flapped her hands.

But Rosa was undeterred. "He's the one," she said. "He did it."

CHAPTER

TWENTY-THREE

Laurie snapped the leash on Rosa and the three of them headed out before more disasters occurred. At the doorway, she waited for Dana to catch up. Her kids were in stitches, laughing their way down the aisle, whispering to each other. Laurie looked up and her eyes snagged on John, who watched her with a bemused expression on his face. He was an island of calm in the sea of chaos Rosa had created. Laurie wanted to run up to him and tell him...what though? He'd walked out on her. Just like he had in high school. Gone off and married the high school cheerleader like in some clichéd romance novel. A surge of anger made her face flush. More heat crept up her neck. Just what she needed. A hot flash on top of everything else. Later. She'd decide about him later.

Outside, they fled across Pioneer Square to a bar that had outdoor seating. The evening was warm enough for light jackets, but the restaurant had their patio heaters turned on. It was still Seattle after all, so Laurie sat away from these. Rosa jumped into her lap and showered her with kisses. "You'll be free now," Rosa said, eager to comfort her. "They'll put that other man in the orange outfit you've been so worried about."

"You are such a wonderful dog." Laurie buried her face in fawn fur, hugging the dog to her chest. "Thank you."

A waitress arrived and Dana ordered wine. Laurie asked for a cold beer from some local microbrewery, but Skye opted for a Hot Toddy. Laurie thought she must not be going through menopause yet. Once their drinks arrived, Laurie put her hands around the cool glass and explained what Rosa had told her.

"So he's behind it. Meek Walter Pearce." Dana was talking to the empty chair next to her. Must be Kimberly. "Something changed him."

Skye looked at the chair. "That humiliation you dished out must have been the final straw for him."

"Uh, she's gone now," Dana said.

"Jerk," Skye mumbled.

Laurie took a sip of her beer. The cold washed away the rest of her hot flash, leaving behind a hint of citrus. She peered at the label and found lemons and oranges. She took another sip and looked up at her friends. "Too bad Rosa can't testify. We have to find hard evidence."

"I have an idea," Skye said.

Which was not always a good thing, Laurie thought.

ON SATURDAY NIGHT, Laurie couldn't decide if she should dress in skin-tight black latex like those black ops people in action movies did or just wear her ordinary joggers and a sweatshirt. Actually, she didn't own any black latex. Or anything skin-tight for that matter. It might smooth out her thighs, though. Maybe she'd get some once they nailed Walter. She found an old black hoodie with holes in it. Probably left over from high school. Poetic justice. She grabbed it to complete her outfit.

She snuck down the stairs, trying to walk without making any noise. Two steps creaked. She needed practice. In the family room, she mentally asked Oliver if he wanted to join them. He lumbered up from his bed and walked to her, his stubby tail wagging his whole rear end. She'd be glad when they stopped docking dogs' tails. It was barbaric. At least he still had his floppy ears.

"I'm going out with Skye and Laurie," she announced to her parents. "Might be late."

Her mother turned around and her brow furrowed. "Why do you have dark smudges all over your face?"

Blast, she'd forgotten. "Uh—" she had to think of something quick "—Dana's kids want to play a ninja game in the park. It will take my mind off things."

Both her parents stared at her in clear disbelief.

"Uh huh," her mother said.

"You're dressed like a burglar." Her father waved his hand at her outfit.

There was a moment of awkward silence.

Her mother fixed her father with a look. "First a defense attorney. Now she's falling into a life of crime."

Her father shook his head. "Whatever you're up to, I hope you three don't get caught."

"Ninja games in the park." God, she was reverting to being a teenager. Laurie turned and fled. Rosa ran after her, yipping with excitement. Oliver trotted along at his top speed. She didn't bother to attach their leashes. They jumped into the back of her rented Honda and waited for her to roll down their respective windows. She complied and they stuck out their heads, eager for the wind in their faces.

"Do we get to bite him?" Rosa asked.

"I wish, but he won't be there. He's at a big event and the house should be empty. That's why we're going tonight," Laurie explained. The event at Galactic should last well into late evening. Dana's crew had found invitations to an after party with some of the city's sparkling elite. Laurie hoped he had an after-after-hours night planned on Baldwin's yacht, but wasn't counting on it.

Walter had bought an older home on the Laurelhurst peninsula, which surprised her. She thought he would go for some all glass house, modern and sleek. The three friends met up at a playground about four blocks in from Lake Washington. "These rich folks don't like people parking on their street," Skye had explained. "Cars at the park won't draw attention. There are footpaths all through this area."

Laurie arrived first and let the dogs sniff around the grass. In just a few minutes, Skye piled out of her Subaru, with Dana pulling in right behind her. "Did you bring everything I told you to?" Skye asked.

Dana patted her sleek backpack. "Rope, flashlight. Mania explained how to turn off the security system."

"I brought the laser light for the cameras and—" Laurie rummaged in her own backpack. Skye had insisted they all have them "—my Swiss army knife has a lot of screwdrivers and blades."

Skye nodded. "Good. Let's go."

The old house turned more into a country manor the closer they got. One man passed them walking a Scottish terrier. They nodded amicably, but the dogs exchanged dark thoughts. Laurie tried to keep her face straight. They walked past Walter's driveway until the man was well around the curve of the road, then cut back.

"I checked this out on Goggle maps. There's a strip of woods between all the houses out here," Skye said.

"How'd you get to be such a good burglar?" Laurie asked.

Dana shushed her. "Don't say that word. You never know who will hear you."

"Jade tells a lot of stories," Skye whispered.

Somehow Laurie thought that wasn't the entire truth.

They snuck through the maple and madrone trees, careful not to get tangled in the thick underbrush, and emerged next to a large garage detached from the house. A green expanse of grass sloped down to a dock with a new boathouse. Laurie had been responsible for researching where Walter's office was and finding blueprints for the house, ridiculously easy these days. Realtors never seemed to take down listings that had already sold with helpful pictures of the rooms. Except this place had been remodeled within an inch of its life.

"His office is on the second floor in the back overlooking the lake. Easiest access is through the kitchen and up the stairs," Skye informed them.

They walked a few feet closer to the house. Skye reached out for the laser light and flashed the red beam into two dark corners and one above the glass double doors leading to the kitchen. Good thing the cats hadn't come, Laurie thought. She asked Rosa to run around the back yard so they could test the motion lights. One triggered, revealing a large deck off the kitchen. They waited for the light to turn off, which took what felt like forever. Oliver sat, a solid, reassuring presence by her side.

Skye had watched to see where they could walk without turning it on again. "Follow me exactly. Do not go any farther to the left." They crept up in blessed darkness to the side of the house. Dana grabbed onto the bottom rail of the deck and pulled herself up. She climbed over and made her way to the back door, hugging the house to avoid triggering the lights.

Skye followed her, surprisingly nimble for her size. Laurie watched, regretting her sedentary lifestyle. And what about Oliver? How was he supposed to get in?

"I'll stand guard," he said, his mental voice menacing.

"Wait here for now. We'll get you in somehow." Laurie pointed at Rosa. "You stay, too."

Rosa sniffed in disapproval.

Laurie turned on her flashlight and found a rock up close to the deck. She stepped on top of it and grabbed the railings. Stretching her leg out to the side, she got her foot on the deck floor and tried to push herself up, but couldn't get good leverage. She put her foot back down and tried to pull herself high enough to get a foothold. On her third try, she made it. Her scramble over the railing was not pretty, but at least she didn't trigger the lights.

She found Skye bent in front of the door, fiddling with the lock. "Yes," she whispered and opened the door. Dana dashed in and pushed in the security code. How her hacker had found it was beyond Laurie. They stood stock still, listening for any sound for a full minute.

"Clear," Skye said.

Honestly, she was getting into this role a bit too much, Laurie thought. She'd imagined it would be Dana who turned all black ops.

Laurie went in search of the outdoor light switches. They seemed to be on a timer, but she figured it out and turned them off. She opened the back door to let the dogs in. Rosa ran across the deck, her fawn coat a blur of white under the moon. Oliver trotted up the stairs and into the kitchen, his claws clicking on the wood floor.

"No barking," Laurie told them. "Let us know if anybody's coming." The dogs sat at attention, ready. With a nod, Laurie walked out of the kitchen, taking the lead. She moved silently down the hallway to the front entry and up the stairs, everyone following. She gestured for Dana to search to the left and she turned right, Skye and Rosa on her heels. Oliver sat at the top of the stairs, somehow resembling a gargoyle.

Most of the doors had been left open. The first room off the stairs seemed to be a guest room. Skye went in to search it. They didn't know what they'd find. Weapons, the black hoodie, probably any correspondence would be in his office. The low blue and green lights of electronics came from the last room on the right. Mania had already cracked Walter's passcode, which was Vengance94$. That should have been enough to convict him, in Laurie's opinion. Not to mention the title of his new novel.

She found Dana in Walter's bedroom in front of the nightstand. She looked up as Laurie ran in. Dana pointed at an open drawer. Laurie moved closer to find an imaginative collection of sex toys.

"He just doesn't look the type," Laurie whispered.

Dana's lips drew up in disgust. "I don't want to touch them."

"Luckily, you don't have to. I found his computer."

Skye arrived at the door. "What are you two staring at?"

Dana pointed. "I need to go hack his computer."

Skye looked at the contents of the drawer, and without a word, took some purple latex gloves out of her pocket and strapped them on like a pro. Laurie had a moment of panic. What was Skye going to do? But her friend started pushing the toys around, looking for a weapon, Laurie hoped.

Dana backed away and the two returned to Walter's office, leaving Skye to her search. Out the window, dark water gleamed under the gibbous moon. "I don't think the neighbors will notice a light," Dana said. She switched on the desk lamp and got to work on the computer.

Laurie looked through Walter's files. The top drawer held financial information. Papers on the house, two cars. Insurance documents. Then she found book contracts. The next file had the movie deal. Curiosity got the best of her and she peeked to see how much he was getting. A measly $50,000 for the rights. At least it seemed small to her. Still, it was a year's salary for an assistant professor. She kept reading. He had a percentage on profits from the film. One percent. Laurie felt indignant on behalf of all writers. Where would these actors and directors be with no script?

Skye arrived about fifteen minutes later. "Nothing in the bedrooms or baths. Need help here?"

"There's lots of files. Might be something in his notes on the books. Take pictures of anything you think might be relevant."

Skye opened the next file drawer, but there wasn't room for them both. "Mind if I take Rosa and search the garage?" Laurie asked.

Dana looked up, her face lit from the glow of the computer screen. "Good idea."

Laurie headed down the stairs. Oliver got up to follow. "You stay. Guard the others," she said. The boxer mix settled at the top of the stairs and put his head on his paws.

"No falling asleep."

He closed his eyes.

253

Laurie retraced her steps down the stairs with Rosa at her heels, making her way through the kitchen and across the deck. The silent beauty of the moonlit lake stopped her for a moment, settling her nerves, then she headed off to the large, detached garage on the side of the property near the tree line. She stood in front of two roller doors, looking for a way to open them. A keypad attached to the side blended in so well she almost missed it. Laurie lifted the top and searched for an emergency override. No such luck.

Rosa barked and trotted down the side of the structure. Laurie followed, looking for a side door, but Rosa was ahead of her. The Havanese sat in front of a door, intent as any bird dog. Laurie walked up to it, but the little dog nipped at her heels.

"What's gotten into you?" she whispered.

Laurie reached for the knob. Rosa growled, a vicious sound she'd never heard the dog make before.

She leaned down. "What's wrong, girl? Why aren't you talking to me?" She waited for an answer, but Rosa seemed fixated on the door. Could there be an animal in there? A skunk or possum, triggering Rosa's instinct to chase like she had in the arboretum the other day? She opened the door and Rosa ran in front of her straight to a shadowy corner. She bared her teeth and snarled.

"Your dog is smarter than you are." A figure emerged from the dark, arm extended.

Laurie froze. The voice didn't sound like Walter.

The figure stepped out of the corner and a beam of light from the moon glinted on the object in his hand. A gun.

Laurie's knees turned to water, but she managed to stay standing. Her hands went up almost on their own.

Rosa barked furiously.

The gun wavered down to the dog.

Now was the time to do something. Laurie remembered the Swiss Army knife. "Please don't shoot my dog. Please," she begged, hoping to distract whoever this was. She unzipped her backpack. The zipper made a sound and the gun came back up.

"Don't try anything stupid." The figure took another step forward and the moonlight fell on her face.

"Peggy Anderson."

"Surprised you, didn't I?"

Rosa whined.

"Come here, girl." Laurie bent down to pick up the furious dog.

Peggy waved the gun toward the side door. "Outside. Head toward the dock."

"Peggy, what are you doing?"

"Shut up. Do what I say."

Laurie turned around, holding the squirming Rosa to her chest, and walked out onto the lawn.

"No, stay over here in the shadows. We don't want your fat friend to see us."

"Really?" Laurie turned her head toward Peggy. "You had to go there?"

"Keep walking."

Laurie watched the ground, careful of her steps. Maybe falling was a good idea. She'd be out of range of the gun. Able to grab her knife. She couldn't believe she had the presence of mind to think strategically. But they were already at the dock where a small motorboat waited, hidden behind the boathouse.

"Get in," Peggy said.

Maybe she could capsize the boat. At least rock it. Make Peggy drop the gun. She angled her body sideways and put her foot on the gunwale.

"No, step into the middle." Peggy knelt behind her, one hand steadying the small craft, the gun pointing into Laurie's back.

It was now or never. Laurie kicked at Peggy's face, but the ex-cheerleader ducked just in time. She surged up, pushing Laurie into the hull.

Laurie fell sideways, losing her grip on Rosa, landing hard on her side. She sat up to see Rosa streaking up the dock toward the house.

"Tell Dana and Skye it's Peggy Anderson," she mentally sent to the dog. She tried to stand.

Peggy slammed her back with an oar. Laurie fell and hit her head on the edge of the seat. She scrambled to sit up, tilting the small craft. A weight dropped into the middle, righting the boat. Peggy revved up the motor and roared out into the middle of the lake, the sudden speed knocking Laurie back down. She reached up and touched a growing knot on her head. Her fingers came away wet, the blood showing up black in the moonlight.

Then Laurie remembered. She was the only one who could hear the animals' thoughts.

CHAPTER

TWENTY-FOUR

ana heard Laurie tell the boxer mix to stand guard, then clamber down the stairs. She turned back to the computer, trying to concentrate. Should she look at his emails first or dive into his word documents? The fake emails between Laurie and Kimberly were sent from Galactic, so she wouldn't find them here. Unless he'd managed to pull a hack. Maybe he had drafts. She opened his word files.

"I mean, Walter Pearce? Who would have thought he had the balls?"

Dana jerked in surprise. She looked up to find Kimberly perched on a chair across from the office desk.

"I guess you changed him," she muttered and turned her attention back to the screen.

"What does that mean?"

Dana's head came up with a snap. "Are you really this clueless? You sexually abuse the guy and leave him tied up naked on a beach, and you wonder how this could have changed him?"

Skye turned around, eyes wide. "What—"

"I'm talking to the blond bimbo ghost who wonders why Walter has changed from a geek into a murderous monster."

Skye made a raspberry sound. "And here I thought people got in touch with their higher selves after death."

"That's rude," Kimberly said.

"Oh, shut up." Dana put her attention on the computer screen, trying to figure out Walter's filing system. Which ones should she copy?

"I have realized some things about myself," the ghost said. "I told you that last time I visited."

Dana rolled her eyes, trying to concentrate, but Kimberly's incessant chattering was making it difficult. Maybe she should just download the whole hard drive and get the heck out. The longer they stayed, the more risk they'd be discovered. She found a port and plugged in the external drive she'd brought. The line indicating the data transfer started to move.

Kimberly prattled on, but she'd stopped listening.

Skye plopped a fat file on a nearby table and flipped through the pages. "It looks like he followed Mr. Wells around. He's got notes in here about the man's habits. Where he'd go for coffee. When he took walks and where."

"You'd think he would get rid of that."

"Exactly. His success has gone to his head. He must think he's untouchable now." Skye had her out snapping pictures of the pages.

The data transfer read thirty percent.

Dana walked over to peek at the files. "Need help?"

"Nah, I'm just taking pictures for Shanks. The financial info should be on the computer. And the book manuscripts probably."

"I decided to copy the whole hard drive."

"Good idea. Looks like he handwrites his first drafts," Skye said, fanning pages. "Jade said they were going to search the place soon. I'll leave the evidence for them to discover."

"Laurie's attorney should get access." Dana went back to the desk and straightened up, leaving everything like she'd found it.

Then she remembered some spy movie where the thief took pictures of everything before searching so they could put everything back exactly like they'd found it. Maybe next time. She laughed out loud.

"What?"

Dana told Skye what she'd remembered about the movie, then said, "I guess I'm planning on doing more snooping."

"Goddess, let's hope not."

The data transfer read one hundred percent. She unplugged the hard drive, pocketed it, and closed the top of the computer. It had been on when she'd arrived. "Ready?"

Scrambling nails sounded on the stairs. Wild barking came from the hallway. Rosa ran into the room, made sure she had their attention, and ran back out into the hall.

"What's happening?" Skye asked. "Where's Laurie?"

Rosa looked over her shoulder and barked furiously.

"Something's the matter." Dana did another check of the room. Everything looked the same. She snapped off the desk lamp and followed Rosa. The little dog led them down the steps and out the kitchen to the deck. Dana switched on the outdoor lights and followed Rosa.

Skye took out her phone and called Laurie's number. No risk of alerting anyone now. Rosa barked and ran in circles, trying to get them moving again. The little dog headed down the steps through the yard, Oliver following at his fast trot. When she reached the dock, Rosa threw back her head and howled.

"Laurie's down here somewhere. I hear her phone." Skye switched on her flashlight. She found Laurie's backpack lying on the deck, half the contents spilled on the damp wood. The phone was lit with Skye's incoming call playing a whale call. In any other circumstances, Dana knew Skye would tease her about it.

They stared at each other. Laurie was missing. And her phone was here, so that meant she couldn't be tracked. They both looked at Rosa, who was watching them with an intent expression. "Sorry, kid. I can't read your thoughts," Dana said.

"I'm calling Jade."

"But then the police will know what we've been up to. We can't report a kidnapping from here. They might think we planted evidence. It will blow up her case."

"We'll let Jade figure that out. We need help." Skye pushed a button and held the phone up to her ear, walking away. She called over her shoulder, "Don't touch anything."

Dana huffed. "I know that much," she muttered. She wrapped her arms around herself. Where was Laurie? Who had been out here? Had Walter come home early and discovered her in the garage? Did he have a security team watching the house? He wasn't that rich yet. Or well known, for that matter. Plus, they would have stopped them before now. Whoever it was must have taken her by boat, which meant she could be anywhere along the lake. Or unloaded on another dock and bundled into a car. Dana took some deep breaths. Panicking wouldn't help.

Skye walked back to her. "Jade said one of us should take the dogs back to the car and wait. Then the other should scream and bang around until one of the neighbors notices and calls the police."

"They'll find the backpack and start looking for Laurie." Dana nodded. "Good idea."

"I'll stay. You take the dogs," Skye said.

Dana reached into her backpack and pulled out a gun. "I can make some noise that will get noticed."

Skye leaned in, her eyes wide. "Dana Preston. I never would have pegged you for a gun owner."

"I got it after Kevin started getting some press. We had a few threatening calls."

"Nice Ruger."

Dana eyed Skye, surprised. "You know guns?"

"My wife is a cop. My dad and cousins hunt." She shrugged.

Dana shook off the distraction. "Here's the plan. You go with the dogs. Cover your license plate with mud or something."

"Mud?"

"There should be a puddle in the park. Or use a cloth, something from your trunk, to cover it up. Drive down here and wait next to these woods." Dana pointed to the patch of trees they'd walked through when they first arrived. "I'll run up there and we'll drive away. You can let me off on the other side of the park and I'll retrieve my car."

Skye nodded. "Give me five minutes. Rosa, Oliver, come." Skye patted her thigh and walked away.

Rosa watched Dana, her brows pulled down around her eyes, clearly doubtful. Oliver stood and looked between the two friends. "Go with Skye. We're going to find Laurie." Rosa huffed and the two dogs followed Skye.

Dana sat cross-legged on the deck and tucked the gun into the waistband of her joggers. She checked her watch. Quarter to eleven. A light switched off in the back of the next-door neighbor's house. Probably a bedroom. She'd be waking them up soon. Her mind wandered to Laurie. Was she hurt? Her friend had probably fought against her attacker, but they hadn't found any blood. It was dark, though. Why kidnap someone you were setting up to take the blame for your crime? It didn't make any sense.

She pushed her worries away and stood, looking for something to make a lot of noise with. Inside the boathouse, two racks held kayaks. Rope coiled on the wall. A sailboat rocked gently in the water. Dana grabbed an oar stacked beneath the kayaks and went back outside. She waited another minute, then let out a bloodcurdling scream. "Get away from me. No, no!" She banged the oar on the deck. "Help, help!"

She ran to the end of the deck and pushed over a box. It only held ropes and flotation devices. Disappointed by the lack of noise, she spied a metal garbage can against the boathouse wall. She ran to it and kicked it over. It crashed over, making a satisfying racket, and fell against a recycling can.

Walter recycled?

Dana shook her head to focus and screamed again. She ran to the lawn and pulled out her gun. Flicking off the safety, she pointed up and fired three times. Lights flicked on, shining through the trees.

Dana raced down the deck onto the lawn, veering close enough to the house to trigger the lights, then cut over toward the garage. She reached the shadow of the trees, running fast, grateful she jogged regularly. She dodged into the strip of woods when she was close to the road. Bursting through the bushes, she found Skye's Subaru waiting. She pulled open the door and jumped in. Slamming the door shut, she pounded on the dash. "Go, go."

The dogs erupted, barking and circling around the back seat.

Skye peeled away. "Think it worked?"

Lights blazed from the house next to Walter's and from two across the street. "It worked," Dana said. "Faster."

Skye raced around a few curves, the dogs scrambling for purchase in the back. After she'd gone a few blocks, she slowed. "How do we get back to the park?"

Dana pulled out her phone and searched for a map. "Turn left at the next street." She continued giving directions until they reached the opposite side of the playground.

Skye pulled over between two houses, these separated by flowering rhododendrons. Dana got out. She could take the path behind the houses to her car.

"Meet at my house. We can listen to the police radio," Skye said.

Dana shook her head. "I've got to get home to the kids. Lord knows what they're up to."

"Jade's expecting me at home. Should I take the dogs?"

"Can you?"

Skye glanced back at their eager faces. "Sure. We've got plenty of room. They'll get along with our pack."

Rosa wagged her tail.

"I'll call when I know something," Skye said and drove off.

· · ·

As soon as Dana walked in the door of her house, Hoa heaved a sigh of relief. "Honestly, Mom. We're the teenagers in this house. We're the ones supposed to be sneaking in late on a Saturday night."

"You are only fourteen, young lady." After Dana's automatic reply was out of her mouth, it hit her that her daughter was right.

Minh rolled his eyes. "At least she lived."

"Of course I lived. What are you talking about?"

"Well, look at you." Hoa waved her hand at Dana's outfit. "You're dressed like a ninja in one of our games. And what is that all over your face?"

Dana wiped a hand over her cheek. It came away stained with the black streaks she'd applied before going out. She'd forgotten all about it with Laurie going missing. "Uh—"

"Yeah, we know you broke into Walter Pearce's house," Minh said.

Dana opened her mouth to deny it. How could they possibly know that?

"And you didn't take us with you." Hoa sat forward, her voice accusing.

Honestly, her youngest was getting as brassy as her brother.

"We could have helped. I just got my license. I could have driven the get-away car." Minh's eyes were bright.

"Don't tell your father." Geez, Dana thought, what a responsible single parent she was turning out to be.

Minh drew his finger across his mouth and shook his head.

"What did you find out?" Hoa asked.

Dana paused in the middle of the living room. Should she tell them? Her impulse was to protect them from worry. And harm. What if these crazy people came after her children? Fury rose up in her. Maybe they should know so they'd be more careful.

Both kids responded to her hesitation. "What happened?" Minh asked. "You can tell us."

"We'll find out anyway," Hoa said.

Based on tonight's experience, Dana had to admit this was probably true. Although how they found out everything was a mystery. She sat down, hands on her knees. "It's bad news. Somebody kidnapped Laurie."

Hoa gasped, her hand flying to her mouth. "Are the cops looking for her?"

"They couldn't call the cops given that they were burglars, nitwit," Minh said.

Hoa threw a pillow at him. "Don't call me that."

Dana held up her hands and told them what Jade had suggested.

"She's so cool," Hoa said.

"I'm expecting a call from Skye."

"We should listen to the police radio." Minh ran upstairs.

"We don't have a police scanner," Dana called after him.

"Mom," Hoa said in a tone that suggested the immense stupidity teens were sure their parents possessed.

Minh reappeared with his laptop and proceeded to type madly.

Dana's phone vibrated in her pocket. She'd forgotten to turn on the sound. Skye's name appeared on the screen along with the silly picture she'd picked for her friend. She answered it and held it to her ear. "What's happening?"

"Speaker. Put her on speaker," both teens shouted.

Dana held her free hand up, palm out. "Okay, geez."

"Okay what?" Skye asked.

Dana clicked to speaker. "The kids know everything. I came home and they knew where I'd been. I decided to tell them about Laurie."

"Are you sure that's wise?"

"Yes," Minh and Hoa both shouted.

"You guys can't say anything. You'll get us arrested," Skye scolded.

"Then you'll have to live with your father," Dana added.

Minh's brows drew together. "We won't tell a soul."

Hoa crossed her heart, bouncing from forty-year-old teen to eight-year-old kid.

"Okay," Skye said. "Here's the scoop so far. The cops came and found Laurie's backpack on the deck. They checked the house and discovered the backdoor unlocked. The house didn't look disturbed, but they called Walter to come check to see if anything was missing."

"Damn it, now he knows," Dana said.

"Language," Hoa mumbled out of habit.

Dana snorted.

"Walter said he was tied up in an important event for the film. He's sending an assistant to look."

"Interesting," Dana said.

"Well, we knew he was at the Galactic party," Skye said.

"True."

"The police are accessing all the security cams that look out on the lake north and south of Walter's house. So far, they found two boats pulling into public beaches and they're tracking the vehicles the people left in. One looks just like a family coming in from a night-time sail. The other looks more suspicious."

"Could they make out faces?" Dana asked.

"It was too dark."

"What if they used a private dock? Took her to a safe house?" Hoa asked.

"Safe house?" Skye repeated. "You kids watch too many movies."

"But they could," the younger teen objected.

"Now they're tracking the two vehicles through traffic cams. We'll see if that gets us anywhere."

"Let us know," Dana said.

Minh went back to his laptop and soon police chatter started up.

Intruder GOA.

Roger that.

He fiddled with the mouse.

10-27.

"That's somebody checking a driver's license. Minh moved his mouse again and another voice said. *10-45?*

10-45A.

"What's that mean?" Hoa asked. They'd all gathered around Minh in the living room.

Dana glanced at his laptop and saw he had a page open with a list of police codes. He checked it and said, "That's probably an ambulance. Something about a patient." He moved the mouse again and another voice sounded. It was like a dial on a radio.

Suspect vehicle found at Shilshole Bay Marina.

"This has got to be them." Minh pumped his fist in the air in triumph.

They huddled around the laptop, waiting for the next report. Dana realized her legs were jiggling and took a deep breath to calm down. She glanced at her children, pride filling her. These kids were smart. Up for action. Of course, that was probably because they'd never faced any real danger. Not like her grandparents, who'd left Vietnam before the war ended, bringing their own teenagers with them. They'd been lucky to escape. She never wanted Hoa and Minh to face anything like that.

The radio transmission crackled.

Vehicle empty. Found a woman's jacket. Checking cams to see what boats have left in the last hour.

Calling Harbor Patrol.

"Blast," Minh said.

"What?"

"Harbor Patrol uses a whole other frequency. I'll have to search again," he explained.

"They're going to the marina. Are they going to put Laurie on another boat?" Hoa asked.

"We're not even sure these are the kidnappers," Dana cautioned.

Minh ran his hand through his hair, his eyebrows scrunching together. "Come on, Mom. Who else could it be?"

Dana chewed her lower lip, thinking.

"Isn't it worth a try?" Hoa asked, her voice quiet.

But Dana sensed her contained excitement. "Oh, no. You two are staying here."

Hoa sprang up from the chair. "Yes. Get your stuff, Minh."

"What? I said you couldn't go."

"Who has a boat docked there?" Minh asked, eyes sparkling.

Dana turned her back on them and walked into the dining room. She took out her phone and looked for John Newman's number. Good, she'd saved it once he'd come back on her radar. She pressed call.

After a few rings, a sleepy voice answered. "Dana? Do you know what time it is?"

She didn't waste any time. "Laurie's been kidnapped."

"What? When?" He sounded instantly awake.

"We think they took her to Shilshole Marina and are heading out into the Sound. Do you have a boat there?"

"Yes, I'll meet you there."

Dana turned to find both her teens watching her, eyes wide. She called Skye. "Meet me at Shilshole Marina."

"I was about to call you. How did you find out?"

"Apparently my teenage son knows how to hack into police channels."

Skye's laughter was loud enough for the kids to hear. Minh's smile was smug.

"John has a boat there. He's taking us out," Dana said.

"See you there."

CHAPTER

TWENTY-FIVE

D ana remembered to slow down before she reached the entrance to the marina. She didn't want squealing tires to draw attention. The place was swarming with cops. She parked at the far end of the lot. Bright yellow crime tape surrounded the area around a black or dark blue van. She couldn't really tell the exact color or make in the dark. Police officers crawled inside the van. Another group stood outside talking. A uniformed officer approached her car.

Dana turned and pointed her finger at the two teens. "Don't say a word or you're grounded for life." Minh took a breath, but she cut him off. "I mean it. The only reason you're here is because I know you'd follow me. Somehow." She mentally cursed all ride services.

Dana rolled down the window and put on the political wife smile she'd been practicing. "Good evening, officer. What's going on?"

"We're investigating a crime, ma'am. I'm afraid the marina is closed."

"Oh, that's disappointing. We were supposed to meet a friend on his boat."

The officer flashed his light over the two teens in the backseat, then moved it to Dana's face. She put her hand up to shield her eyes. "Sorry, ma'am. It's too dangerous to go out on the docks now. Kinda late for the kids anyway."

Minh snorted and Dana shot him a warning look. She started the car. "Thank you officer. Stay safe." She immediately felt stupid. What kind of thing was that to tell a cop?

The man turned and walked back toward all the activity. Dana backed out of her spot and turned right, resisting the urge to peel away. They had to get to John's boat and find Laurie. Her life was at stake. The police were wasting time combing through the van looking for evidence. They had her jacket. What more did they need?

Minh had looked up Baldwin's yachts on the internet. If one was out on the water, he'd find out. "So, you're just going to leave? Give up?" he asked.

Hoa leaned forward, gripping the back of the passenger seat. "Mom, we have to go back."

"I can't make a scene. He'll remember and be on the lookout for us sneaking back in. We'll figure it out. John knows this place." She'd seen a good turnout back the way they'd come. As she pulled out onto Seaview Avenue, she ordered her SUV to call John and Skye. Was it was sophisticated enough to place a conference call?

John answered immediately. "Dana? Are you there yet?"

"Who is this?" Skye asked. "Let me talk to Dana. You'd better not hurt her." Barking erupted from Skye's connection.

"Whoa. I'm fine. John's on the line. I called you both." Dana smiled at her friend's fierce words. "The police have shut down the marina. They asked me to leave. What should we do?"

"Head for Dock D & E parking. The south end," John said. "My boats are docked on E."

"Roger that," Dana said.

"Roger that," Hoa repeated in a whisper. She high-five her brother in the back seat. Dana was regretting her decision to let them come.

269

Skye laughed. "Oh, goddess. For a second, I thought Dana had been kidnapped, too."

John ignored this. "Drive slow. Turn off your headlights about one hundred yards before the turn off. We don't want to draw any attention to ourselves."

"But I don't want to run into anything," Dana objected.

"The place is well lit, so you'll be fine. And keep those dogs quiet, please."

"These dogs—" Skye started to say, but John had already hung up.

"This is so exciting," Hoa whispered.

Dana saw a sign for Ray's Boathouse and realized she'd already passed their new rendezvous point. Her fast U-turn had the kids whooping in the back. "This is serious, you know. These people probably have guns. I should have left you at home."

"You need me. I can dial up Harbor Patrol," Minh said.

He was right, Dana realized. She spotted the sign for the parking lot ahead and cut her lights. There was no traffic, so they would probably be okay. The opening to the lot was visible under a dim streetlight. She turned in and saw Skye just getting out of her Subaru. Dana pulled in beside her. Rosa and Oliver ran to the kids and licked their hands, then sat beside Dana. She wished she could hear their thoughts, but found Oliver's solid weight reassuring when he leaned against her leg.

"You brought the kids?" Skye whispered.

Dana matched her tone even though no one was around this late. "Like I said, they knew where I'd been when I got home. That we broke into Walter's house."

Skye shook her head. "Smart."

"I told you Minh scanned the police channels. Found out they'd discovered the van. I knew they'd find a way to come if I didn't bring them with me. At least this way I can keep an eye on them."

"We both will."

Another car pulled into the lot and parked next to Skye's old Subaru. John jumped out and gave them a quick wave.

"Whew, glad it was him," Dana said.

John opened the back of his vehicle and pulled a net filled with what looked like orange life vests and rope.

More orange. Laurie would be thrilled.

"We'll need these." He narrowed his eyes at the kids, then with a shake of his head, headed toward the docks.

Kimberly popped into view. Just what Dana needed. A prissy ghost.

"I heard that," Kimberly said. "I'm here to help."

"Then you better. Laurie is in trouble."

They trooped after John through the parking lot, keeping to the shadows as much as possible while trying to look like normal people. Not easily accomplished as they fell all over each other. Just out for a late night sail. The thought made her pause. Did John have a sailboat? She hoped it had a motor. They needed speed.

"Yes, a sailboat. He loved it more than me." Kimberly said.

A stab of sadness for both of them sliced through Dana. Kimberly had found the love of her life, but died before she could spend much time with him. And here Laurie's life was at risk just when she and John had reconnected. Wait, did that mean she thought John and Laurie were meant for each other? She had, but he'd acted like a jerk when Laurie needed reassurance. She shrugged off the thought. He was here now. What mattered was saving Laurie. She'd let them sort out the rest.

Dana ran to catch up to John. "The kids were determined to come."

"This could get dangerous," he cautioned.

"Yes, but they would have found a way and at least they'll be with me."

"When we get there, they stay on the boat."

"Agreed." Dana wondered if he had handcuffs.

John pulled a key fob out of his pocket as they approached the gate to the docks and pushed a button. The gate unlocked with a click and John pushed through and headed to one of the long docks. He broke into a run once they passed the first couple of boats, and they clambered after him, Rosa fast on his heels. Dana kept up easily, following Hoa's white shirt that shone under the moonlight. Maybe she should have gotten the kids to change to ninja black. They would have loved that. She kept her eyes on the dock, trying not to trip, and ran straight into a soft, but solid wall.

"Oof." Skye let out a whoosh of air. "You almost pushed me in."

"Sorry, I didn't see you."

John had stopped next to a slip with a sailboat on one side and something bigger on the other. He took out a set of keys. "We're taking the company cruiser tonight. No time for sailing."

Dana heaved a sigh of relief. John motioned them toward the stern of a mid-size cabin cruiser with some logo and a name written on the side. She couldn't make it out in the dark, but police spotlights would. "Do you want to implicate your company in this?"

"Seems like somebody already did that. Wasn't my company listed in the shell corporations that bought that mansion Sandy Jones told you about?"

"It was."

"I'm coming for them now." John picked Rosa up, holding her under his arm and stepped on board first. He set her down, then helped Oliver on board, leaving the rest of them to their own devices. They clambered on. Dana had kept her cross trainers on and was glad of the traction. She moved up the ladder to the glassed-in cockpit while John untied the lines mooring the boat. Minh stood on the slip, helping with the process, then jumped on at the last minute. She watched her son stow the ropes. Where had he learned how to do all this?

John arrived in the cockpit and started the engine. He backed the cruiser out from the slip carefully, then turned and headed around the water break toward the open water. Shilly, the sea monster sculpture, gleamed under the gibbous moon, oddly comforting.

Dana stood next to Skye in the cockpit, the kids crowding in behind them. Kimberly hovered behind John. Dana wondered if he could feel the ghost's energy. The dogs yipped at the foot of the steps to the cockpit. She looked around. There was plenty of room up here. Benches ran the length of one side of the cabin and a worktable with a clear top sat in the middle. Minh had already stationed himself there and had his laptop open. She motioned to Hoa. "Go get the dogs before they run around and fall overboard."

"Everyone needs a life vest." John pointed to the marine net bag he'd brought. "There are ones for dogs, too."

Of course he'd have vests for dogs, Dana thought. Her heart warmed toward him. Once everyone had shrugged into the contraptions, Skye bent down and put the dogs in theirs.

"Do we have any idea where they've taken Laurie?" John asked.

"We know Walter Pearce is involved and he has regular parties on Baldwin Cress' yacht."

John gave a whistle. "That's some boat. Walter, huh? Little weasel."

Dana had a lot more to tell him, but now was not the time. "Is there any way to track his yacht?"

"Are you sure he's taking out the gigantic superyacht? The one with the sails or the support boat with the heliport?"

Dana had seen pictures of both boats. "I can't imagine he'd take the huge one. Does Baldwin have like an everyday superyacht he loans his friends?"

John gave a wry laugh. "Probably. He'd keep it at the same marina. Baldwin docks at Terminal 91."

"Checking," Minh said.

"How?" Dana asked.

"I'll hack into their security cams, Mom." Minh said it like any idiot would know that.

"Good man," John said.

Dana looked from John to her son. Was John right? Had Minh

become a man and she hadn't noticed? Still, he was only seventeen. She'd keep an eye on him, but pride warmed her heart.

"I'm in. Looking for Cress or Galactic." Minh concentrated on the screen, sucking in his lower lip.

"How can we find them out here?" Skye gestured around at the wide expanse of water. The lights of West Seattle sparkled in the distance.

"Boats have locator signals. I also have an idea. The Center for Whale Study tracks where the pods take their babies during calving season," John said.

"We're looking for people, not orcas," Dana objected. She took a breath to continue, but John raised his hand to stop her.

"NOAA has issued two tickets for harassing whales to the same yacht recently. It's registered to Galactic. Not the super yacht, but big enough."

"How does that help us?" Skye asked.

"They were at Fern Cove and Spring Beach when the incidents took place. Local residents say they see this yacht often. Those parties get noisy, and you know how noise carries over water."

A ferry horn sounded as if to illustrate. Dana had lived on the crest of Capital Hill when she was in college and loved the sound—loud, but pitched low and somehow grounding.

"Found the area designated to Galactic," Minh reported. He hunched closer to the computer screen.

"We've gotta move. There's a merchant ship coming in."

Dana glanced out and saw the headlight of a huge freighter. John maneuvered their boat far enough away, but the sheer size of the cargo ship left them in awe. Except for Minh, who had eyes only for his computer. "One of Galactic's yachts is missing from its slip," he said. Then looked up. "Whoa, that is one big ship."

"It is. Gotta keep your eyes open out here and watch your AIS system."

Dana had no idea what that was, but Minh nodded sagely.

"Great job. Now, see if you can find the transponder for that boat. I'm heading to Fern Cove. It's closer."

"Aye, captain."

Dana smiled. Minh was enjoying himself.

"Grab the dogs. I'm about to take off," John warned.

Skye scooped up Rosa. Hoa sat down on the floor next to Oliver and wrapped her arms around him, probably taking more comfort from his presence than keeping him safe by the looks of it.

The boat cut through the water, gaining speed. Dana gripped the bar in front of her.

"Isn't he amazing?"

Dana's head snapped back to see Kimberly standing behind John, her eyes admiring.

"He is," Dana mentally sent to her. "You were lucky to have him."

"I guess. Too bad we didn't really love each other."

"Why'd you keep the baby? Force him to marry you?"

"My parents are Catholic. No abortion. I didn't want to have a child and give it up for adoption, so it seemed like the best solution."

"Marry somebody you didn't really love? Why not just keep the baby? Raise it yourself?"

"My family is old fashioned. Besides, I was young. Still living in that fantasy. Marry the quarterback and live happily ever after."

"Found the signal," Minh shouted over the noise of the wind. "They're near Fern Cove."

"We're headed that way. ETA thirty minutes at this speed, but it's going to be a bumpy ride. Hold on."

Dana sat down next to Skye. Hoa stayed on the deck with Oliver, but leaned against her mom's legs. Minh stood next to John, both oblivious to Kimberly. Skye finally settled on the bench and put Rosa between her and Dana. They watched the stars and lights on the shore as they flew through the water, trying not to worry, not talking about what might be happening to Laurie.

The boat suddenly slowed, raising Dana out of her daze. The glow of the Milky Way spread across the sky in an intricate display of stars. John throttled back and soon the boat drifted in the gentle swells. He turned to them and said in a low voice, "The yacht is anchored right round this point. You two are coming with me." He pointed at Dana and Skye.

"No fair," Minh said.

"I need somebody responsible to stay with the boat. If we're not back in an hour, call the police and Harbor Patrol."

"But—"

"Your sister is too young for this and you have a good head on your shoulders."

Minh squared his shoulders. Dana had to admire John. He knew how to handle her kid.

"Hoa, keep the dogs quiet."

"Aye, captain," she said, her voice was shaky.

Skye took out her phone and handed it to Minh. "I want you to call Jade and tell her we found them. She'll know what to do."

Minh's eyes gleamed. "Yes, ma'am."

Dana snorted. When had he started calling her friends 'ma'am.'

Skye just nodded. She opened her backpack and took out a Sig pistol. Tucking it into her waistband, she pulled out what looked like a thin hunting knife sheathed in leather. She stuck this between her pillow breasts.

John gave her a nod of approval. He took out a Glock and stuck it behind his back in the top of his pants, then pulled up the leg of his pants and strapped a knife to his calf. Dana was surprised she recognized both gun makes from her recent research.

"Wicked," Minh whispered.

John studied Dana. "What do you have?"

She showed him her Ruger.

If John was surprised both she and Skye had a handgun, he didn't show it. "Good. Let's go."

Dana didn't tell him she'd only fired it once.

They followed John down the steep steps to the deck where he unlashed a dingy and lowered it into the water. He held onto Dana's forearm as she got into the boat. Skye climbed in behind her. They positioned themselves to balance the small craft. John got into the back and pulled the start cord. Just as he started to pull away, Rosa leapt into the boat and crouched down in the hull.

"I guess you want to save your mistress." John pointed a finger in the little dog's face and said, "No barking."

Rosa gave a quiet yip to indicate she understood. At least it seemed that way to Dana.

CHAPTER

TWENTY-SIX

L aurie woke up slowly. She was lying on her side. Her shoulder hurt and her hands felt numb. Opening her eyes, she only found darkness. She squinted, trying to focus, to see something that gave her a hint about where she was. The last thing she remembered was trying to throw herself into Lake Washington and Peggy whacking her in the head with the butt of her gun.

Where was she now? She tried to sit up, but something stopped her from getting her hands on the floor to push up. She jerked them and rope burned her wrists. They were tied behind her. She tried to get her legs under her so she could stand up, but her arms pulled down when she moved them, bending her into a bow.

She was trussed up like a Christmas goose, hands tied to her feet with a piece of rope. She stretched slowly, testing how far she could move. Her feet thumped on a solid wall that sounded like wood. Shit, she was trapped in a tiny space. Visions of Victorian heroines buried alive flashed through her mind. Panic seized her. At least they left bells in the coffins back in the day. She struggled against the ropes, trying not to scream, but her movements only succeeded in tightening the knots, rubbing her wrists raw.

Laurie made herself stop thrashing. She had to calm down and think if she was going to get out of this situation. Taking long, deep breaths, she lay still until her heart rate calmed. Opening her eyes, she waited while they adjusted to the dark. She noticed a line of dim light in front of her. It was in the wrong place for a coffin lid. It was a door. Relief flooded her. She was in a closet.

Her relief was short-lived. How was she going to get out? She scooted her whole body back against the long wall and worked her way to an upright position. Sort of. Now what? To hell with helpless Victorian heroines, although that was a cliché. They were pretty feisty if you read between the lines. What would Lara Croft do? She'd have some nifty knife secreted somewhere she could reach so she could cut the ropes, open the door, and karate-chop anybody who tried to stop her escape. But Laurie didn't have a knife and had only studied aikido for six months when she'd first moved to Boston.

She looked around for a sharp edge, squinting in the dim light. The closet had a woody scent with a hint of citrus. Cedar. Above her head stretched a bar to hold clothes. No coat hangers. Maybe there was a hook. She couldn't quite see all the way to the top of the tiny space. It was so much like a coffin. Laurie shook the thought away.

She pushed against the wall with her shoulder and got her feet under her. She tried to stand. Smooth planks lined the way. No splinters. No rough spots. Struggling up, she straightened as much as she could. If she leaned to one side, she could keep to her feet. Then the floor rocked beneath her. She fell against the wall. She stayed leaning, trying to get her balance back. Just as she felt stable, the floor rocked in the opposite direction. She waited, paying attention to the movement. The floor moved back and forth in long, gentle rolls. She was on a boat. Probably on the Sound by the feel of the waves.

Footsteps sounded in the hallway and the lock on the door clicked. It pulled open before she could prepare for—what exactly? To attack whoever opened it? Tied up like this? Laurie squinted against the blinding light.

"I see you're awake. And standing. Quite industrious."

Laurie recognized Peggy's voice. As her eyes adjusted, she saw dark shapes behind her that resolved into two men with bulging biceps. They studied Laurie, their expressions neutral. A chill ran through her. They looked like they'd just as soon kill her as help her out of her bindings, depending on Peggy's orders. Where in the world did she get these guys? They'd severely underestimated this woman.

"Step out," Peggy ordered.

Laurie shuffled forward, walking like a woman in a tight courtesan dress.

Peggy gave an impatient huff. "Untie her legs. She's harmless."

A surge of indignation ran through Laurie. She wasn't harmless. She could do some damage. Maybe not against these mountains of muscle. She bemoaned all those aerobics classes she'd wasted her time on when clearly she should have been studying something more lethal like Taekwondo.

One of the muscle men bent down and undid the knots on the rope so fast she wondered if she could have gotten them untied herself.

"Follow me," Peggy commanded. She walked away without so much as a glanced behind her, certain of command.

Laurie would be annoyed if she wasn't too scared. She walked behind Peggy, obedient, the two guards taking up the rear. Dark wood lining the narrow hallway gleamed under the recessed lights in the ceiling. Carpet cushioned her steps and dampened the sound of the engine to a low hum. Peggy pushed through a door at the end of the hall and climbed a set of white oak steps with black non-slip strips. Then emerged in a glass-enclosed corridor that seemed to run the length of the boat. Laurie blinked, even in the early morning light. No clouds today. The snow-capped Olympics rose from the blue water of the Sound, the rising sun turning them dusty rose.

It was a beautiful day to die.

Now that she was above board, she could take in the boat's size. Laurie was bad with numbers. Like when she was driving somewhere and the GPS told her to turn in fifty feet, she had no idea how far that was. She couldn't estimate how many feet this bot stretched. It was longer than a trailer truck, but not quite a football field. However long it was, though, it was impressive. Could this be Baldwin Cress's yacht, famous for Walter's wild sex parties?

Eww.

Toward the front of the boat—Laurie knew there was a proper term for the front, but couldn't think of it in her current state—Peggy veered right and went into a room. One of the guards held the door open for Laurie and gestured for her to enter. In passing, she noticed a chain tattoo around his neck.

The space looked like a regular living room, except the walls were all glass. One far corner sported the same dark wood as the lower hallway with a big screen TV mounted above a credenza. The TV was turned off. A bar area took up the right wall. An island separated it from the rest of the living space. White leather sofas stretched in front of the island and along the back. At least it looked like leather. Was that practical on a boat? Laurie would have to consult the internet when she had this much money. Like that was going to happen.

The other muscle man escorted her to a dining room chair that had been set in the middle of the room and untied the ropes around her wrists. She remembered she should examine everyone carefully so she could have a police sketch artist draw an accurate picture. Because she was going to escape. No tattoos that she could see. The man looked up at her, arctic-blue eyes devoid of emotion. A scar ran under his eye to his jaw. Her stomach turned as cold as his eyes.

He attached her feet and hands to the chair, this time with zip-ties. Now they were getting with the times, Laurie thought. Rope was old-fashioned. Except people who were about to be tortured were usually bound like this. She looked around for implements—sharp spikes, hypodermic needles, plyers to pull out fingernails, a bone saw. Laurie's body tried to fold into itself. She didn't see any devices her brain had so helpfully pictured. Resisting would be futile as the Borg were fond of pointing out. She wondered about her mind's running commentary. Maybe she was cracking under the pressure.

Peggy sat on the edge of a cushy sofa across from Laurie and crossed her ankle on a knee. Not ladylike at all. Boy, had she fooled them. She stuck her face close. Not close enough for Laurie to sink her teeth into her nose unfortunately. "I know you three bitches have been investigating me. What have you found out?" Her breath smelled like mint and orange.

"Nothing about you," Laurie said. "You could have stayed hidden. Left me alone."

Peggy sat back and nodded at the man with the scar. He slapped Laurie across the face. Hard. Her head snapped to the side, eyes watering.

"You need to take this seriously, Dr. Olson." Peggy did not say her name like a student who wanted a better grade would. Her voice dripped with contempt. "Answer me."

Laurie wished she could put her hand to her burning cheek. Who should she throw under the bus?

Her delay earned her another slap across the face and her head snapped to the other side. She stifled a cry of pain. If she survived, she'd have to find a new chiropractor in Seattle. "We discovered there were two people in black hoodies at the reunion."

Peggy narrowed her eyes. "How did you figure that out?"

"The security cams."

Her forehead creased, then she shook her head. "You're lying."

"Why? Because you think you took all the cameras offline?" Laurie couldn't keep the spite out of her voice.

Peggy nodded to her henchmen and Tattoo Man stepped up. Laurie flinched when he raised his hand. He gave a grunt of satisfaction and didn't strike. "Watch your mouth," he hissed.

Laurie hated the rush of gratitude in her chest. She closed her eyes to get some control of herself. She took one deep breath and then opened her eyes. "The person who tried to collect money from

Kimberly was shorter than the guy who pushed her off the high balcony." She left out the fact that they knew the first person was a woman.

"I see. What else?"

Laurie decided to skip Sandy's involvement. "We found out who was following us."

"Name?"

Laurie hesitated and the guy with the chain tattoo took a step toward her.

"Carl Simmons," she blurted.

Peggy's face didn't change. It seemed that she already knew this. "What else?"

"Well, obviously the emails implicating me are fake."

"What did these supposedly fake emails say?"

Laurie suddenly laughed. She tried to stop, but couldn't control herself. The laughing escalated, growing higher in pitch, bordering on hysteria. One of the men moved toward her and she bit her lip to force herself to stop. "Threats against Kimberly."

"And you claim they're fake." Peggy put both legs on the ground and leaned forward. "How do you know that?"

"Because I didn't write them," Laurie spat out.

"Yes, but can you prove it?" Peggy leaned forward like some trial lawyer who'd landed an incriminating point, her perfect bow mouth forming a predatory smile.

So Peggy was behind the emails, too. Laurie's heart rate doubled. For some reason, this petite, mid-aged cheerleader was more frightening than her hired hit men. Oh, God. Please don't let them be hit men. Laurie steeled herself. "Whose boat is this, anyway?"

Peggy cocked her head, looking just like one of those baby velociraptors in *Jurassic Park*. "Why can't it be mine?"

Laurie gulped. "I just didn't think you had this much money is all. Sorry." You shouldn't show fear to a velociraptor. You shouldn't be sitting in front of one either. She closed her eyes for a second.

"So you discovered that Carl Simmons was following you. Who hired him?"

Laurie opened her eyes. Maybe you could lie to a velociraptor. "Don't know."

"So why were the three of you at Walter's house poking through his files?"

Was Peggy trying to confuse her by jumping from topic to topic? Laurie pretended to be confused. "Wait, are you saying Walter hired him?" Laurie made her eyes and mouth round, trying for a look of surprise.

Peggy just stared at her.

Laurie guessed her ploy hadn't worked. "We went there to talk. He wasn't at home, so I walked out on the –"

Peggy slammed her hand down on the coffee table in front of her. "Do not lie to me."

Laurie felt a rush of warmth in her lower abdomen, and it had nothing to do with feeling the least bit attracted to anyone in this room. She squeezed her lady muscles together just in time. She would not wet herself in front of Peggy f-ing Anderson. "We thought Walter might be behind the emails."

"Now, why would a successful author like D.J. Stone be interested in an insignificant English professor like you?"

"Exactly," Laurie said.

Peggy sat back, surprised by her answer.

"Can I go to the bathroom?" Laurie asked in a small voice.

"No."

"Look, I'm just trying to clear my name. We remembered that prank Kimberly pulled on Walter. We thought maybe he was behind the blackmail attempt. That he wanted revenge."

"Prank?"

"You remember. You were a cheerleader then. Walter was assaulted—"

Peggy's eyebrows climbed into her hairline.

"—uh, left tied up on a gay beach naked."

Peggy studied her.

The pressure in her bladder increased. She jiggled her legs to hold it. "I don't want to go to the Big House. I can't wear orange all my life. I did not kill Kimberly Woolridge." The desperation in her voice was real.

Peggy blew out a sound of disgust. "Take her to the head, but watch her the whole time."

Laurie stood once the ties around her feet and hands were cut. Scar Man grabbed her forearm and half dragged her toward a small door off the bar. She sagged with disappointment. She was hoping to get out of this room. Make a break for it.

"When you get back, you're going to answer all my questions or we're going to get serious," Peggy said.

DANA'S EYES widened when the dingy rounded the spit of land and the Galactic yacht came into view. It wasn't the grand super yacht built in the Netherlands that showed up in all the news-feeds, but it was big enough. The white hull gleamed in the moonlight, revealing a streamlined design. The graceful bow tapered into a pointed stern. Running lights showed the sleek and sophisticated profile. The yacht rose elegantly from the hull, featuring three tiers with large windows. Somehow it resembled a sports car, built for speed, exuding sophistication and prestige. And menace.

John cut the engine and lifted an oar out of the bottom of the boat. He guided them toward the rear of the yacht, not making a sound. A guard with a gun in his lap dosed at the top of a handy set of steps. John pulled up to the vessel, staying in the shadows. He put a finger to his lips and climbed out, pulling his gun out of the back of his jeans.

Dana strained to see what was happening, desperate for John not to shoot the guy. She started to stand up, but Skye put her hand on her shoulder and pressed down. Dana looked at her. Skye shook her head and made a flipping motion with her hands. Oh, right. Better not capsize just yet.

"What the—" the man said. Then came a grunt and some scuffling.

A minute later, John looked over the edge. "Come up and bring the rope next to the motor."

Dana grabbed the coil of rope and climbed up, glad of the non-slip strips in the wet. Skye followed her carrying the intrepid Havanese mix. The guard lay on his side, unconscious, his temple bleeding, a blue handkerchief stuffed in his mouth. John held his hand out for the rope. Dana gave it to him and John made short work of tying the man's hands and feet behind him, then lashing him to the chrome handrail.

He picked up the guard's gun and tucked it in his waistband, keeping his own Glock in his hand. "Let's go."

They climbed up to the aft deck on silent feet, checking for crew. Seeing no one, they made their way up a few steps to a long promenade that stretched the length of the vessel, passing dark windows. Dana hoped that meant nobody was inside. Skye set Rosa down. The little dog put her nose to the deck and started sniffing. "Let us know if anyone's around," Skye whispered.

Light leaked down from the deck above. They glided down the outside passageway, checking for more crew. A man with a chef apron stood at an open door smoking. John hid his weapon behind him and approached. The man just nodded and offered him a cigarette. "We're looking for a friend," he whispered. "Have you seen a woman with blond hair, about so tall." He held up his hand.

The man shook his head. "I see nothing, señor. I say nothing."

"Good man. Just be careful." He pointed up. "They might object to us taking her with us."

"No hay problema, señor. I no get involved."

John nodded, then motioned them forward.

"Buenas noches," Skye said as she passed him by.

He nodded. "Señora."

Dana crept up to Skye and whispered. "Imagine what he's seen. I guess he just wants to keep his job."

"Might not even have a green card. Works for us, though."

Rosa's ears perked and she disappeared up the steps to the third deck. Skye called after the little dog, but had to keep her voice low. Rosa appeared at the top of the steps and crouched, her fluff of a tail high. She caught everyone's attention, then trotted away.

"Think she found something?" Dana asked.

"Probably," Skye said.

The three humans crept up the stairs and sheltered against the wall of the boat. Rosa watched them closely, then turned and trotted down to the lit windows. She sat, apparently waiting for them to catch up. Dana was relieved she didn't make any noise. John pointed his gun in front of him and flitted closer. He moved like a ghost. Dana winced and looked around. Kimberly leaned against the railings, her back to the water, both arms supporting her—did she weigh anything though, Dana wondered—looking like a model or a trophy wife. Dana snorted.

Voices drifted out to them. "We need to find out what she knows."

The voice was familiar, but she couldn't place it. Dana was surprised it was a woman.

"More important is who she's told. Does her lawyer know? Because if he does—" She left the implication hanging.

Then a male voice replied, "Just tell us what you need us to do, ma'am."

Skye took her phone out and pressed a button. At Dana's questioning look, she whispered, "I'm recording this."

Dana had such brilliant friends.

They moved closer, Skye holding her phone out.

Behind her, Dana heard a thud followed by a grunt. The sounds of a scuffle, but before she could turn around, something poked into her back. "Don't move or I'll shoot." Her hands flew up on their own.

She looked over at Skye. A man stood behind her, gun pointed at her head. "Hands up," he said. Skye stuffed her phone in her pocket before she complied.

A third behemoth of a man had John's arm behind him at what looked like a painful angle. John's mouth bled. "Stop struggling," the guy said. A fourth gunman stood behind them holding an assault rifle. And here she thought they'd been doing so well.

Dana took her captors in with a quick glance. Huge shoulders and biceps. All taking too many steroids, that was for sure. Probably small man parts, she thought. They'd die young from the side effects, but given their profession, that was likely with or without the steroids.

"Move," the last man said, waving the barrel of his gun toward the room where the voices had come from.

Dana gave herself a shake. She was the one likely to die faster than their captors. All three of them. And Laurie.

CHAPTER
TWENTY-SEVEN

L aurie delayed in the tiny bathroom as long as she could, but a loud knock on the door announced her respite was over.

"Time's up," said a muffled male voice. One of Peggy's muscle men.

Laurie opened the door and walked into Scar Man's fist. She fell back, her hip hitting the side of the sink. He grabbed her arms and pulled her up, backhanding her.

Her arms flew in front of her face. "Stop it. Why are you doing—"

Tattoo Guy pulled her arms away from her face and pushed her into the living room. She fell at Peggy's feet. Not a position she loved. "You're going to answer my questions now, Dr. Olson. Who were the two people at the reunion?" Peggy asked.

"I don't know."

Scar Man kicked her in the ribs. "Answer her."

She put her hands in front of her body. "Okay, Sandy Jones. She was forced to collect the blackmail money so she could get paid for a real estate deal."

"And?"

"I don't know who the other person was."

Tattoo Man had moved behind her. He kicked her low back, sending a shock of white pain up her spine.

"Stop," she panted. "We never found out."

"Do you know where the emails originated?"

"Galactic. Somebody's got an in with the techs there." Then Laurie remembered the look on Peggy's face when she'd told her they had accessed the security cameras. Now she was certain. Laurie lifted her head and stared at Peggy. "It's you. You're the one who turned off the cameras. Did you push Kimberly over the ledge?"

"No, that was me." A rich baritone voice came from the door behind her. She'd heard it before. Reading a book. She craned her neck and saw Walter Pearce standing in the doorway.

"I see I didn't miss all the fun. And look who we found outside."

Dana, Skye, and John walked in, hands in the air. More guards followed them, with automatic rifles pointed at their backs. John's lip was bleeding. One carried Rosa under his arm. She growled, lips back, white teeth bared.

Laurie's heart sank. Her hope of being saved sank to the bottom of Puget Sound where they'd probably hide their bodies.

"So your friends came to save you," Peggy sneered. "And now we have you all."

"The police called me. They said you broke into my house." Walter laughed. "They have no clue what's really going on."

"What is going on, Mr. Stone?" Dana used Walter's pen name, her voice dripping with derision.

"You were all so superior with your nose stuck up in the air all the time. And fatso over here—" he gestured toward Skye "—big clumsy dyke. Begging to be included in the in-crowd, just like a dog."

Skye didn't react to Walter's taunts, but kept looking down at her jacket pocket. Did she have a weapon hidden in there?

Peggy whirled around and asked Laurie again, "What does your lawyer know?"

"Who cares? They'll be dead soon enough," Walter said.

"We need to know so we can construct an alibi, darling."

So, that's how Peggy was connected to this. She wanted Walter's money and to bask in the fame coming from his movie, so she'd struck up a relationship with him.

"He has enough to clear me," Laurie said.

Peggy nodded. Tattoo Guy grabbed her hair and hauled her to her feet.

She screamed, her scalp on fire.

"Leave her alone." John ran forward, but Scar Man grabbed him, twisting his arms behind his back.

Tattoo Guy pushed her down in the interrogation chair and jerked her head back. Her eyes watered. He leaned in close to her and said, "Tell her what you know."

"We know who sent those fake emails for you. Same person who sabotaged the security cams," Laurie said.

"Reginald?" Walter spit out.

"That's right." They hadn't known, but now Walter had revealed a name. She glared at him. Fat lot of good it would do her being eaten by sharks and wolf eel. Laurie stopped herself from shuttering and spit out, "And we know how you came up with the plot for your last book."

"Mr. Moss said you'd be the great writer, but turns out I am." Walter strutted in front of her.

"You're just a hack."

"And you're just a second class English teacher. You've never written anything original in your life." Spittle flew from Walter's mouth. "That asshole deserved what he got."

"What did he get?" Laurie goaded him on.

"He got killed. That's what he got. And I did it."

"Walter, don't," Peggy shouted, but Walter ignored her.

He stalked up to Laurie. "Moss was the hack. He wrote those simpering romance novels. Pretended to be a woman." His eyes glazed as if he were remembering the scene. "I made him take it all back. Every nasty word he ever said about me before I killed him. He groveled before me, but I showed him no mercy."

Laurie screwed up her mouth. "God, Walter. You even talk in clichés."

Tattoo Guy backhanded her.

John yelled her name, struggling to break free.

Rosa barked furiously.

"And Kimberly?" Dana shouted. "You killed her because she invited you out with the cheerleaders and football players. But it was a ruse. They stripped you down and humiliated you. Did unspeakable things to you."

Walter lunged for Dana, but one of the guards stopped him.

"It was horrible," Peggy said. "Nobody deserved to be treated like that."

"But you did what she asked, didn't you Peggy?" Skye said.

Peggy stared at Skye, her eyes wild. "You don't know how awful she was. She tormented me. Criticized every move I made on the squad. Told me I'd always be second best. Never good enough."

"Is that such a big deal?" Skye asked.

"You'd never understand. You were such an oaf."

"At least I was happy."

"I was always the runner-up, second place, consolation prize, supporting cast—to Kimberly. Kimberly thought she won because she got the quarterback. She ran our group like she was the leader, but I was the brains behind the throne. She never could get a professional job. Failed in her career. Always messed up. She was a pretty receptionist. That's all she was good for."

Peggy's eyes had a maniacal gleam. "But I showed her. I was successful. Became a personal trainer. Worked my way up to high-end clients. They showed me how to live. I got bored with my steady husband and his middle income. I started to do secret jobs for customers. Even studied with their security teams. That's when I saw my opportunity with Walter. We could make Kimberly pay."

A tear ran down John's cheek. "She loved her kids. She was a wonderful mother. A better woman than you'll ever be."

Laurie smiled at him, glad to see him defending Kimberly.

"Did you intend to murder her?" Dana asked.

Peggy stopped short. "She was a sadist. That bitch deserved to be killed."

"I loved pushing her over the ledge," Walter said, then turned on Dana. "I saw you there and thought, 'Why not?' I'm just sorry you got rescued."

Dana lunged for him, a punch landing under his chin, sending him sprawling across the floor. Peggy ran to his side.

Rosa sank her teeth into the man holding her.

"Damn dog." He shook his hand and she sprang free, running toward Laurie. She launched herself at Tattoo Guy, who fell back in surprise.

John elbowed the man holding him. The guard's arm flew up and the rifle spewed round after round into the ceiling.

Skye and Dana hit the floor, covering their heads.

"Drop your weapons," someone shouted.

Uniformed police officers flooded the room, guns out.

Jade stepped forward.

"Thank the goddess," Skye said.

"Walter Pearce, you are under arrest for the murders of Joseph Moss and Kimberly Woolridge."

"You can't prove—" he shouted.

Jade spoke over him. "Peggy Anderson, you are under arrest for accessory to the aforementioned murders—" she lifted a shoulder "—among other things."

Two policemen handcuffed Walter and Peggy, then started reciting their rights.

Rosa jumped into Laurie's lap and covered her face with kisses. "Puppy dog, it is so good to see you."

"I'm sorry I was late. Do you want me to bite anybody else?" the dog asked.

Laurie stroked her soft head. "No, I think Jade will do that."

"I always liked her," Rosa said.

One of the policemen walked up to her. "Do you need medical attention?"

She started to answer, but John reached her first.

"I'm so sorry. I can't tell you how sorry I am. Are you hurt?" The policeman stepped back, letting John kneel in front of the chair she was in. Rosa regarded him with solemn eyes.

"I think they might have broken a rib, but I'm alive."

He took a deep breath. "I was an idiot. I thought you suspected me. That I would be involved in killing Kimberly. I should have stayed and listened. You were the one under arrest."

She put her hand on his face. "Thank you for finding me. You saved my life."

"It was a team effort." He swept his arm toward where Skye and Dana were talking with the police.

The officer who'd approached her said, "We'll take you to Bayview ER to be checked over. Is there anyone we should call?"

"I'll take care of her," John said. He looked into Laurie's eyes. "If you'll let me."

She melted. "Yes, John, I'll let you take care of me now. And when I'm better, we'll take care of the whales together, if you'll let me."

"It would be an honor." His eyes shone. John took her arm and eased her to her feet.

Dana and Skye stood with Jade. Some of the police were leading Peggy's henchmen off in cuffs. Others secured the scene.

Laurie limped up to the group. "I recorded it all," she heard Skye say. Skye handed her phone to her wife. "Walter confessed to both murders and Peggy said she helped him. I recorded it all."

"Thank you, sweetie." Jade looked around to see if anyone had overheard this pet name, but her colleagues were too busy to notice. "We've got his files and his computer. It was enough to get a warrant."

"That was fast," Dana said.

"With a kidnapping involved, the judge fast tracked it."

"Thank God you're safe," Dana said and wrapped her arms around Laurie. Skye joined in from the other side.

"Careful of my ribs," Laurie squeaked out from the friend sandwich.

Rosa stretched up, wanting to be included in the group hug. John picked her up and ruffled her ears. He got Jade's attention. "Can we give our statements later? We need to get Laurie to the hospital."

"That will be all right. Is that your boat back there?"

"Yeah."

"We can give you a ride to it. Or should we call an emergency chopper?"

Laurie shook her head. "No need. I'm not that bad off."

Jade gave her a tight smile. "You were brave."

Laurie tightened her eyes to keep the tears from falling. She couldn't fall apart now. Maybe later.

John put his arm around her and said to Jade, "If it's not too much trouble, could you collect my dingy please? I don't want to lose it."

"I'll see to it." Jade said, then motioned Skye, Dana, and Laurie to come over to a corner of the room. Once they were far enough away so nobody could overhear them, she said, "There's one more thing we need to do. Help Kimberly cross over."

"Oh, yes. Please," Dana said.

Jade smiled. "Meet me tomorrow night at Discovery Park. I'll text you the exact place to meet."

DANA SAT against a large log on one of Discovery Park's secluded beaches. The hike down the forest trail had warmed her up. The days were getting longer and the sun had just set behind the tips of the Cascades. The breeze from the Sound was cooling her off again. She pulled on her favorite wool sweater she'd bought in Cornwall on a trip with Kevin and the kids a couple of years ago. Memories of the trip tore at her heart. It had been the last time she and Kevin were close. Before his political career had ramped up and he'd gotten busy. And distant. She pulled the beige fisherman's sweater over her head. Jade had asked them to wear white and Dana had complied, but she wasn't going to freeze for Kimberly Woolridge. Beige was close enough.

She and Laurie had met in the parking lot and followed Skye's directions to the beach, Rosa and Oliver enjoying the early evening romp through the woods. Rosa only chased one rabbit. They'd broken out of the trees to find a secluded stretch of beach. A fire crackled in the middle of a rough circle of tree trunks large enough to lean against. Jade stood with her back to the ocean, the waning sun illuminating her white robes and trailing blue scarf. She nodded at them as they approached.

"Hi. What should we do?" Dana asked.

Skye and two of her family members Dana hadn't met before welcomed them with fingers to their lips. So no talking. A tall man lit a bundle of sage and, with a bundle of bird feathers, wafted the smoke over both of them. After being thoroughly saged, Dana and Laurie were ushered to their places around the fire. Apparently, the dogs did not need saging. They settled down near Laurie, surprisingly quiet and attentive.

Skye's family helpers went to the opposite side of the circle and took out hand-held drums. They began a quiet, heart-beat rhythm. Dana kept looking for Kimberly, but she hadn't appeared yet. What would they do if she didn't come to her own ceremony? Dana didn't know how to call her. Once Kimberly had appeared when she thought about how annoying seeing her was, but other than that, she had no idea. She'd have to ask for help, but she wasn't supposed to talk.

Jade raised her hands out to her sides, palms out, like those images of Mother Mary that Dana had seen in Catholic churches. She'd read a bit on Vodou and Santería online. There was a Brazilian version called Candomblé. The spiritual practices had come from the West Coast of Africa, especially from the Yoruba tribe. Enslaved peoples had mixed their traditions with Catholicism, imposed by the Europeans, and the ceremonies had lived on, transformed, but with the same spark of the original belief system. Some of it reminded Dana of Buddhism and Hinduism.

Jade's voice interrupted her train of thought. "Welcome, friends and family. We have come tonight to help out our friend, Kimberly Woolridge, recently departed from this life. Her death was sudden and violent. I'm sure she is confused. That she has questions."

Jade's voice took on a trance-like rhythm, soft and steady, but easy to hear above the drums. "We invite her to come. For comfort. For help. To reconnect with her Orisha and her ancestors." As she spoke, she threw handfuls of what looked like herbs into the fire. Dana couldn't be sure. Pleasant smells mixed with the salt of the ocean and sharp tang of kelp along the waterline.

Jade picked up a bottle. Was that rum? She poured a generous amount into a silver chalice and threw it into the fire. Flames shot up, devouring the alcohol. She called out a name, Echú, and laid down a plate filled with, of all things, popcorn. The dogs sniffed, but Laurie put out a restraining hand and they settled again. "Bring our sister Kimberly to us. Let us hear her suffering so we can help calm her spirit."

Jade and Skye started humming. If there were words, Dana wasn't familiar with them. She joined them, sticking to quiet vowels. Laurie started humming as well. Rosa let out a howl that sounded much like her ancient wolf ancestors. Oliver looked at her as if he was deciding whether he should add his voice.

Jade then took a large conch shell and filled it with white flowers. "Yemayá," she called out, then sang the name. Dana had heard this spirit's name in feminist circles. There were songs to her. She knew Yemayá ruled the oceans, maybe all bodies of water. Even the faucet water, Dana wondered. She hunched her shoulders, thinking maybe that was sacrilegious.

Jade laughed, the sound trilling through her chant, and Dana wondered if she knew what Dana had been thinking. Her heart opened with Jade's laugh and she saw a figure walking from the water toward them. Was it Kimberly or Jade's—she tried to remember the right word—Ori-something.

"May Echú find her. May Yemayá bless her," Jade intoned.

Skye and the group repeated it. Dana and Laurie joined in, trying to get the pronunciation correct.

The humming chant continued. Dana swayed with the drumming. The urge to dance swelled up and she stood up and moved in a circle, arms out. When she was facing Skye, she noticed a ball of light around her. Her friend looked radiant. Dana's gaze moved to Jade and she stumbled. Beside their priestess stood a beautiful woman in a flowing blue dress. The sleeves and hem faded into white, making it look like she was clothed in waves.

Dana's mouth fell open. Was she—was that—? She wouldn't call this being a ghost. She radiated too much light. The spirit caught Dana's gaze and deepened their connection. This was Jade's Orisha. The word popped up clearly in her mind. Along with the being's name. Yemayá.

This ritual was real. All Dana's doubts left her and her hopes soared. This would work. Kimberly would get help and leave for the spirit world. Then Dana could go back to normal. Yemayá smiled at her, then turned her head.

Down the beach, two misty figures emerged from the fog that had crept in. The closer they came, the more distinct they grew. The taller one came into focus. A dark man with a red cloth draped around his waist that fell to mid-thigh. He wore a plethora of cowry shells around his neck and carried what looked like a torch. But as he came closer, Dana realized it was a living flame. Kimberly walked beside him, unfazed by his appearance. She looked almost like she had appeared in life. Solid, brimming with health.

"The spirit of the crossroads, the messenger, has come." Jade threw another cup full of rum on the fire. "Welcome, Echú. Papa Legba brings our lost friend. Welcome, Kimberly Woolridge."

"She comes," the rest of the group chorused.

Dana and Laurie repeated this phrase, Laurie looking at Dana, her eyes bulging. "Can you believe this?" she mouthed.

"I know," Dana replied sotto voice.

The two spirits joined the circle next to their priestess. Kimberly bent her head to Jade, listening. She answered a question in a voice so low Dana couldn't hear. The two Orishas spoke to Kimberly for a few minutes, keeping the conversation private. Then Jade picked up a stick of incense and danced around Kimberly with it, singing in a language Dana didn't know. After a few passes, Kimberly broke into tears. She sobbed, her face in her hands. Yemayá wrapped her arms around the ghost, although she looked like a flesh and blood person by this point. Warmth filled Dana's heart. She was glad Kimberly was getting comforted.

Jade finished her passes with the incense and the wind picked up. Lightning forked out over Puget Sound, almost unheard of in Seattle. Something unusual was happening. The Orishas walked Kimberly closer to the fire, then backed away almost reverently, leaving her standing alone. Dana could see the tracks of tears on her cheeks. The wind strengthened, blowing tree limbs near the beach. Small pieces of driftwood danced down the shore. Lightning struck again, closer this time.

A figure materialized next to Kimberly, dark and shining like polished ebony, dressed in a flowing red dress and wearing a head-dress with horns that reminded Dana of the water buffalo in Vietnam. She moved around Kimberly in a sinuous dance, cracking a whip of what looked like lightning at each of the cardinal points. Then she turned to Kimberly and merged with her.

Dana gasped.

"Oh, my God," Laurie cried out.

Kimberly lit up like the lightning in the sky. After a minute, she smiled at Dana, sending her gratitude. Then she turned and started walking back down the beach the way she'd come, the woman in the red dress beside her.

"Kimberly Woolridge has been reunited with her Orisha, Oya.

299

The mistress of wind and lightning. Lover of flirtation. Protectress of children."

Dana nodded her head. Well, that summed up Kimberly all right. She waved goodbye to her ghost. The two figures kept going, thinning out as they walked, until they melted into the mist.

Dana sighed in relief. She figured Kimberly was gone for good now. She and Laurie walked back up to their cars, quiet after their experience. Laurie was free now that Walter and Peggy had been arrested for Kimberly's murder. Dana could return to normal, whatever that would be now. She needed to figure out what to do about Kevin, but that could wait.

Dana took Laurie's hand and they walked out of the forest together.

"Just a little while ago, I couldn't have imagined all that we've experienced," Laurie said.

Dana squeezed her hand. "It's been amazing."

CHAPTER
TWENTY-EIGHT

Two weeks later, the three friends plus Laurie's parents, Hoa and Minh, Rosa and Oliver sat on John's company cruiser enjoying the sun. "L-pod has been hanging around Bainbridge of all places with their two new calves. If we're in luck, we'll see them."

"We've had good luck lately." Laurie reached over to the teak parapet. "Knock on wood."

"I still can't believe how much the college offered you to settle your suit," Laurie's father said.

"I could never go back there after the way they treated me," she said. "And both Walter and Peggy go on trial soon."

"The mountain of evidence against them is damning," Jade said.

Hoa giggled. "She said damn."

"Language." Dana shook her head, but couldn't help smiling.

"Seen Kimberly lately?" Laurie asked.

"She's gone," Dana said. "I think for good."

Laurie's mother's eyes widened. "What? Kimberly, but she's—"

"Dead," Dana confirmed.

301

"Dana started seeing Kimberly's ghost after she died," Laurie explained.

"Now she's disappeared. I think she's satisfied with the outcome and that's all over for me now."

"Are you sure it wasn't just your imagination, dear?" Laurie's father asked, his forehead wrinkling.

"I wish. It started after I fell off the top deck at Galactic," she said.

"Sometimes near death experiences can open up the brain's extraordinary abilities," Laurie's mother explained. "It's been documented."

"She's not the only one." Laurie figured it was time to confess her own new ability. She explained about the near plane crash and how she could hear Rosa's thoughts afterward, watching John where he leaned against the hull.

Her parents seemed to sense they should be quiet.

"Only Rosa?" John asked.

"I can hear Oliver and Natasha. And Dana's cat so far."

He studied her. "I wonder if the whales will talk to you."

She rushed over and wrapped her arms around him. "You believe me."

"Of course, I believe you. I love you." He leaned down and kissed her.

A loud, whooshing noise accompanied by a spray of salt water broke them apart. Laughing, they looked over the starboard side and saw the back of a whale sliding down into the water. The tail followed, and the orca gave a playful slap, the spray drenching everyone on board.

"Wow," Skye wiped her face. "That was close."

Another whoosh sounded and they leaned over the side to find an orca spy hopping, the black eye staring at them. "Of course we can talk to her," the whale said.

Laurie jumped up and down, hugging herself. She laughed. "I heard her. I heard her."

"Seriously?" Jade asked.

"I did."

"Want to meet my baby?" the whale asked.

"She asks if we want to meet her baby," Laurie said.

A smaller head bobbed up beside the larger mother. Oohs and aahs filled the sailboat. The dogs put their front paws up on the side to watch. Rosa's tail wagged and Oliver's butt wiggled so hard he almost lost his balance.

Hoa pointed her phone at the two. "Epic. I'm videoing this."

John hugged Laurie to him. "Yes, life is going to be epic."

DANA PRESTON's marriage is falling apart—but that's the least of her problems when the dead come knocking. Click here to read *Ghosts, Garters, and Grimoires*, book two of the Emerald City series.

WANT TO READ ANOTHER LAURIE, Dana, and Skye adventure? Claim your copy of "The Antique Shop"and get my newsletter. Not spamy and you can cancel any time.

Thank you for reading *Murder, Mystics, and Menopause.* Your honest review will help future readers decide if they want to take a chance on a new-to-them author. Just click here to leave a review.

About the Author

Best-selling author Theresa Crater writes compelling supernatural suspense and paranormal fiction. Her series include the Spirit Springs and Emerald City paranormal series, the award-winning Power Places supernatural suspense series, and the Mystic Assassin series. She has published several individual novels, many short stories, and a spiritual memoir (the story behind the stories) which can all be found on her website. She lives in Boulder with her Egyptologist partner and their cat who is naturally named Cleo. www.theresacraterbooks.com

ALSO BY

Theresa Crater

Spirit Springs Paranormal Women's Fiction

The Crone and the Stolen Orb

Emerald City Paranormal Women's Fiction

Murder, Mystics & Menopause

Power Places Series

Under the Stone Paw

Beneath the Hallowed Hill

Return of the Grail King

Into the City of Light

Power Places: The Complete Series

Yuletide Tales: Holiday Short Stories

Stand-Alones

The Star Family

Three Awakenings: A Spiritual Memoir

Other Books from Crystal Star Publishing

T.L. Crater

Mystic Assassin Series

Assassin Awakens

Breached: A Mystic Assassin Novella

Louise Ryder

God in a Box

School of Hard Knocks

Acknowledgments

Thank you to all my readers. You make it possible.

A special shout out to my advanced readers for their eagle eyes and helpful suggestions.

Special thanks to Stephen Mehler and Cleopatra Iset.

www.ingramcontent.com/pod-product-compliance
Lightning Source LLC
Chambersburg PA
CBHW070631260626
47161CB00007B/2665